DE

The Hellstromm Legacy

Book 2

LOVE, WAR, and DIVINITY

Kelly Ross
Visit me on Facebook: World of Delveon
Email: Worldofdelveon@gmail.com
ISBN# E-Book: 979-8-9876127-2-9
ISBN# Print: 979-8-9876127-3-6
Copyright © 2023
First published 2023

The world doesn't end here. Check out more of Delveon with Legacy's, Chronicles, and Tales.

Timeline

- 1850 Penelope's Chronicle: I am Shadow (Out Soon)
- 1865 Hellstromm Legacy: Book 1 The Knight and the Half Dragon (Out Now)
- 1866 Hellstromm Legacy: Book 2 Love, War, and Divinity (Out Now)
- 1868 Hellstromm Legacy: Book 3 Fate of an Empire (Out Soon)
- 1886 Hellstromm Legacy: Book 4 Secrets of Titania (Out Soon)
- 1887 Hellstromm Legacy: Book 5 Wayward Journey (Out Soon)
- 1887 Hellstromm Legacy: Book 6 (to be determined)
- 1888 Dominex Tales (18+) Devils Bounty (Out Soon.

TITANIA

ZATHEILES

DRUSO ESCARIA

KOBLAND

AUSOTH

VASPERALD

SHESOA

BACARIAN

VELIDAR

N
W E
S

4

CHAPTER 1

(A new beginning)

The sun sets over the vast desert, casting long shadows in the pristine, white-walled city of Portstown. Light furred Catfolk don't notice the cool fall air blowing in from the ocean, but alas, the same can't be said for most of their visitors from Rose Harbor. The days are still warm, peaking in the mid-eighties, but the nights drop into the low fifties. These visitors have been in Portstown for just over eight months and now feel it as much as home to them as Rose Harbor. Walking the streets, the Catfolk, Centaurs, Sand Elves, Dwarves, and some darker skinned Humans, all meld together, save for their visitors.

Walking the streets is a woman, white as marble save for the bright red flowing dress with gold magical runic patterns. Her obsidian-colored hair, braided and bound with gold lace, hangs from two black horns that curve from her temples around the front, covering her brow. Several braids with a gold lace binding them together, hang from her horns framing her face. Walking next to her arm in arm is a tall, tan skinned man wearing a red and gold suit of his own matching her. Crystal smiles as they stop for dinner at their favorite seafood restaurant, with William holding the door.

Two others follow the odd couple at a distance. One, an Asian Human of average height, and the other is a female Minotaur that towers over all but the largest Catfolk. Both wear white wushu outfits from their days living at a monastery. Tom and Tyra, having a habit of following the couple, walk in a few minutes later, and soon find Crystal's table. Tom unceremoniously plops down and grabs a breadstick, as Tyra circles around and finds a chair big enough to hold her. This grabs Crystal's full attention. "What's the plan now that the treaty is signed, and we are now all one big, happy family?"

Crystal picks up her goblet of wine and glances at Tom over it. "Baron Tenishar must select a representative for Portstown, and all the official documents will be returned to Rose Harbor." She sips at it and lets out a note of approval. "After that, we move on to New Haven. We must solve this Black Rose problem before it leads to war." She leans back and swirls the liquid in her goblet, admiring its intoxicating fragrance.

Tyra sits down and exchanges glances with everyone, then motions in a circle. "So, what about us? Are we just going to stay at Captain Blakley's home till we redeploy?"

A waiter arrives and takes Tom's and Tyra's order. William smiles at the thought. "You're welcome to stay, but when we go back, we will need a few weeks to prepare and resupply for the trip to New Haven. We could drop you off at the monastery in the meantime."

Crystal leans forward. "That's not a bad idea. I can stop by my house there and pick up more tomes." She holds a hand to herself. "I'm not going to improve if I don't start getting back to my studies." She sips her wine, leaving a slight red stain on her lips that reminds them all of what she went through earlier this year.

William swallows some calamari, and the tone of his voice darkens. "Is that wise? The last tome you studied almost got you to take lichdom seriously and gave Tia the willies."

She waves him off with a half grin. "I'm reminded of something Master Monzulo said: *failure is a chance to begin again smarter and wiser*, or something like that." She leans back, crossing her legs and finishing her wine. "Now that I know what to look for, I can avoid it." She looks around the table. "And if I can't," she takes in a deep breath. "I have you all to pull me back to reality again."

Tom grins with a slight nod of agreement. "Glad some of Master Monzulo's teachings are becoming useful to you, countess." He glances down and mutters under his breath. "Now, if we can get you to stop taking your anger out on the little folk." This gets a scolding glance from Crystal that he catches from between the braids hanging from her horns. "Yeah, like that."

They continue some small talk, and Tom's, and Tyra's food arrives. Crystal and William had finished some time ago, but hadn't left. A Halfling woman in a white shirt and black vest and pants walks between the tables, being cautious of taller individuals to prevent getting hurt. She must constantly tilt her head, so her elongated ears doesn't get caught on something, as people move chaotically about. Arriving at the group's table, she taps Crystal's leg, getting her attention. Crystal turns to her, "What is it, Shadow?"

Penelope internally grimaces at her alias being used out in the open. "Captain Zylra wants to know your departure schedule so she can prep the ship for the journey home."

Crystal wipes her mouth with a napkin and tosses it to the table. "We were just finishing up. Where's Tia?"

Penelope glances westwards, and a slight smile crosses her face. "She's at the new Church of Daniel. I believe she knows we're leaving soon and is making sure everything is in order. She's always been a serious person, but she's giving this extra detail."

Crystal nods and gets up, prompting William to follow. "Let's stop by there first on the way back to the ship." They turn, thanking Tom and Tyra for their company and depart the establishment, Penelope follows closely behind them. Crystal places her arm once again into William's, as if daring anyone to make a move to harm her.

Penelope herself is ever watchful since the Black Rose has made several attempts at assassination and sabotage. She looks at how confident Crystal is with William right there. *I can tell from the small flinches that she's scared all the time, but she's putting on quite the show by acting uncaring. She's projecting confidence so others can't see how shaken she really is.*

They reach the new church, built on the west side, far from the center of town. Illuminating the building are candles that cast flickering shadows that remind them of home. Several converts of Sand Elves and Catfolk are wearing white robes, the only real difference from the church back in Rose Harbor. Looking upon the dais, they spot a tall, full figured, Half-Elven woman in brown robes speaking to the congregation. They walk up and sit in the front pew, waiting for her to finish. Technically, there are no services today, but Tia enjoys giving words of wisdom to the new converts.

Tia follows the trio with her eyes as they sit down, then dismisses the worshipers to start on their chores. She walks over and engulfs the smaller, petite woman in her arms. "I don't know how Priestess Lyndis can do this job. I'll be glad to be back on the road for once!"

Penelope interrupts, bringing all the attention to her. "You look like a natural leader up there. They hung on your every word." Penelope gestures towards Tia. "Who's going to take your place when you leave?"

Tia breaks off and glances down at Penelope. "Lyndis is supposed to send someone who can lead this church." She turns her attention back to Crystal. "She offered it to me, but my place is here with you guys, making sure you stay out of trouble."

Crystal huffs and makes a pinching gesture. "Dear Provider. I make one minor error in judgment, and everyone thinks I'm the bad guy!"

William speaks up from his seat. "Technically, you've had a few errors in judgment."

She turns and looks at him, red faced, and crosses her arms. "What's that supposed to mean?"

8

He counts off his fingers. "You stepped out of the wagon while a demon possessed plant was attacking, putting yourself in danger. Stood on top of the wagon when we were being attacked by giant chickens that turned people to stone. Picked a fight with a Minotaur. Fought off rioters when you should have been escaping. Almost gave into necromancy..."

Crystal stops him there, grabbing his hand. "You made your point, Will!" She turns her head to Tia. "We are planning on leaving in the morning, so gather your things. I'll be leaving my Vardo and stuff here since we will be back. You don't have to take everything, just what you might need for the trip home."

Tia bows her head. "As you wish, countess." William and Penelope stand, and they hug Tia.

Crystal hugs Tia and gives an enormous smile. "See you in the morning around ten?"

Tia grins, turning to look at the church and back again. "I'll be there." She waves as they walk away.

Crystal and William lock their arms and exit into the streets. The night has come, and the stars are appearing. The bright white buildings glow with the rising moon, showing little need for streetlamps. "Shadow, could you inform the captain of our departure plans? I don't feel like going out there with how far the embassy is."

"As you wish, countess."

"And be careful."

Penelope notes the hint of worry in her voice. "I will, countess."

Crystal and William take their evening stroll and return to the embassy, taking several flights of stairs up to her room. William opens the door for her, and she smiles up at him as she walks by, but he doesn't enter. She continues over to the end table by the bed, pulling the gold lace from her braids, causing them to unravel. Turning her head, she gazes over her left shoulder at William and pulls her hair to the side, exposing her nape. "Close the door behind you. I have a feeling I'll need my bodyguard to protect me tonight." William blushes and steps in, pulling the door shut. She smiles and tosses the gold lace on the tabletop as the latch on the door echoes throughout the chamber.

The next morning, a banging at the door awakens them both in a panic. Crystal rolls off Williams's chest and he sits up. Penelope's muffled voice calls from the other side. "Countess, I have your breakfast."

Crystal whispers with fear filling her voice. "If she finds you here, she will tell my dad. Oh, this isn't good." William is busy trying to gather his clothes, but she stops and points at him. "I have an idea."

He stands up, holding his clothing. "I'm open for suggestions."

Penelope raps on the door again. "Ms. Hellstromm, is everything alright?"

Crystal yells at the door. "Yes, give me a moment! You woke me up, and I got a cramp in my ribs. Give me a second to pull it out!"

Crystal speaks an incantation as low as she can then touches William, making him and his clothing vanish. "Go stand in the corner so she can't bump into you and stay quiet."

William does as he's told. *I hope she doesn't take too long. I hate myself for this, but what choice do I have?*

Crystal throws on her nightgown, but it's so sheer that it leaves nothing to the imagination. She opens the door but stands behind it, so no one in the hallway can see more than just her head. Penelope walks in, setting the silver tray on the table in the middle of the room. She looks around, scanning slowly, then shoots a glance at Crystal. "Where's William?"

Crystal's heart jumps. *How does she know? She can't know, she's guessing.* She holds her hands out. "What do you mean?"

Penelope points to a pair of briefs under the bed. "I know he's here; I can see his underwear under your bed." She walks to the window, looking over the edge. "And I don't think William is walking around without them."

Crystal swallows and cold creeps over her body. *She spotted that because she's shorter than us! Can't believe months of hiding and we left a detail like that in the open.*

Crystal opens her mouth to respond, but Penelope interrupts. "You two should know better than to be doing such things unmarried. I thought for sure his honor would have kept him in check." She shakes her head, then looks slowly around the room again. "Invisibility? I'm disappointed in you, William."

Crystal boils, grabbing Penelope and putting a finger in the small woman's face. "I'm not a kid anymore. A month from now, I will be twenty. I think I can make my own decisions."

Penelope gets red faced herself, raising her own finger. "That's not the point." She waves to the outside. "What if you get pregnant out here? What if word gets back that the daughter of the Third House is sleeping with a man out of wedlock? It could ruin your father's business."

Crystal quips back. "I'm not going to get pregnant. I have a spell just for preventing that." She crosses her arms and turns her chin up. "And besides, I love him and only want to be with him. I'm not going out and sleeping with *just* anyone."

"You know I must tell your father. It's one reason I'm on this trip."

Crystal grabs the Halfling, holding her in place by the shoulders. "Don't you dare!" Fear grips Penelope as this is anger she's not seen before. "If you tell daddy, that could mean the end of our relationship, and I can't handle that."

"Your father likes William. I doubt he will make you stop seeing him."

Crystal takes a hand off and points at Penelope's face again. "You know my father better than that!" She steps away, turning her back. "You know where I get my temper from. Daddy would challenge him to a trial by combat and there is no way William could beat him. Dad's personal power armor is way too powerful." Crystal turns back and lowers herself down to Penelope's level. "I never had a use for honor. I always looked at it as something that holds someone back, but they would fight because of me." Crystal closes her eyes briefly and opens them again. "Please, for me, just keep this to yourself."

Penelope softens, understanding what she means. "Fine, I'll stay quiet, but you better say something to your father. If I tell him, there won't be any reasoning, then." She turns, scanning the room once again. "And you better fess up too, William." She leaves, closing the door behind her.

Crystal dismisses the enchantment, and William reappears, turning his attention to the door. "What do we do?"

Crystal lifts the lid on her breakfast. All the concern in her voice vanishing. "Eat breakfast with me?"

"I mean about Penelope. I know Tia will keep things to herself because she's understanding of these things, but Penelope is under orders. She's loyal more to your father than you."

Crystal takes a bite of her pancakes. "Killing her is out of the question. She's too good of a cook." William looks at her with surprise on his face. "It's a joke." Crystal drops her fork and glances up at William. "Am I really that bad that people think I'm serious about murder?"

William shrugs and sits down. "You're just really hard to read sometimes."

Crystal feeds William a piece of sausage with some syrup dripping from it, and he smiles. "We have a good thing going here, don't we?" Crystal grins, picking at her eggs. "We're happy, we're satisfied, our careers are going well, and I'm becoming more famous and powerful just the way I wanted."

William smiles. "Nothing else could make you happier?"

She shrugs. "I would be happy if we would stop getting caught." William nods, deep in thought. They gather their things and William has his armor taken to the ship. Waving to the people of Portstown from the deck of the ship, they retire to their cabins after lifting off. Crystal places the paperwork in the ship's safe then informs Captain Zylra that their first stop is the monastery, to drop off the monks. With the fanfare below fading, they head homeward.

Late on the eighth day, they cross into the mountains, maneuvering around them like icebergs. Tyra comes out and stands next to Crystal, leaning on the banister. "We are getting close to home finally." Crystal nods in agreement, taking in the cool mountain air. "Thanks for bringing us home, countess. It's been a fun experience."

Crystal turns her head to look up at Tyra. "You're not going to join us when we go back to Portstown?"

"Oh yes. I didn't mean for it to sound like we were leaving permanently. Who's going to find these people if I don't track them down?" They talk as they watch the last mountain pass by and the ocean comes into view. A steamship flying the colors of the Seventh House on its mast is a vast contrast with the snow-covered countryside. "Looks like William's father won the bid to take over shipping from Black Rock. I bet that boosted their House significantly."

Tyra looks at Crystal. "I don't understand."

Crystal points, and Tyra follows. "That ship out there with the smoke coming out of it is from the Seventh House, meaning William's dad is making money from shipping." She smirks. "Finally, some accountability is in some expert hands."

CHAPTER 2

(Home)

The sun is just above the ocean when the monastery comes into view. The sky turns shades of red and orange, making the clouds wisps of flames. Captain Zylra starts the landing procedures, finding a place behind the house. Tom and Tyra can see the monks gathering below and are the first to disembark into the snow once they touch down. Crystal and William descend slowly and walk to the house and enter, leaving the monks to speak with their friends.

William lights a lantern, casting eerie shadows over the building's mystical contents. "What are we looking for?"

Crystal rifles through the library, browsing the spines and pulls the ones she wants. "These tomes are sources of magic and information. Like this one here." She shows him pointing at passages. "This shows how to increase the potency of a spell by adding a little extra to the incantation by pulling more from my body or adding extra spell components." She flips her hand over as if she was stating the obvious. "It's a type of metamagic to improve on existing spells or change their effects and or looks." She puts it down on the table and pulls another. "This is a book on Cyromancy. I'm sure there are secrets in here knowing Olovira." She sets it down too, then jumps as a knock at the door interrupts them.

Grasping her chest, William pats her on the shoulder. She nods, looking down, and waves at him to answer it. He opens the door to see Master Monzulo standing there. He bows to them, and they return the gesture. "I see you've taken my advice and pursued happiness and love, but it seems power is still a desire, Ms. Hellstromm."

Crystal's voice shakes as she responds. "If you knew what I've been through, you would understand."

"I've heard. When Tom arrived to get our water, he explained it all to me. I'm glad to see it worked and you're back to your old physical self."

"Then you know why I have to gain more power. People keep insisting on doing things for me like I'm fragile." She turns back to the books. "I'm... well, I don't even know anymore." She turns back to him, pointing to her horns. "I'm more Dragon than my mother."

"Yes, Olovira was like you under all those robes. One of a kind." He takes a deep breath. "But power alone will not fix what ails you inside." Crystal turns away and continues going through tomes, prompting him to exit.

William points a thumb at the door. "I'm going to take a walk since you're busy and don't understand any of these things. Call me when you're done." She nods and waves him off, but he can hear her breathing heavier.

He steps out and Master Monzulo walks with him. "I sense that she's found her purpose, but you're resistant to your own."

William looks down at Master Monzulo. "Yes, I'm not sure what to do about it. She's a countess now and her entire career is ahead of her. I'm afraid anything I do to involve myself more in her life could derail that."

Master Monzulo folds his hands into his black wushu. "And you think if you weren't there at her side, it would help her?"

William's voice drops. "That's what I don't know. If I wasn't there, she would be gone or worse, but then, being here

15

now, she might pass up her dreams." He glances back at the old place. "She wants more than just settling on being a countess."

"You're letting fear cloud your judgement. She is pursuing happiness and love, and your souls are in harmony. You must feel it." They continue to walk along the path a bit and he stops, prompting William to stop too. "You must ask yourself a basic question of life. What is it you want most from it?" He looks back to the old house with Crystal still in it. The old man looks up at William. "And we both know what it is you desire most. So much so that it causes you inner turmoil that's only settled by her presence." He pauses a moment as Crystal steps out and waves at them from the doorway. "And she will need you more now than ever."

William smiles and places his hand on the old man's shoulder. "Guess I just needed to hear that. Thank you."

Master Monzulo bows and walks away. William returns and steps in, seeing a stack of books on the table, along with a staff carved of white wood. He picks it up, looking at the intricate carvings in it, and she promptly takes it from him. "Don't break that. It's for Tia."

"What is it?"

"It's a staff that stores and enhances healing magic. This way, Tia can be a better healer. With the way things have been going, we could use all the help we can." She thumbs behind her. "I found this sitting under a cloth in the corner back there." She points to the stack. "Now I need to get these books into the ship. I have homework to do."

William lifts the tomes. "Wow, these are heavy. It's like being in the academy all over again."

She looks up and glances over her shoulder at him. "What's that supposed to mean?"

"I'm carrying some pretty girl's books, trying to impress her."

She smiles and smacks him on the butt, giggling to herself. "Yah mule!" They take off once again and within a few hours, they can see the gold and silver spires of the palace at the center of Rose Harbor. The city is ringed in snow outside the magical dome that keeps it the same temperature year-round.

Descending through the magical barrier, the ship lands in the airfield behind the palace, and the ground crew moors it to the ground. Crystal puts on a royal purple dress, and takes the treaty from the safe. With William at her side, they descend the ramp, spotting Marcus and his advisers waiting for them below. Before Crystal could kneel, Marcus motions for her to join him at his side. The eagerness is evident as he speaks. "I can't wait to hear how things went."

They get inside and Marcus chats it up with the female Catfolk from Portstown and is all excited about them joining the Empire. He motions to his staff, and they take her to another part of the palace. Marcus watches her leave, then turns to Crystal. "Countess, you pulled this off just as I thought you would. My instincts about you are right." He holds his hand out. "Where are the official documents?"

Crystal pulls them from her white handbag, having expected this request, and hands them over. "It was a strenuous journey, but only the first half of the empire's objective is complete."

Marcus' grin grows, but Crystal notes the curiosity in his voice. "I didn't expect you back till after you dealt with New Haven and the Black Rose. Why are you back so early?"

"My birthday is coming up soon and William's and Tia's has already passed. I figured we could return home and connect with family before heading out again. Maybe put on a party for family." She takes a deep breath and lets it out. "Plus, we've been almost killed several times."

"Exciting, isn't it? I wish I could still do stuff like that, but I'm too busy running things." He folds the paperwork and hands it to an attendant. "Put that with the rest of the treaties and return to me." He looks back to Crystal. "When are you planning to head out again?"

She looks down for a moment and then back up at him. "Provider's day is three weeks away, and my birthday is just two days after that." She swallows, searching for a hint in his eyes. "So, after that. Gives plenty of time to be with family before my next trip."

Marcus grabs her tiny shoulders with his large hands, giving her a start. "A party is a great idea, for there is so much to celebrate. It will be my treat for all that you've done for the empire." He turns, putting his hand behind her back and pushing forward gently. He snaps with his other hand, getting William, Tia, and Penelope to focus on him. "I want you four back here on Saturday with your families. That gives you three days to prepare. You are to be my guests of honor. Just send word on how many are coming, so I can get place settings." The excitement in his voice echoes through the large hall. "This is a momentous occasion for the Empire, and your first successful negotiation."

Crystal beams. "Thank you, Your Highness."

"William, your horse should be unloaded and Penelope, I took the liberty of having a riding dog brought out for you. The rest of your things will be brought to you by nightfall. You go on and have fun and I will see you in three days at six p.m." He waves them on to leave.

Once they're gone, Skylar wraps her arms around Marcus's shoulders, appearing behind him. "So?"

He sighs. "The next few days will be telling." He turns and looks into her eyes. "Let Daniel know it's time for him to act."

Skylar grins. "And then what?"

Marcus shrugs. "Then we wait and guide her when the time comes. Her power is increasing."

18

The group walks out of the palace into the midafternoon sun. The Royal Guard brings around their mounts, and Tia waves, taking off into the streets.

Crystal watches her for a moment, then turns to William as he mounts his horse. "I miss the snow already."

William laughs, offering his hand to pull her up. "You can always go back outside."

Crystal squeezes him and her voice turns playful. "You going to come with me?"

Penelope gets on her own mount. "Stop it, you two."

Crystal frowns. "Mood kill."

Penelope pulls alongside William's horse. "That's the point." William looks down with a smirk, then kicks his mount.

Riding home through the streets, the evening sounds and the magical lamps give a small feeling of familiarity. The evening also brings the smells of so many cooked meals from dozens of cultures. They have been away so long that the city seems more of a fond memory that they are revisiting. Riding into the Hellstromm's manor gates, the guards welcome them home. The trio dismount and the guards take the animals as they walk up to the front door. Crystal lets herself in, but William stops on the porch. Crystal notices immediately that he hasn't followed her in and turns around. "What's wrong, William?"

"I must get home myself. My parents are worried about me, too."

"I know, but I'm sure father will want to know how the armor held up."

As if punctuating her words, the sounds of heavy tools being set down echo from another part of the house. A short black man with several short braids strolls up to the door, his leather overall's covered in grease and metal shavings. "Thank the Provider you're back alive." Crystal turns just in time to intercept a hug from Jack. He lets go and grabs William's hand. "And thanks to you for bringing her back to me once again."

William's heart leaps. "It was an honor guarding her and being at her side. She's quite remarkable."

He thumbs at himself with pride and a laugh. "Oh, I know. I raised her." Jack drags the large man inside, patting him on the back. "How did the armor hold up? You're alive, so I'm assuming it worked well?" William feels uncomfortable with the interrogation.

Moving to the main room, a woman of bright white in a black dress joins them, sitting down in Jack's lap. Jasmine is eager to hear of her daughter's exploits. They discuss everything that happened in Portstown, except for Crystal's kidnapping and involvement with necromancy. A knock at the door interrupts them. Cline, their butler, walks over and answers it. "Sir, Miss Crystal's things and Mr. Blakley's armor are here."

Jack turns and looks over his shoulder. "Have the armor taken to my shop and place it on the stand. I'll look at it later."

"And what about all these tomes, sir?"

"Tomes?" Jasmine gets up and walks over to look over them. "What are all these, Crystal?"

Crystal gets up and joins her mother, leaving Jack and William alone in the room for the moment, but comes back and motions for William. Shrugging to Jack, he gets up and walks to her. "Mom wants your help." She pats him on the shoulder. "Good luck." She leaves him and sits down next to her dad, picking up about the negotiations as William enters the foyer.

He sees the stack of tomes and Jasmine smiles. "Could you grab these and follow me? I want to go through them before my daughter does. She's eager, but I fear she wants to accomplish too much over a short time, and that makes her reckless."

William nods in agreement, and his eyes widen for a moment. *You have no idea.* He picks up the tomes, and she beckons him to follow. *Jack mentioned she's as strong as several men put together, but yet she needs me to carry these? Now I know where Crystal gets it from.*

They take a flight of steps down and into her lab. "I know my husband has already said this, but thanks for bringing Crystal home to us."

"It was my pleasure, Mrs. Hellstromm."

She turns and looks at him, then points to her desk. "You can place them here."

He puts them down and turns to her. "Is that all you need, Mrs. Hellstromm?"

She places a hand on the tomes and then turns, beckoning him to follow her. "You're a good man, William. My daughter is lucky to have you at her side." They get back to the foyer, but she stops him short of going back into the main room. They can overhear Crystal and Jack talking. She's animated about the battle she and he fought together and bounces around a little. Jasmine keeps her voice low but watches her daughter and husband. "You make her incredibly happy." She turns William to face her by grabbing his broad shoulder. "And you make us happy, too."

"Thank you, Mrs. Hellstromm."

She cuts him off. "Call me *mom.*" His face flushes with embarrassment and she nods in approval. "And that confirms it. You are madly in love with my daughter. By her being this animated," she pauses, looking back into the room. "I can see she is in love with you. I know you're biding your time because of what's happening." She turns back to him. "But as far as I'm concerned, you're my son." She straightens his shirt up. "She wouldn't have risked it all to bring you back if she wasn't."

"Thanks… *mom.*" This brings a larger smile to her face, and one crosses his too. He liked how it sounded.

"We need to get back in there before they get suspicious."

They reenter the room, and Jasmine sits with Jack and William takes his place next to Crystal. They talk more and eat, laughing and exchanging stories for several hours. "As much as I would love to stay all night, I really must be going. I was expected home some time ago and I'm sure my parents are worried about me." William stands and Crystal escorts him to the door, waving Cline away.

"What did you and mom talk about?" She looks up at him with her piercing blue dragon eyes.

"Just how ambitious you are, bringing all that magic stuff back. She's hoping it doesn't overwhelm you, that's all."

She cocks her head. "You're hiding something from me."

He smiles. "Just the urge to kiss you, but not in front of your family. It's not the right time yet, I think." He takes a step down, almost putting them at eye level. "Although it is really difficult to resist the urge." She pats him on the chest and he turns, mounts up and waves goodbye. Not wasting time, he makes his way home and finally relaxes as he passes through the gates.

Dismounting, he hands off his horse to the stable master and enters his home. Sally, the Blakely's Elven maid, welcomes him home. After he settles in, she leaves to fetch his parents, Gerald and Muriel. They come running in and practically tackle the man. They spend hours talking and catching up, but William leaves out some of the more gruesome details. "In three days, Emperor Marcus wants us to be there at the palace as a big celebration of our accomplishments."

Gerald and Muriel exchange glances, but Gerald breaks in first. "Wow, dinner with the Emperor. You must've made a great impression on him."

William looks down, pulling on his clothes. "This means I need to get another suit and I need to do some other shopping tomorrow." He looks at his mom. "Will you join me? I would like your opinion on things."

She grins, knowing her son all too well. "Sure honey. Would be happy to."

CHAPTER 3

(Fury and Rage)

Tom and Tyra watch the *Bastion* take to the air and head south to the capital. Turning, they walk through the ankle-deep snow and get back to their cabin. Tom kicks up some dust just opening the door. "Looks like the spiders have taken over our humble home." Tyra snorts and places her Lajatang in the corner, then tosses some wood into the furnace. Tom finds a mop and some water to wash the floors.

She picks up a rag and gets it wet. "I'll get to dusting. Master Monzulo will expect this place to be pristine and orderly." Cleaning doesn't take long for the pair as the moon rises over the mountains.

They decide to get some dinner and head outside, the icy wind nipping at them. Walking along the pathways. Tom quips to Tyra. "You know, she's probably miserable right now, being back in the heat of the city."

"Why do you say that? She's going home to see her family and to be with her toyfriend."

Tom looks at her quizzically. "Toyfriend?"

"Those two have been all over each other for months. I almost can't tell them apart anymore unless I actually see them."

Tom smiles. "That's a possibility. Think he's going to ask for her hand? He is a man of honor, after all."

Tyra nods in agreement. "He would be a fool to give up a woman like her." She looks down at her little Human friend. "Think he can save her from herself?"

Tom's tone fills with hope. "Only time will tell. She went to a dark place, and it changed her. Hopefully, he can take her to a place of light and change her back. Her love for him was stronger than her need for destruction." They walk into the dining room and get some rice and water. They sit down and eat their meal. "I miss Portstown already."

Tyra laughs lightly and snorts. "You're spoiled."

Tom motions to his bowl. "Admit it, the food there was so good."

Tyra eats her rice and nods, not arguing. They eat, continuing with the small talk and about how fun it was being out there. Another man sits down with a cup of hot green tea. They both turn to see the distinctive black wushu of Master Monzulo. They both stand and bow as years of training kick in. He smiles, bows his head and waves them back to sit. "Please sit. Have some tea with me and tell me all about your adventure. Worldly experience is as much of a teacher as any instructor."

Tom and Tyra resume their seats, telling him every detail. "To be honest, Master, I don't know what was worse for them. Crystal almost being tortured to death, or William, who thought he would never see her alive again. If it wasn't for Tyra, they would have never found her."

"Then it was fate that led you to be there. I have a feeling you two are going to be crucial in their future." He sips at the steaming tea. "They didn't show up here by chance. Destiny has a plan for you. It's now your task to find out what that is." Master Monzulo whiffs at the tea's fragrance. "Hot tea on a chilly day is one of life's truly wonderful experiences." He stands up and they follow suit, bowing to each other. "I take my leave." He turns and walks out.

A few days pass and they both decide to bathe that night to get the dirt and dust off of them from cleaning. Tom sits in the pool, his body still aching from the cleaning and training, when something doesn't sit right with him. He can feel something is out of place and gets out of the water. He checks on Tyra and she's asleep in the warm water, snoring away. *She had a long week.* Looking out over the courtyard, the moon has the snow lit up. He stares at the beauty and how pristine it is when something catches his eye. He squints and sees movement. *That doesn't look like a student.* He goes back to the pool and wakes up Tyra.

She snorts and thrashes awake, then stares up at him. "What?"

"Get your clothes on. I think we have unwanted guests."

Tyra gets out of the water and towels off. Being wet in this sub twenty-degree weather is bad news for any humanoid. Tom turns around to leave when a black clad individual swings a knife, catching him in the forearm. He reacts instantly, grabbing the assailant's hand, putting it into a lock, twists, and forces them to drop the knife. A quick knee to the liver knocks them to the ground. Ripping off the mask, it reveals a Human female. *Who is this?* He looks out and sees more figures moving. *No time for that now.* She goes to make a move, but Tyra kicks her in the face, dropping her back to the floor, unconscious. Tom looks at his arm and it's not bleeding badly. He rips a strip from a towel and Tyra bandages him. "Trouble followed us. We need to act now!" Tom looks up at her. "You alert the others; I'll try to get to the sanctuary and let Master know." Tyra exits with him, heading into the night.

They first head to their cabin to grab their weapons. As they exit to go their separate ways, an explosion echoes from the northern wall and within moments, they hear fighting. Tyra rounds the cabin and can see hundreds of invaders rushing through a hole in the wall. Awakened by the bomb, monks, both masters and students, grab weapons to repel the invaders. Younger students with little training try to find shelter as the invaders attack indiscriminately. Tyra goes into a rage and rushes in, swinging her Lajatang. The sharp half-moon blade severs limbs with the sheer brute force of her swings.

She intercepts a sword strike on the haft of her weapon with a loud clang. She releases a hand from the weapon and grabs the man's sword hand, flinging him into the air as if tossing a doll. More monks arrive with their own weapons, giving her reinforcements. The back of her leg stings as a short sword cuts deep. *I'm over exposed here. Too many at once.* She blocks and counters, sending another attacker to the ground. A sword comes in aimed at her midsection and she realizes she's out of position to stop it, but a Katana flashes in front of her, mere inches from her chest. She looks down and Master Mori is standing there holding the other's blade at bay.

"We need to start a fighting retreat. There are too many at once, so we have to fortify the main building and bottle them so they can't use their numbers." Tyra nods slowly, stepping back as blades and clubs come swinging in. Metal on metal rings out in the frozen night. The once pristine snow is now stained red with the blood of the dead and wounded.

Tom rushes up the steps to warn Master Monzulo about what's happening. He already knows who it must be, given he's seen this twice now. *Black Rose must be desperate to attack our monastery.* The sounds of battle are well below him as he takes the steps two at a time in a dead run. Pulling on his chi, he forces himself to move at speeds no normal Human could muster. Getting up the one thousand steps in a few minutes, he rushes to the massive doors, legs burning from the exertion of pushing his body beyond its limits.

He enters and there are a few awake. He finds the closest master and informs her of what is happening. She runs to find Master Monzulo and Tom sounds the alarm by smashing the gong outside. The ringing echoes across the monastery, alerting the others that reinforcements are on their way. Master Monzulo comes out along with the other highly trained masters and top students.

Master Monzulo places a hand on Tom, getting his attention. "What is going on?"

Tom points down the hill where fires have started as the attackers are now torching cabins. "We are under attack, Master. I fear it's the Black Rose making this assault."

"Then we must repel them." He turns to the other masters. "Arm yourselves." Different weapons like staffs, swords, and spears are given out, but Master Monzulo doesn't take one.

Tom is on his heels. "Master, you aren't going with a weapon?"

He shakes his head. "My hands are more dangerous than any sword." His voice sounds regretful. "Today, you get to see a grand master in action."

Tyra hears the gong, and they continue to fight in retreat. She and Master Mori have taken several hits, bloodying their robes, but many attackers have fallen to their blades. Several larger attackers smash open the hole in the wall and make their way in. "Master, Ogres approaching." She can smell their pungent stench, knowing exactly what they are. *How is the Black Rose getting them to cooperate?* The Ogres attack haphazardly, hitting friends and foes alike with their weapons. One rushes at Tyra, and she smiles at the challenge. "Come on, big guy, let's see what you got."

He comes at her, bringing his large club down on her head, and she raises her Lajatang in response. The impact dents her weapon and her hands and arms hurt from the sheer force of the blow. *Finally, a worthy adversary to test my mettle on.* He raises his weapon to take a second blow, but she spins, kicking her leg out, catching the giant in the solar plexus, doubling him over. Following through, she brings the crescent moon around and plants it in his chest, burying it deep. He grabs the weapon and yanks it from her hands. Jerking it free of his chest, he roars with pain and anger. "Oh, hell." He swings it at her, knocking her back and snapping the shaft.

He moves forward and brings his club to bear on the Minotaur. Rolling away, she feels the impact with the ground where she used to be. Sweeping her leg under his, he falls, giving her time to pin his left arm. She grunts with everything she has, snapping his elbow. He brings the club over and knocks her flying. *I think he broke some ribs. It's hard to breathe.* She gathers herself as he stands up and starts beating his chest with his club, lets out a roar, and charges again. She lets out a battle cry of her own and charges back. He swings for her head, but she ducks it, lowering her horns and impaling them through his throat, stopping him in his tracks. She can feel his warm blood soak into her fur, but his weight is too much, and the pain in her chest causes her to fall to the ground with him.

Master Monzulo, Tom, and the others make their way down the steps, sliding along the side as Tom and Tyra did back in Portstown. The fires have spread to the almost all the buildings but the younger monks are trying to put them out. Older students watch their backs, taking on the Black Rose to buy them time. Master Monzulo and Tom cross the training field and see the massive brawl going on at the north wall. Tyra is taking on a massive Ogre as several others have smashed cabins and devastate everything in their path. Master Monzulo issues orders for containment. "Tom, you come with me. Tyra has taken on more than she can handle."

Tom pulls his Sai and follows Master Monzulo into the battle. The old man's wispy white beard flows with his moves. Catching a sword hand mid swing and with some movements barely perceivable to the eye, turning the man's thrust into another attacker. The man swings again at the grand master, only to be pummeled with a quick series of precision strikes, dropping him paralyzed to the ground. *I've never seen the Grand Master in action before and it's amazing watching him flow, landing blows, incapacitating one enemy after another.*

They reach where Tyra fell and can see her struggling to get the Ogre's body off her. Tom breaks a sword with his Sai and lashing out with a kick, taking down another invader. "You ok down there?"

A muffled response comes back. "I could use some help. I have some broken ribs and can't muster the strength to get out." There is a slight pause. "And I think my horns are stuck in him, too."

Master Monzulo looks at the downed Tyra. "And what have you learned?"

"That Ogre's stink more after they have died. Get me out of here before I puke and make this worse."

Master Monzulo smiles and kicks up a fallen half spear to his hands. Whirling it around, he thrusts outwards past Tom's head and into another attacker. Tom looks at the shaft of the spear, then turns and sees the dead man standing there. Master Monzulo pulls the spear free, and the body hits the ground. "Thanks Master."

"Keep your focus, young one. The tide is turning, and they are retreating. Help me get this thing off Tyra." Tom moves over and the two men, along with Tyra, roll the dead Ogre over. Tyra is soaked in the giant creature's blood and has a look of disgust crosses her face. Tom helps her to her feet and, in a fluid motion, lashes out with a left jab, cratering another man's face, breaking his nose and several facial bones at once.

Master Monzulo gives a single nod. "I'm off to take down their leader."

Tyra wipes away some gore. "How do you know who the leader is? They all look the same."

"I can feel his intent." He looks at them both. "Come with me, you two."

Tyra picks up the Katana dropped on the ground Master Mori who saved her earlier. Grief hits her. *He must have stayed here defending me till he fell to the overwhelming numbers. Thank you, master. I will honor you.* They make their way through the huge melee, taking targets of opportunity, and

30

another Ogre stands in their way. Master Monzulo looks at the two students. "I'll handle him. You two focus on the others." Tom and Tyra nod as they engage with smaller targets. The Ogre growls and swings his club down at the tiny old man. He rolls back, then leaps onto the club after it hits the ground. The surprise on the Ogre's face is short-lived as the Grandmaster runs up his arm and leaps at his face. The Master hovers there and lashes out with several quick kicks to the Ogre's face and it falls to the ground.

The Ogre clambers to its feet, but Master Monzulo warns it. "Stay down. You cannot win this." The brute gets up anyway, not understanding the request. Master Monzulo sighs. The Ogre is almost to his feet when he lashes out, hitting the gigantic creature on the knee, snapping the joint. The Ogre lets out a yelp of pain and swings his club, but the old master redirects the blow away. What Tom and Tyra witness next will stick with them for years to come. The old master assumes a new stance and focuses. An indigo-colored ball of chi forms around his hands and he lashes out, punching the Ogre in the chest. The energy discharges, knocking the larger monster away several feet.

Tom blinks away the flash. "What was that?"

"That is the power of opening your chakra and letting your chi flow outward. It takes many decades to master properly." Master Monzulo turns to him. "Something you shouldn't try for some time. The color of the energy depends on where you draw your energy. I will tell you more about it after we finish here." They make their way, dispatching more foes till they finally confront the guy who's running this operation by the breach in the wall.

Master Monzulo points out one invader. "You there." A man in black armor turns his head. "Call your people back and they will live, but if you keep this up, we will have no choice but to defeat you totally."

"You will pay for helping the White Dragon lady and the Rose Empire." The unidentified man pulls his sword and swings it at the master's head. Tom intercepts the blow with one of his Sia, but he can't seem to break this one.

"It's ok Tom. This is between him and me." They separate with the ringing of metal on metal. Master Monzulo takes Tom's weapons from him. "Go with Tyra and help the others. I won't be long." Tom and Tyra nod and leap back as the leader draws his weapon back. The Grand Master knows this one isn't fodder like the others. He's skilled with weapons and is much younger than himself. Master Monzulo waits and the two circle each other, fully knowing that the other is more dangerous than they are letting on. The younger man loses his patience first and strikes out with his sword. Master Monzulo catches it with the Sai and whips the blunt side of the other one around, lashing out with it at the man's face, but it's blocked by the younger man's hand. The clash of metal on metal ring out in the darkness.

Master Monzulo catches the blade yet again and goes to sweep the man's leg, but he raises it and puts it back down right after the strike. "You've had some training in martial arts."

"You could say that." The sword swings at Master Monzulo's face and he ducks back as the blade passes through his wispy beard. "More than enough to drop an old master like yourself."

"Perhaps."

His sword thrusts outwards and the old master catches it. More indigo colored energy appears in his hand. The discharge knocks the dark knight's weapon away. Stunned from the shock of the energy release, Master Monzulo spins and lands a blow to the young man's chest with the other Sai. It pierces the armor effortlessly, sliding all the way to the forks. The young man coughs up blood and pulls back, the needle point of the Sai sliding from his body. "Give up now, and I can save your life."

"I rather die, then go back a failure." He coughs up more blood. He drops to his knees, holding a hand over the hole in his chest.

Master Monzulo shakes his head. "Such a waste of talent and skill, to use it for such evil." He steps away from the black knight. "You could have been a good man." The other warrior falls to the ground as the snow slowly stains red. With their leader no longer giving them directions, the remaining invaders retreat. They take count of the dead and wounded, getting those who are still alive to the pools and start recovery. Master Monzulo's voice is mournful as he issues more orders. "Get these fires out and start making arrangements to shelter those in the sanctuary. Until we rebuild, we need to get as many as we can inside."

He looks around and sees the only remaining buildings that are untouched by fire are the main temple, the bathhouses, and Olovira's place. "Master Monzulo?" Tom interrupts his introspection. "If they attacked us like this, what about Crystal and her companions?"

"It's a good possibility, but Rose Harbor is much more fortified than we are. Be that may, they could still be in danger, so we should warn them." He hands Tom his weapons back.

"Also, we could get help from Rose Harbor. I'm sure Crystal will send aid to us." Tom bows his head. "Can't hurt to ask."

Master Monzulo agrees. "You and Tyra will set out in the morning. See if you can find some horses."

CHAPTER 4

(Dinner with Royalty)

Three days pass and on the morning of the dinner with Marcus. William gets a box delivered to his door. Sally brings it to him and has a spring in her step as she knocks on his door. He answers and without waiting, she brings it into his room. Setting it down, he can tell she's excited. He opens the box and pulls out a red and gold outfit made of the same Titania cotton from Mithport. The embroidery is done with actual gold and mithril thread, giving a little weight to it, but the effect is noticeable in the light.

Sally whistles in appreciation. "Crystal sure knows how to pick those, doesn't she?"

"Actually, mom helped me pick this and design it. Crystal doesn't know about it and it's for the dinner tonight." He turns and looks at Sally, holding it up to his chest. "Do you think she will like it?"

"If she doesn't, you should stop dating her."

"I'll put this on later tonight. Right now, I need to check on something else."

"What's that, Master William?"

"My armor. Jack said he was going to be working on it and it's been a few days. I would like to see how far along he's gotten."

Sally nods, and her smile fades as he leaves. *He's lying to me, but why?*

The Hellstromm's arrive first to the palace in the armored steam car. A Royal Guard helps Jasmine get out first in a pearl green evening dress with gold and adamantine accents. Crystal gets out next with her signature hair style with her horns in a crimson red dress with gold and mithril lace around the cuffs, collars, and embroidery. Precious stones embedded in the dress sparkle in the light. Crimson red lipstick and highlights in her makeup around her eyes punctuate the outfit. Jack is wearing a simple black tuxedo with onyx cufflinks and a crimson undershirt. Penelope is the last to disembark wearing a sky-blue evening dress, and tugs at it as if it was a clingy alien.

The guard ushers them in when Tia and Andrew arrive. They greet and exchange hugs. "Where's your family, Tia?"

She looks down shyly and Andrew speaks up. "She was an orphan. The church is her family. So, she came here with me."

Jack gives her a hug, and surprise crosses her face. "Oh, I'm sorry Tia, I didn't know." He steps back. "But if it makes you feel better, you can be part of ours. The things you did helping Crystal, it would be wonderful to have you as an honorary member."

Tears well up in her eyes and Jack looks confused. "I thought that would make her happy. Did I say something wrong?"

She shakes her head. "No, this makes me happy." She wipes away a tear. "Let's get inside."

William and his family arrive in their carriage minutes later. Muriel wears a pearl white dress that shimmers and changes shades in the light. Gerald wears a white formal suit with a black tie, and William steps out in the crimson red suit with the mithril and gold embroidery. The Royal Guard escorts them to the dining area. They make a left instead of heading straight into the throne room and then a right at the end of that hall. Tapestries and paintings of far-away lands line the corridors, depicting all kinds of exotic sights and actions.

Entering the dining room, Marcus and his five wives, the Hellstromm family, along with Tia and Penelope, are all waiting. Marcus motions at the table that has small cards labeling their seats. William notices his seat next to Crystal's and his parents are across from the Hellstromm's.

They get seated and Marcus starts by standing holding up his jewel encrusted gold goblet. "A toast to these fine young people who, against all odds, pulled off an amazing mission." They toast and everyone has smiles and the stories start. Crystal brags about the ship and how smooth it performs. William talks about the armor Jack constructed and how Crystal saved his life by killing the Ogre at the last second. That story gets exchanged looks from Jasmine and Marcus, but the mirthfulness of the dinner doesn't change.

Penelope speaks up. "This is excellent, Your Highness. This food is as good as mine."

"I should hope so," Marcus guffaws. "My chef was the one who taught your master how to cook."

Marcus has a band playing in the background for them as they retire to the entertainment room. They settle into couples, leaving Penelope sitting with Tia and Andrew. Muriel motions to William and Crystal. "I find it uncanny that Crystal could guess what my son was wearing tonight. She matches him so perfectly, almost by instinct."

This prompts a larger smile from Crystal, exposing her sharp fangs. "Thank you, but it wasn't coincidence or instinct." She drinks some wine. "Asorin told me what William ordered the day he ordered it. He figured I would like to know since Muriel mentioned they were going to a dinner party with us." She leans back into him and looks up into his eyes. "I like to keep my bases covered."

This prompts some laughs from those who've traveled with Crystal, and Andrew tugs on his robes. "Tia and I match too." This causes some more laughter and Tia to flush red and bury her face in her chest.

Marcus' third wife, a black woman wearing a gold dress and a solid gold and jewel encrusted neck corset, speaks up addressing William and Crystal. "You two vook very happy togethier." She turns to Tia and Andrew. "And vou two as well. I can feel that vou have a good bond between vou."

Tia just continues to turn a deeper shade of red and Andrew replies to her. "Our faith requires us to be devoted to our god, so we can't pursue each other. Faith comes first."

She leans back in her chair. "Shame. The way vou two talked at the table, vou would think vou've been dating for years."

William stands up with that, bringing all attention to him, and the conversation stops. He looks nervous and rubs his hands together. "I've been a part of this since the beginning and ever since Emperor Marcus chose me. We've grown together, had our trials, our brushes with death and our victories." He turns looking at everyone, but none interrupts. "I've fallen in love with a wonderful woman." He turns to Crystal, his heart pounding in his ears. "And I've come to a decision."

He reaches into his right pocket and pulls out a small black box. Everyone in the room knows exactly what it is, and with a wave of his hand, Marcus quiets the musicians. The tension is so thick you could almost grab it with your hands as William pulls Crystal to a standing position, then kneels before her. Inside is a gold ring with a diamond attached, causing Crystal's heart to flutter and skip. Tears of joy are already forming in her eyes as he asks the most important question of his life. "Countess Crystal Hellstromm, will you marry me?"

Crystal can't stop the tears. "Yes." She stammers. "Yes, I will Sir William Blakely." Holding her left hand out. William takes the ring, and it magically resizes to fit her finger as he slides it on. He stands up and they kiss passionately, not having to hide it anymore. Both mothers, along with Tia and Penelope, cry with Crystal. They stand and congratulate the couple, hugging and shaking hands.

Marcus' booming voice brings everyone to a standstill. "I cannot allow this to happen." He looks around with his eyes, shock on everyone's face. Then a grin crosses his own. "Unless I get to be the one to officiate the wedding." He stands up, hugging the couple as well. "Congratulations, you two." He points a finger at them. "But I'm serious about this. As my countess, I'm the one who will marry you two, so there is no way anyone can say it's unofficial."

Crystal, tears still in her eyes but with an enormous smile, hugs him. "Thank you, Your Highness. I look forward to it."

He nods and sits back down, placing his arm around Skylar and his third wife. "William, you're a braver man than most, giving up your family name for her."

This brings the room to a standstill a second time. Jack breaks the stalemate. "What do you mean? Isn't it traditional to take the man's name when getting married?"

Marcus turns casually to Jack. "In a traditional marriage, yes, but she is a countess and is part of the First House. Being that she is your daughter, she is also of the Third House and William is from the Seventh. There is a law I implemented years ago that states that when marrying into a House, the higher standing name is kept. This dissuades men with ill intent from taking advantage of daughters, to promote their own names into places that wasn't earned."

He looks at William. "So, by law, you will take her name. Are you still interested in this union, knowing what this means?"

William turns to Crystal. "It doesn't change my mind at all. She was willing to give her life for me. Giving up my family name for hers is a small sacrifice I'm willing to make."

Marcus' Forth wife, an Elven lady wearing a gold and silver dress, speaks up. "Do you have a date in mind?"

He sits back down. "I haven't thought of it that far. I figured I would get Crystal's opinion on the matter before deciding." Crystal sits in William's lap and leans into him as if she's been practicing it for some time.

They continue to talk as the night progresses on. Marcus bids them adieu and thanks them for coming. They stand up and file out, but William hesitates, hanging back a moment. Marcus addresses him. "Something you need, young William?"

"Yes, Your Highness. If I'm not out of line, I would like to borrow a horse to take Crystal home. I would like to spend some time with her tonight and with the moon half full, it should be romantic."

Crystal beams a smile, and Marcus nods. "Yes, you may." He snaps his fingers, and one attendant takes off, knowing what he was going to ask before even asking. "It should be out front for you momentarily. Enjoy your night together."

Crystal and William speak at the same time. "Thank you, Your Highness." They bow their heads, and he waves them out. Jack and Gerald talk about the events of the night while the women share their feelings about how things have advanced. Gerald and Muriel's carriage is waiting and the Hellstromm's steam car pulls around.

Marcus watches them go and Skylar leans into him. "So far, so good." She glances up at him and their eyes meet. "But I feel she's not ready yet."

Marcus wraps his arm around her. "I agree. She needs a few more nudges in the right direction, but her power spiked when he proposed." He turns looking out the window down at their exiting guests. "We must be careful or there could be unforeseen ramifications. Daniel has his own part to play tonight as well."

"How is he going to do that, exactly?"

Marcus smiles. "The same way we all promote a prophet." She grins.

Outside, Gerald looks over the Hellstromm's unusual steam car. The whole thing is painted adamantium black with a long hood with large chrome electric lamps for headlights. Chrome signal lights and large silver conical horns on either side of the large chrome grill, topped by a silver eagle for ornamentation. A spare tire in a nook on the passenger side just in front of the door matching what's on the car. Long curved sweeping fenders cover the wheels. On both ends are steel backed chrome bumpers. Very dark opaque windows close off the passenger compartment, but the driver's windows are crystal clear. Topping it off are two small round mirrors behind the tiny signal lights on the fenders, allowing the driver to see behind them.

Gerald runs his hand along the metal. "Amazing vehicle you got here, Jack. Very different from all the other steam vehicles around."

"Thanks." Jack taps the roof. "I built it myself. Took almost a year to scrounge up the Adamantium for the doors and imported the Mithril from Mithport on Titania. Wasn't cheap, but my family's safety comes first."

"Have you thought about going into steam car manufacturing?" Gerald runs his hand along its smooth fenders. "This is some real high-quality craftsmanship. Odd how you went with such small metal wheels when others are using easily produced wagon wheels."

Jack shrugs. "Lower profile means better stabilization. Besides that, I've got my hands into so many things I couldn't think about mass car manufacturing at the moment. For right now, I design farm equipment and get royalties from the Second House who build them."

"That's interesting. How about a joint venture then? You know I build ships, but with your technical knowhow and my foundries, maybe we can work something out?"

Jasmine pipes in. "Anything to get him out of the war business." Jack glances at her and she places a hand on her hip. "If he would build cars instead of power suits, I would be thankful."

Gerald nods. "As tough as this car looks, you could almost put some small cannons on it."

A smile creeps onto Jack's face, and Jasmine's evaporates. "Don't you even think about it, Jack Hellstromm!"

Jack holds his hands up. "What?"

"You know *what*!" She crosses her arms. "I know that smile."

He looks back at Gerald. "She's just mad that I don't buy her flowers."

"As nice of a guy you are, Jack. Why would you never buy her flowers?"

"She never has any for sale when I have money."

Gerald laughs. "I'm going to use that next time Merial gets upset about that." He shakes Jack's hand. "I'll talk to you more about this mass production of cars thing later. It's late and she's tired."

Tia and Andrew are already walking back to the church and William mounts up, pulling Crystal up with him. Jack's voice takes on a warning. "Don't be too late, you two. Just because you're engaged doesn't mean you're free to frolic." This gets Crystal and William to exchange glances as to ask, 'who us?'

Penelope shakes her head and gets in the car, still pulling at her dress, ready to be rid of it. Jasmine and Jack follow Penelope, and Gerald and Muriel get into their carriage and depart. William and Crystal wave at them as they are last to leave.

CHAPTER 5

(Uncertain future)

William turns his head and looks back at Crystal, and speaks teasingly. "So where would you like to go, Mrs. Hellstromm?"

She teases him back. "Anywhere you want to take me, Mr. Hellstromm."

With the moon above their heads, they ride slowly through the empty streets, illuminated only by scattered magical lamps high above. "It's going to be hard for me to get used to that."

"Of having my family name instead of yours?"

He takes a deep breath, letting it out slowly. "It's an odd law that I hadn't heard of, but then again, it's only meant for a very select group of people, so it's not something I would have thought about looking up."

"I know, I didn't know it was a thing either, but if you listened to Marcus' reasoning, it makes sense. He has five daughters and three sons. So, when his daughters get married, by traditional means they would lose that Rose name and it would be replaced by whomever they marry. If they fall for a lower-class person, they will get name recognition unjustly." She hugs him tighter. "I can see why he did it, and by making it apply to the other Houses as well. It keeps it fair."

"But I'm marrying you because I love you, not to promote my name." He turns his head to look at her. "Guess that's why I'm ok with it. My love for you is more than that."

This causes her to squeeze him and press herself against his back. "We have a lot to discuss tonight, darling. So, what are we doing for my birthday in two weeks?"

He turns back. "It's a surprise."

Tia and Andrew make their way across town, casually walking, the flickering of the magical streetlamps guiding their way. "I can't believe how long it took William to finally propose to my sister. You could see those two were meant for each other."

"Yeah, it was pretty obvious." She pushes her hair behind her ear. "I've seen them out in the field together. They make a good team."

"I can see that. She's changed some from the little girl I knew who was all brash and power hungry." Andrew glances at her. "They are going to be happy together."

"Have you ever thought about what they have, and want that too?"

"Of course. I think everyone wants that at some point in their lives, but I have my faith, so those things aren't my concern anymore." As he speaks, she gives a small shake of her head. "Why do you ask?"

"I don't know. I've been in the faith all my life and thought I would never have to worry about such things myself. They have so much more in life together and it's made me wonder what else is out there."

Concern fills Andrew's voice. "Sounds like you're questioning your faith."

She shrugs, looking at the ground. "Daniel chose me for these missions to help them. What if this is the point?" She stops turning to him. "What if we got his wishes wrong and we aren't supposed to only love him? What if his teachings were a way for us to connect to others?"

"That's an interesting notion." He motions to her to give him more. "Has Daniel provided you with any other hints?"

Tia looks away. "I believe so, but I could be interpreting it very wrong."

"Don't keep me in suspense. What was it?"

"When we were on our way to Portstown, Crystal mentioned taking control of her own destiny." She paces a little. "That the gods shouldn't decide everything for us, and I should take control of my own, too. I thought long and hard about that." She gazes up at him. "I went with her to give her council, but instead, she's giving it to me."

"So, what kind of conclusion did you come to?" Andrew's voice is filled with intrigue and Tia catches it. She glances around and notices they are close to an alley. Grabbing his hand without warning, she drags him into it and presses him against a wall. "Tia, what are you…" is all he gets out as she leans into him, pressing her lips against his, with a passion she couldn't hold back anymore.

Her heart races, and joy fills her mind. *What is this feeling? I can't explain it, but it feels right.* Andrew wraps his arms around her, holding her tight, and pressing his lips more firmly. *I'm supposed to be faithful to my god. Did I just throw that all away?* After a few minutes, they separate, breathing hard.

"Interesting conclusion."

"You felt it too, didn't you?"

"I did, but this is taboo in our faith."

"That's just it. I don't think it was meant to. I think that is what Daniel has been trying to tell us all these years, and that's why he chose me to go with Crystal and William. To bring us together and change the way things are done."

"You have a hard argument ahead of you." Andrew presses his forehead against hers. "The leader of the church isn't going to just take your word for it."

Tia's body shakes. "I wonder if I go to Emperor Marcus with this; he can do something. He says he values Daniel's guidance. Maybe he will have some answers for me."

"That would help." He looks out of the alley for a moment. "But for now, we have to keep this between us."

A male disembodied voice comes from the darkened alley. "Keep what between you?" Andrew and Tia look around but can't see who said that. A short man comes out of the darkness looking at them. "Are you Tia Moonglow?"

Tia looks at Andrew and then back again. "Yes?"

The man lashes out quick as lightning, stabbing her in the gut with a sneer on his face. He pulls back and her blood spills to the ground. Tia grabs her stomach, dropping to the ground. Andrew reaches out and punches the guy, sending him reeling backwards. He turns back to see blood seeping from between her fingers.

William and Crystal travel through the streets and cross over a stone bridge that separates the city into two parts. Out of the darkness, an object careens off William's head, knocking him and Crystal to the street below. Blood oozes from the wound as he is partially conscious and disorientated. A group of four people, three males and one female, come out of the dark, and all wearing black. One man speaks up, taunting them. "Nice night for a moonlit stroll, isn't it, countess?"

"Who are you?"

"You don't need to know, but we know you." The man and his cohorts draw their weapons. William pushes Crystal aside and leaps to his feet. He reaches for his sword, only to realize he's not wearing it. The female mocks them. "An unarmed knight and a countess alone in the dark. Bad move." She's lunges but William grabs her weapon hand and twists it. She lets out a scream of pain, as the snapping of bone forces her to drop her short sword.

The other three charges in, but a shadowy figure of an ogre materializes from the darkness and backhands the first man clean out of his boots. His sword drops to the ground with a clank as he sails through the air and into the river. William turns seeing Crystal getting to her feet, hands wreathed in black flames. The other two stop and face the hulking shadow, not knowing what it is they are looking at. William grabs the dropped sword and stabs one of them through the back. The woman on the ground grabs her short sword with her good arm and swings it. Crystal screams and falls back to the earth as the sword breaks through her scales, drawing blood and cutting muscle.

Andrew glances at Tia and back at the man. *She needs my help, but if I turn my back, he will stab me, too. Daniel help us*! From the ground behind him, he hears a prayer and turns to see Tia holding out a red-glowing, blood-soaked finger. A ray of pure searing light lances out, bright as the noon sun, and strikes the assailant in the chest, burning a hole through him. Her hand collapses as she loses the battle with the void. The man looks down at the hole in his body, drops his bloodstained dagger and collapses.

Andrew turns and kneels over her body. He feels for a pulse and its feint. He prays, and his hands glow with a blue light. Touching her, the light envelops her body, and he continues to pray, repairing the damage. The bleeding stops, but she doesn't awaken. "Something wrong. She should be awake if the wound is healed." He chants a second prayer, and she glows purple seeing that she is stable, but there is something else he can't explain. He holds her head up and weeps, knowing how close he came to losing her and the realization that she was right. *There must be more to her claim, but right now, her safety is most important. Need to take her to Lyndis to see why she's not reacting to my healing.* He picks her up and carries her away, running as fast as he can back to the church.

William parries a sword strike from the last remaining man, but the guy gets in a second hit, stabbing him in the right flank. His victory is short-lived as Crystal growls in a dark voice from the ground. "Get that one next." The shadow moves and grabs the assailant, picking him off the ground and slamming him back down into the brick street, crushing his skull. Crystal ignores the pain from her calf and rolls on top of the lady, planting a blood covered knee on her arm and pinning the other with her hand. She backhands the woman, knocking out a tooth.

Blood spilling from her leg, Crystal deactivates her bracelets, bringing her claws to bare. Bloodlust builds inside her as she reaches back, ready to rip the woman's throat out when William grabs her arm. She looks up at him with hate and anger in her eyes, causing him to step back. Within that moment, all her rage evaporates, and she relaxes. She waves her clawed hand in a dismissive gesture, and the shadowy Ogre vanishes, along with the black flame, from sight as if made of smoke. Standing up with William's help, she kicks the girl on the ground, and the sound of bones fracturing assault their ears.

"That wasn't necessary."

"I disagree. She hit me with a sword and tried to kill us." She looks down at the woman, flexing her claws. "She should be happy I don't turn her into a sideshow."

"Speaking of." He looks down. "Why did you attack us?"

The woman spits up blood. "I'm not telling you anything."

Crystal starts an incantation and holds her hand up as if she was holding something and a ball of light appears in her hand. "Don't you recognize her, darling?"

William looks down. "She looks familiar."

Crystal reaches down and rips her shirt off, exposing her chest and the distinctive scars from her claws. "I thought I killed you at Black Rock when you stabbed William."

"You nearly did. I was in recovery for months because of you."

William interrupts. "So, you're a member of the Black Rose."

She lays there on the ground in silence, not bothering to cover up. Crystal reaches down and traces her claws across her scars. "You better tell us what he wants to know, or I'll kill you permanently and animate your corpse. Then you to tell me whatever I want." Her voice is cold and sends a shiver up William's spine. "I don't even need your whole body. I can cut your head off and get the answers I need."

William places a hand on her shoulder. "You promised to never do that again." He pulls her back up. "And what's the deal with the Ogre? Where did he come from?"

Crystal looks away. "I…" She turns, taking a few steps away, and crosses an arm over herself. "That was the Ogre we fought in Portstown."

William shakes his head. "But he's dead. How?"

She cuts him off. "I summoned his soul." She turns and faces him, just to see confusion on his face. "When I killed him, I." She hangs her head. "I did it by removing his soul."

Anger crosses his face. "What do you mean, 'removing his soul'?"

"I used magic to pull his soul from his body, and now it's at my service."

48

William's hands flop to his side. "You enslaved another being's soul?"

Anger and grief fill her voice. "I had no choice."

"There was always a choice."

She balls her fist up and hits him, but it's gentler than he thought it would be. She looks up at him with tears in her eyes. "No, I didn't. It was that or lose you again. And I." He wraps his arms around her. "I can't do that again."

He holds her close. "And with this ambush, you used it again to protect me." He can feel her nod, with her horns grinding against his chest. "You can't keep giving into that power, or you will just be right back where you started." She pulls away and takes a few steps. "Just don't do that to this girl. As bad as she is, using that awful gift would only make things worse."

Crystal looks at William and back to the girl. "Looks like you're lucking out a second time in a row." She walks around William and looks at his wounds. "I guess she's not going anywhere. Go get a guard and have her arrested. Let them interrogate her. Emperor Marcus will praise us for taking in such a valuable prisoner."

"What about you?"

"If she tries anything, there won't be enough of her body left to identify the species."

"That's what I'm afraid of."

William retrieves some guards, and they haul the woman away. They get back to Crystal's home and he helps her down. Carrying her to the door, she stops him from putting her down. She gazes up at him, worry in her eye's. "Please stay here tonight. After what happened, I fear there could be another attempt."

He shakes his head. "That's not a good idea. I know you all too well and I don't want to be killed by Cline or your father because you can't control yourself."

"You need medical attention and I forbid you to leave." He walks with her inside and closes the door with his foot. "We were attacked by *would be* assassins and I don't want to be a widow before I'm even married." She grabs a passing maid. "Get the doctor." The maid nods and hurries off.

CHAPTER 6

(Right vs Wrong)

Andrew carries Tia all the way back to the church. This late at night there is no one up, so getting in was a hassle. He carries her to the back and lays her in front of the altar. Leaving her there, he rushes and finds Lyndis. Returning, she prays over Tia, then looks up at him. Andrew kneels down too. "Do you know what's wrong?"

"I don't know." She glances up at Andrew. "Her body is here, her spirit isn't. I've never encountered this before." She looks down back at Tia. "I need to consult the texts. Stay with her."

From the void, a light appears to Tia and steadily gets closer. As it approaches, it takes shape of that of a Humanoid man wreathed in light. Tia is confused for a moment, then realization comes to her. She kneels before him. "Daniel."

"Yes, my child." The being's words echo through the darkness. "Our time together is short, so I must be brief."

"Am I to join you in the afterlife?"

"Not this time, my child. Instead, I'm speaking to you to guide you on your purpose." She realizes she can't feel her heart and places a hand on her chest. "You are on the right path, but the path is not an easy one. There will be those who will doubt your words, are my words."

"And what path is that, my lord?"

"You already know the path. I was not meant to bear the torch of love, but hold for the one who will be. When one worthy of the torch appears, it will no longer be my burden, and things will become clearer." The voice fades a little. "You've taken the first step. Don't be discouraged by those who doubt you. Trust your instincts." He fades away.

"But how am I to prove I spoke to you, that this is what you wanted?"

"Those nearest to you will know, and you will get help from an unexpected source."

"Daniel!" She reaches out as if to take hold of him, but bolts upright with Andrew, and Lyndis kneeling next to her jump back and yelp. Several others standing there all praying behind them come to a sudden stop. Tia's heart races and is panting, still holding her arm out as if she's reaching for something.

"Calm down." Lyndis eases her back to her floor. "You were gone there for about an hour and thought you passed on. You're body was alive, but your spirit was gone. We were praying for your soul to have peace with Daniel."

Tia looks to her, and swallows. "He spoke to me, said I was on the right path, and to trust my instincts."

Lyndis looks at Andrew and back to Tia. "What do you mean, child?"

Tia sits back up and feels something in the hand that she reached out with. Bringing it up to look at it, it's the holy symbol of Daniel, but it's not made of wood, but of some silver-like material. "He said I discovered the true path for his followers." She hands the holy symbol to Lyndis, and she can feel it's not natural, but divine.

"Where did you get this?"

Tia shakes her head and Andrew shrugs. "She didn't carry it in here." Andrew takes her hand, helping her to her feet. "Maybe he gave it to her to put weight to her words, to prove she communed with him?"

Lyndis can feel Daniel's presence in the artifact but feels it's not hers to keep, and hands it back to Tia. "What are we supposed to do?"

"I don't know. He said I would get help from an unexpected source, but that's ambiguous."

"You know how many churches there are of Daniel?" Lyndis indicates for Tia to follow. "And I'm not admitting you're right or that you even have a point, but why commune these wishes with you and not with someone like me who's at the head of the church?"

"I don't know what one either. He said the path ahead of me was going to be a hard one, that there will be those who doubt my words." They go into her office and Tia sits down. "He said he was only meant to carry the torch of love till another is worthy." She looks to Lyndis "And no, I don't know what that means either. I thought that was his role, but he makes it sound like he was never meant to have it." Tia grabs her head. "It's all a whirlwind in my head, and I can't make sense of it."

Andrew sits down next to her and rubs her back. "I believe you, but the thing is, how do we change the dogma without causing the church to tear itself apart?"

Tia shakes her head, then looks up. "Why did he have to pick me? I'm not good at these things."

Lyndis stands in front of her. "We will figure it out together. I'm not completely convinced of your words, but that holy artifact in your hands tells me I should listen to you. We can go over the holy scrolls and give them some scrutiny to see what we find, but let's do that in the morning. Right now, we should get back to sleep."

The Hellstromm's doctor applies some healing salve that stops the bleeding and kills off any would-be infection. Then grabbing some bandages, he wraps William's wound and tells him to sleep it off and, in the morning, get proper healing from a church or hospital. He then applies the same salve to Crystal's leg and bandages it. "Will do, doc." He looks at Crystal. "Looks like you're getting your wish, but I'm not sleeping in your room. I'll crash on the couch."

"Nonsense." She thumbs to the backyard. "You can stay in the guest house out back. We keep it ready for whenever Grandma and Grandpa drop in. You can sleep there tonight where you will be safe."

The doctor gets up and packs up his bag, tips his hat and walks back to his quarters. William stands with some help from Crystal. "I really shouldn't. It would look bad."

Crystal cuts him off, and the tease in her voice returns. "William Hellstromm, that's not a suggestion. It's an order." She looks at him in all seriousness.

"Ok, you win."

"Damn straight I do."

He smiles. "I'll go to my room now." She takes him outside and across the courtyard to the guest house. It's almost as big as a normal upscale dwelling, which he finds is probably normal for them. She leads him inside and back to the master bedroom that has its own bathroom. He sits on the bed and removes his boots and socks and starts with his pants and stops himself. "Maybe you should go to bed. If you're caught in here with me, the Black Rose will be the least of my problems."

She leans forward and kisses him with a renewed passion that gets him to wrap his arms around her. A few minutes pass and she breaks it off so they can both breathe. She pulls his face into her bosom and strokes his head. He can hear her heart beating and it brings a smile to his face. "We will figure out what these people want and how to stop them." She pulls back to look down at him. "Get some rest, darling." She lets him go and takes

54

a few steps. "And I promise I won't sneak in here, despite how badly I want to."

Jack is waiting for her when she comes back inside the main house. "What is going on, monster?" She spins towards his voice and sees him appear, wearing his newest iteration of his armor, larger and scarier than ever.

A tear starts in her eye and walks up to him. "Daddy!"

He exits his armor and steps out, and she hugs him. "The Black Rose attacked us on the way home. He was injured."

Jack looks down at her legs. "You were hurt too?"

"Not as bad as him. We are going to go see Tia and Andrew in the morning for magical healing, but we should be ok overnight."

Jack pats her on the back and escorts her to her room. "Good idea. I'll alert the guards to be doubled and hire more to beef up the security. They might make a move on any of us at this point."

The next morning, Tia awakens in her bed with the other females of the church, but she feels different. She can't explain it, but it feels as if it has lifted a burden from her chest. She meets Lyndis and Andrew along with a few others. They go through scrolls as regular clergy do their normal tasks of cleaning and preparing. Lyndis flips through ancient papers. "I'm hoping that somewhere in the archives is proof that supports or denies your claim, Tia. The library dates back as far as the founding of the city." She picks up a new stack. "This is a monumental task to read all these books and scrolls written over the centuries by so many clerical scholars."

Andrew shrugs. "Maybe that's how we lost our way without knowing. Too much was ignored and/or simplified."

Crystal and William limp into the church, followed by Jack in his power armor during the midmorning. A marvel of steam and magic standing over seven feet tall, painted red and black. On his forearms are the tips of what look like swords, and a nozzle attached to the underside of the left arm with a flexible metal tube leading to the back. The power armor sparks an alarm from those gathered, and clerics come out and surround the trio. Tia and Andrew look out and see the massive armor with William and Crystal standing there under guard. Tia hurries across the floor, followed closely by Andrew and Lyndis. "What happened?"

William groans as she undresses his wound. "The Black Rose attacked us last night." He winces as the bandages stick to the injury. "They almost got me a second time. I'm not going anywhere unarmed ever again."

"Crystal, you're hurt too?"

"Yeah, I caught a short sword on the back of my leg. Thanks be to Daniel that Olovira did this to me, or I would have been an amputee."

Tia cries, causing everyone to look at her. "We were attacked last night, too." She lifts her robes and showing the scar from the stab wound she took. "I almost died." She turns and looks at Andrew and a small smile appears. "Thanks to Daniel, Andrew was with me and saved my life."

Andrew heals Crystal the best he can, then stands. "You've become resistant to healing magic. There isn't much I can do for this."

Crystal puts on a fake smile. "It's fine. What about Tia?"

"We thought we lost her. I healed her, but she didn't wake up. I brought her back here and not even Lyndis could bring her around. We were about to pronounce her dead because her soul had left her body. Then she bolted upright and took a deep breath, scarring us half to death."

William shakes his head, and Tia continues her healing. "Sounds like you had it worse than us." She backs away, and he rubs the spot and can feel the scar. "Good as it's going to get."

"Daniel came to me when I slipped into the void. I was waiting for him to take me to the afterlife but instead..." Tia holds up the silver like artifact. "He gave me this." She hands it to Crystal. "He told me he I have a new purpose."

Crystal looks at it mutters and incantation and waves her hands in gesture. Her eyes glow purple for a second and she looks at it. "It's magical, but I can't tell you what it does without researching it."

"That's ok. I'm sure I will discover whatever it does when the time comes."

Jack points at it. "Emperor Marcus has something similar to that given to him by the Provider." He motions to the palace. "I've seen it a few times when I've been in his office negotiating contracts. Maybe he can help you with it. He seems to like you kids, so he could give you more of an explanation."

They all stop and turn to him. "Are you saying this is a legit item from a god?"

Jack shrugs, the heavy metal scraping together. "Could be. Emperor Marcus would know for sure." He thumbs outside. "You want a ride to the palace? My car is outside."

Lyndis looks at Tia. "It would help to know." She turns to Andrew and the others. "Keep searching the library for answers in the meantime and make sure your chores are done."

Crystal interjects. "I want to go too; I want to know what this Black Rose prisoner has to say."

William pulls her close. "I'll come too."

Crystal shakes her head. "No, you should go see your family and make sure they are ok. If Tia and Andrew were attacked, then they could have been assaulted, too." Her voice turns dark, making a crushing motion with her hand. That turns

Jack's head. "The Black Rose has made this personal, and I'm going to crush them to dust." She looks around and sees everyone has taken a few steps back. "What?!"

William places a hand on her shoulder. "Honey, you're scary when you do stuff like this." She frowns and turns her face up and away, closes her eyes and crosses her arms. He grins and leans down next to her ear and whispers to her. "You're cute when you pout."

This causes her to peek one eye open and smile. "I can't stay mad at you." Her tone is flat and unemotional, getting everyone there to exchange glances. "I'll just take it out on someone else later." She hooks her arm through Williams. "Let's go."

Lyndis leans over to Tia. "I can't tell if she was being serious or not."

Tia shakes her head. "I don't know either."

William helps Crystal into the car, and then the same with Lyndis and Tia. Andrew stands there. "I'm going to go with William just in case there is a need for me. If not, then I can always come back."

Lyndis glances up at him. "Just be careful." Jack shuts the door and informs the driver to head to the palace.

William and Andrew start their journey and make it a few blocks when Andrew breaks the silence. "How did you know Crystal was the one for you?"

"What?"

"You and my sister. How did you know she was the one for you?"

"At first, I didn't. I thought of her as a pompous brat that was full of herself." He tries to hide his grin. "But as the days and weeks went by, I was seeing past all that." William checks around him before crossing a busy street and the two run across, avoiding an ox driven cart and a newer model steam car. "But I don't know what exactly triggered it. She's beautiful, smart, skilled, and had a life goal. It was respectable, even if some of it made her standoffish." He checks around himself. "When we got to the monastery, Master Monzulo spoke to us and said that it's not power and protection that was important, but love and happiness." He looks over at Andrew. "Then it clicked after I woke up on the cold floor. That old man saw something that we didn't see ourselves." William looks distant and his grin fades. "I think Crystal came to that realization when she was willing to give her life for mine." He turns to Andrew. "That's why she started spending more time around me and making excuses to do so."

"It wasn't just sudden but something that you felt grow over time?"

William and Andrew continue to walk and grab some fruit to snack on. "Spending time with her here at home, on the airship, and eight months in Portstown made me realize that no matter what, live or die, we were connected forever." He looks at Andrew and laughs. "And the nudge that pushed me over the edge to make the plunge was when your mom called me son. I knew then I needed to do the right thing." Andrew motions to stop traffic as they cross another busy street. "Why do you ask Andrew, if you don't mind?"

Concern crosses Andrew's face. "I think I have a connection like that as well, that I was only vaguely aware of that came to a head recently." He opens his mouth and stops, then starts again. "What started as a small flame has now grown and I'm having a hard time controlling it."

"I don't understand. You're in love with someone?"

Andrew nods in confirmation. "I'm afraid so, and I can't shut it out."

William stops and grabs Andrew by the shoulder, spinning him around. "Why would you want to shut it out? Love is a wonderful feeling."

"Because of my faith. We are only supposed to love Daniel, not another." Andrew looks down and kicks at the ground. "But Tia said she saw Daniel last night and told her the texts have been misread or misinterpreted. That he was only meant to keep something called the *torch of love* till another comes to take it." He shakes his head, trying to clear his head. "It doesn't make sense."

"Maybe not." Andrew looks up at him. "It would be a hard life not getting to love those around you. It would drive me nuts if I weren't allowed to be with your sister. I wouldn't have a purpose to live." He places a hand on Andrew's shoulder and gives it a little shake. "Maybe that's what he means by misinterpreted? Maybe you're not supposed to just love him?"

Andrew thinks about it. "I know how that feels, and you're right. It is rather maddening not being able to express love for another."

"For what it's worth, brother, I was told by a wise old man that you must find your own purpose in life, right? That applies to you too." William lets him go and they walk again, leaving Andrew in thought the rest of the way.

They get to William's manor and walk in. Gerald and Muriel are there in the main room sitting and reading the news. The sarcasm and the fact that his father doesn't look at him makes William's heart sink. "Glad you could make it home."

"Sorry father, I'm glad you're sitting down. I have news you're not going to like."

CHAPTER 7

(Law and Dogma)

Jack and the girls arrive at the palace and exit the car. The guards almost don't let Jack pass with his armor, but Crystal shows the signet ring Marcus gave her. "We need an audience with Emperor Marcus. It's of great importance."

The Royal Guards escort them to the throne room and hold a hand up. "Please wait here, and I will inform His Highness of your arrival."

Long moments pass and Marcus and Skylar enter the room. His voice booms through the room. "When I said to let me know when you were ready, I wasn't thinking it would be the next day."

They go to kneel to him, but he dismissively waves his hand sitting on his throne. "Please don't. I think we are way past those formalities at this point." They step forward. "What brings you four here? I see you brought a new one with you this time I'm not familiar with."

Tia motions with her hands and bows. "This is Head Priestess Lyndis of the Church of Daniel, Your Highness."

"Oh? I've only heard of you. Glad to see you've finally visited." He leans forward. "What brings you to my humble palace, Head Priestess Lyndis?"

"Your Highness. Last night Tia, Andrew, Crystal, and William were attacked, and Tia was almost killed. As a result, Tia claims she was visited by Daniel and gave her some conflicting information from what we normally believe."

Marcus leans back, glances at Skylar who gives the subtleness of nods, then turns back to Lyndis. "And what does this have to do with me? This sounds like an internal church matter."

Lyndis turns slightly to Tia. "Show him." Tia pulls out the silver looking artifact and holds it out. Marcus' demeanor changes from dismissive to interested. "Daniel gave this to her when their communion was over."

Marcus stands and walked over to Tia. He takes her hand and raises it to get a better look at the artifact but doesn't touch it himself. "I see why you came to me." He looks at Crystal and Jack. "Why are you two here, then?" He points to the artifact. "It can't be because of this."

Jack's voice is muffled from inside his armor. "Crystal and William killed three of their attackers, but one survived and was arrested. We are here to see if the Royal Guard had any luck extracting any information from her."

"So why the power armor? You showing off for me? If so, you have my interest. That's rather impressive."

"I'm protecting my daughter and her friends. If anyone pulls anything, they won't be pulling it for long."

Marcus stands upright and gives a subtle nod of approval. "Very noble of you, Jack, but I believe that responsibility is going to be passed to young William soon. Are you ready for that?"

"Till then, she's still my responsibility. William will have to be prepared from the day he says his vows, that if anything happens to my daughter on his watch." Jack puts hit thumb in his chest. "I'm his biggest threat." He looks down at Crystal. "But I have faith in him to lay his life down again if he must. That's why I'm proud to have him as my future son."

Marcus smiles and turns to the guard. "Take these two down to the detention area and get what they want. I'm going to help the girls here figure out their god problem." The guards snap to attention and motion for Jack and Crystal to follow them. Marcus waves the two priestesses to follow him into his office. Skylar sits silently, watching things unfold.

He has them sit down and closes the door for privacy. Walking around his desk, to the wall behind it, and takes down a silver like object hidden among the rest of the decorations. Had you not been looking specifically for it; you could easily miss it. "The provider gave this to me in a vision as well. In a similar situation, I too was near-death." He waves his hands, gesturing around him. "It gave me a new purpose, and it helped me build all this." He puts his artifact down on the desk. "And I can tell that's from Daniel, so I can confirm he visited you. I know when you walked in here that day so long ago there was something special about you, but this amazes even me."

Tia nods and she puts the artifact down next to the holy artifact of the Provider. They react to each other by softly glowing a white color. All three stare at it for a long moment. "What does that mean?"

Lyndis shakes her head, stupefied. "I don't have a clue. Till today, I have seen nothing like this."

Marcus sits in his chair. "It looks like they are acknowledging each other's presence." Marcus shrugs. "I've only had the one all these years, so this is a first time for me too. It's fascinating, isn't it?" He leans back. "One prophet to another, tell me about this vision and please, be as detailed as possible and why you're having an internal crisis."

Crystal and Jack follow the guard down to the main office. It's busy with the clanking of armor and people talking and exchanging information, and they are brought to a desk. A mid-sized aging Human male with dark skin, graying hair, and with several scars across his face sits there. He stands, reaching out and shake their hands. "I'm Major Steiner. What can the Guard help the Hellstromm's with today?"

Crystal takes his hand first. "A prisoner was brought here last night with a broken arm that is with the Black Rose. We were wondering if you got any information out of her yet?"

Steiner shakes his head. "She's been pretty stoic about keeping quiet, but we haven't tried to really push her yet." He takes Jack's hand and steps out from behind his desk. "You could come back tomorrow, and we should have more information then."

She shakes her head in disapproval. "I want to see the prisoner."

"I'm sorry Ms. Hellstromm, I can't allow…"

She cuts him off, flashes the crest of the First House and anger fills her voice. "That's Countess Hellstromm to you." She puts a finger to his armored chest slightly, pushing him back. "You will address me properly and give me access to the prisoner." Jack raises an eyebrow, but no one can see his face in his armor.

The room goes quiet as all eyes focus on her. She stares the other man down with those icy blue eyes and fear races up his spine. "Right this way, countess."

They follow along and Jack leans down to her. "You learn so well, Crystal. Just remember not to take it too far."

Her tone comes across as sweet and innocent. "I know daddy."

They get down to the cells, and there are many people in there. The noise picks up as the prisoners start cat calling Crystal and making obscene remarks and gestures. Unfettered rage breaks loose from the cage inside her and she turns off the bracelets, allowing her fingers to grow into long, taloned claws. One man reaches out and with a swift, unperceivable fast motion, she swipes his arm, slicing through effortlessly. He lets out a scream of anguish, but her claw has hooked through his arm and bone, making him unable to pull away. She yanks him violently; the ringing of the bars drowns out and ends all other noises. She bares her sharp teeth in a sneer, changing from beautiful and innocent to something born from the most sinister of nightmares.

The Major hears the scream and metal bending from behind him. He turns and eyes widen at the horror unfolding. He reaches out to stop her as she is racking the prisoner against the bars. Blood gushes outwards in all directions as she rends flesh and breaks bones. Jack grabs her hand, trying to pull her away. "Let go Crystal!" Gears in the suit grind and pressure valves blow open, preventing catastrophic failures as his attempt to control her is futile. *How strong is she? This is insane*! The Major grabs on as well, but she effortlessly pushes him away with her left arm, sending him sliding several dozen feet across the stone floor.

Crystal focuses on her prey, ignoring the fact her father has latched onto her. Bloodlust floods her mind, but some measure of control comes back at the last moment. "YOU WILL NOT TOUCH ME. YOU WILL NOT TALK TO ME. YOU WILL NOT LOOK AT ME. IF ANY OF YOU CRETENS VALUE YOUR LIVES YOU WILL BE RESPECTFUL OR I WILL RIP YOUR GOD DAMN ARM OFF! DO I MAKE MYSELF CLEAR?!"

Jack continues to pull on her. "That's going too far, Crystal!" She pulls her claw out, blood splattering in all directions. Major Steiner yells for a medic as he gets back to his feet.

She brings her claw to her mouth, licking the blood from it. She turns, walking away, examining her work with delight. "If you knew what people like this did to me out there, you would kill them right now." Crystal looks over her shoulder back at him. "Scum like this only knows one language, pain, and I've gotten extremely fluent in it."

"You're scaring me, baby girl. I don't know what happened to you out there, and I wish you would tell me. But this…" waving his hand at the pool of blood. "This is not the answer."

She buries her claw in his armored chest. "You've wiped an entire city off the face of the planet. Don't tell me about going too far and what's scary." Jack is glad she can't see his face and how much that hurt him, hearing her say that.

She turns and finds her prisoner farther down, sitting in a cell with other women. "So, you've come here to ask me more questions? Save your breath. I'm not getting close enough to those bars for you to grab *me*."

"You think I need my claws to hurt you?" A malicious grin appearing on her face. "Bitch, you don't know who you provoked."

She raises her hand and starts an incantation, and Jack grabs her hand, interrupting her spell. "Not like this. This is what I mean by taking it too far."

Crystal looks at her father and the Major comes running back down the hall. "Countess, your authority doesn't allow you to harm prisoners unjustly."

She looks at him and back at the Black Rose woman. "In this case, you're correct. I don't have 'just cause' to splatter her brains out all over the wall." She turns back to Steiner. "But the guy whose arm I lacerated was trying to grab me; that was self-defense." She looks at the unknown woman in her cell. "Saved by the law. You might want to tell these guys what they want to know and you want a long prison sentence." Her voice drips with vindictiveness, gripping the bars so tightly that they bend. "Because once you hit the streets, I can freely hunt you down." The girl visibly swallows. Crystal turns and leaves. Jack looks at the Major and shrugs.

They are about to exit to the squad room when the Black Rose lady yells from her cell that she wants to talk to someone from the Guard. Crystal smiles, knowing she got what she wanted. They walk in and Jack pulls Crystal to the side. "What has gotten into you?"

"You heard her, she ready to sing like a canary to the police to get the maximum sentence she can so I can't get her.

Her greatest fear right now is being free. As long as she's in custody, she's protected from me."

"You almost ripped a man's arm off and made that entire speech just to intimidate her into giving up the information they wanted?"

"And it worked." She shrugs. "Well, we will know if it did in a few hours, anyway."

"I don't know what's gotten into you, but you're not the sweet little girl I raised." Even in the power armor, she can hear the shift of him being disappointed.

She points to the holding cells. "Dad, that lady in there? She killed William in Black Rock. It's her people that captured me and tortured me almost to death. Had William not shown up when he did, we wouldn't be having this conversation."

Jack steps back. The helmet flips back and the arms and legs open, allowing him to step down and he hugs his daughter. "I'm sorry that happened to you." She puts her arms around him, and he sobs a little. "But this, this anger, this miasma you carry about you about it isn't the answer. It's one thing to scare your enemy into peace. It's another to inflict pain for the sake of inflicting pain. Don't become the people you're fighting."

She looks thoughtful and her expression turns from anger to sadness, then wraps her arms around him and hugs him. "I'm sorry, father, you're right. I didn't mean to disappoint you."

"I'm just glad I'm here to still offer you guidance. I'm just glad I could talk you down."

"William had to hold me back as well when we were in Portstown. I almost went too far then, too."

"Then he's the perfect man to marry you. He needs to guide you and keep you off this dark path." Jack steps back and climbs back into the power armor and it closes around him. "Major, we are sorry for the interruption. We will go back up and speak with the Emperor and if you get any news, please inform us." Jack turns and ushers his daughter back upstairs.

CHAPTER 8

(Hard choices)

William and Andrew sit down opposite Gerald and Muriel and William looks to them and back to Andrew. "Did anything happen last night while I was gone? Anyone you didn't know show up or look out of place?"

Gerald looks at Muriel. "I didn't hear anything, did you?" She shakes her head and Gerald turns back to William. "What's going on, son? Why weren't you home last night?"

William leans forward and looks to the floor, gathering his words and wringing his hands. "The Black Rose attacked us last night. Tia almost died, and Crystal and I fought off a group of four, capturing one for interrogation."

Gerald and Muriel gasp and Gerald leans in. "You were all together?"

Andrew jumps in. "No, Tia and I were walking home and went into an alleyway for a shortcut. From the dark, a man asked for her name, then stabbed her. Around that time, William and Crystal were being assaulted themselves."

"They tried to assassinate you?!"

William nods. "Thankfully, they didn't know what they were doing, or underestimated us." He looks up at his father. "Crystal and her father are talking to the prisoner. I expect they will talk, or they will wish they never laid eyes on her."

"I know you Will. You're coming up with a plan, right?"

William covers his brow with his right hand and tilts his head back. "Been trying to. This entire ordeal is at the worst possible moment in my life. I was hoping to have the wedding before we left, but if we don't deal with the Black Rose, they might target us there when we are most vulnerable."

Andrew shakes his head. "Why would they do that? It's a sacred thing."

"Because if I was going to strike the enemy, I would when they were most vulnerable." William brings his hand down and looks at Andrew. "And you can't get more vulnerable that a large gathering of people with no weapons or armor."

Andrew nods, as that sounds logical. "What about the engagement?"

William smiles. "I love her, and I'm not breaking that off, if that's what you're asking." He sighs. "But I will not put her or anyone else at risk till the threat is neutralized." He looks at Gerald. "What would you do, father?"

"Advice?" Gerald gets deep in thought. "I'm not sure, but if these Black Rose people will not leave you alone, then you're right, you're going to have to deal with them sooner rather than later."

Andrew looks helpless. "I wish I could guide you on this, but I'm not wise in the ways of war."

William stands up. Andrew, Gerald, and Muriel also stand up and William heads to the door. "In any case, we need to get back to the palace. I came here to check on you two. Double the guard, increase rotations, and make sure they report anything suspicious. If they can't get to us, they may target you. Jack has already done that at his manor."

"Be careful, my son." Muriel hugs William and kisses him on the cheek. "We worry about you."

William walks out with Andrew in tow. "It's just another deployment, but at least the company is wonderful to be around." William gets his steed and another for Andrew and ride to the palace.

William speaks with Andrew as they exit the gates. "How do you think your sister is going to handle the news that we have to delay getting married?

"That's a good question. No one has ever proposed to her before and lived to talk about it." William turns and looks at him and Andrew laughs. "In all seriousness, I don't know. She's not unreasonable and will understand, and it's not like you two bought a home yet. Where would you go? Not back to one of our parents' places."

William watches the road. "You're right. We need our own place together, don't we?" He looks thoughtful. "A lot to do, but first, we need to get some peace."

Marcus rubs his chin. "It would be difficult to prove what a god says when he only spoke it to you, and this is some very convincing proof. How would you prove your theory, Tia?" She casts her eyes to the ground, and Marcus can see her blushing. "Is there a problem?"

Lyndis looks at Marcus and back to Tia as if Marcus knows something that she doesn't. "Am I missing something?"

Tia shakes her head "I don't know how to prove what he said besides the artifact."

"There is obviously something different about you than the others. He chose you for the mission and now is coming to you to change his church." Marcus rests his elbows on the desk. "What have you done differently that would have gotten your god take notice?"

Tia shrinks into the chair "I-I don't know."

Marcus leans back in his chair. "I think you do, but you're too afraid to speak up." He wags his finger in the air. "Remember what I said the first time you were here?" She shakes her head. "In here, there is no judgment. You can speak your mind without reprisal." He looks at Lyndis. "This applies to you, too. No matter what she says, you are not to judge her for. It's between her and Daniel."

Tia doesn't look up. "Before my vision, I…" She pauses, struggles and pulls at her robes. She looks up at Marcus and just spills it out. "I think I'm in love with someone else and I kissed them." Tears well up in her eyes.

Marcus and Lyndis trade glances. "That's all?"

"It's not that simple, Your Highness." Lyndis takes Tia's hand. "When you become a member of the church as a clergy, you swear to only love Daniel, forsaking all others for him. She broke her vow and when she got stabbed, Daniel gave her this artifact and told her she was on the right path." Lyndis turns back to the artifact. "Could we have been mistaken on his teachings, or maybe there are some stipulations we overlooked, long and forgotten in antiquity?" Marcus sits there pondering the answer when Jack and a blood covered Crystal enter the room.

Tia leaps from her chair. "Crystal, are you ok?" Crystal cocks her head and looks down at the blood on her dress and notices her right claw has blood on it. "Or should I ask if your assailant is still alive?"

Crystal frowns and places a hand on her hip. "What's that supposed to mean?"

"You're covered in blood, and giving how calm you are, I'm assuming it's not yours."

"No, one prisoner made a grab for me, and I defended myself." She lifts her arm and turns the bracelets back on. "I scratched him up to force him to reconsider life choices."

Marcus raises an eyebrow. "Did you actually fear for your life?"

Crystal bows her head. "I don't know what he was capable of."

Marcus' eyebrow doesn't drop. "I know your strength, young lady. I doubt anyone short of William, your father, or myself can match your current physical prowess. You needed a pin cushion to prove a point?"

Jack scoffs. "She's actually stronger than my power armor. Me and the Major couldn't peel her off the prisoner. She tossed him like an angry toddler would a doll." This gets Marcus to raise an eyebrow.

She doesn't look up. "I'm sorry, Emperor. That is correct. We need the information from the Black Rose prisoner. When the cat calling and obscene remarks started, I lost control." She glances up at him. "But I used that to get her to think I'm some kind of crazed vengeful killer and it would be better off staying in jail."

Marcus sighs. "I don't approve of your method." She bows a little farther on reflex. "But I know it gets results. Don't do that again. It's not befitting a countess to get her own hands dirty."

"Yes, Your Highness, it won't happen again, I swear it."

Marcus switches the subject. "Tia seems to have caused a stir within her church."

Crystal straightens up. "With the vision thing? I didn't get to hear the story about that. Tia was keeping it to herself." Tia's face flushes and she sits back down, burying her face in her chest. "What's the short version?"

Lyndis places a hand on Tia's shoulder. "Tia said that she was falling in love with someone else besides Daniel, and she kissed them. After that, she was stabbed and had her communion."

Crystal smile grows across her face. "You took my advice and kissed Andrew? Good for you, girl." She tilts her head to look Tia in the eyes. "Finally took my advice and took control of your destiny."

Lyndis leans back and scowls. "This is you're doing?"

Crystal shoots a dirty look back. "You make it sound like two people being in love is a bad thing. Relax, there is no greater feeling that love." Marcus looks to Jack and gives a subtle nod.

Lyndis stands up, and Crystal straightens up on reflex. Lyndis steps forward and puts her finger on Crystal's chest. "Because of your 'advice', my church is being turned upside down trying to figure out if centuries' worth of teachings is wrong."

Crystal looks down at the Elf's finger and then looks back up at the tall priestess. "Two things." Crystal's voice turns cold as the mountain tops. The smile fades and the row of sharp teeth become visible as she speaks. "First, remove that finger before I feed it to you." The seriousness in Crystal's voice gets Lyndis to pull her hand back. "Second, people should get to love who they want." Crystal steps forward and puts a pointed finger in Lyndis' face. "She loves another being and that should be celebrated, not repressed by an outdated barbaric church dogma."

Marcus coughs, grabbing everyone's attention. "Ladies, please don't fight in here. If you want to brawl, take it out back." He stands up. "But I think Crystal has a point and would explain a lot. It makes one wonder how many of your members regret their decision, but still want to serve Daniel."

"There was another part of the vision." Tia speaks up from her chair, drawing everyone's attention. "Daniel says he's carrying the torch of love, waiting to pass it to another." She looks up. "What did he mean?"

Lyndis shrugs, but Marcus gives her a comforting look. "There are only a handful of gods now. According to the legends, there was a war in heaven and several gods fell and the gods of magic, love, knowledge, and evil still don't exist. But seventy years ago, a new god of war, nature and destruction have risen and taken their places among the pantheon." Marcus glances at Jack, then back at Tia, then Crystal. "Maybe it's an artifact that's waiting for the day a new 'God or Goddess of Love' will appear?"

"I'm not very knowledgeable about religious matters." Crystal points to Tia. "But she is."

Tia's eyes go wide. "Oh, no." She puts her hands up. "I don't know anything about other gods or that legend. This is the first I heard of it."

"Well, how about this?" Crystal casts her gaze at Lyndis. "The church can let Tia and Andrew pursue their relationship and give love a chance. If this anger's Daniel, he would take their divine powers, wouldn't he?"

Lyndis glowers back. "What you ask for is blasphemy."

"But you don't know that." They turn and look at Marcus. "I believe Crystal's proposal has merit."

Lyndis looks to Marcus and bows her head. "Yes, Your Highness. I'll agree under protest. For what it's worth, I hope she's right, and this is what Daniel wants. I still have to disagree on principle, being that there are old teachings to counter what we already know."

Marcus points to the artifact from Daniel. "It's settled then." Tia lets out a long breath of air, having realized she's been holding it this whole time. She stands and picks up the holy artifact.

William and Andrew make it to the palace and walk in with their escort as Tia turns with the artifact. "What did we miss?"

Crystal beams and steps up to him, wrapping her arms around his neck and giving him a passionate kiss. It carries on till Jack speaks up. "I'm right here, you two."

"Sorry Mr. Hellstromm." Jack coughs, interrupting him. "Father." William pulls at his collar. "Sorry, habit and all." Crystal steps back and he can feel something sticky on his neck. He touches it and sees blood on his fingertips and then realizes her right hand and her clothes have blood stains. "What happened to you?"

She tilts her head down and looks up at him with her eye's her voice going soft. "Nothing."

Marcus buts in. "There was an incident down in the holding cells. Crystal had to make an example out of someone, apparently."

William looks to him then down at Crystal. "Do you enjoying wearing someone else's blood?"

"Not really, but it sends a message that I shouldn't be messed with." She cites an incantation and waves her hand. The blood stains vanish from her garments and hand. "Better darling?"

"Yes, much."

Marcus clears his throat. "So, while we are all here, have you two decided on a wedding date, or do you still need time?"

William jumps in as Crystal is about to speak. "We haven't had a chance to talk about it, Your Highness."

Crystal turns and looks up at him. "I thought…" William shakes his head, stopping her there.

"We need to talk about it. I've had some ideas after talking to your brother and my parents, and I want to run them by you before we make any final plans. I think it's important." He looks at Marcus. "I'm sorry to ask this, Your Highness, but is there a place we can speak privately?"

"Step out and go straight across the throne room. There is another office there I use for diplomatic dealings."

"Thank you, we won't be long." William takes Crystal's hand and leaves.

They cross the throne room, with the group staring at them. Skylar watches them as they cross the room. Tia turns back. "Wonder what that is all about?"

Marcus shrugs. "You tell us. You've spent the most time around them."

Andrew pats Tia on the shoulder, and Lyndis gives him a dirty look as if silently scolding him for something. "So, what did I miss?"

Lyndis bows to Emperor Marcus. "I'll leave this to you." "If I may be excused, Your Highness." He nods and waves her out, leaving Jack and the unusual couple.

Andrew watches as she closes the door behind her. "What was *that* about?".

"My vision. Remember last night when you said you felt what I did when we had our moment?"

Andrew looks to his father and then to Marcus. Fear creeps up his spine as he looks at Tia. "Yes, are we in trouble?"

Marcus interrupts. "Not at all Young Andrew." He indicates to Andrew and Tia to sit down. "We talked about the artifact, the vision, and the circumstances they appeared in." Marcus retakes his seat. "You're being allowed to court Tia here, if that is your wish. You're released of your vow and if her vision is correct, then you two have nothing to fear." He holds a finger up. "If Daniel doesn't like it or she misinterpreted it, well, repent, and things will go back to how they were." He leans forward, resting his elbows on his desk. "This is an opportunity a man like you doesn't get often. Lyndis has given it her blessing and hopes Tia is correct. What do you say?"

Andrew looks at Tia and can see her trying to hide her smile by looking down. "I would like to court her. She's amazing." He looks at Marcus. "How will that work with us staying together at the church?"

76

Jack opens his helmet. "You could come home, son. Your room is still there, untouched after all this time."

Andrew shrugs, opening his hands out wide. "So do we just date as if we were normal people who worship Daniel?"

Marcus speaks up. "That's the idea." Everyone turns to him. "But with her going back out into the field, you won't get to date much, so better get cracking on that." He turns to Tia. "And that means you're going to need some other clothes beside those robes." He looks back at Andrew. "This doesn't release you from your duties. You're still a cleric of the Church and are expected to fulfill your duties to it as if nothing changed." Andrew nods in agreement, not knowing what to say.

Tia looks up. "I've never had to buy clothes before. I don't have any money."

Marcus grins. "I'm sure it will thrill Crystal to help you with that."

William and Crystal walk into the office and he shuts the door. "Are you going to tell me what's going on, Will?"

"I think we need to delay the wedding. At least till we deal with the Black Rose."

Crystal becomes enraged. "Why? They wouldn't dare attack me on my wedding day."

"Wouldn't they? These people waited for us. We've hurt them in Portstown and almost killed all of us in Black Rock. A wedding would invite trouble."

Crystal's anger fades to heartache thinking about the first time he died. "I know you're right, but I still want us to get married. Maybe we can vet everyone who enters and station guards. Make it to where an attack would be futile?"

"And what about the reception, the honeymoon, the trip there and back? Are we going to honeymoon with an army surrounding us all the time when we should cherish each other's company?"

Crystal flops down in a chair. After a moment, she looks up. "How about we get married in secret? Our parents, Tia, Andrew, Shadow, and Cline. Keep it super simple, don't tell anyone, no guest list. Then when we get back, we have a real wedding with all the bells and whistles, and it be like a celebration?" She looks down at her hand. "My engagement ring will serve as my wedding ring till we do it right. As far as anyone knows, we are only engaged except to those closest to us." She looks up at him with her icy blue eyes, pleading for a compromise and William can't help but breakdown.

He kneels, taking her hand. "Ok, ok, you win."

She jumps up and wraps her arms around his neck, holding herself off the ground and kisses him. "We need a date. I was thinking about the sixth."

He stands pulling her off the ground. "Why the sixth?"

She ticks off her fingers. "Well, Providers Day is the thirty-first, my birthday is on the second and the sixth is a Friday, meaning we can have a honeymoon for the weekend before leaving the following Monday." She turns and grabs some parchment and a pen. "With January being a slow month for most places, we should find a nice place easy enough." She scribbles some notes. "And it should be easy for you to remember our anniversary, since it would be so close to my birthday."

"And it would give you three days within a week you get presents."

She rubs her nose against his. "You know me so well."

He lets her down. "You know, we don't have a place of our own, and where are we going to 'honeymoon' for the weekend?"

"The guest house could work for now. We can live there temporarily until we build our own place." She makes a few

78

more notes, then takes his hand. "But we can worry about that after we destroy the Black Rose for good. Let's go tell them the news."

"So why are you so intent on getting married before we leave?" William resists her pulling. "The real reason."

She looks up at him and he gives in and walks with her back to the other office. "Because if I have to spend another week with you only next door to my room instead of in it, I will go mad."

William and Crystal return to the other office and explain to the others what they are planning on doing. Marcus gives a devilish grin. "That's a brilliant plan. Just to be clear, I'm still going to be the one to marry you two, right?"

Crystal pulls her braids back behind her. "The first time or the second time?"

"Both. The second time will give me an opportunity to get you a proper wedding gift, since you won't be getting one this time."

William turns to her. "This means you won't be in a proper wedding dress; you know that right, honey? We have to make it look like a normal meeting with the Emperor."

She bows her head. "And Mom and Cline will get your parents, along with Tia and Andrew, then just teleport straight here so they aren't seen coming or going." She puts on her impish grin. "You're almost as deceptive as I am, darling."

Jack steps out, and William follows, but Marcus asks Crystal to stay. "I need a moment alone with my countess, if you don't mind." He closes the door, sealing them in.

Crystal swallows. *Why is dread filling me right now? I did a lot of wrong. Hope it's not coming back to bite me.*

"What happened down in the holding cells has me worried." He steps around the desk and stands in front of her. "Are you feeling, ok? I heard what happened to you in Portstown

79

and it can affect you negatively." Marcus puts a hand on her shoulder and his voice is comforting. "I know someone who can help you, if you want it."

Crystal bites her lower lip. "I've been doing my best to deal with it." She looks down at the floor. "William and Tia have helped me with some of my inner demons." She looks into his eyes with courage she doesn't really have. "I'm strong, but if you order me to, I will get outside help." She perks up a little and her tone shakes. "Guess that is why William proposing to me has been so positive. It's given me something else to think about, and our future together."

He pats her shoulder. "I won't order it for now, but you really need to control that inner Dragon. It might lead to future problems." He leans down and gives her a hug. "I might be a big scary Emperor, but I think of all of you as my children. If you need anything, just ask." He stands upright. "If you keep on this dark path, you will lose everything." He sighs. "Don't retreat to the dark place when you have bastions of hope like William, Tia, and Penelope ready to show you a better way." He reaches behind her and opens the door. "I will see you on the sixth at one p.m."

"Thank you, Your Highness." She bows and exits.

Marcus closes the door behind Crystal, and Skyler walks in through a hidden door behind him. "So, she has a dark side." He nods. "Is she still the one?"

He nods again. "She's willing to fight, even to the death, for it." He turns and takes hold of his wife. "Everything is still going as planned. Every day, her power is growing, and now it's starting to leak into the world around her."

Skyler wraps an arm around his shoulder. "Right as always, my love. Need to keep a close eye on this one."

Crystal walks out of the office and hooks her arm into William's as if she owned it. "Shall we go home, darling?"

"What about Tia and Andrew?"

Crystal waves her hand dismissively. "Oh, I figured they would be off to get a hotel room or something."

Tia and Andrew both turn a bright red, and Andrew leans down. "Why would we do that?"

Tia takes Andrew's arm like Crystal did to William, and they walk out. "You two need some private time to talk about your future together." She takes on a tone of authority. "And what your destiny is going to be, but first, you some better clothing. You're going to be the first fashionable priestess."

Tia pulls at her robes, looking down at them. "But I don't know anything about clothing. I like my simple robes." They walk out into the late afternoon sun. "Besides, we must get back to the church. The others have probably dug up the entire library by now and we should look that over."

Crystal stops and grabs her, turning Tia to face her. "Tomorrow morning I'm coming to get you, and we are going shopping."

"But where am I supposed to put it? I can't take that stuff back to the church."

"That's true." Jack gets them all to jump, forgetting he was there. "You're taking a girl who's known nothing but the convent her whole life and throwing her into our 'civilization'. Where is she going to stay?"

"She can have my old room." Crystal turns to William. "William and I are going to move into the guest house temporarily till we build our own home together." Crystal walks up to the door of their car and the driver opens it for her.

Jack holds a hand up. "Hold on. When were you going to run that by me?"

"Run what by you? The moving into the guest house or Tia moving into my room?"

He puts an armored hand on his hip. "BOTH?!"

William helps her down in the car. "On the ride home?" Her impish grin appears, and she reaches past him, grabbing Tia by the robes and pulling her into the car.

Jack shakes his head in disapproval. "That's not how this works." Jack looks at William. "What do you think?"

"Of?"

"Moving into my backyard. You two aren't married yet, so living together would be a challenge for any man. Can I count on you two to keep each other innocent till the sixth, or do I need to have guards posted?"

William shakes his head. "I'll be honest with you, sir. I love your daughter to death, but being that proximity, there is no way I could resist her advances for two weeks."

"Advances?" He turns and looks at Crystal. Tia buries her face in her large chest and turns a bright red, and Crystal flushes pink.

"He's very strong willed. Very honorable. I've been testing him for some time." Crystal fabricates the lie like a skilled artisan and Jack doesn't detect her deception.

He turns back to Will. "Well, being Tia is going to be staying with us. Maybe Andrew can stay with you? I don't think it would be a good idea to have these two with rooms next to each other. Wouldn't be anything stopping one from sneaking into the other."

William can see Crystal doing her best not to give herself away and he just nods with a straight face. "Wise decision. I can see your point has merit."

Tia and Crystal both start laughing, getting Jack's attention. "Something funny ladies?"

"Nothing daddy. Inside joke between me and Tia."

"How about this?" William counters. "Tia, can stay at my estate in one of our guest rooms instead of making Andrew move all his stuff? It would be easier that way and my mother can look after her and make sure she gets to the church in the morning to do her duties as required?"

Tia doesn't say anything but nods in agreement, but Andrew speaks. "She can stay in my room, and I should stay at the church, so the others don't think I'm getting special treatment. Tia is gone a lot, so her not being there won't raise suspicion and I don't want to turn the church upside down. Heck, I'm not even sure if we even should do this, but if Tia is right, then we could take the first steps in the church's rebirth."

Jack shrugs. "Good enough for me. I'll make sure Cline knows to have you ready for church every morning."

"We have lots to do, so I'll see you all in a few days." William closes the door and Jack gets in the other side. He turns to Andrew. "Mount up. Looks like you're going back to the church."

CHAPTER 9

(Carefree)

Tia wakes up in Andrew's bedroom. Sitting up, she looks out the window, getting a good view of the mountains. *I don't know what to think about my situation.* She looks down at the bed. *Feels strange to be sleeping in a man's bed, even if does feel like a cloud.* She lays back down, mind racing at how different her life is from just a year ago. *This is all so surreal. I just wish I could have gotten some decent rest.* A knock on the door scares her out of her thoughts, and her heart races. "Y-Yes?"

"Ms. Moonglow, it's time for breakfast. What will you be having?"

I've never had a life like this, either. What do I say? What do I do?

Another knock at the door. "You ok in there Ms. Moonglow?"

"I'm fine, just thinking." She gets up and slips on her robes. Opening the door, Cline is standing there with a notepad and pencil.

His voice is deadpan and serious. "I was going to take your order so Ms. Penelope can get it started. Anything you want in particular?"

"What does he mean?" She fakes a smile. "Like what, exactly?"

Visible confusion crosses Cline's face for a moment. "Would you like milk, or orange juice, or some other beverage? As for food, you can ask for just about anything. What are you craving?"

"I don't know, to be honest. This is the first time I have had a luxury like this. I don't want to impose."

Cline waves away her concern. "Nonsense. You're an honorary member of the House and are to be treated as part of the family. So please ask for whatever you want, and I can get it ready for you downstairs."

"I'll take some milk and I guess two eggs, sunny side up and some sausage and bacon if that's alright?"

Cline writes it down. "Anything else, ma'am?"

Tia shakes her head. "Is Crystal awake yet?"

Cline puts his notepad away. "I don't know. She stayed in the guest house last night. She probably wanted to see what it would be like to live on her own. After I dropped off your order, I was going to check on her."

"I can go check on her so you can do your other duties, Cline. I'll bring her in for breakfast."

"Thank you, Ms. Moonglow. I appreciate that. Breakfast won't be too long." He turns and leaves. Tia follows behind and walks out into the back courtyard to the large guest house as Cline continues onward to the kitchen. She knocks on the door and long moments pass. She was about to knock again when Crystal peeks through a curtain. The door opens and Crystal is standing there in her nightgown. Tia comes in and closes the door behind her.

"Cline was wondering what you wanted for breakfast."

"Guess that means I need to get dressed. I kind of like being able to walk around like this. I feel so free having the house to myself."

Tia shakes her head. *How anyone can be so comfortable being so exposed all the time like this will never sit well with me.*

Crystal walks off to the bedroom, dropping her nightgown along the way. "After breakfast we will find you some new clothes, alright?"

Tia turns away, embarrassed. *She really has no modesty when she's comfortable around others.* A few moments pass and Crystal comes out in a nice dark blue backless dress with silver accents that form fits, showing off her petite body. It covers up to her breasts and ties behind her neck, but leaves the arms, shoulders and back exposed, and drops to just past her knees. Her hair hangs loosely behind her.

Crystal does a little twirl. "Like it?"

"Like what?"

Crystal responds as they leave the house. "My dress. I think something like this would work well for you. You're so 'blessed' that you might as well show it off a little."

Tia blushes. "That's too revealing." She looks down at the grass. "I couldn't be seen in something like that."

"You're too modest." Crystal opens the door to the main house. "And yes, I know that's ironic coming from me. I would run around naked all day if I was allowed." She shrugs. "But if I can wear decent clothing to appease others, so can you. Just have to get you a little out of your comfort zone."

"I just don't know about all of this." Tia turns to Crystal, flustered. "I don't even know if this is what my god wants. I have yet to pray this morning."

"Don't worry. Do your prayers after breakfast and then we will go out and have a fun day. It will be just us girls, so no Andrew, no William. Just me, you, and some dress shops and maybe some lingerie?" The mentioning of the lingerie turns Tia red as an apple, getting an evil laugh from Crystal as they walk into the dining room.

Jack is sitting in his spot reading the morning paper with his reports and looks up at his cackling daughter. "Something I miss?"

Tia and Crystal both sit down next to each other. Crystal elbows Tia a little. "I'm teasing her. She's been a woman her whole life, but doesn't know how to *be* one. We are going to have fun today." Penelope walks in and places their food down and takes their order. "Shadow, why don't you come with us?".

Penelope raises an eyebrow and sounds skeptical. "Come with you, *where?*"

"We are going out dress shopping and Tia should get another opinion besides mine. You're an older woman. Help by giving a different perspective." Crystal teases the Halfling. "Who knows, maybe you will meet someone too?"

"I have my duties here, I'm afraid. So, I won't be able to."

"Actually Penelope, you're going."

She slowly turns to Jack. "I am?"

Crystal perks up but says nothing as she eats. "Yes, you are. They have both been attacked and your 'skills' will be useful. I'll send a normal bodyguard, but you're going to be the secondary that will look out for trouble." Jack looks askance at Penelope. "So go out dress shopping and have a good time, but if you sense danger, you get them out of there."

She bows. "I will get changed then, to be sure I'm prepared."

She exits and Crystal swallows. "Good thinking. I was just wanting her there for an opinion, but as a secret bodyguard is a good spin. I like it."

William awakens to a knock at his door, and Sally gets his order for breakfast. He grabs a shirt and looks out his window as he buttons up. He can see the bay where he used to work before the Black Rose business and spots a large ship in port. It sports an emerald green and silver-colored hull with the flag of the Silvian Empire flying from its mast. *Odd, I don't recall a shipment from the Silvian Empire today. Then again, that doesn't look like a cargo vessel.* He reaches over and opens a drawer, pulling out a collapsing telescope.

Peering through it, William can see Farvrak Steelpelt, and his kobolds, arguing with the Dwarven shipping crew and the new dock guard that took his place. *He doesn't seem to be able to keep a lid on things. If he doesn't calm them down, there's going to be a fight on that dock.* He looks to the Silvian ship and a shiny emerald-colored armored individual with four escorts descends the docking plank. *I've never seen armor that color before. It's the same tint as the color of the Silvian's flag with silver accents. The other four knights are wearing traditional looking mithril Elven armor, swords, and service pistols. The leader's armor is very different with sliding plates.* He continues to observe as they turn towards the fight, and he zooms in for a better look. William is astonished. *That the green knight is a woman? Judging by the Silver Holy Symbol of Johnathan embedded on top of the armor near her neck, she's possibly a paladin.* He watches as she moves. *Those extra sections must be to keep her flexible. The way they slide up and down means she must have wanted her armor to be as with her while keeping the protection. That's rather ingenious.*

She approaches the arguing factions, and they turn to her. He can't hear what she is saying, but this causes Ms. Amberjaw to become more agitated and hefts a crowbar as if it was a sword. The green knight reacts instantly, pulling a scimitar from the scabbard on her hip in an instant, hitting the Dwarf with the hilt and knocking the Dwarf down. By the time her ass hits the dock, the sword is back in its scabbard.

William shakes his head. *Damn, that was fast. Impressive.* She offers her hand to the fallen Dwarf as some sort of apology. *She has a knightly code like me. This makes me wonder why she and the Silvian Empire are here. It's sure not to settle shipping disputes.* She motions with her hand in a circling fashion and the others round up and they walk away. Whatever was going on was solved, and now the shipping containers are being loaded up.

Sally calls from the hallway. "Your breakfast is getting cold."

He puts his telescope down and places it back in his drawer. *This day is going to be interesting.*

Crystal, Tia, and Penelope ride in the car with the Half-Orc bodyguard driving. They get to one of the less expensive, but still upper-class shops in the area. Crystal glances at Tia. *I want her to look good, but till she finds a style she will wear, there is no reason to go all out just yet.* The driver opens the door and helps the ladies out and then stands there by the car, watching the only way in or out.

They walk in and an Elven woman greets them. "Welcome ladies. How can I help you today?"

Crystal motions to Tia and Penelope. "These ladies need some fashion. What can you show us that will make these two more feminine?" Penelope and Tia both turn red, but for different reasons.

Penelope shoots a glare at Crystal. "You said I was here to give Tia a second opinion, not to play dress up!"

Crystal sounds dismissive and shrugs. "I lied?" Penelope's frown doesn't go away. "If you're going to be my secret bodyguard, you can't *look* like one, can you?"

Penelope doesn't let up. "You didn't know about that till *after* Master Jack suggested it." Crystal smiles and turns back to the Elven seamstress.

The Elven lady stands there with a forced smile. "I guess we need to start with taking some measurements unless you already know yours?"

Tia looks at Crystal. "What does she mean?"

Crystal gives her an impish grin. "She means you're going to have to have to stand on that raised platform over there and take that old robe off, so she can measure you. Your arms, legs, breasts, waist, stuff like that." Tia's eyes go wide, and Crystal can hear her thinking, and rolls her eyes. "No, it's private. Just you and her. They aren't going to have you strip to your underwear in front of the entire store." She indicates to Penelope. "And Shadow is going to have to go through it, too. You're not alone in that boat."

Tia nervously goes with the Elven lady into the room with the pedestal, and she closes the door. "I understand you're nervous, but a proper fitting of a dress is important. It's the difference between things popping out that you don't want to, or being too snug, being unable to breathe. You can put your robe back on after I'm finished, I promise." Tia nods and undoes her robe, tossing it to the floor. She stands there, not knowing what to do. The lady moves Tia's body, taking her measurements. "Arm twenty-nine, neck thirteen, shoulder eighteen, chest thirty-two H, waist twenty-five, hip forty-two, inseam Thirty-two, and height sixty-seven. Half-Elves sure get the best of both worlds, don't they? You can put your robe back on now. Now that I have an idea, I can find something better for you." Tia slips her robes back on and the Elven lady peers out and motions for Penelope to take her place.

I hate this, but if I don't do it, Crystal will run me ragged. Stepping in, the Elven lady closes the door. She removes her clothing and hidden daggers clang to the ground, along with a revolver and some other things. She looks down at it and back at Penelope. "You saw... nothing." The malice in Penelope's voice gets the lady to swallow hard. "Just do your thing so I can get this over with."

"Sure." She walks around the Halfling for several minutes. "Arm fifteen, neck seven, shoulder eight, chest sixteen B, waist thirteen, hip eighteen, inseam thirteen, and height thirty-three inches. I'm done here if you want to put your stuff away."

Penelope gets dressed and hides all her stuff again. She walks out and she motions to Crystal. "Next?"

Crystal smiles. "I already know my measurements." She waves the woman away. "I have custom dresses made all the time."

Penelope elbows her hip, causing Crystal to look down at the Halfling. "We had to go through that. Why not be a team player here and show Tia that you are willing too?"

Crystal looks at Tia and sighs. "Fine, but I don't think I've gained any weight. Hell, I think I might have lost some after my ordeal."

She walks into the measuring room and drops her dress, revealing all to the poor lady. "You didn't have to remove everything, just the dress."

Crystal quips back. "That's why I didn't want to do this. I *only* wear the dress. It's backless to expel heat. I don't feel the need to wear anything else."

She shakes her head. "I don't think that's how that works, but I'll deal with this as best I can. Arm twenty-five, neck ten, shoulder thirteen and a half, chest twenty-nine B, waist eighteen, hip thirty, inseam twenty-two, height fifty-nine. You're tiny, borderline anorexic. Just as a warning, your waist should be about twenty-two at the least. So better keep that in mind." She stands up. "You can get dressed now, please."

Crystal puts her dress back on and has the seamstress tie it back up behind her neck, then exits. She joins the other two. "Happy? Apparently, I lost some weight. My waist is only eighteen. Guess we are going out to eat after this?"

The Elven lady interrupts. "Who's trying on the first dress?"

Crystal pushes Tia forward. "Let's see something that shows off her figure." Tia turns back to Crystal with a look of betrayal. "Don't give me that look. You know exactly why we are here." Crystal finds a seat waiting for Tia to emerge.

"I'm going to go take a look around." Penelope steps outside and looks at the passing traffic and the surrounding people. Falling back onto her training, she scopes out the people around the area. *Anyone who looks like they are paying more attention than they will be noted, but with the big steam car here, it's more difficult to know who's interested in it, over us.* Walking around the car, she checks it to see if anything looks out of place. She knows the Half Orc could be distracted, and someone could place a magical tracking device on the car when he's not looking. Not long later, Crystal calls her, so she crawls out from under it and turns to the driver. "Keep an eye on the car as well. Don't let anyone near it."

Walking back in, Crystal is looking at Tia who is in a new lime green dress. It shows a lot of her chest and reaches halfway down her calves. It has some frills to it but otherwise doesn't look too remarkable. The back is open; the sleeves are short, and the color goes with her green eyes. "What do you think, Shadow? She shines up like a newly minted penny."

"It's amazing, actually. This is the same Tia we came in with?"

Tia is trying her best to keep her composure. "I think it's too revealing. My bosom is exposed."

Crystal bites her lower lip and sounds jealous. "Girl, you've been blessed. I have to work at getting mine noticed." Tia flushes again, looking away. "I'm kinda jealous of Andrew, honestly. I wish I had hips like that." She turns to Penelope. "Ok Shadow, your turn while Tia here changes and finds something else."

Penelope's head swivels around, eyes wide. "Wait, you're serious about getting me fit to wear a dress?"

"Yep. You have to blend in, remember? Maybe something in a canary or golden yellow?"

Penelope sighs. *This is going to be my whole freaking day, isn't it?*

William sits down and has his breakfast. His father speaks up. "What's the agenda for today, son?"

"Thought I would swing by the docks. A ship from the Silvian Empire docked there this morning, and I'm wondering what's going on." William chews his food, giving him time to think. "I know we're allies and get shipments in, but that is no container ship, but a military vessel."

Gerald shrugs. "No one told me there would be a Silvian ship in port today. Let me know what you find out, but be careful. Take your sword with you in case you're attacked again."

William nods in agreement, pointing his fork at his father. "Yeah, I'm not going anywhere without it again. At least till the Black Rose has been dealt with." He chews on some bacon and swallows. "Crystal wants me to move in with her."

Gerald drops his fork in surprise, then recovers. "I'm sorry, what?"

Muriel walks in. "Did I miss something?"

William wipes his mouth with a napkin. "Crystal wants me to move in with her at her estate. They have a guest house that's decently large till we get our own place built. Guess she wants to see how I am in daily life without any separation. Not that I think it would differ from being out in the field." Muriel's face reflects the shock of such a question.

Gerald turns to her and back to William. "Living with someone is very different from working with them in the field, son." Muriel sits down. "But you're an adult now, and you're betrothed to this woman. If you want to move in with her, then I can't stop you."

"That's why I'm asking if it's a good idea. I know the temptation of being with her in such proximity will be a lot, but being we are getting married in two weeks, I can't really see the harm in committing early."

"Is it your fear can't keep to yourself, or her? If you're moving in with her, that would suggest you're going to be sleeping in the same bed?"

William nods, still enjoying his food. "And at that proximity, it would be easier to storm the palace than keep her off me. Then again, we've been through hell and back with each other. Nothing can separate us."

Muriel smiles. "In that case, do what you want to be happy. We want grandchildren, but at least try to wait till after you're married before going that far?"

William stands up. "I'll do my best, but Crystal is a force of nature. Until we get married, I will try to keep her at bay. I don't want Jack or Cline killing me beforehand." He gets up and hugs his mother and tells them goodbye. "I'll head to the docks and get the story there, then find Crystal."

CHAPTER 10

(No Rest for the Wicked)

Tom and Tyra make it to Rose Harbor in just under four days, not stopping to camp by taking turns sleeping on their mounts while the other guides their horse. When they get to the gates and the guards stop them. "Names please for entry and reason for visit?"

Tom sits upright. "I'm Tom and this is Tyra. Reason for the visit is our monastery was attacked by the Black Rose and we need to see Countess Hellstromm immediately."

The guards exchange glances. "The Black Rose?" He opens the gate. "I'll have someone guide you to the Hellstromm estate."

"That's alright, we know the way. We've been there several times."

"I must insist on an escort. Just in case you aren't who you say you are."

Tyra snorts. "Fine, but this is an emergency." A guard armed with a service revolver and a short sword mounts up and follows them to the Hellstromm estate. Jack's personal guard receives them back to his workshop, where he's busy fixing the battle damage on William's armor. They walk in and Jack perks up immediately with the light from the outside being blocked.

Jack puts his tools down and walks over to them and gives them both a big hug. "Didn't expect to see you two here." He turns to the Royal Guard. "And you are?"

"Nobody sir. Just making sure they are legit. I'll take my leave."

Jack's smile fades as he sees the somber looks on their faces. "What happened?"

"The monastery was attacked. We lost almost seventy students in the battle, along with several masters."

Tyra picks up from there. "We won, but the Black Rose has proven they will not stop at nothing to cause destruction." She places a hand on Tom's shoulder but continues to look at Jack. "We need help there."

"Whatever you need, I'll get it out to you. I owe you and your monastery that much."

"Where is Crystal? She might be in danger."

"She's out shopping with Tia and Penelope." Jack puts his tools down on his anvil. "And the Black Rose attacked here, too. Crystal and William by the river and Tia and Andrew near to their church a few days ago." He wipes some grease off with an old rag. "I put my guard on high alert ever since and sent a bodyguard with them."

"So, it was coordinated from the beginning. They attacked all of us at once. We struck a nerve with them if they did this much to try to kill us all."

"We need to find Crystal. They could target her again."

"She's out dress shopping in the Seventh House District. Guess she wanted to check on William while she was there. Grab some fresh horses. She has my only working car right now."

Tyra keeps her nose in the air, tracking Crystal and Tia's scent for an hour till Tom spots the car outside a medium-sized shop with pink siding. "This is definitely a place for women."

Tyra snorts and looks down at Tom. "All three are in there."

That comment perks up the Half-Orc and he uncrosses his arms. "What do you want here?"

Tom walks up to him, projecting a smile. "We are friends of the countess on official business."

"I can't take your word on that."

"Then come in with us. If we cause trouble, a big guy like you shouldn't have a problem dealing with us."

"Fine. Surrender your weapons to me first" Tom nods and hands over his Sai and Tyra hands him her Katana that she hasn't let go of since the battle. They walk in and Crystal turns to the noise of the bell. Tia is standing there in a forest green, back and sleeveless dress, with the center from just above the navel to the neck open just barely covering her bosom. The rest of it hugs her form and shows off her hips down to her knees where it loosens up, allowing her to walk around.

Tom lets out a whistle of appreciation and forgets why he was there. "I would have never thought that a woman that beautiful was hiding under those robes."

Tyra slugs him in the arm as Tia turns pink all over. Penelope places a hand on her hip. "So, what am I, chopped liver?" Tom and Tyra turn to see Penelope in a bright Canary yellow dress with a silver beltline. A V-cut going from the belt to the shoulders, leaving the middle open. The sleeves reach to her hands and are open in the front from the elbows down. The dress reaches to the floor, cut along the sides to allow for movement, and showing off her legs.

Tom's jaw becomes unhinged, and his voice turns to a tease. "Penelope is a girl?" This earns another slug from Tyra. "That's starting to hurt, you know."

Penelope does a little spin showing the back was open too. "I didn't think I would like to wear a dress, but something like this, I can hide all kinds of weaponry."

Crystal waves her hand in front of his face. "What brings you two here?"

"Sorry what?" Tom blinks for the first time in several minutes.

Tyra scowls. "You were drooling."

"Was not." His voice goes to a whisper, so only Tyra can hear him. "Was I?"

She pulls back, and he flinches, but Crystal grabs him first, turning him to face her. "Focus. Why are you two here?"

"Sorry, been a rough few days, and then I walk into a shop with three attractive women. My mind got overloaded there a second." He shakes it off. "The monastery got attacked four days ago. We came here to check on you and to see if we could get aid."

The smiles on the girls vanish. "Was Master Monzulo..." She stops, unable to finish her thought.

"He's fine. He asked us to come here to ask." Tom recounts his story. "In the end, we lost over seventy students and a few masters. The enemy took much larger casualties."

Crystal gasps. "We need to go see the Emperor immediately."

Tia steps down. "Let's get changed then."

Crystal shakes her head. "No, leave them on. We don't have time for you two to change."

Penelope looks down and up at her. "But we haven't paid for them."

"I'll worry about that. Grab your clothes and get in the car. Besides, they look great on you two. Tom's whistle convinced me they are perfect for you two." Crystal signs off on some papers. "Send the bill to my father. We have to go."

The Elven lady smiles, writing it all down. "Thanks for your patronage." They exit and clamber into the car and Tom and Tyra reclaim their weapons, following on their mounts.

William makes his way to the docks and spots the Hellstromm's car leaving a pink shop and what he can swear is Tom and Tyra riding behind them. *It can't be them. We dropped them off at the monastery. But what if?* He shakes it off. *This day is getting weirder by the minute.* He makes his way down and stops and talks with Ms. Amberjaw. "What happened here an hour ago?"

"Farv's kobolds were trying to pull a fast one again, and we were trying to stop them. Then this green knight lady comes out of nowhere and gets between us. I suspected she might be trying to help them and said as much." She gets angry and animated. "She shot back at me about being a dishonorable wretch that was probably just harassing the kobolds because we are Dwarves and should just drop the matter. I got angry and was going to put a dent in that fancy armor. Then she knocked me on my ass and left it at that."

"Well, did you think that maybe perhaps she was right? You don't have this problem with anyone else but them, and I know they aren't the only smugglers in the business."

"It crossed my mind as that hilt crossed my forehead. She was unnaturally fast with that draw. I think she might be dangerous."

"I think she's a paladin going by her ornamentation. Did she say where she was going when she left?"

"Yeah, the Palace. She said: 'let's get going before we are late to the meeting with Emperor Marcus'. Then she rounded up her people and walked away."

"Any idea why they are here?" He motions to the Silvian warship. "As the shipping and receiving boss, did you get any paperwork for that ship?"

"No sir, I didn't. Didn't even know it was going to be birthed here. Only orders I had was to leave that spot open for today." She rubs her chin. "Guess I know why now."

"Thanks Ms. Amberjaw. Looks like I'm heading to the palace to track down your assailant."

Crystal and the others arrive at the palace and exit the car. Tom and Tyra dismount and follow the well-dressed ladies inside. The guards greet and escort them along the way. They cross the great map and enter the throne room. There they see four normal looking, heavily armored mithril knights standing back, armed with revolvers and long swords. Crystal's focus is drawn to the knight with emerald armor with silver trim, standing before Marcus and Skylar. *Who are these people? I don't want to cause a scene, but this is important. I really don't want to cause a diplomatic incident.* She doesn't have to wait long. The Emperor catches sight of them and motions the green knight to take a step aside. As the knight turns, Crystal's eyes widen for a moment. *That's a woman under that armor, and it's form fitting.* As she approaches, Crystal note's the emerald woman is just about the same height as her.

Marcus waves them forward and groans as they go to kneel, stopping them. "Oh, come now. Didn't I say we were past that?" He leans forward on his throne. "I wasn't expecting you for another week and a half." He points to the monks. "And give this week's track record; dare I ask what's wrong?"

"Your Highness," Crystal turns and motions to the monks. "These two bring word from the monastery to the north." She turns back forward, bowing her head slightly. "The Black Rose attacked them and both sides took heavy casualties. I would like to request aid to help them recover their losses." Crystal sees from the corner of her eye a subtle nod from the green knight. *Wonder why she's still wearing that helm., That can't be comfortable.*

100

"Of course. They were instrumental in your mission's success. I shall provide anything they need." He looks at Tia and Penelope. "And I see you're doing well with getting your friends to wear clothing like yourself. You're having an influence on them."

Crystal smiles with a giggle in her voice. "I had to drag them out almost at claw point, but yes, I got them into dresses." Tia blushes, realizing others are seeing her in it.

Marcus turns to the green knight. "Crystal, this is Princess Zarra Silvian of the Silvian Empire." Crystal curtsies to the princess, showing respect. "And this is Countess Crystal Hellstromm. She's been helping me grow my empire and stamp out some… nuisances."

The green knight holds her hand out, and Crystal takes it. Her voice is muffled through the helm as she bows her head, but it's soft and almost calming. "Pleased to meet you."

Marcus glances at Skylar and back at them. "Why don't you remove that helm, princess? We are all friends here."

The green knight turns back to him. "Is that wise, Your Highness?"

Crystal's brow furls a little. *Odd question to ask. Why the secrecy?*

Marcus reassures her. "Yes, you don't have to worry about them."

Crystal holds up a hand. "Is she trying to conceal her identity because she's royalty?" Marcus just holds his open hand to the female knight.

She reaches up and removes her helm. Braided red copper hair falls from inside and gold studded jewelry pins hold it all together. They clink against the armor as her long hair rolls halfway down her back. A large silver ring hangs at the end, pulling it all straight. Tia and Penelope step back on impulse, but Crystal stands stoically as the green knight turns to look at her. Her obsidian skin is flawless, and eyes are as fresh cut rubies.

The copper hair color is even present in her eyebrows, meaning it's all natural. The short, elongated ears finish the story.

Crystal smiles. *She's rather beautiful. No wonder she hides under that armor. Must be to keep the guys at bay. With all that jewelry, that helm must be magical to hold it all.*

Zarra looks at Tia and Penelope and back to Crystal. "You're not afraid like your friends?"

"Afraid?" Crystal turns to see Tia and Penelope are not where she left them but several paces back. She sighs, pointing to the floor. "Get back over here, now!" This gets a smirk from Skylar seeing Tia and Penelope react instantly. She turns back to Zarra. "My apologies, Princess. I thought I raised them better than that."

Zarra glances at the three of them. "They are your children?"

Crystal shakes her head but laughs at the notion. "No, but they might as well be. I've been trying to teach them etiquette and proper dress code for being around royalty."

This gets Zarra to crack a smile. "I know how that goes, but that's a common reaction to my presence. That's why I don't remove my helm unless I'm sure it's safe."

She has a beautiful smile. I bet she breaks a lot of hearts. A woman this attractive would wear it for more than that reason alone.

William walks in and sees Tom and Tyra first, then the four knights that were escorting the green knight. He passes them to see the ladies talking to the green knight. Surprise catches him as he sees she's a Dark Elf, and not a Tree Elf. *What is going on here?* Then he takes in more and spots Tia and Penelope are in actual dresses, causing his mouth to open a little.

A hand lands on William's shoulder and he looks to see Tom holding him there. "You already got the best looking from the lot. Give the rest of us a chance." His hand leaves his shoulder as Tyra slugs him, knocking him several feet away.

102

"One of these day's I'm going to stop aiming for his arm." A faint 'oooww' comes from Tom from the ground.

Marcus and the others look up at the commotion coming from the monks and see Tom laying on the floor. "Is there a problem?"

Tyra answers sarcastically. "Not anymore."

"Good." He turns his attention to William. "Is there something you need, William?"

"I was coming here because of her." He points to Zarra. "She assaulted a Dwarf on the docks, and I was filing a report and needed her side of things."

"She's a princess and has immunities, but I don't believe she would just randomly assault someone without good reason."

Zarra's voice turns flat. "The Dwarf in question was about to hit me with a crowbar. I beat her to the punch."

William nods in agreement. "That's what eyewitness accounts say, as well as Ms. Amberjaw." William shrugs. "I'm still a member of the guard so, I was just following procedure."

"Very noble of you, Captain." Zarra sounds impressed. Crystal glances at her askance. "That's some commitment when you're willing to track me all the way here."

"Yeah, he's something isn't he?" Crystal walks up to him pulling him down and they lightly kiss, but enough to display that they are a couple.

"He must be very special to have captured your heart, countess." She stands more rigidly. "Tell me about the monastery."

Tom gets up off the floor and explains for a third time what happened. Marcus and Zarra ask some questions, and Tom and Tyra try their best to fill in for them. Marcus snaps his finger, and an aid arrives. "Get the *Bastion* loaded with relief aid of blankets, construction materials and a work crew to help them rebuild." The aide bows her head and turns, but Marcus grabs her. "And also get my architects and city planner." She writes it all down.

Crystal speaks up, getting Marcus' attention. "If it's all the same to you, Your Highness, I would like to go with them."

"If that is your desire, I won't stop you, countess. You love those people, and I know you want to help them."

"I'm going with you then." William looks down at her. "Where you go, I follow."

An unexpected voice joins the conversation. "I want to go as well and help." Zarra turns her head to Crystal. "You've piqued my interest, countess. I've heard some stories of you even as far away as the Silvian empire and was hoping to meet you while I was here." She turns fully to address her. "But to get to see you and your band in action will be a genuine experience." Looking to Crystal and William. "If you will allow me to travel with you."

Crystal lets go of William and walks over to Zarra. "It would be a pleasure to have you along." She turns to the aide that's still standing there. "How long till the *Bastion* departs?"

The aide looks at Marcus, who nods, then looks back at Crystal. "About three hours."

"Thanks, get under way." She turns to the others. "Tia, Shadow, better go get changed after all." Crystal walks up to William and places a hand on his massive chest. "And you, my love. You need to go get your armor from my father. Not sure how much he's gotten done, but let's hope it's enough to get you by. I'll see if I can pick up some 'wands of repair' so we can do some damage control."

Tom rotates his sore shoulder. "What about us?"

"Can you two help with loading? Tyra is stronger than a dozen Dwarves, so she could speed up the loading and you can help her."

Crystal looks to Zarra. "Princess Zarra, I don't dare give you a command, but as a suggestion, bring a change of clothes, a bathing suit if that's your thing, and any personal care items like soaps. I don't know how long we will be gone, so anything you think you might need for a long outing is recommended."

A look of bewilderment crosses Zarra's face when Crystal mentioned the bathing suit. "Why did you mention 'a bathing suit, if that's my thing'?"

The silence in the room is only broken by Penelope. "Because she refuses to wear one while bathing, even with others around her."

Zarra smiles. "That's pretty bold to be that comfortable in ones on skin."

"More like they are the uncomfortable ones. I don't do that with men around." Crystal waves a hand flippantly. "But they act like they don't even look at their own bodies."

Zarra shrugs. "No judgment from me. I'll get my things. It's going to be nice not being pampered and get out."

Crystal looks at Marcus, who has a smile on his face. "You're a natural born leader, Crystal. Make the empire proud."

Zarra rolls her hair up and dons her helm. Crystal hooks her arm into William's and walks out with the others following behind. Zarra turns to the other knights. "Let's go."

They exit into the midday sun, and Crystal's car is waiting. "William, why don't you let Zarra use your horse, and you can come with us back to the manor to get your armor? That way, she can get her things and meet us back here sooner?"

"That's not a bad idea." William turns to Zarra. "Do you need help to get up on it? It's a large horse."

She leaps up, putting a foot in a stirrup, and throwing herself up onto it with the grace of an acrobat. "Thanks for the offer, but I've had to do this before. Don't let my tiny size fool you, Captain."

He pats the horse on the head. "Take good care of him. See you back here in an hour?"

"Sure, that's more than enough time."

"Be careful." Crystal can't hide the concern in her words. "The Black Rose has been targeting me and those I associate with. So, if you're joining me, you're going to be a target soon."

"I'm not worried. Johnathan will protect me from evil." She kicks the mount into motion, heading for the docks.

William watches her go. "She's defiantly a paladin of Johnathan. Brave to fault."

Crystal pulls him down. "Let's get moving ourselves. The longer we take, the longer the monks suffer."

CHAPTER 11

(New and Old friends)

Crystal and the others return to the palace in just over an hour, having packed up some things and gotten needed items along the way. They exit the car and unpack, noticing William's horse is already back. William opens the trunk. "She didn't take very long."

Crystal nods, pulling the staff from the back. "Tia, this is for you."

Tia takes it, looking it over. "What is it?"

"It's a staff that will focus your healing spells. Should help you get more from your abilities." Crystal pokes her in the chest and feels the chain mail under her robes. "Good."

They get back to the throne room, and Marcus is speaking with Zarra and he waves them over. "That was quick. I figured you would have taken longer, countess."

"Not today, Your Highness." She sounds somber. "People are in trouble, people who helped us. We need to see what we can do to repay the favor. I didn't want to waste time with the minor details."

Marcus smiles. "You continue to amaze me, countess." He stands. "You've grown much over the last year, and will be quite the woman in your own right." He walks up to her, putting his large hands on her bare shoulders. "Make the empire proud.

Anything the monks need, send for, and I'll make sure it gets to them."

Crystal smiles. "Thank you, Your Highness."

Marcus turns to William. "They could use your strength to help get crates loaded, if you wouldn't mind?"

"Not at all, Your Highness."

With an air of command, he waves them on. "Then let me not keep you kids. There are citizens to save."

Zarra falls in step next to William. "You're going to bake in that armor if you're going to be working. If you need help to remove it, I can assist you."

This draws an askance glance from Crystal, and William smiles. "Thank you for the offer, princess, but Crystal knows this armor very well." He smiles at the attention. "Plus, her father built it, so she should be the one to help."

Zarra leans forward to look at Crystal, unable to hide the surprise in her voice. "So, you're the daughter of *the* Jack Hellstromm?"

Crystal smiles. "I am." She looks at Zarra. "You know my father?"

"Not personally, but many of his inventions are used in the Silvian Empire. Mostly his farming equipment. Makes the planting and harvesting seasons so much easier and increased our yields by three hundred percent." Zarra sounds excited. "I knew your name sounded familiar, but I didn't want to assume you're related, till William here mentioned his armor built by the man. I can see his artistic flare in it."

"Thank you, always happy to meet someone who appreciates my father's work."

They continue to walk and get out to the airfield where Zarra sees the *Bastion* sitting there along with two other airs ships. One looks almost finished, and the other is still a skeleton in production. "What are these?" She doesn't hide the wonderment in her voice. "They look like ships, but we are nowhere near the ocean."

Crystal hands her things off to some Dwarves who are loading the ship. Penelope taps her on the hip. "Countess, I'll go check out our rooms, just in case we have a nasty surprise, then the rest of the ship."

"Thank you, Shadow. Glad to have you watching out for hidden threats."

"Crystal, if you wouldn't mind?" William reaches up to unbuckle his armor.

An impish grin crosses her face. "Sure." Starting an incantation, she's stopped by him grabbing her hands.

"No, no, no… none of that." This gets a laugh from Crystal, who stretches up and kisses him.

"Kill joy."

William's voice shakes a little. "I'm sure Princess Zarra here wouldn't want to see that."

Zarra glances between the couple. "Wouldn't want to see what?"

This gets a laugh from Tia and Penelope as they take their leave. They can't see Zarra's face, but they can imagine her confusion. William holds up his hands and makes air quotes. "Crystal has a 'special' spell that can remove all clothing from a person, leaving them bare to the world." He turns to Zarra. "So had she completed that, I would be standing here in my birthday suit."

"I still can." Crystal pats him on the chest. "But we have more pressing issues. How about this? We go to our room where I can remove the armor, and then you just put back on what you need to work. Be a lot faster than having me pull one piece off at a time."

William nods, and Zarra's helmet turns to one, then the other. "You two are married?"

William shakes his head. "We will be next week."

"Congratulations, I'm happy for you two." She pauses. "Must be a local custom that one can fraternize before marriage."

They turn and look at her, and Crystal turns pink. "It isn't, but I've never been known to always play by the rules."

They enter the airship, and Zarra is filled with wonderment. All the noises, the dials and copper tubing. "You could get lost in here if you're not careful."

"Yeah, but it's home away from home. We've had a lot of time on this ship. I know most of it just from wondering around looking at it all when I had to think about different situations." They walk into Crystal and William's cabin, and Zarra looks around. "So where am I staying?"

"Through that door is William's old room on this ship. It's very nice and private, with plenty of windows. He won't be needing it anymore. With us finally getting married, I don't think we need to hide our love anymore."

Zarra examines the room and notices the Dwarves have already placed her stuff near the bed. She closes the door behind her and removes her helmet. A few moments later, there is a sound of metal crashing against the deck plate from behind her. Dropping her helmet in a panic, she turns and throws open the door. Her jaw drops and eyes widen, getting a view she wasn't prepared for. William is standing there with Crystal's arms wrapped around him, his armor and clothing lying on the floor. She gawks at his bare muscular body and realizes what just happened. Crystal turns and lets out a gasp, and William grabs a sheet off the bed, wrapping it around himself.

She panics and holds her hands up while looking away. "SORRY!" She darts back into her room, slamming the door. *That is a lot of man. I can see why Crystal is so fond of him. No*

Elven male is built like that. She takes a few deep breaths, trying to calm down.

A knock at the door breaks her from her thoughts as she turns around. The door handle moves slowly, and the door creeks open just a smidge. Crystal peeks through the door, her voice friendly. "Can I come in?"

Why doesn't she sound mad? Zarra steps away from the door. "Yes, countess." Crystal steps in and shuts the door behind her gracefully. Before Crystal can start, Zarra bows her head. "I want to apologize countess, I heard the noise and with Shadow hinting there is danger, I thought you two were in trouble. I wasn't trying to see him vulnerable like that."

"I know. Everyone else is so used to the noise that I forgot you haven't heard it before. We should have expected it, and informed you ahead of time, so it's not your fault. I'm not mad."

Crystal can see Zarra's face is flushed, even though her obsidian skin. "You're not mad? I heard Human women are very protective of their men."

"Protective yes, but I assure you, I'm not mad. He's probably dressed by now. Are you planning on changing out of your armor into something more comfortable?"

Zarra flushes a little more, not understanding what she's proposing. "It had crossed my mind; how long will it take to get to this monastery?"

Crystal shrugs a guess. "Several hours. We should get there by midnight if we leave soon."

"Then I should remove my armor. I don't want to be baking in this all day."

"You want help?" Crystal opens her hands apart. "I know what a pain it can be to get armor off dealing with William's."

Wait, did she? She's beautiful, but she couldn't be. Zarra shakes her head. "Thank you, but I'm fine. I've gotten used to removing it on my own. I had servants that helped me for a long time, but I always wanted to get into the field, and knew one day it would happen, so I would have to know how. Thank you for the asking."

"Let me know if you decide to change your mind. I'm off to watch William work." A grin crosses her face. "That always brings a smile to my face."

"I can see why." Zarra realizes what she just said. She turns wide eyed back to Crystal, who cackles and walks back into her room. Zarra changes into a button up, short sleeve ruby red blouse and matching shorts. *I'm finally away from all the royalty crap and can be the paladin I was called out to be. I should be out helping the others.* Exiting her room, she realizes the Dwarven and Gnomish crew are looking at her funny. *They obviously recognize my signet ring know I'm from the royal House of the Silvian Empire, but I'm still a Dark Elf.* She sighs. *I can't really blame them. Centuries of war and the atrocities my ancestors committed aren't going to be erased in a few hundred years.*

She exits down the gangplank. *Crystal was the only who didn't react fearfully. Wonder why?* She gets outside and glimpses Crystal standing there; the breeze blowing her crimson dress about. *William didn't react either, but he recognized the holy symbol. Maybe that put him at ease?* She turns her head, watching the large man lifting crates. *Speaking of Crystal, you are one lucky woman. If he was mine, I would be jealous of every woman that glanced in his direction.*

Zarra looks around and can see they aren't the only ladies who seem to be fascinated by him. *Then again, that would be very unpaladin like of me. Even some of the Dwarven females are distracted and stumble over themselves.* Zarra walks up to a Dwarven male with an unbraided beard hanging all the way to his knees. "What can I do to help?"

He looks up and steps back on reflex. "Sorry there miss, didn't hear you walk up. I'm sorry. What did you need?"

"I would like to help. I'm with the countess and her crew, so I want to pitch in."

"That's noble of you." He smiles and points. "You can grab some of the smaller things, I suppose. I can give you some lot numbers."

She flexes her arm, trying to show off. "I can carry larger things."

Crystal had already turned to observe the Dark Elf's shapely figure, her taut muscles moving under her dark skin. *She's trained hard to get a body sculpted like that.* She turns her focus back to William. *But then again, she's wearing heavy armor all day training. She would have to be physically strong to complete a task like that.* Penelope brings Crystal some lemonade and the two of them drink and watch the men work.

The Dwarf nods. "Well, in that case," he points to a stack where Tyra and William are taking from. "You can help them, but those are really heavy. If you decide you can't do it, then there is no shame in it. Those two are one hell of a team for moving things. Most of my crew can't handle anything like those two, but there is plenty to do." He flips through paperwork. "Don't hurt yourself trying to show off."

Zarra steps over to where Tyra and William are working. "What can I help with?"

Tyra looks down at the tiny Dark Elf that barely stands above her waist, snorts a laugh, and shakes her head. "These things are very heavy, loaded with steel parts for repairs and building materials. I'm not making fun of you, but you're tiny. You should help the tiny Dwarves with their projects." She thumbs herself I the chest. "Leave this big stuff to me and William."

William overhears and walks over. Using his shirt he has tied to his belt, he wipes away the sweat that has built up on his

113

brow, but his muscular chest still glistens. "What's the problem?"

Zarra licks her lips she now finds dry. "I'm wanting to help, but she thinks I'm too tiny."

William glances at Tyra. "Princess, if you get hurt, we could all get in trouble."

She cuts him off, pointing a finger at him. "Don't refer to my title, please. Out here, in the field, I'm one of you. I've been a princess for two hundred and seven years and yearned for another purpose." She puts that finger in his chest and her heart races, but she keeps her composure. "Now I finally have it, even if for only a few days, I want to be like the rest of you. So put me to work."

William smiles and shrugs helplessly. "Alright, Zarra. Let's see what you can lift then. I don't want you to pull a muscle and be out of commission the first time you're acting as a commoner." He points to a box that is marked seventy pounds. "That's a good one to start on." She bends over and William glances away, changing three shades of red and then glances towards Crystal, whom is now busting up laughing with Penelope. "Zarra, lift with your knees. Bending over like that is going to cause you some back problems later." He tries to only see her in the very corner of his vision.

She stands back upright. "Could you show me?"

"Sure." He steps in front of the box and crouches down, bending his knees, putting him just about neck high to her and grips the box with both arms and lifts standing back up. "By doing it this way, it saves on your back. This places all the weight on your knees that can bear the load. When you turn, turn your whole body. I've seen plenty of healthy men twist carrying something like this and it just destroys their spine." He places the box back on the ground and backs up. "So, keep that in mind." He indicates to the box. "Your turn."

She smiles. "Thanks for the instruction, Captain. How do you know all this?"

114

"My House runs the shipping docks, so I've worked there most of my life. Firsthand experience."

She bends down as he had showed her and grips the box. She heaves and lifts it off the ground, her muscles rippling under the strain. "Where to, boss?"

He takes one up marked as its tare weight as one hundred and ten from the ground as if it was effortless. "Follow me, young lady."

With the added labor of William, Tyra, Tom, and Zarra, the ship is loaded almost forty-five minutes quicker than estimated. The quarto walks back to Crystal, Penelope, and Tia who've been watching the whole time. All four of them are covered in sweat, or at least one would have to guess with Tyra under all that fur. Crystal walks up to William and wraps her arms around her man's neck, kissing him. "You put on one hell of a show, darling."

"He's very informative too. Brains and brawn, few blessed with such a combination." She looks over herself. "I need a bath."

"We all do." Tom shrugs and grins. "They don't have a bathhouse on board, but if you need someone to wash your back, I'll happily volunteer."

Tyra rears back, ready to punch him back up the boarding ramp, when Zarra laughs, wraps her arm around his shoulders, and pulls into the ship. "You must be the comedian of the group. That was good." Tom's grin disappears and concern crosses his face. He looks back as she continues to talk and his face screams 'help'.

Penelope shakes her head. "Looks like his witty remarks finally caught up to him."

"Or she was saving his life?" Tia looks at Tyra, who's fuming. "Are you two romantically involved or something?

Every time Tom makes a comment about a woman, you punch him."

This brings her head around as if she was just shot. "NO!" She sighs. "But he's always making asinine remarks like that to every female he runs into. One of these days, he's going to get more than a slug to the shoulder for opening his trap like that. I want him to find a nice girl, but not making dumb comments like that."

Crystal's tone gets mirthful. "It's sweet how you're looking out for him." Crystal motions to move out. "We should get on board and make sure she hasn't killed him and hidden his body."

Tom is in his room who is bunking with Tyra, having traded Penelope to Tia's room. Zarra is in her room, having left Tom in there safely from Tyra. The alarm goes out that the ship is about to take off and Crystal walks out onto the top deck with William. He changed his clothes and is wearing a nice white shirt with red pants. Zarra joins them a few moments later along with Tia as the two have been talking. Tia wears her normal Cleric's robes but Zarra changed into an emerald colored, tight fit long dress. Crystal glances at her askance. *If she's trying to hide that she's a princess, she's doing a good job.*

Zarra looks down as the trees pass under them. "When you told me the ship could fly, I was thinking you were saying so in jest, but this is a wonderful view."

Crystals braids flow in the breeze. "Yeah, it never gets old. I'll stand out here for hours watching the landscape pass me by. Gives me time to think."

They can see the snow line around the dome is approaching and William and Tia head inside. Zarra watches as they leave and just looks out the windows instead. "What's with them?"

"It's going to get really cold, really fast, and they can't stand it." Crystal watches as the snow line gets closer. "But I relish the cold. The heat from the dome is nice, but the cold is

116

where I thrive." As if to punctuate her point, the ship passes through the magic barrier, going from a nice seventy-five degrees down to twenty in an instant. Zarra takes in a sharp inhale of freezing cold air and her skin erupts in goosebumps. The moisture on the deck freezes within seconds. Crystal's smile grows, feeling the cold air against her skin through her silk dress.

"Well, I-i-i- hav-v-v-e to ag-g-g-ree with your f-f-f-f-riends." Her teeth chatter. "I-i-i- would-d-d-d love to t-t-t-talk to you m-m-m-ore, but without a park-k-k-a, there's no way I c-c-can stand out here. Sorry C-c-c-countess."

Crystal turns to the Dark Elf and utters an incantation. Her hands, glowing white, lays it on Zarra. The white glow transfers to Zarra, enveloping her body. Her teeth stop chattering and she feels comfortable, as if it was back to seventy again. "Better?"

"Yeah, amazing spell you have there. Environmental protection?"

"It's handy if I want to speak with someone alone. The freezing cold can keep most at bay." Crystal turns to her. "You said back at the Palace that you heard of me?"

Zarra shrugs, leaning on the banister with Crystal. "From the reports I saw, you're a powerful magic user, quick-witted, and have a way with words. Those around you love you, and your enemies fear you."

"I think both reputations are well earned." Crystal looks at the setting sun to the west. The pristine snow on the trees and fields beneath them as the yellow sun touches the cold blue of the ocean, casting shifting colors from the warmth of the sun. "I've done things I'm not proud of. I'll admit that."

"I heard you were almost tortured to death." Zarra looks at the sunset with her. "It would take someone with a true steel resolve to not be affected by such an experience." She turns to the ivory woman. "I don't blame you if you've made poor decisions, but how did you keep from going mad if you don't mind me asking?"

Crystal smiles but doesn't turn away from the setting sun, watching it slowly dip into the ocean. "I didn't. After surviving, I tried to kill myself. I couldn't live with what I became. I hit a low spot, that I had no right to survive." Tears freeze to her face. "But William, Tia, Shadow, even Tom and Tyra picked up the broken pieces of my soul and did what they could to put me back together. Now I know how Humpty felt." She turns to the Dark Elf. "That's why I HATE the Black Rose so much. They threaten those I love most and my empire. I will stop at nothing till they are destroyed." The malice spewing from her catches Zarra off-guard.

"I understand what it means to hate an enemy."

"I'm sorry, I'm still trying to control that part of me." Crystal looks away. "Ever since that day, there has been a part of me that wants nothing more than to destroy everything in my path. I've been trying to deal with it on my own, but I don't know how to keep caged inside."

"Maybe that's why I'm here." Zarra puts a hand on Crystal's. "I've been there."

Crystal turns to the Dark Elf. "What do you mean?" She wipes away the icy tears that's messing up her mascara.

"Ever since I saw the reports, something pushed me to come to the Rose Empire. A calling, if you will. To meet you and your band of hodgepodge friends." She shakes her head, looking down at the passing tree's. "You're a countess, a member of the third House and practically royalty." She steals a glance at Crystal. "But instead of hanging with other rich and nobility types, you've surrounded yourself with common folk." She stands up straight and turns to Crystal. "I've been looking for a place to belong. I'm a Dark Elf princess, born in the darkness of the deepest tunnels of Naerth, and from an empire ruled by High born Elves who live in trees. If anyone knows about being out of place, it's me."

"Well, you will fit in around here." Crystal laughs. "I consider myself a Half-Dragon, but depending on who you ask,

I'm a Dragon 'reborn' or 'awakened' or a 'ritual gone wrong'."
She smiles and turns to Zarra. "Are you hungry? I could use a
medium rare steak right now and a tall glass of wine."

"Sounds wonderful." The two walk into the cabin where
William and the others were watching from the windows.

"Let's eat and share stories."

CHAPTER 12

(Reminiscing)

They all go down to the mess hall where Dwarves, Gnomes, and Halflings are eating. The clacking of forks and spoons die down and all conversation winks out. Crystal looks around and notices they are all staring at them. "Go back to your dinners, don't mind us." Moments go by and no one moves. Crystal looks over at them and seriousness takes over. "Fine, if you're not hungry, then you can all leave. Either you can enjoy your meal now or wait till tomorrow." This prompts the crew to go back to eating, knowing they won't get to eat later. They all sit down, the crew making room. "I've been on this ship for months now, but I've never actually eaten down here." They place their orders knowing they get special treatment on food. Normally her food would go to her chamber, but this time she's eating with her crew.

Penelope sits with a smile. "Nice to be served for once."

Crystal starts first, talking about how she, William, and Tia were selected out of dozens of candidates. "So, then I show up with my Vardo to the palace. William had told me to bring what I needed to survive, so naturally I needed a place to stay." She places her fingers to her chest. "I'm not going to sleep on the ground like some savage."

She stuffs a chunk of steak into her mouth and chews. "And when I get out, it's Emperor Marcus helping me down." She points her fork at Zarra. "At the time I was so afraid of the

Emperor, I almost passed out on the spot in fear. I was more afraid of him taking me off the trip if I did, so I was trapped in this loop of 'what do I do'?" As she parts her arms that show surrender. This gets a chorus of laughs from not just her group but from the crew of the ship. "I tried to say something, anything, but it just comes out as a mess of sounds like I was a babbling idiot, when Emperor Marcus told me to just breathe."

"Yeah, I wasn't thrilled that she brought the mobile home, but to be honest, I should have expected nothing less of the *princess*."

Tia laughs. "I remember all that. I thought you were about to blow a gasket, but you handled yourself well. You two were such opposites; it was comical. You have any idea how hard it was not to laugh when you two are arguing in whispers at each other."

"Wait, you two didn't grow up friends? Your union was just happenstance?" Zarra looks between them in wonder. "The Emperor picked you three for a simple recon mission, and you two fell in love along the way?"

Crystal leans on William. "Guess you can say that. It wasn't like that at first. I was teasing him a lot along the way. Testing him and his ideals. His soldier training making him all straight arrow and proper irked me a little. Guess because it reminded me of myself." She looks up at him. "But you can't stay mad at a man like this. Once I saw him with his shirt off, I was hooked."

Tia, Penelope, and Zarra all nod in agreement at once. "So, how did you know he was the one for you? If you don't mind." The atmosphere of the room changes immediately as smiling faces fade and she picks up on it immediately. "Did I ask something bad?" Her own smile fades away. "It wasn't my intention"

"It was one of my low points and I think for all of us, really." She tightens her grip on William. "William swore he would protect me, even if it meant giving his life. In Black Rock, he did just that." She sniffles a little, recalling the memory. Tia dips her head. "I only knew him for a few weeks at that point, but spending every waking moment with him, in his presence, it felt like I knew him my whole life." She wipes away a tear and Tia wraps an arm around her, tearing up herself. "I watched William die, fighting to get my Vardo free of the attacking Black Rose." She struggles to get the words out. "And in that moment, something in me broke loose." She cries, remembering the moment.

Tom picks up from there as William comforts her. "This crazy woman leaps out of the back in a rage I've never seen before and just goes nuts. Tyra and I jump to grab her, but she refused to leave him behind. If that's not love, I don't know what is."

"So, what happened?" Zarra leans forward. "If it's not too personal. He's alive, so something isn't right here."

Penelope picks up from there. "We rode all night back to the monastery. We were all exhausted, beaten, and crushed." She sips some of her wine. "Then she gets some crazy idea to sacrifice herself in some ritual to bring William back, but didn't tell any of us. She got us to go skinny dipping with her in the pool, then stole our clothes."

Zarra's ruby eyes widen and turns to Crystal. "You skinny dip?"

She smiles, but the tears are still there. "One of my many quirks. I think I have a beautiful body and damn anyone who thinks I should bathe with it covered up. I did mention that earlier about the bathing suit." She catches nods from some of the male crew in the corner of her vision.

Penelope continues. "Anyway, that's the point where I'm walking around a monastery, bare as the day I was born, surrounded by monks who probably haven't seen a naked female body in decades. I'm ducking around corners trying and finding something, *anything*, to cover me and Tia up in. Then I have to figure out why Crystal here," pointing with her fork for emphasis. "Went weird out of the blue." She takes a bite of her steak, savoring the flavor. "I run into Tyra and Tom, and she tracks her to the old lady's place, which is good because I had found Crystal's suicide note and had to stop what was happening."

"I would do it again." Crystal nuzzles William's arm.

"May I finish my story?" Penelope gets a nod from Crystal. Zarra looks around and can see the crew is paying attention, too. She even sees some tears in some of the female crew's eyes. "So, we couldn't get past the door. Tyra might be as strong as an ox, but she couldn't break the magical barrier holding the door closed, so I got in through a high and tiny window." She emphasizes more by making a climbing motion with her arms. "And opened the door from the inside, *but* the barrier didn't come down."

She stabs some green beans and holds them up, about to shove them into her mouth. "I rushed to the basement, hoping to stop this thing alone, but Olovira had a barrier there, too. She thought of everything to stop from being interrupted." She looks so somber. "All I could do was beat on the invisible wall as Olovira raised the dagger and brought it down, finishing the ritual. I couldn't look, but when I heard her body hit the floor and then fell over from the barrier vanishing, I realized something wasn't right."

Crystal picks it back up from there. "She gave her soul, instead of mine, to bring William back. She gave me back the man I loved and joined hers in the afterlife."

Zarra breaks down and can't hold back her tears anymore, as can hear the same from several other crew members. "You two literally been through hell and back together." Zarra tries to hold her composure. "No wonder the Emperor speaks so highly of you all. We would all be so lucky to have friends willing to go through these kinds of trials in life."

"So, Zarra, what's your story? You mentioned you're a Dark Elf princess from a city of tree dwelling Elves. How did that come about?" Crystal takes a bite of her own steak.

"For several thousand years, there was a war between the High Elves of the Silvian Empire and *my people*." She makes air quotes when she says, 'my people.'

Tia tilts her head. "Why the air quotes?"

"I don't consider them my people. I share looks with them, but their ideals are not mine. Being raised by the Silvian's, they gave me a different outlook." She glances around and notices she's the center of attention. "About one hundred fifty years ago, give or take a decade, the war was getting bad. The reason behind the fighting between the two warring factions was lost to antiquity, having gone on for almost five thousand years. The only thing remaining was the deep hatred, but not the reason why."

Tia frowns. "That's horrible."

"Yeah, it was. Then something changed. The Emperor of Rose Harbor arrived at the Silvian Empire, and funny enough, his description is almost dead on for Emperor Marcus, so if I had to guess, it was his great grandfather." She takes a drink of her wine and realizes the glass is empty and holds it up to get someone to take it. "Anyway, he talks to the High Elves, and he talks to the Dark Elves, comes up with a proposal to end the fighting and end the hatred." She looks at the people surrounding her. "Me, and several dozen children were 'traded' for High Elven children to take each other's places in each other's respective homes. Being I was a Princess, as denoted by my unique hair color." She motions with a hand at her head. "I was traded for the Emperor Silvian's daughter. Well, one of them. He and his wife have seven children, including me."

William asks before anyone else. "But why the exchange?"

"The idea was twofold. First, that one side wouldn't attack the other, knowing their children were there, and that

124

makes sense. I wouldn't launch a full-on assault knowing children were there, much less if they were mine." She looks down at her food. "And the other is to influence and teach the children the other side of the ordeal. I was but thirty-five when I joined the Silvian's as their adopted daughter. They took good care of me, gave me an excellent education, and treated me as if I was their biological daughter. I love them to death for it."

Tyra buts in. "What about your actual parents?"

"I visited with them regularly and got to play with the other children who were 'traded' so it wasn't a horrible experience. And he was right, we learned a lot, and our people grew closer together." She takes a bite of her rare steak. "We still don't agree on everything, but now we have open adoption and immigration between us. There is still deep resentment between the two people, but it is lesser now than it was two hundred years ago."

"I'm curious about two things about you."

"Only two?" Tom looks at her plate. "Is one of them about her eating steak when Elves are vegetarian?"

Zarra laughs. "Tree Elves are vegetarian. I'm not and require meat to survive. Few plants grow in Naerth." She turns to William. "What do you want to know? I keep very few secrets."

"The first and most obvious for me is you're a Paladin of Johnathan. Its thrills me to meet one, and I'm wondering how that came about?"

Tia chimes in as well. "I was curious about that, too. You must be extraordinary."

Zarra smiles. "That's my proudest moment. I've learned of several gods and found Johnathan to be my calling. Brave, good, and honorable. Everything my people weren't." Her hands are on the table, but animated. "And I figured if I could become this beacon of good, that it would show both of our peoples that there was another way. I trained hard, even as a princess, in sword combat, armored combat, horseback, archery, gunplay and

125

strength trained." She flexes for emphasis as she continues. "I know I'll never be on par with someone like William as far as physical strength, but I have other advantages." Zarra takes a deep breath. "What's your other curious question?".

"Well, it's the design of your armor. It's not a solid metal plate, but multiple smaller plates that look as if they slide along each other. Is that for weight reduction?"

Zarra's smile grows. "That's where another strength lays. I am 'flexible'." This gets the group to exchange glances as she stands up. "I'll show you what I mean." She then bends over backwards, contorting her body till her head rests on the floor. Everyone looks astonished, and Tom's mouth hangs agape. Tyra reaches out and claps the man's jaw shut, bringing him out of his un-monk like thoughts. Zarra stands upright again, then reaches behind her back showing that her joints don't move naturally. "I'm not sure why, but I can bend in ways that if anyone else would try, would land them in the hospital."

Tom whistles. "You would have made a great martial artist, being able to flex like that."

She sits back down and makes a few popping noises as she shrugs. "Had there been a monastery over there, maybe I would have been."

William grins. "Maybe you and I can spar some time? Show me how it works in combat? Being able to fight smaller, faster opponent would be good practice."

Zarra nods. "Sure, maybe after we're done rescuing the monks."

William looks at Crystal. "Are you ok with this, honey?"

She blinks, coming out of her introspection. "Yep, anything to help you protect me better, I'm all for. Just expect me to laugh if she knocks you on your ass."

He smiles. "I would expect nothing less."

126

Crystal turns to a Gnome. "How long till we land at the monastery?"

He shrugs. "I don't know. I'm off duty."

"I didn't ask if you were on duty, I asked how long. Now go and find out." She makes a shooing motion. He gets up and takes off. "Sometimes you just have to prod the help a little to get things done."

The Gnome comes back and informs Crystal that they will be there in just under an hour.

"Thank you, crewmen. That will be all." She turns to the rest of them. "It's late. If you want to get some rest, go ahead. I'll talk to Master Monzulo if you all want to get some sleep. We won't be starting any projects in the middle of the night, but I would like to inform him we are here and get an idea of what he needs done."

"I can go inform him if you want to sleep, countess." Tom stands. "I'm faster than you are, anyway."

"I know you are Tom, but I think this would mean more to him, and myself, if I went."

Tia stands as well. "At least take someone with you. We don't know if more of these Black Rose people are around."

Crystal nods, and Zarra speaks up. "I'll go with her." She stands next followed by the others. "As a Dark Elf, I can see in the dark, so it's much harder to hide from me. If someone is out there, I'll see them coming."

Crystal turns and looks at William, and she smiles. "Sounds good to me, unless you have an objection, my love?"

"She has the advantage in the dark. I'll grant her that." He looks at Zarra. "Be careful. She's a handful."

"Why are you warning me of her? You mean to be careful about watching for bad guy's right?"

"No, watch out for her. I feel bad for anyone who gets caught in her crosshairs when she's angry."

Zarra looks at Crystal and she shrugs. "Long story, I have 'anger issues' remember."

They all retire for the night, and William helps Zarra get her armor back on over her leathers. "This armor is light, but strong. Is this mithril?"

"It's a mithril, titanium alloy. It's stronger than steel but weighs only three quarters of full steel, and with the sliding plates, I get almost full range of motion in it."

"That's interesting. Wonder is Jack would want to see this armor, maybe make his power armor more mobile."

"Maybe someday I'll get to meet the great man himself, but for now, I have a countess to protect." William has a look of worry on his face, and she can tell. "I know it's difficult not being at her side. I promise to you she will be fine, but you can always come too."

Crystal smiles. "That's true honey. If you're that worried, come with us. We could always head to the bathhouse and soak for a while."

"I don't think that's the proper time to think about that."

Crystal shrugs. "It's your fault. You're too handsome for me to keep my hands off." She leans in and gives him a kiss. Crystal catches a small nod from Zarra as she finishes getting the buckles done. "See, even she agrees."

This gets Zarra's head to come around. "I meant no disrespect. I was just, uh."

Crystal laughs, cutting off her stammering. "Oh, this is great. She's just as easy to tease as you were, my love." Crystal's smile doesn't leave her face as one of her fangs is bare. "You know how hard it is to keep women from looking at him? It's impossible. So, I don't get mad over it." She shrugs. "If I got jealous every time another woman ogled my man, I would never get any rest. I don't need those kinds of wrinkles by the time I hit twenty-five."

Zarra casts her eyes down. "Thanks for understanding."

"Nothing to be ashamed of." She places a hand on Zarra's shoulder, comforting her. "It's how we are built." She looks back to William. "Beauty comes in many forms, and who doesn't enjoy gazing upon something that is pleasing to our eyes." She moves to him, wrapping her arms around his neck and kissing him. "I'll be back soon. Keep our bed warm."

"Yes, countess." A crew member comes and informs them they are landing. William waves them off.

Crystal lets go and turns to Zarra. "Shall we go?"

Zarra rolls her hair up and pins it, then dons her helm, covering her face. "I'm ready. And thank you for not treating me as royalty."

Crystal addresses William. "If we get into trouble, I'll signal you. A simple flare spell can be seen for several minutes, so if you see one, come running. I'm sure we won't have any problems. The monks have a way better night watch going by what we had seen from the windows as we came in." William nods and escorts the girls to the gangplank leading to the ground. The door opens and the cold hits Zarra like a wall.

Zarra pulls her blanket tighter around her armor. "I should have brought some gambeson to wear under this. I forgot I was going to be working in the snow."

They start down the ramp and Crystal asks if Zarra would like her to cast her endurance spell again. Zarra accepts. "It must be zero out here, this blanket will not hold up."

"Advantages of being Half-White Dragon." She chants her incantation and motions with her hands. "And I know that's not the correct term for me, but I'm not going to repeat myself over and over about the ritual. So that identity is fine with me and easier to go with." They glow white momentarily, then envelopes Zarra.

"Thanks. It is still cold, but not so bad that I think I'm going to die now."

CHAPTER 13

(Rebuild)

They make their way across the snow-covered ground, lit up by the half waning moon. A short monk intercepts them and bows. "Countess, we've been expecting you." He turns the emerald knight. "You are not William."

She points back as he is still standing there. "I'm Zarra. I'm one of her friends. William is on the ship."

"Of course." He turns. "Master told us that no matter when you got here, he should be notified. If you will follow me."

Crystal motions for him to lead, and they follow him up the steps. As they climb, Zarra starts having reservations halfway up. "Why are here so many steps?"

"To whittle out the unworthy." Crystal lets out a laugh. "You need me to help you?"

"I should make it, but this is brutal."

Crystal smiles, casting her gaze up the steps. "I remember the first time I had to walk these steps. My legs cramped hard. William had to massage them to get them to relax, but put me in an awkward situation."

"Really? I thought you loved him?"

"Not at that time. I was mad that he thought he had the right to touch my legs when we still barely knew each other and thought he was using it as an excuse to feel me up." Crystal giggles, thinking about it now. "But as he kneaded them, the pain went away." She continues to giggle. "But he was right on his assessment that day. I had thought of many ways to kill him as he massaged my calves." She addresses the monk. "Last time I climbed these steps, a nice man with a sword escorted me up. I take it he's asleep, and that's why he isn't doing it?"

The monk doesn't turn back nor slow down. "Master Mori fell during the attack."

Crystal's smile fades. "I'm sorry for your loss." She casts her eyes down. "I didn't know him personally, but he felt like a good person."

They get to the top, and Zarra can feel her calves and thighs burning. "Johnathan, help me. This is something else." She almost sounds like she's begging. "Can I have a minute to rest?"

The monk nods. "I'll wake Master Monzulo. Have a seat here."

As Zarra takes a minute to rest, Crystal surveys the monastery and gasps at the destruction. Even in the dark, there is enough light between the half-moon and the snow to see most of the carnage. Disdain and vitriol fill her voice. "I'll make them pay for this." She can feel the rage building in her, then a cold metal hand lands on her shoulder, getting her attention.

"Please, countess." Zarra speaks soothingly. "I get your angry, but fighting evil with evil will not vanquish it. It will only make it stronger."

"I couldn't have said it any better myself." A familiar voice comes from behind them. Crystal was expecting it, but Zarra jumps. Crystal turns and bows to the Master and Zarra follows suit. Master Monzulo bows in return. "I'm glad you came, and sooner than expected. I figured you wouldn't get here till after the New Year."

"You helped me and William in our darkest moments. It doesn't matter to me that tomorrow is Provider's Day. You and your monks are more important than a few presents. We will stay until we restore everything."

He smiles and turns to the new girl. "I see you brought a new friend. Who's this new lighthouse guiding you through these turbulent times?"

"My name is Zarra. Crystal and I only met today, but her cause is noble. So, I volunteered to join the relief efforts."

"I feel it's going to be much more than that. Her intentions are good, even though some of her methods are not." He looks back at Crystal. "I'm glad you're getting many sources of wisdom, so you will continue to grow. You will be a fine leader someday, and many will flock to your flame seeking your guidance. I can feel it."

"What would you like to start on first? I brought a crew and supplies for rebuilding, and depending on the damage, we can have this place back to normal in a week to a month. Emperor Marcus is throwing his full support behind my efforts here."

"We will discuss that in the morning over some hot ginseng tea. For now, enjoy your night and, as always, our facilities are at your disposal." He bows to them.

Crystal and Zarra return the bow. "Good night, Master Monzulo." He turns and heads back inside and the girls start back down the steps.

Crystal laughs as an idea hits her and Zarra turns in her helm at her. "What's so funny?"

"I was thinking of how fun a floating disc spell would be on this hill with all this snow."

"Oh, lord Johnathan, you would die hitting the bottom."

"Maybe." Crystal surmises. "It's controlled by thought so you could keep it a foot above the ground and just slide into the courtyard."

"Doesn't it only stop when it gets so far away from you? You would keep going till you hit the wall."

"I didn't say it wasn't without its perils, but the thrill would be awesome."

Zarra looks down the hill. *Maybe she needs more help than I know.* They get to the bottom and Zarra heads towards the ship, but notices Crystal has taken a separate path.

"Where are you going?"

"To check on my house."

"You have a house?"

"Yep." Crystal points to a small house across the yard. "Olovira left it to me before she died, and it's been a well of knowledge."

"What are you looking for? Study material?"

"Something like that. Marcus mentioned that there was a war between the gods, and there are several no longer in existence. With Tia's vision saying Daniel is 'carrying the torch of love, but is waiting to pass it on', has me curious."

"Curious about what, countess?"

"What actually happened, and why hasn't there been any new gods to replace the ones that were lost? Something isn't adding up to me. It might take me years, decades, or I might die never knowing, but there is more to the Emperor's story." She arrives at her door. She places the magical key that she always has on her in the lock and the door opens.

"Have you thought that it might not be a good idea to delve into this?"

"I'm not looking for a way to kill a god. I'm just wondering why there are gods missing and why other gods are taking on followers and powers they don't know how to use." She turns to Zarra. "Maybe that's what's wrong with this world. It's out of balance and has been for a long time. If Emperor Marcus is right, there might be something bigger than the Black Rose, causing all our problems."

"I don't know. Sounds like you're onto something, but what if it angers the gods?"

Crystal is digging through the extensive library. "Olovira had to of had the knowledge of the gods to of researched and used that spell to bring back William." She points at the ground. "The knowledge is here, but *where* is the question?"

Zarra shrugs and looks around. She goes to pick up an interesting looking stick when Crystal grabs her hand. "That's a wand of max lightning. You set that off and it could blow a hole right through the wall."

Zarra looks down at the unassuming stick and back at Crystal. "Sorry."

Crystal's face softens. "It's ok, just don't mess with anything in here. I haven't cataloged everything and some of it can be very dangerous. I don't want to see you or anyone else I consider a friend, being hurt by these objects." Crystal takes it from her and places it in her handbag. She looks at the library and it's just row after row of tomes. "I'll come back tomorrow. I was hoping something would just reach out to me, but I have a feeling something like this is going to hide itself." Crystal sighs and walks out with Zarra and locks up behind her.

"But why do you want to know so bad?"

Crystal shrugs. "I want Tia to be happy. Besides, Emperor Marcus mentioned it, and something I've learned is if he speaks of something, it's worth checking into."

They head back to the ship and William is still standing at the door, having stood watch the whole time, her stoic protector. He opens the door and embraces Crystal. "How did it go?"

"Uneventful. Monks have really stepped up security around here. We should be safe as we do our job." They retract the gang plank and seal the door, then head back to their rooms. "Master Monzulo wants to meet us all for tea in the morning and start a plan of action to get things going." She opens the door to their room. "While I was up there, I had a look and it's bad, Will. They suffered a lot here, all because of me."

"That's not true." William wraps his arm around her shoulder as they walk into their cabin. "If it wasn't you, it would have been someone else giving them a reason to do this. Stop blaming yourself for what the Black Rose has done."

"That's good advice, countess. Evil will do evil; it doesn't need a reason."

Crystal nods, looking at them. "Let's get some sleep. I need to clear my head." Zarra walks into her room and beds for the night, removing her armor with soft clinking trying to be quiet so late at night. Crystal removes her dress and looks up at William. "Carry me?"

He grins, lifting and cradling her in his massive arms and carries her over to the bed, laying her down, and then sliding in with her. He strokes her cheek with his massive hands. "I love you."

She nuzzles against it, putting her own hand on his. "I love you too."

The next morning, the sun creeps its way over the mountains to the east, shining down on the airship and its crew. The morning rays blast through the windows, signaling to those aboard it's time to start the day. William awakens to Crystal laying on top of him as he's become accustomed to. He strokes her hair gently to get her to awaken. She inhales deeply and looks up at him, almost getting him in the face with her horns.

He's gotten used to dodging those pointy instruments, and she pushes upward to give him his morning kiss.

"Good morning, my love."

"Always is when I wake up to you."

She lays her head back down on his chest, hearing his heart beating. Its steady rhythm puts her to sleep at night with its comforting presence. "Have you ever wondered what our lives would be like if we just gave all this up? Just went back to Rose Harbor and settled down?"

"Not really. I know we've been through a lot, but before, our lives were so bland, don't you think?" He shifts his head to look down at her as he feels her move her head to look up at him. "Think of all the people we've met, the differences you've made in the lives of the common folk. Of people we haven't met."

She runs her hand along his chest, feeling the hair run through her fingers. "But what about a family? We are going to be married soon. Shouldn't we plan for our lives together, raising children, teaching them the ways of sword, magic, and technology?"

"I've given that a lot of thought. I want to be a proud father." He runs his hand over her head. "But till we vanquish the Black Rose, us and our future children will be in danger."

"I hate them." She curls her hand into a fist, pulling some of his hair. "We don't even know what they really want, but all they do is torment people. I'll show them torment and pain."

"Honey, honey, leave my chest hair."

She lets go, realizing she was starting down that dark path yet again. "I'm sorry, darling. I need to work with Tia, see if she can help me gain control of this, before it leads me to doing something truly horrifying."

"Let's start with breakfast first." They get up and get dressed. William puts on some leathers, then some heavy brown wool clothing over them. Crystal puts on a pearl white sun dress the fits loosely and comes down to her knees. The straps are tiny coming over the shoulders, leaving her arms and upper chest open. It's almost the same color as her skin.

"Don't fall in the snow wearing that. We will never find you."

Crystal counters with a smile. "Maybe that's the point."

Tia and Penelope are waiting at the top of the gangplank, while the crew unloads crates of supplies from the cargo bay. The morning light makes the snow extra bright, making it hard for everyone to see. William covers his eyes to tone down the snow blindness. "Where are *our* monks?"

Tia answers him. "Tom and Tyra are already out there working to unload."

"Better get out there, William. They are going to need your help and leadership." Crystal cinches up his collar. "I'm going to go see Master Monzulo myself and formulate a plan." He leans down, gives her a quick kiss, and descends the ramp to find the Dwarven foremen. "Shadow, I have a special mission for you."

"What do you need, countess?" Penelope is dressed in all white clothing and furs, keeping with her theme of staying hidden.

"I want you to sweep the perimeter, see how they got in, and where they came from. Gather as much intelligence as you can. They couldn't have come from Black Rock because that city is fortified now. So, they had to of had something else, a ship at the coastline, a hidden base in the mountains, something."

"You can count on me."

"Then get some breakfast and get started. I look forward to your report tonight." Crystal then turns to Tia and Zarra. "I want you two to accompany me back to my place and help me find some things. I might not be good at architecture, but maybe we can find some magical support that's already here. Plus, I could use you there to steer me clear of any more evil. I'm
138

already tainted and don't want to be drawn down that path anymore."

Tia envelops her in a hug. "Glad to help with that."

Penelope leaves first, heading across the field and climbing up onto some crates. Crystal can't begin to guess what she is doing. She, Tia, and Zarra descend into the snow. "We must see Master Monzulo first. He said there would be hot tea, so I'm hoping their cafeteria is in decent order. Going by what I saw from the top of the hill last night, the Black Rose tried to burn the whole place to the ground."

"We will make it right, and it looks like Johnathan, Daniel, and Provider are with us as we bring gifts of aid."

Crystal nods, flexing her hands as they walk through the ankle-deep snow. "I want so badly to destroy the Black Rose. I hate them, but I know it's wrong." She sighs. "But every time I even think of them, this rage builds inside, and eventually I lose control."

"After what they did to you, I don't fault you. You admitting this is a problem is a tremendous step to recovery. I've been praying to Daniel for you every day." Tia looks at the staff. "And I've done some studying of my own to become a better healer, and I want to try a few things."

Crystal's hands relax and she gets a small smile. "Like what?"

"Since we are here at a monastery, meditation for one. First step in recovery is trying to get your inner demons identified." Tia turns her head to address Crystal. "So you need a place of silence to relax and focus. I know the devastation and the reason behind coming here isn't ideal, but spending time here among the monks might help you relax."

They walk into the cafeteria and Master Monzulo is there with a steaming pot and several nice porcelain glasses. He stands up and bows to the ladies and they return the gesture. He motions for them to sit down opposite him, and he pours them a cup each, sliding it carefully in front of them. "Having morning tea, with three beautiful women, is one of life's wonderful pleasures."

"Thank you, Master." Crystal and Zarra say in unison, steam rising from their cups and then giggle about it. They sip lightly at the hot tea as they start their meeting. They speak about the events of the night they were attacked. Crystal's jaw clenches as she glowers at her hands. "I'm sorry I brought this down on you, Master."

"Do not accept blame for something you didn't cause." He waves the thought away. "Had you not come along, they would have attacked anyway us for supporting the Emperor and the Rose Empire. If anything, your presence accelerated their plans, and they weren't ready. That's why the attack failed."

Her shoulders slump and casts her gaze downwards. "That's nice of you to say, but I still feel responsible."

Master Monzulo looks at Tia and Zarra. "Crystal has a very troubled soul, and I can feel your eagerness to help, but you two are not much better off than she is." He strokes his beard. "I have an idea. I'll hand off the work orders to Captain Blakely, and you three meet me at the sanctuary. We have much work to do."

CHAPTER 14

(Information is Strength)

Penelope surveys from atop the crates. *I need to start where they breached the wall. I know it's along the north face somewhere.* She holds a hand in front of her, blocking the glare from the blinding snow. She pulls her hood over her head as well and it helps reduce some glare as well. The crate under her shifts and she looks down, realizing Tyra had just grabbed the whole stack and is moving it elsewhere. She carries the crates, along with Penelope, over to the cabin area where the burn damage is the worse. Penelope hops down and skulks about the cabins, then locates the breach. *That's what I'm looking for.* She studies the ground along her walk there and shutters looking at the crushed snow and the frozen blood stains. *This was one hell of a fight.*

She finds what's left of the outer wall, boarded up and not very secure. *That won't be a problem once the Dwarves get over here and start working. But before they do, I need to go over this place and see what I can find.* She picks up chunks of splinters from the old wooden wall and feels it in her frozen hands. Some chunks have burn marks. *Black powder explosion.* She holds it up to her nose. *This black powder isn't used in firearms. This is a fast burning, high yield powder I've seen Jack use in some of his more 'adventurous' products.* She tosses the wood to the ground and stands up. *This was a possibly professionally made, not something they just tossed together.* She walks up to the boarded wall and looks along the charred edges. *And it was a big one, going by how thick this wall is.*

She clambers over the shoddy patch job, finding plenty of holds, and drops to the other side. *This was one hell of a blast going by the melted snow and crater left behind.* She can see dented and broken armor and weapons along with remains of those too close. *Looks like it detonated early. Several here were too close to the blast when it went off.* She checks the ground and for several yards around the area; finding pieces of melted and charred metal. She picks up a large piece and examines the torn metal, all twisted and mangled. *Vaporized in an instant. Looks like a standard hammered steel plate. Could have been made by anyone, but I should take this to Crystal and see if there are any magical properties.*

She looks around the grounds, looking for the greatest concentration of footprints, recalling her training at the hands of Henry. The old man's voice echoes in her head. *"When tracking an enemy, you can tell a lot by how they move in formation. If they are spread out, then it is an informal, ragtag group of people who haven't trained together."* He holds a single finger in the air as he paces. *"But a single line formation is actual trained soldiers meant to hide the number and composition of said troops."* She smiles as she looks over the trail. *This is way easier to tell in the snow than in plain grass.*

She tracks their steps and can tell these were not professionals. The large footprints of the Orcs and Ogres they brought with them are clear, along with the pathway is about as straight as a bunch of freezing Humanoids can do. She walks the path back slowly, hidden, taking in every detail. She travels it for some time and the cold is biting at her nose and extremities. *What I wouldn't give for one of Crystal's weather protection spells right now.*

She walks the trail for a few hours. Green pines scatter around the land along with dormant maples and elms. Stepping around a large pine, she notices a trail branch away from the primary group. *Those are some large animal prints, possibly a mount, but definitely not a horse. I'll have to come back to this.* She looks up and gets an idea about how much daylight is left. *I don't like how this looks. I need to find where they came from first.* Tracking it further for another couple of hours, she notices the trail stops with a large circle of melted snow. She continues to look around and find more of these circles and signs of a camp. Picking through the remains of campfires and left-over tents that had collapsed, she searches for evidence of how they got here. *They had returned here when they were defeated and grabbed what they could.* Picking through the remains, she comes to some conclusions. *There is still frozen food, supplies, and all kinds of stuff still here.*

She can hear Henry in her mind. *"When an enemy has been beaten, and their leadership killed, they tend to loot and run away. Survival becomes the singular goal in mind."*

She stands up. *Going by how much is left behind, those who fled were very few, and very amateurish.* She finds the remains of the commander's tent, whips out a dagger, and cuts the canvas open. Crawling in, she gets a better picture of what was going on. *Maps, documents, and some very interesting items.* She lifts a rod that has some magical writing. She deciphers it, matching up symbols she's seen around Jasmine's lab and the ones she was taught by Henry.

"Mass teleportation." She tucks it into her belt. "Few can pull off a magic of this caliber." She scans the area. *Wonder if there are any other goodies around here?* She turns some stuff over and checks loose papers on the ground. *This stuff is ruined, but maybe Crystal can restore them.* The wind blows the flap she cut open and the freezing cold flows in, reminding her that time is short. She grabs the maps and any other important looking documents. Then anything that looks fancy and sticks it where she can. Removing a section of the tent, she crafts a makeshift bag that she can drag behind her.

As she clambers over the fallen boxes, only to spot a black clad individual standing there with a revolver. *Great, I accuse them of being armatures and I fall into this.*

A masculine voice calls to her. "Step away from the tent."

She raises her tiny hands. *The fact he didn't kill me on sight means he isn't afraid of me. That's something I can use.* Her training kicks in as Henry's teachings come back to her. *"Try to get information without looking like you're an unimportant nobody. Sometimes you get lucky."* She steps forward. "Doing some salvaging yourself?"

"What? No." He points the gun to the mess and back at her. "This is my camp."

"Oh, sorry." She glances around, trying to look unassuming. "I'm just a drifter looking for salvage. I saw the knocked over tents and there was no one around, so I figured something bad went down and it was abandoned." She digs into her training, trying to look like a potential ally. "Where you and your friends attacked? Maybe I can help?"

"How would a tiny scavenger like you help? Just drop what you took and leave, and I won't hurt you if you go now."

"I'm a survivor, like you. I've had my share of bad dealings. Some of this stuff looks valuable." She emphasizes by shaking the bag, causing it to jingle. "We could travel to Rose Harbor and sell it, split the cash, and go our separate ways."

His hands are shaking from holding the gun for so long. *His muscles are getting tired. If I can keep him talking and not shooting, he will end up dropping it on his own.*

"I'm not in this for the money. I'm waiting for my friends to come get this stuff."

"So, you're guarding the place? How long have you been out here? You look frozen, you poor thing." She puts the bag down.

He finally drops the weapon to his side and sighs. "I am. I've been out here for five days, waiting." He sits down on an overturned crate. "I've been thinking no one is coming to at this point."

"Does anyone know you're here?" More of her training from Henry tells her to get friendly with the target. *"The more*

144

sympathetic you are to their problem, the less likely they are to get defensive about any probing questions later. Just don't get emotionally attached. It makes it harder for you to do your job later."

"I don't know, honestly. I could be out here freezing to death waiting on nothing."

"Why are you out here? You're miles from anywhere. Had I not been out looking for some something to eat, I would have never found this place."

He holsters the revolver on his hip. "Why are you so far from the road?"

She walks closer to him, keeping her smile on and sounding friendly. "I was walking to Black Rock and ran out of food. I was wondering the hillsides here looking for edible berries or maybe small game I could eat and got lost. Then I found this campsite, looked abandoned and hoped I could find some food and things I could sell later." She looks up at him. "Girl has to eat, doesn't she?"

"I guess so. Can't fault you there." He pulls his own mask off, showing how young he is. "Look, I don't want to hurt you, but if the people who are paying me to be out here come back, they are going to want their stuff, so I have to watch over it."

"But you said it's been five days." She points to the mess. "Sounds to me you've been left for dead." She sits down next to him, looking friendly. "You even said it yourself, that you could be out here for nothing. Why not take what you can carry and just leave? Better than freezing to death. There is a monastery near here. I saw it a day or so ago, maybe less. They could take you in. Monks are normally good people willing to help." She studies his face, judging his reaction.

He waves his hands in front of him. "Oh no, I can't go back there."

She puts concern into her voice. "Go back? They kick you out?" She places her hand on his, trying to comfort him. *If I can get him to confide in me, he will continue to tell me everything I want to know.*

"No, not exactly." He turns to her. "Look, you seem like a nice person, and I don't want you to get mixed up in this. I was hired along with others to mess the monks up for helping the Rose Empire and an evil they were harboring at one point." He takes a deep breath. "I don't think they are evil, but they are helping it by helping some lady named Hellstromm and her friends. They are terrorists who have killed people for no reason."

She senses no hint of deceit from him. *He actually believes this nonsense?* She pats his hand some more. "You really think monks would help someone who is evil?" She shakes her head. "I'll admit I don't know a lot of monks, but helping evil isn't a descriptor I would use."

"I know. It doesn't make sense." He shakes his head. "But I've heard stories of her and her friends, carving people up, shooting up homes, and torturing innocent people. She has to be stopped."

"I'm well-traveled and haven't heard of this lady. How do you know of her? Where are you from?".

"I haven't seen it firsthand, but I've heard stories all the way up to New Haven. That's where I'm from."

She leans back to give a look of incredulous at him, blinking to add to the effect. "You're from New Haven? That's got to be a six month walk one way. You walked all the way, cross the continent and a mountain range to attack a monastery?" She turns away from him. "I wish I could find a man with that kind of dedication. Maybe I wouldn't be a scavenger living off of the land." He laughs for the first time. *Good, this means any lingering defenses are lowering. He thinks I'm his friend.*

"No, I didn't walk that far. There was this circle I had to stand in with some others that were hired for the job. Was

146

supposed to be a way back once we got here and completed the job. This lady said some things, and the floor glowed blue, and we popped out here. Then the guy in charge said to get the camp set up." He sighs. "We sat here for a week, not doing anything, just meandering about, and a scout would watch the monastery." He licks his chapped lips. "Then this floating boat came out of the clouds one night. Never saw anything like it before." He points towards the monastery. "It landed way off in that direction somewhere. Stayed for about an hour maybe, then took off again."

He turns to her. "At that moment, I was scared out of my mind. It matched the same floating ship description that had shelled one of our camps months earlier. None of us believed that such a thing was possible, but seeing it hanging there in the sky, like the angel of death, scared me to my boots." His eyes turn full of fear. "That's when I realized the stories were true. No good person would make such a thing, to rain fire down on helpless people who were just minding their own business."

He was fed some good quality propaganda. I remember that incident, and they were not helpless people minding their own business. They were terrorizing people and almost tortured Crystal to death. This guy was convinced the opposite was true with a carefully crafted lie. She looks up. "It's getting dark. We need to start a fire if we are going to survive the night here. I'm sorry your people abandoned you here, but I think the monastery is still our best chance of long-term survival. The fact you made it this long in the frozen hell means you're not stupid. Let's help each other. We can go there together and pose as passing travelers. If they look shady, we can steal some horses and leave."

He looks to the setting sun. "Yeah, you're right. It's getting late, and I think you're right about the fire. I dug out a large hole over here and put a tent5 over it. Its looks like the tent collapsed, but it's more insulated being under ground and keeps it from being seen from a distance."

She nods in agreement. "How do you know these survival tricks? Were you a farm boy before coming here?" She follows him to the hole he dug out.

"Something like that. My dad was a soldier, but that life wasn't for me. He taught me some survival tricks if something ever happened." He breaks up some boxes and grabbing some lumber from a broken ox cart. She follows him down into his hole and at the back is a shaft going up that looks like a makeshift chimney. He tosses the lumber and other flammables and starts a fire. "As long as we don't let this be too big, it will heat this hole up nicely without choking us out."

She does her best to sound grateful. "I'm glad you found me. I would of froze to death out there."

"Wait here. I'm going to get more wood." He heads up, and she follows, peeking above the ground to see him grabbing more wood from the cart and some blankets. Coming back, she ducks back down. Handing her down the blankets first, then the extra wood for the fire. "This should help keep you warm." He gives her a sigh. "Look, I don't trust you, but if you had the intent to kill me, you had more than enough chances to do so. I know you're at least not a murderer." He turns away. "I'll go with you to the monastery in the morning. I hope you're right and they are good people, but I'm dead if I stay out here."

He heads up to gather more wood, and she joins him. "I might be tiny, but every little helps right?" They work together, stacking wood for the night as the sun dips below the trees, plunging the area into the sub-zeros. They sit opposite each other, chewing on ration bars scavenged from the camp, and exchanging small talk. *He's so young, can't be over nineteen. How did he get mixed up in all this?* This leads to another train of thought. *I'm surprised no one has come looking for me. I figured Tyra would have been enlisted to come look for me. It's been hours, and now it's close to midnight.* Even with the fire, it's still cold in their makeshift cave and both of them are shivering.

He lays against the dirt wall with some padding between her and it, trying to sleep upright. More of her training fills her

148

head. *"In the field, sharing body heat is one of the best ways to survive the wintry nights."*

She watches as he continues to try to get comfortable. *I'm going to have to do something that I know I'll regret later.* She takes the rod and other items from her belt and buries them under some loose dirt, then crawls across the small dugout to him. She pulls back his cover, waking him.

"Don't get the wrong idea." She settles in with her back against his chest. She pulls the covers back over, adding her own blankets to his. "If we share body heat, we will live longer." She gives him a stern look. "But if those hands of yours go wondering, you're going to find handling that iron a lot harder without them."

"I understand. My dad didn't raise me that way." He wraps his arms around her but keeping his hands on his own arms. "I'm Chuck, by the way. If we are going to be friendly like this, you might as well know my name."

"Penelope." She sits there till she hears him fade off to sleep, warmed by his touch, but only out of fear of freezing to death. Leaning back, her large ears rest against him and she fades to sleep.

She's awoken by vibrations in the ground. *There is a large animal nearby, I can feel it.* She slides a hidden dagger out, but leaves it under the blanket. She can feel the kid's arms around her, limiting her movement but keeping her warm. *I'm going to have to wake him. If this is a bear or a mountain lion, I'm going to need his help.*

She squirms a little and whispers at him. "Wake up. There's an animal out there."

He arouses and shakes his head. "Animal? Where?" The tent above them is ripped off.

They look up and the head of a Minotaur peers down at them. Penelope shouts in joy. "TYRA!"

Crystal peeks over the side and sees the couple, his arms wrapped around her tiny frame. "Should we come back later and give you two more alone time?"

CHAPTER 15

(All work and no Play)

Crystal, Zarra, and Tia follow Master Monzulo up the stairs and into the main building. Tia feels like her legs are going to fall off after climbing all those steps, but Zarra is doing so much better not wearing her armor this time around. They remove their shoes and heavier clothes. "Thank you, Master, for letting us use the sanctuary so that I can start Crystal's healing. My magic can heal physical wounds, but it's the one's we can't see that's troubling her. I appreciate the help."

Master Monzulo leads them through the sanctuary. "Often, the best way to solve one's personal problem is by helping someone else with theirs."

Tia looks confused. "What personal problem do I have?"

Zarra interrupts Tia. "I believe he means me. I have my own issues."

"All three of you do. And together, you will solve them for one another." They walk into the Master's personal meditation room. The last time Crystal was here was when he gave her and William the candle. "You have much self-doubt, Tia. Your soul is bright but fearful, being unable to do what is best for your future." He turns and points to where they are to sit. "Even if you already know what that is." He turns to Zarra. "You run from your problems. Instead of facing them head on. You are brave in the face of physical danger, but fear your own emotions." He then looks at Crystal. "You have the greatest trouble. You cannot find a balance between the love in your heart and the rage in your soul."

Tia, Crystal, and Zarra sit on the floor, legs crossed. Master Monzulo lights some incense, filling the air with a sweet fragrance. "I don't know about this, Master. I usually handle my problems on my own."

"There is nothing wrong with getting help. All the better from those who love you."

Crystal continues to question the Master. "So… we can help each other?"

The master sits cross-legged and closes his eyes. "The first step to reaching inner peace is proper breathing."

Tyra, Tom, and the other monks get their orders and start carrying lumber, tools, and crates of building materials to the cabins first. The female Dwarf and a male Elf contractor look over the remains of the buildings. Speaking amongst themselves, they determine which ones can be repaired and what must be demolished. They go from building to building, checking each one for integrity, arguing about what can be done, but they usually come to a consensus within a few minutes. The Elven man looks at the collection of cabins. "It looks as if they just kept building new ones as more people arrived."

"I concur." Dwarven lady takes notes. "We need to draw up something new for them. Maybe a barracks like structure with a few personal cabins for travelers and some of their leadership?"

"If it were summer, I would agree with you on that, but those projects could take a month or two to complete. If we restored the cabins that could still be inhabitable with a few repairs, it would let them move back in as we move along. Then when summer comes around, we can come back and do the barracks."

William towers over them both. "Why don't you two draw up some proposals and I'll run them by the Grand Master? It is his monastery, so he should pick how to proceed."

"That would be fair." The man agrees with a nod. He turns to his female counterpart. "But we must agree on construction materials to use. Right now, we can repair the cabins as is, but if we imported some masonry, we could upgrade them to brick that would be more fire retardant."

The Dwarven lady holds up a finger. "And a tile roof, instead of wood, so anyone tossing a torch on top can't cause any structural damage." The Elf nods in agreement.

"Like I said, put your proposals on parchment and add some sketches, and I will hand them off. Just for now, let's at least restore the kitchen and dining area."

Tom sits down on a box nearby. "But Master Monzulo's orders were to restore the cabins first."

"Yes, I know." William looks over the site. "But we are at an impasse. Master Monzulo didn't know we could make improvements while we are here and assess the situation first. Since we aren't changing the dining area, we can at least get it fixed. Then we can start with the living quarters tomorrow."

Tom stretches a bit. "I guess you're right. I just don't like the idea of them being homeless in the cold."

"Me either, but if we can make improvements, we should. If you get attacked again, we should be able to minimize the damage they take. An extra day of sleeping cramped up at the top of the hill isn't going to kill them." William waves the contractors off to get started.

"That makes sense. You know more about this than I do, Captain." He stands, picking up the next crate.

The three girls sit meditating with the Grandmaster. "Clear your thoughts. Push out the bad thoughts and focus on breathing. Take in the good air and expel the bad." His voice is soothing and calm. "We are finding balance within you. With proper breathing and focus, you can tune your mind to calm yourself."

They sit in silence. *I've been breathing my whole life. How would I not know how to breathe?* Crystal's hands twitch. *This is a waste of time and should be out there helping or doing some research.*

"Crystal." The grandmaster interrupts her thoughts. "Focus. If your thoughts wonder, the meditation will fail."

Her eyes are still closed. *How does he always seem to know?* She focuses on taking in deeper breaths and letting it out slowly as he instructed. *I feel silly, but I guess it's something that works if he's been doing it for so many years.*

"That's better. Now focus in your mind on something positive, something or someone who brings you joy."

The three girls have different ideas about what brings them joy. Tia focuses on Daniel and the joy he brings to her. Crystal focuses on William and her friends. Zarra focuses on having her freedom and having met these interesting individuals.

Tia goes into a trance. *I feel rather peaceful. It's not too dissimilar from prayer.* She empties her mind of everything but her god when she gets a feeling of joy and warmth. *Wonder if this is what the Grandmaster was talking about.*

A disembodied but familiar male voice speaks to her. *You're doing well, my child. You've taken the first steps to correcting the path I had originally laid out.*

Tia's heart skips. *Daniel?*

I'm here with you, child. I am with all my children.

What is my purpose, Lord?

You haven't one purpose, but many ahead of you. The torch of love will be passed on soon, to one who can use it properly. Your work has just begun with changing my church to see my vision. Once I pass this torch, the vision will be easy to be seen by all. Stay strong. Images bombard her of families born within the church, expanding his influence through them. His divinity spreading the healing and warmth of his gifts through his followers.

All of this, because of me? But why me? I don't understand my Lord.

You will in time. Events unfold as we speak.

"Daniel?" She feels her body being shaken. She opens her eyes and Master Monzulo and Crystal are standing there. Zarra stands across the room, not wanting to get in the way. "What happened?"

"You tell us." Crystal pulls Tia to her feet. "We've been trying to get you to come out of your trance for three hours."

"That can't be right" Looking out a window and noticing the sun is indeed setting. "I don't understand" Panic fills her voice, looking back to Crystal and the Grandmaster. "That only felt like a few moments, not hours."

Master Monzulo strokes his beard. "What did?"

"I think I had another vision of Daniel. I saw families being born within the church, and he said he would soon pass the torch of love to another who will know how to use it properly. Then he showed me his vision of the church will be possible for all his followers to see."

Crystal shakes her head. "Slow down, take a breath." She looks to the Grandmaster, letting Tia go. "Passing the torch? Is this some kind of relay?"

He shrugs. "That's a question I have no answer to." He turns and walks to the door. "I have to look over some proposals brought to me by your people. Now that you're back with us, I can look those over." He smiles. "Then I will teach you how to make tea properly." He steps out of the room, leaving the three women to themselves.

"There's a proper way to make tea?" Crystal shrugs, turning back to Tia. "I thought it was just water strained through some leaves."

The master calls from the other room. "I heard that."

Tia laughs. "I think for him, it's a bit more complicated than that, countess."

"Anything else your vision tells you?"

"Just that my friends will guide me." She sits down. "Not sure what that means, either. You just tell me where to go. That's not much in the way of guidance."

"Gods are always cryptic." Zarra steps up to them. "It's like they are bound by some weird law to never say what they mean."

"There is something I want your help with." Crystal turns to look at them. "After we are done here today."

William pulls some roofing materials up on top of the dining hall and hands it off to a monk. Dwarves, Elves, and a few monks are up there patching and repairing. The sounds of hammering, sawing, and some not so child friendly banter can be overheard. Tom and Tyra are up there with him trying to help, but carpentry isn't one of their skills, but still doing well. "Everything going smoothly over there?"

"Yeah, it would surprise you how much of our training revolves around common housework." Tom hammers in some more nails, taking on a mocking tone. "Focus you mind, be one with the hammer, drive the nail into the wood, feel the joining of metal and nature." He chuckles, getting Tyra to join in.

"Tom, you're something else. Not what I would think would be a typical monk. How did you keep your humor in a place that's so serious all the time?"

"I don't really know, to be honest. Guess part of me is just a renegade." He turns and looks at William. "And life isn't worth living without a little danger from time to time, don't you think?"

"Can't argue that, I guess, but how is it dangerous being humorous?"

"Have you met Tyra?" He chuckles, thumbing her direction. "She's chased me more than once around this place for things I've joked about." He hammers in another nail. "You could say she 'won't put up with my bull'-"

A slug sending him sliding across the roof, interrupting his sentence. He lets out a yelp of pain. Tyra fumes. "I'm going to kick your ass back to Rose Harbor."

"Have you thought of not talking like that around her?" William chuckles. "Would save you a lot of pain."

"What's the fun in that?" Tom rubs his arm. "If I keep this up, one day I'll be able to dodge it, then nothing will touch me."

William shakes his head. "Looks like undue punishment to me."

"Think of it like sparing, can't get better if you don't fear the sting of an opponent."

They continue to work and banter. Trading stories of their childhoods. As the sun comes down, the temperature does too. "I'm getting hungry." Tyra flops down. "How close are we to being done?"

"We can finish up without you." The Dwarven contractor looks through some papers. "We just need to put the finishing touches on it. So, if you want to go get something to eat, feel free."

"Thank you." She crawls across the roof and jumps down with Tom.

The three girls kneel on the floor across from the old master. Next to him is a kettle of hot water. Four white porcelain cups sit in the center of a cherry wood colored slatted uprising. On the wooden rise, but not on the slats, is an oddly shaped green bowl filled with long dry leaves. Opposite that, on the other side, is a long stick with a small curvature at the end. On the slats themselves is a white teapot with a lid and a small glass pitcher.

"Making tea is about energy and focus. I will show you a very simple tea ceremony that will help channel your chi." He starts by lifting the small lid off the porcelain teapot and setting it aside, then lifts the hot water and pours it in. "Your bodies' chi flows like water into a reservoir, where the energy is ready to be used."

He then places the pitcher of hot water down and replaces the lid back on the kettle. He lifts the kettle and pours the water into the tiny pitcher. "The purity of the water represents the purity of your energy. As it's able to flow freely, so must your energy." He then puts the kettle down and lifts the pitcher, pouring the hot water into each of the four small cups. Taking the leftover water, he empties it over the closed white teapot. He then lifts each of the cups and pours the hot water over the closed teapot as well, letting the water flow over its lid and through the slats. "Once the energy is used, it cannot return to the source, thus it is gone."

He then picks up the lid to the teapot once more and places it to the side, showing it is empty. Picking up the green bowl with the tea leaves in it with his right hand and the small wooden stick with his left, he continues. "The tea leaves represent your body. You don't force the leaves into the kettle, but guide them to slide out on their own, the same way you want to guide your body's natural energy to move on its own." He prods with the tiny stick gently, pushing the leaves around and letting them fall from the dish naturally till all of them are in the teapot. He then places the empty dish and stick back on the raised wooden platform.

Lifting the hot kettle, he pours slowly into the teapot, watching carefully not to overfill it. "Let your chi flow with the water into the teapot, influencing the flavor. With balance and focus, the tea will be sweet and will flow well. If it is not, it will be bitter and clog up." He puts down the hot water and replaces the lid. He then lifts the teapot, holding the lid down with his left hand, refilling the pitcher. A golden-brown liquid with a sweet aroma pours from it.

He puts the empty kettle down and lifts the tiny pitcher, using it to fill each of the smaller cups. After the last one, he places the now empty pitcher down and hands Crystal, Zarra, and Tia a cup, and takes the last for himself. He raises it to his nose and inhales, smelling the sweet tea. They do the same and can smell how good and calming it is. They all drink at the same time and can't believe how great it tastes.

Crystal closes her eyes, enjoying it. "This is a truly wonderful tea, Master."

Tia nods in agreement. "Thank you so much for showing us this."

Zarra sips the hot liquid. "Never thought I could become a tea drinker. This is amazing."

"I show you this so you can practice on your own. The lesson doesn't end today. It's a lifelong journey. Tomorrow I would like for you to be back here and practice making tea. It's not as easy as it looks. You must learn focus to make truly great tea."

Crystal nods, taking another small drink, then her eyes go wide, and puts the cup down. Tia notices Crystal's distress immediately. "What is it?" Zarra perks up, taking interest.

"Shadow has been gone all day and should have been back by now." She looks to Master Monzulo. "I don't like it when she doesn't report in. Can I borrow Tyra and go look for her? I would feel better knowing if she's alright."

Master Monzulo smiles. "You're on the right path. Go find your friend."

Tom, William, and Tyra are having dinner in the cafeteria. Surrounded by workers and monks, they can hear the noise of the gathering for some distance. Crystal, Zarra and Tia walk in and see the throng of people, but William and Tyra stick up among the shorter people. They make their way to the table, with Tom and Tyra on one side, and William sitting on the other, laughing and having a good time. William looks up and offers a seat, giving Crystal a place to sit next to him. "How did it go, honey?"

"I don't know about me, but Tia had a flashback or something. So that was exciting." She leans in for a kiss. Tia sits down next to Tom, and Zarra sits on the other side of William, boxing him in between them. "Have any of you heard from Shadow? She should have been back by now, and I was wondering if she was here, but I don't see her."

Zarra looks around the table. "Maybe she went back to the ship?"

"I doubt it. She wouldn't forget to check in." Crystal looks at the ship. "But I don't want to leave any possibilities unchecked." She looks at Tyra. "You're the best tracker I know. Let's go retrace her steps." She looks at the others. "You look around here just in case she came back. If you find her, run me and Tyra down and bring us back. It shouldn't be too hard to see where we went in the snow."

William stands. "I should go with you."

"I know, but Tyra here can handle herself, so I'll be ok. If we get into trouble, she can just pick me up and run. Besides, she's one halfling and the Black Rose fled. It's not like they are sitting out in the cold for five day's hoping I go into the woods

160

alone." Crystal sighs. "Also. I'm the one who put her out there to do this job. I should be the one who finds her."

He leans over and kisses her. "Be careful. If something happens to you, I'll be the one going nuts on people."

CHAPTER 16

(Healing old wounds)

Penelope stands up. "Very funny countess."

Chuck stands up, looking at the ivory woman. "Countess?"

Penelope slips the revolver from its holster before he can grab it. "Chuck, this is Countess Crystal Hellstromm."

The look of shock on his face tells everything, and fear grips him. "You told me you didn't know this woman. You lied to me?"

She holds the weapon up. "I had to. If I had told you I was friends with her, would you have shot me with this thing."

"Yeah, your point is taken. So now what? Going to kill me right here, or torture me to death."

Crystal looks confused looking between them. "Why would we do that?"

"He is one of the surviving members of the failed assault five days ago." Penelope sighs. "But he signed up under false pretenses. They lied to him and made it sound like we are the bad guys, and made you look like a monster. When they fled, they left him here to die." She tosses him the revolver, showing some trust. "He's a good kid at heart. We need to help him."

Crystal shrugs and jumps down into the hole. He looks down at the gun in his hands and back up to her. "Well, the *monster* is here. If you want to kill me, now's your chance. I've been chased, shot at, tortured, branded, sliced, and stabbed, all while trying to figure out why, when I have done nothing but defend myself after leaving the comfort of Rose Harbor." She grabs his weapon hand and points it at her chest. "I'm tired of fighting people whom I'm trying to help. Pull the trigger, and you'll be a hero to your friends, but even after I'm dead, just remember they still left you here to freeze to death." The gun shakes in his hands and her cold icy eyes look up at him.

Tyra reaches out and Crystal slaps her away. "Let him choose." She looks back at him. Their eyes lock. "You can accomplish the Black Rose's primary goal with the twitch of a finger, or you can let go, and let me help you."

"I'm in a no-win situation. I stand down; you could kill me. If I shoot you, they kill me."

Penelope puts a hand on his hip, getting his attention. "Chuck, if I wanted you dead, you wouldn't have woken up, but you're not the enemy. You're a mixed-up kid that should get to go home to his parents."

He looks at each of them, visibly weighing his options in his head. He sighs and drops the gun on the ground. "Fine. I'll go back as your prisoner. If I don't freeze to death along the way."

"You're not going to die, Chuck." Crystal's demeanor changes. She cites an incantation and her hands glow white and touches him. The freezing cold no longer bothers him. *That was much harder than it should have been. It's becoming that time again.*

"What did you do?"

She speaks the words a second time, touching Penelope, and she glows white a moment and it fades. "Thank Provider you have no idea how bad I needed that."

Yeah, it's closer than I think. Need to wrap this up fast and get back. "It's an environmental endurance spell. For a few hours, the temperature of the environment won't bother you. You could run naked in the snow and it would be no different from a warm summer day." She holds her hand up for Tyra to take. "You could use it to get a few hours a sleep here before it wears off, or you can come back with us. I honestly don't care. We came for Shadow. You're just a kid lost in the woods, as far as I'm concerned."

He turns wide eyed to the Halfling. "You're Shadow?"

"Yeah, why?" She grabs the stuff she hid and tossing it up to Tyra and Crystal.

"Shadow the slasher, the killer of men and stealer of souls?"

Penelope tosses him a look of complete absurdity and Tyra and Crystal bust up laughing. "What have you been doing when you're not cooking my dinner?"

"I've got no idea what he's talking about. I don't kill people, and last I checked, I'm not a necromancer. How would I steal souls?"

He sighs. "Never mind, I should know better. You're so tiny you couldn't kill someone."

Penelope gives him a stern look. "Tiny doesn't mean harmless."

Tyra pulls Crystal out of the hole. "Are you sure you don't like him?"

Penelope glowers up at Crystal. "He's a nice guy, but the wrong race, and way too young."

Crystal reaches down to help Penelope out of the hole, but she tosses Chuck's gun and bag of loot up first. "What does race have to do with anything?"

"I'm a Halfling. It would be like you dating…"

164

"William?"

Penelope pauses. "Doesn't matter how nice he is. Humans and Halflings can't mix." Penelope picks up her bag of loot and his gun.

Tyra yanks the young man from the pit. "You find anything useful, Penelope?"

"Plenty. Would have been home hours ago, but this lug here was feeding me intel. Couldn't give up the banquet."

"Then you slept with him."

Penelope groans and puts Chuck's revolver back in its holster. "I'm never going to hear the end of this, am I?"

William and Zarra search the ship, Tia and Tom search around the area along the wall. Tia's prays and creates a sun like glow that moves with her, making their search outside much easier. William sounds frustrated. "She's so tiny. If she was hiding, we would never find her, but to be honest, I think she hasn't returned."

"I agree with you, but I don't know her, so I was just guessing. She would have been making Crystal's dinner by now."

"That's reasonable thinking, but I think Penelope got into trouble and is stuck out there somewhere. And I think Crystal knows it too."

"But why only take Tyra and herself, and not you?"

He looks her over. "Because of the weather. It's damn near zero out there. Either of us in our armor would freeze to death out there, away from the warmth of a fire. She's Half-White Dragon and immune to this cold." They walk out of the mess hall. "And Tyra has a natural fur coat. So she didn't decide in earnest." William and Zarra head back to his room and take drinks from their mini cooler. "You want something?"

Zarra looks in his direction. "What do you have?"

"Water, orange juice, milk, and some kind of strawberry drink, I think?"

"Strawberry sounds good."

He grabs a few cups and brings them over to the table. He pours her a glass, then himself one. "I don't even know where she gets half this stuff, to be honest."

"She's really special to you."

"Yeah, she is. We are getting married in six days. At least that was the plan till this deal with the monastery." He takes a drink and looks at the glass. "This stuff is sweet, almost hard to drink."

"I like it. Your betrothed has wonderful taste." She downs the whole thing. "In everything. She would fit right in with royalty."

"That's how she was raised. I think Jack had big plans for her."

"Like what?"

"He's the head of the Third House. He was probably hoping she would marry up. That's why he had her so prim and proper, but instead, she's marrying me."

"Do you think Jack is upset about her choice?"

"Oh, no." He lets out a short laugh. "He made me a personal set of armor, and Jasmine, his wife, was calling me son before I asked Crystal to marry me. I think once he saw how happy she was, that any plan he had for her was tossed out the window. He loves her as much as I do." William smiles and chuckles a little. "He even got upset when Crystal wasn't allowed to take my name, but I have to take hers. I didn't let it phase me."

"You have to take her name?" Puzzlement crosses her face and he pours her another glass. "I thought it was traditional

166

in Humans for the female to take the name of the male. Was I misinformed?"

"No, you weren't." He sighs, rolling the glass around in his large hands. "It's a name protection law that only affects marriages between or into ruling Houses. The House name of a higher status always has predominance, regardless of how the couple is married. Unless she marries someone from the First or Second House, the Hellstromm name carries on. Since I'm from the Seventh, her name trumps mine." He leans back, the chair creaking a bit. "It makes sense. You wouldn't want your name and the House you built to be replaced by someone who could only marry in to gain power, not love. With me taking her name, I prove I'm marrying her for love, not status."

"You're lucky you get to marry for love." She sounds downtrodden. "As a princess, chances are I'm going to be part of an arranged marriage for some treaty somewhere and have to spend my life with some man or woman I don't even know."

William's smile disappears. "Sorry, I know Emperor Marcus has several wives, and that's how he got them, but he treasures each one."

She nods, swirling the glass in her own hands, watching the light pink liquid slosh around. "Not everyone gets that lucky." She takes another sip of her drink. "That's why I'm out here. I'm at the age where I can be married off for some power play. A Dark Elf princess, adopted daughter of a high born Tree Elf and paladin of Johnathan. I would be a grand trophy wife."

"What if you were to get married beforehand, or find someone before they can marry you off?"

"If I find love beforehand and get married, I don't know. Doubt my father would let such a thing happen." She looks up at him with those ruby red eyes. "Why? Are you offering?" She teases with a smile creeping across her face. He shifts in his chair, looking away. *He's uncomfortable with my joke. Must be thinking of Crystal and what she would think.* "I'm just teasing William. I wouldn't dare try to take you from Crystal. If half the stories about her were even partially true, I would wash up on some distant shore somewhere."

"Yeah, she's very territorial." He leans forward. "But she's getting good at noticing if people would match each other. She figured out that Tia was in love with her brother just by observing them, and then she got Tia to make a move, against her vow." He grins. "And that's causing the Church of Daniel to go through changes now."

"Really?" Zarra leans forward, too, making them close. "Crystal turned an entire church upside down to get two would be love birds together?" She shakes her head, sitting back upright. "She is something else."

"I think it's a gift she has. She's far from perfect, but she has this gift for getting people together who need to be together. If she ever gets over this problem with the Black Rose, she might make money as some kind of dating service."

"Maybe I should hang out with her more and find someone for me before my father decides I'm worth some territory in some far-off land."

"Well, I know how you can get her all to yourself for hours."

"I wouldn't want to intrude like that."

"She needs someone like you to be around, to be honest. Tia is shy, Penelope is a cook, and Tyra, well, she's Tyra. You, on the other hand, are true royalty, and way more girly than anyone else I know. Maybe it would be good for you to tag along with her over us."

She looks into his eyes for a moment. "Think so?"

"You're into fancy clothes, dinners, and looking good, right? As well as being an armored badass?"

"Well, yes." She puts her glass down. "She wanted to talk to me about how I got over my personal demons to become a paladin. A big part of me coming here was to meet her and the

168

rest of you." She leans back. "So where do you say I should be to be with her for hours, besides meditating, that is?"

"Well, Crystal loves to do three things." He finishes his drink. His face contorts from the over sweetness of it. "Shop, bathe, and …"

"That's only two. What's the third?"

He starts, then stops. "Never mind, my mistake."

She has a look of confusion on her face, but drops it. "It's been a while. Maybe we should go looking for her."

"I agree, but we would freeze out there."

"What about Tia? I know she uses divine, but our priests have ways to protect ourselves from the extreme, too. Maybe she can help?"

"Doesn't hurt to ask, I suppose. You have some good ideas. It's going to be nice having you around." William stands up. "Let's get our armor on and go find Tia, if you wouldn't mind helping me get into mine."

"Sure, if you help me get into mine, it's not any easier for me."

They locate Tia, which isn't hard since she's walking around with a miniature sun above her head. "I've had no luck out here."

His teeth chatter. "I figured as much."

"Why are you two out here in your armor?"

"We are going to go find Crystal. She's been gone for hours, and to be honest, I shouldn't have let her go." His teeth still chattering hard. "Do you have a spell similar to Crystal's that removes the extreme cold so we can function out here?"

"I believe I have a prayer that would work. I've never used it before, so give me a moment to remember?" William and Zarra nod in unison and she closes her eyes. She begins her prayer and her hands glow white and reaches out and touches William, then Zarra, encasing them in a white glow for a few seconds. Their teeth stop chattering and both look comfortable.

"Thanks, Tia." they say in unison. They don their helms and are about to leave.

"Hang on, you two need a light."

"No, I'm a Dark Elf. I can see in the dark. We'll be fine." They turn and head over the hole in the wall.

Tia watches them go into the darkness. "Why do I feel this is a bad idea?"

Crystal and company, walk through the ankle-deep snow. Clouds have come in, blocking out the moonlight and making the woods even darker. Crystal concentrates hard and summons a magical ball of light works as a makeshift torch. *I'm getting worse. Need to get back soon.* Penelope holds up the rod to Crystal to see "Is this what I think it is?"

Crystal takes it from her and looks it over. "It's a rod of mass teleport. Highly advanced. I'm going to have to study it a bit to use it. Do something wrong, and you could end up anywhere." She looks at the tiny woman. "Where did you find this?"

"I found a bunch of things back at that camp. Maps, items, charts." Her tone shifts lower. "A survivor."

"So, what's going to become of me?" Chuck interrupts. "Am I going to prison?"

Crystal looks over her shoulder at him. "No. We going to ask you some questions first, and then we will determine what to do with you." She faces forward again. "But if you weren't lying to Shadow earlier, we will get you home somehow."

He tilts his head in disbelief. "You're serious? You will just let me go?"

"If you're truly an innocent, yes, I will just simply let you go. We can someday get you home, or if you want to stay in Rose Harbor, find you a job and start a new life." She motions to Penelope. "Maybe Shadow here will take you on and give you a job as a member of her staff cooking."

"Wait, you're really a cook?"

She nods. "Yep, and one of the best in Rose Harbor."

"You have many talents, I see."

Her tone goes flat. "You have no idea."

They walk for several hours when Tyra stops short, holding her arm out. "I smell something."

"What is it?"

"There is an unfamiliar scent out there."

Penelope pulls her daggers, and Chuck looks around. "What's happening?"

"We aren't out here alone, but being we haven't been shot at yet, means either they mean us no harm, or they are wondering if they can take us." Penelope scans the area slowly. "You should ready your gun."

Crystal turns her head to Tyra. "Is it Humanoid?"

Tyra continues smelling the air. "I don't think so. It's unfamiliar, but the scent is getting stronger. Coming from…" She turns and sees a reflection of light near to her. Before she can bark a warning, a huge creature burst into the light, pouncing on Tyra and knocking her to the ground. The thing is larger than the Minotaur. White and brown feathers cover its body. Its large beak comes down on Tyra, tearing into her shoulder. She lets out a scream and punches the thing, but it doesn't seem to have any effect.

Chuck freaks out and fires wildly into it. It swivels its head around and they can see feathers surrounding its face.

"Owlbear!" Penelope steps back. "And a damn big one at that."

Chuck fires the last few rounds into it and reloads. "What do we do?"

"We kill it before it kills us. There is no retreat from this thing!" Crystal starts an incantation and waving her hands and points at the beast. She finishes and then, nothing happens. "Oh, you've got to be kidding."

Penelope leaps, digging her daggers into its back. It lets out a yelp of pain, stumbles off Tyra, and bucks Penelope away. It turns and rushes Crystal. Claws bigger than her head reach out for her as she closes her eyes. She feels her body take the hit, and she's lifted from her feet. *Wait, having my head ripped off would hurt more, wouldn't it?* She peeks an eye open and William is standing there, holding her with the thing's claws sticking into his armor.

"Miss me honey?" The thing makes another cry of pain, causing her to look past William's massive pauldron and spots Zarra's emerald armor in the faint light. Her blade dug into it's back and hanging on.

Zarra grunts. "So, is this what you guys do for fun?"

The owlbear pulls its claw from the back of William, and he lets out a grunt. Penelope pulls her own revolver and aims. Fire erupts from the antique firearm and the owlbear has a new hole in its neck where blood pours out. It thrashes, tossing Zarra back, then turns to face her. Zarra's eyes flash wide as the massive creature bears down on her faster than expected. With a single huge paw, its claw rends the metal of her armor's flank and tosses her several feet away.

William puts Crystal down. "Blast that thing with everything you have." He turns drawing his sword and planting it in its back next to Zarra's.

"I can't."

He grabs Zarra's sword and pulls on them both, lacerating its back and cutting a slice through its tough hide. "What do you mean, you can't?"

It kicks on instinct, stabbing William in the leg with its back claw and sending him flying, dropping both swords in his wake. "Bad timing, you know?" It turns to him and goes to charge, but Tyra gives the thing a right hook that thunders from the force. Its head swivels away, knocking it to the ground.

Chuck sounds horrified. "Is it dead?" Its head swivels around and looks at Tyra and snaps at her, but she pulls away before it makes contact. Chuck finishes loading and fires again, hitting it in the eye. It screeches in pain, causing them to grab their ears from the noise.

Zarra gets back to her feet, clutching her right side. "How do you kill this thing?" Zarra grabs William's sword and rolls away as it takes another swipe at her.

Penelope fires again and again. The tree's echo from her and Chuck's pistols firing into the huge thing. "It's not a natural animal. Its instinct is to kill everything in its path."

Crystal steps back, shaking her head. "Thought I had more time."

Penelope calls out to Crystal. "Why aren't you casting anything? Help us!"

"I… I can't. My magic is gone, temporarily." Penelope nods understanding just how the situation got worse. William gets back to his feet and looks at the situation. It's bleeding badly but doesn't look like anything they are doing to it is slowing it down. He rushes the thing, colliding with it, and the clash of his armor against the thing's tough hide reverberates off the trees. The large man brings the thing to the ground on its back. It flails wildly slashing at him, but it can't bring to bear its full strength against him.

Chuck looks at Penelope. "Does this thing block magic?"

She shakes her head. "No, it doesn't. It's… personal."

Zarra sees an opening as it bites down on Williams's helmet with its massive beak. She stabs it in the skull with his sword and blood splatters over her armor. It screams and spasms, letting William go as he drops to the ground next to it. Tyra jumps in, stabbing it in the heart with her Katana. It's thrashing, rakes her, opening several long wounds. Tyra falls, but it stops thrashing, laying there dead. She looks down at the wound, then her eyes roll back and she lays still.

CHAPTER 17

(Family)

Crystal runs to Tyra's side. "Tyra, stay with us." Tears form in her eyes. "You're going to be fine. We aren't that far from the monastery." She turns to Penelope. "You pick up anything that could help? Health potions? Healing salves, healing bandages?"

Penelope tosses the bag on the ground and starts digging, and a tearing noise comes from behind them. They turn and Chuck had ripped his shirt off and walks over to the fallen Minotaur. He places the cloth against the wounds, trying to stop the blood flow. "I can do first aid, but this looks bad."

Zarra walks over and knees down. "Hold pressure on the wound. I need a moment." She rips her gauntlets off. Chuck looks the dark obsidian color of her hands, and she reaches up and removes her helm, revealing her face and copper head hair. He lets off and leans away as if he's about to run, but she snaps at him. "Keep pressure on or she will bleed out!" He snaps out of it and reapplies pressure. She places her hands over his, the warm blood of the Minotaur staining their hands as she prays to Johnathan. Her eyes close and hands glow blue, and soon it envelops the Minotaur's body. Her face shows the strain as she keeps her prayer going, till she finally collapses backwards, exhausted.

Tyra coughs but stays laying on the cold ground. Chuck still holding her down with the cloth over her wound. "Thanks Chuck."

"It wasn't me, it was the Dark Elf."

William stands up with help from Crystal and they walk over to Zarra, who's laying on the ground with a blood seeping from her right side. "You're hurt too." Crystal offers her a hand.

Zarra takes it and stands up. "Tis but a scratch." This gets them all to laugh and hurt.

"You're going to fit in fine around here."

Penelope hides her weapons again and gathers up the dropped loot. "How far are we from the monastery?"

William looks around. "About forty minutes' normal pace, so probably an hour with us wounded like this. Why?"

"Because my environment spell just wore off."

Chuck nods in agreement. "I'm starting to freeze again, too. You got any more of those enviro spell things left?"

Crystal shakes her head. "My magic is out for the time being."

Zarra winces as she takes a step. "So, an hour in the freezing cold, wounded and magicless." She looks at everyone. "Should we start a fire and sing a camp song?"

Crystal holds her hand out to Penelope. "Give me the rod"

Penelope hands it over. "What's on your mind?"

"I'm going to try something."

"Countess, you said you needed to study that before you used it."

"I don't have much of a choice. Those two are bleeding badly, and Tyra is barely fighting off death." She looks it over.

"I'm not leaving anyone out here to die in the cold alone. A regular teleportation spell relies on a clear vision of the area you want to go to." She holds the rod up, looking it over. "I need to concentrate. This will teleport everyone within twenty feet of me, if they are willing."

William is skeptical. "What happens if you're wrong?"

"We could end up anywhere. But no matter what, you three aren't going to make it. Luckily, these things usually have a low failure rate if you know your location very well." She looks up at them. "Besides, I've seen Cline use this spell hundreds of times, and nothing ever happened to him, and my mom has used it to get out of harry situations." She shrugs. "So, how bad can it be?"

William looks at everyone else. "Well, let's get popping. Where are you planning on taking us?"

"Right in front of the bathhouse. I'm hoping with a short jump and being one of my favorite places, the success rate should be very high." She looks at everyone. "Everyone ready for this?" She holds the rod in her hands, with the inscription facing her.

She gets nods from everyone, and she reads the activation word, picturing the bathhouses at the monastery. A flash of blue fills their vision as the trees fade and are replaced by the familiar-looking buildings of the monastery. She looks around and smiles. "Holy Provider, that worked!" She looks at them. "You three into the bath."

Zarra looks down at her armor. "We going to take a bath now?"

Crystal turns to Penelope. "Take care of your boyfriend. I'm going to get these guys into the pool. Alert Tom and Tia, we might need them."

"He's not my boyfriend!" She reaches up and grabs his hand, pulling him along. "Come on, Chuck, let's find you a spot to sleep for the night." This gets a laugh from Crystal as she helps William, Zarra, and Tyra into the bathhouse. With the bleeding trio getting inside, Tyra wastes no time getting in the water. The healing spring stings, but does its job.

Zarra looks weary and weak, tries to remove her armor, but is interrupted by Crystal. "Just get in and remove it there. It's a healing pool alongside just being good for bathing." Crystal helps lower her into the water. "Stay here and take in the healing. It's not as potent as a healing spell, so it will take longer, but will restore you as if nothing happened." Zarra sinks neck deep into the water and visibly relaxes.

Crystal helps William into the next room meant for men, and Zarra can hear the crash of his metal armor hitting the ground one piece at a time.

Zarra lays there in the water and can feel the healing solution working its magic. "So, what do you know about her?"

"Crystal?" Tyra snorts. "When I first met her, she was snooty, over the top, and pushy. Everything about her made me want to punch her in the face."

Zarra looks at the large woman as she removes her own armor. "What changed your mind?"

"She's still over the top and pushy. You've seen that firsthand a second ago."

"But she had a good reason. A little pushy is a small price to pay to save a life."

"Yeah, suppose so." Tyra relaxes. "And she's driven. She fought me in hand to hand before she became a full Half-Dragon awaked thing. I got to punch her in the face after all, and by all rights, I should've easily beat her." Tyra takes in a pained breath. "But I let overconfidence get the better of me, and I think she was betting on it."

Zarra giggles and then winces. "That sounds like an interesting story."

"She didn't get away unscathed, but she earned my respect that day. She took one hell of a beating from me before her magic brought me down." Tyra smiles. "She's tougher than she looks."

"You respect her for beating you?"

"No, I respect her for a lot. She needed my fur and would fight me for it. Any other person would have tried being underhanded, and she's a kind of mother figure now. Over the last few months, I've seen her change." Tyra turns to Zarra. "She's still self-centered and thinks she's better than everyone, and at time's I still want to punch her in her perfect face." She settles down in the water more and puts her head back. "But now she's protective of us."

"It's been several minutes. I figured Crystal would have been back in here by now." Zarra partially stands up. "I hope William is ok."

"Don't bother. The other door is closed. I barely heard it before the metal armor started hitting the floor. She's taking care of his wounds personally."

Zarra sits back down. "I can appreciate that. He's a good man."

Tia and Penelope come in and Tia rushes to Tyra as she's covered head to toe in blood. She speaks a prayer and her hands glow blue, conjuring the magical healing and sealing Tyra's still oozing wounds. "How are you hanging on, Zarra?"

Zarra looks down at the gashes in her flank, watching them as they are closing on the own slowly. "I'll live, but the scars will be a little hard to explain when I get home."

Penelope laughs and sits down on the edge. "Oh, don't worry, this place is unique. There won't be any scars left over."

"I thought magical healing didn't remove scars, just sped up the healing process."

"Yeah, but this water is different. It removes the scars, too. It's bizarre that way, as if the wound never happened in the first place." Penelope looks at Tia. "You got things here?"

"Yeah." She walks over to Zarra and starts a prayer of healing. Penelope nods, stands and heads to the door. "Where are you headed?"

"To check on William and Crystal."

Tyra laughs when Penelope walks around the corner, and Zarra and Tia look at her. She holds up her hand and counts down from five. Reaching one, the sound of the door sliding open is punctuated by a shout from Crystal. It's muffled, but they can distinctly hear Crystal's ire. "Shadow, get the hell out of here! That door was closed for a reason!" The sound of something metal striking the wall and Penelope slides around the corner.

"Hang something on the handle next time!"

Tyra is still laughing and wincing when Penelope returns. "You're some kind of investigator, and didn't see that coming?"

Penelope looks and smiles. "I guess I should have. They weren't doing anything *yet*." She shakes her head. "There is a lot of blood in that water."

"Probably because he's wounded and doesn't want him to die." Tyra continues to laugh.

Tia and Penelope laugh, too. "Think she was aiming at you, Penelope?"

"No, I'm alive. That was a warning shot."

Zarra sits upright. "She almost killed you?"

"No, she didn't. If she wanted me dead, I would be. I caught her in a vulnerable state and she was just scaring me off." Penelope grins. "Besides, that was payback for all the teasing she's done to me tonight." She checks around the corner. "I'm off to bed. I'll see you girls in the morning." She waves and exits.

Zarra shakes her head. "You're an interesting group."

Tia tends to her wounds. "You're part of this group now, too."

Zarra smiles. "Thanks, feels good to be truly welcome for once." She looks at Penelope. "Can I ask a personal question?"

"Sure, shoot."

"Everyone calls you Penelope, but Crystal. She refers to you as Shadow. Why?"

Penelope sits, but before she can speak, Tia stands and walks to the door. "I'm going to check on William's wounds." This gets Tyra and Zarra to giggle. "She won't get mad at me." She exits and a few seconds later, knocks on the door.

The next morning, Crystal and William wake up in their bed and get dressed. She looks over his armor and the hole in it. "Looks like I'm going to be busy today."

"You're going to be busy?" William buttons his shirt. "Doing what?"

"Master Monzulo wants me, Zarra, and Tia for a second lesson, but your armor needs repair, and I'm sure Zarra's doesn't look much better."

"You're going to fix my armor? How with you being, you know, magicless?"

She pulls out the wands of repair. "That's why I bought these."

He smiles. "You're going to get your hands dirty fixing my armor?" He leans in, kissing her passionately.

"Oh, please, I've gotten dirty before in my father's shop. This is nothing." She wraps her arms around his neck and pulls his face close. "Now you have some barracks to build, I have armor to fix, and Tia is going to be making us tea today."

There is a knock at the cabin door that brings them both to look. Opening it, Zarra is standing there decked out in her winter gear. "Are we ready to go?"

Crystal looks back at William. "Yeah, he's about to build some barracks with the others, or are you going to be questioning the kid?"

"I think Penelope should question the new guy, see what he knows." William pulls his coat on. "From what you told me, he's just a mixed-up kid." He sighs. "Shouldn't be hard for Penelope to continue to get answers from him and then get him home." Walking with Crystal, they exit the room. "You two should get going. Penelope knows what to do today, and then tomorrow, we can head home and celebrate your birthday."

"I forgot all about it, actually." They make their way to the gangplank. "The big two zero. No longer a teen. Feels weird." He smiles and motions for them to get going. "Maybe Tia should help Penelope question the kid. Leaving her alone with him might cause her to make mistakes."

Zarra stretches. "If Tia goes with Penelope, who's going to make the tea, then?"

Crystal shrugs. "Figure that out when we get to the top. William, just tell her to go with Penelope. She likes the kid and without Tia, may go easy on him." William nods and exits first, leaving the two ladies at the top to survey the land. They see William speak with Tia, then motions to Penelope and Chuck over by the construction site. "Guess they are putting him to work as they talk."

They walk down the gangplank taking in all the activities. "If he really feels guilty about what he did, making him fix the damage might do him some good." Zarra yawns as they walk towards the stairs. "Guilt is a motivator." The two girls make their way up the stairs to the sanctuary. Zarra stops at the top and her legs are burning. "How do you get used to this?" Zarra heaves hard.

"It helps to have magically enhanced strength from being a Half-Dragon."

"Guess that would help." She stands back upright. "Let's go, only a few more steps and we get to sit all day."

Crystal gets a smirk on her face. "I feel it's not going to be so easy."

The two girls walk into the sanctuary and are guided to the master's training area, where he sits in meditation with incense burning. "I sense two souls entering this room, both in disharmony." He stands and turns around. "I feel Tia isn't here. Is there something wrong with her company?"

"No, Master." Crystal walks to the center of the room. "Shadow found a survivor who was part of the attack here five days ago. Tia is helping her with some questions."

"You brought him back unharmed?"

"Yes Master. He was slowly freezing to death, and we think they tricked him into joining."

"You controlled your anger at him for being part of the Black Rose?"

"Mostly. I started to lose it, but I calmed down after Shadow started talking about how he was mixed up." She hangs her head. "Part of me wanted to hurt him, but I stopped myself." She looks back up and makes eye contact with the Grand Master. "I got to talk to him and he could be just on the wrong side of things, fed lies. If that's how the organization is, then I have to approach this differently."

"I'm glad to hear you are opening your mind to new possibilities." He turns to the sweating Dark Elf. "You can go ahead and remove that heavy clothing." Zarra nods and strips down to her regular tight fitting forest green shirt and short pants. "Why do you seek to help her?"

Zarra shakes her head. "Crystal has a problem with her inner demons and was wondering how I dealt with mine. I've been where she is now, so I'm here to help."

"You two are like the Yin," he points with an open palm to Zarra, "and Yang," he points to Crystal. "Dark and light, seeking to balance the other. You're drawn to each other seeking this balance." He motions them to come to the center of the room and they take their places. "Crystal, before we get started, you're going to want to change into something that is more giving. That dress of yours isn't going to work."

"What are we going to be doing that I can't wear this for?"

"Kata." Turning to Zarra, he motions to the outfit he is wearing. "And you will change as well. You both will wear common white wushu for this."

"So why are we learning a Kata?"

"Crystal had a lesson in proper breathing. You, having some military training already, don't need the basics for that. By learning a simple Kata, you will learn to control your body along with your chi. You will better find balance. Mind, body, and soul must be in balance for good health." He turns to the ladies. "Once you two have changed, we will begin." He points to an empty room. "When you're done, come back here."

CHAPTER 18

(Redemption)

William and Tyra gather up Tom and they work on some cabins. The master decided to keep any cabins that could be repaired to be so, and others knocked down. Then build three new barracks with modernized equipment. This way, they could move some out of the sanctuary and the cafeteria and back into regular places while the barracks were being constructed. The contractors split the work, knowing that Elves are better working with carpentry commonly found in the cabins. The new barracks will be brick and mortar, that the Dwarves are clearly more adept with. Penelope and Tia take Chuck and find a nice spot in the cafeteria to talk about his involvement with the Black Rose and the assault.

"No, you're not in trouble, Chuck." Penelope sits down across from him and Tia prays, casting the area in yellow light. "But anything you can tell us about who recruited you and why will go a long way to cleaning this mess up and bringing about peace."

"But why did she cast that spell that made the area light up?"

"Tia made it to where no one here can lie about anything. Not me, not you, not her, no one walking in."

"I'm a cleric of Daniel." Tia sits next to Penelope. "I'm a healer, and councilor. We know you're scared, but you shouldn't be. Once we are done with you, you're free to do what you want. We just need to know some things first."

"Is your name really Penelope?"

"Yes, it is. I wasn't lying to you about it. In fact, had Crystal and Tyra not showed up, I was just going to leave you alone that morning with the stuff I found, if that's what you wanted."

He nods. "That Crystal lady, why was she accusing you of liking me?"

"Because she can be a real bitch sometimes and loves to tease those around her for her own amusement."

This gets Tia to snicker. "That's a proper assessment, but harsh."

He glances at Tia and back at Penelope. "So, you don't?"

"You're cute. I won't fault you there, but my reasoning is sound. We are way too different. As much as I would like to date you, it wouldn't work." She realizes what she said and clamps her hand over her mouth. She composes herself. "If you're the good man we suspect you of being, you're going to find a nice girl someday."

"I'm convinced the truth thing is working." He looks at the girls. "What are you wanting to know?"

Penelope starts with her questions first. "The person in charge, who was he or she?"

"I don't know the guy personally. In fact, I know little about him at all. I know when we were brought to a location with lots of other people and were told to listen to him."

"And where was that at?"

"There are some ruins several miles outside of New Haven to the west. I was originally in New Haven when I was recruited and after several weeks of meeting there. They took us out to the old ruins and lead down into a room that was

186

excavated. There, a lady wearing all black and had her face covered, talked to us." He cups his hands in front of him and looks down at the table. "There she told us about the evil the monks had committed, how they supported the evil that attacked our..." He takes a deep breath. "Their people and killed them in cold blood with the help of the people from Portstown."

"So that's when you came here?"

"No, she had supply wagons and the other stuff you saw brought in. We were told to stand still. She would chant something and her hands and the floor glowed blue like it did in the woods yesterday. Then we appeared where we did where you found me." He looks at the girls. "He told us to set up camp, that it's going to be a few days before we are ready. And while we did that, a team of about twenty mounted some horses and took off."

Tia interrupts. "So why did he have you wait?"

"One night while we were around the campfire, he sort of explained the plan a little. That the Emperor's attack dog, the countess, was on her way home in her flying death machine, and we were to attack after we saw it. They knew you were coming here first somehow, and it was going to be coordinated with your arrival. The night we saw the ship, we were to attack as soon as possible. The other team was to attack the countess, and anyone attached to her as a message that we won't be afraid of your evil."

Penelope turns to Tia. "That's why you, Andrew, Crystal, and William were all attacked at the same time." She turns back to the boy. "What can you tell us about the lady who sent you here?"

"Not a lot, but I know I heard her name spoken a few times when talking to the leader guy. Zala, Zalrra, Zalrear. Something like that."

Penelope guesses. "Zalreria?"

"That's sounds right."

"That's what the lady in the ruins told us when we questioned her. She must be the grand architect behind all of this, but why?"

"They think you people are evil butchers who have no care for sentient life, and the Emperor is some kind of immortal demon who needs to be slain."

Penelope continues her questions. "The stuff back at your camp. Do you know what's there?"

"No idea. I was just a lowly pawn in this, it looks like."

"These ruins you spoke of west of New Haven. Could you draw us a map of the place and how to get to it?"

"Sure, for a cute girl like you, anything." He realizes what he said as Penelope's face reddens. "That truth thing really drags things out of you, doesn't it?"

Tia shakes her head. "It only prevents you from lying, not compel you to speak. You did that on your own."

"I'll go get some parchment and something to write with." Penelope bails from the table.

Crystal and Zarra are both wearing fresh white wushu's standing in the Master's private dojo. Master Monzulo has them both throwing punches and turning methodically. "Feel your inner strength flow through the stances. Each throw, each turn, each bend, allows your chi to flow from your body's core." The two women are sweating heavily as they go through the motions again and again, with the Grand Master correcting their stances and movements. "Focus your mind on the movements, controlling your motions. Breath in time with your movements to keep your mind clear." He circles them as he speaks. "Let the stress leave your body through the energy of each kick, each punch, and the fluid motion of the body."

He eyes their every movement. "Your stance controls your balance, too wide or narrow, and you can easily be knocked over." He demonstrates by lightly kicking Crystal's feet, and she topples to the ground. "A proper stance is important in everything." He offers his hand and pulls her back to her feet. "Your feet were too far apart. I know you're not a physical combat person, but even with magic, stance can mean the difference between getting a spell cast or being on your back with the magic gone."

"Thank you, Master." Crystal gets into her stance again. For a moment, she felt her anger rise, then squashed it. She inhales and takes a deep breath. *I know it's all part of the lesson. Just stay calm.*

"Much better, now if someone was to come at you, you could still use your spell without risking losing it." The old man smiles. "Let's take a tea break. Crystal, is you would do the honors?"

"I don't know if I'm ready for that."

He places a hand on her shoulder. "No one is ever ready for everything. Doing something when you're not ready is one way to gain experience."

Crystal looks at Zarra and she smiles. "And I'll learn to make tea by watching you. Just do your best."

She has little confidence in her voice. "Guess I will give it a try."

"I want you to do. Trying means to attempt something. If you do something, then you've accomplished something, even if it's not the result you were looking for."

She nods, contemplating his words. He motions with an open palm out of the room. They follow him to the same place they had tea the day before. This time, Crystal is where he was then. She kneels, and Master Monzulo and Zarra kneel across from her at the table. "I'm a little nervous."

"It's ok to be afraid. Fear is a natural emotion, but when it controls you, you become the vessel for your deepest instincts." He smiles warmly. "Start by breathing properly and find your focus. Feel your chi inside and get a good center, then you can proceed."

She closes her eyes and meditates a bit, feeling her nerves calm. He smiles as he feels the turmoil inside her smooth out. Zarra watches and listens, and Crystal opens her eyes and begins. The Grand Master gives her encouragement as she goes through the steps. She feels she is calming as she goes along, pouring the hot water, picking up the cups, and then putting the tea leaves in. She does her best in trying to get them to fall on her own, but gets frustrated forcing them out. *Can't be that big of a deal. Their leaves.*

She pours the hot water into the kettle and from there to the small pitcher. Some of the smaller broken tea leaves are in the otherwise pleasant-smelling golden-brown liquid. *That should be fine. I wouldn't notice if I wasn't looking for it.* Then she pours the tea into the three glasses with some still resting in the pitcher's bottom, showing she got the amount of hot water wrong. She hands the cups to the Master and Zarra.

They all lift their cups and drink. Crystal can see on their faces that she messed up somewhere as it's bitter, not sweet like how the Master did it. But he smiles all the same. "This wasn't bad for a first time. I've seen it much worse than this." He watches her become disheartened as her head points to the floor. "Crystal, you cannot expect to master everything on the first try. You're naturally gifted at magic, but practice is everything. It will take you months to master your chi and make exceptional tea." He stands up and offers his hand to the two ladies, pulling them up as well.

"As the tea gets better, the more you will know about the status of your control and focus. This is a way to test yourself to see how your progress is coming along." She looks up and makes eye contact with him. "Tomorrow we will continue, but for now, we will go back to practicing your kata and breathing exercises. I can see how little practice is getting both of you girl's results. I can already feel your souls harmonizing with each other. And once they are in sync, you will be a united force, able to withstand anything."

Crystal and Zarra look at each other, then back to the master and speak in unison. "Let's continue then."

Penelope returns with parchment and a pen, and Chuck gets to work. Tia informs Penelope that she's going to go check on William and his crew, leaving her alone with Chuck. She asks him details as he goes along; he does his best to explain. She taps on the map, pointing to a row of wiggly lines. "These are the mountains?"

"Yes. This area here is the Dry Sea desert on the other side, and this is the Krasnaya River." He points to the line he drew going through the New Haven city. "You have to cross the mountains to get to New Haven, so it's a secure area." He looks up at her and she looks at him in his brown eyes. He reaches out and covers her tiny hand with his. "But the place you're looking for is north of there in the swampland on this peninsula." He takes her hand, guiding it to the spot. She feels her heart rate increase, but quickly suppresses it. *No. He's a Human, and I'm a Halfling. We aren't compatible. I've learned this lesson. Just let it go.*

"It's an old fortress that was the city a few hundred years ago, but a massive earthquake or something caused it to sink, flooding the land, so it was abandoned." He smiles at her, but she doesn't return it.

She slides her hand out from under his. "I really appreciate the information, and I know you think I'm cute." Looking at him, she sees the happiness fade to disappointment. "I know what you're seeking, and I'm going to let you down now before it grows too much. We are too physically different. I'm barely waist high to you." She can see his eyes betraying the sadness he's feeling as she continues.

"But you saved my life. I thought I meant something to you?"

"I save a lot of people." She straightens out. "Right now you're feeling infatuation, not love." He casts his eyes down. "It will fade. But some day you will find a nice girl who will make you happy. We can be friends. I'm ok with that." She reaches out and lifts his chin. "At least you're alive and can start looking when you're ready. It's just not going to be me."

His face saddens, and she sighs. *I broke his heart. Humans and Halflings don't mix in a relationship. I learned that lesson long ago. Those feelings don't matter. Besides, my profession would keep us apart, regardless.*

He goes back to the map. "There are about twenty to thirty people on the grounds at any given time." He sighs. "As far as total below grand and all, I haven't a clue. But there are Orcs and Ogre's acting as heavy guards."

He leans back and looks into her blue eyes. "That's really all I know. The road going in is under water or covered in mud. I suspect that had it not frozen over, we would have had to use special flat bottom boats to make it across." He puts the pencil down. "Wish I had more for you, but they didn't tell me much."

"This is good intel." Penelope takes the map. "You're going to help us put an end to these hostilities and find some common ground." She rolls it up and sees him just sitting there. "So have you thought about your future, like where you want to go and what you want to do?"

He looks down away from her. "I did till it was torn apart."

She leans forward on her elbows. "Chuck, don't beat yourself up. Even if we worked something out, my job wouldn't allow it."

He looks back up at her. "What do you mean?"

"I'm an investigator, and Crystal's personal chef." She reaches out and takes his hand. "I've accepted that and love what
192

I do." She locks eyes with him. "Maybe someday, I'll give it all up and settle down, but for now." She shrugs. "I just can't. My life has gotten exciting." He smiles. "You should find what you love, so if you want to go home to the farm, we will get you there. If you want to stay and start over here, we can help you get a job doing what you like."

"What is it like, being a personal chef?"

She sits back, letting go of his hands. "I have to exercise a lot. Having to sample every dish to make sure it's perfect means I'm constantly eating something, and being as tiny as I am, I could easily gain weight." She chuckles. "And you have to eat a lot of food to get a good palette, so that takes its toll too."

He smiles. "Is that all?"

"The pay is really good, but I work my tiny ass off for it. But I want for nothing."

He counters, muttering under his breath. "Except a meaningful relationship."

She sighs as he's circling back around to this again already. She expected it, but was hoping he would just let it go. "Yea, and being on call isn't the greatest either, but I get to travel and it's never boring."

"Is it hard being a chef?"

"Oh yeah, it is. Very challenging, but hard work means good pay." She grins and looks up at him. "Before I was a chef, I was a thief and was barely making it, but one day I got help from an unexpected source, and some encouragement then my life got better."

"You were a thief before a chef, but why?"

"I was stealing so I could save for lessons, because I always wanted to be a cook. I loved the idea of taking things and turning them into something that people would enjoy." She looks at him and picks up her glass of water to take a drink. "Not the best idea in hindsight."

"What happened?"

"I was saving up to go legit already, and I decided I could pay for it all at once if I hit a rich guy's house. But instead of making off with a score, I was caught and sent to jail. He took pity on me and paid for my schooling in exchange; I had to work for him." She puts the glass down. "I got lucky. He didn't mistreat me, he didn't underpay me, and he got me out of a bad spot in my life."

"Why are you with this Crystal lady instead of with him?"

"She's his daughter, and grew up most of her life with me cooking for her, so she wanted me to come along. So here I am."

Tia returns and sees the two of them getting along. "The crew could use some help with the cabins." She looks at Chuck. "And it will go a long way to show you're sincere about the wrong you did if you help them with the repairs."

Chuck nods. "I know, and I want to help. I've built plenty of barns, a few cabins won't be hard. It's nothing new to me."

Penelope continues to smile. "There you go, get into the construction business. City is constantly expanding, so it's a solid job and pays well."

"Yeah, and who knows, maybe someday I'll have my own business someday." The sarcasm doesn't escape the two ladies.

Penelope leans over and takes his hand again, getting his full attention. "If you believe in yourself, anything is possible." They lock eyes again and her heart skips a second. "If you hope to go into business for yourself, then learn the job, get an apprenticeship, learn the trade, and go for it. Nothing can hold you back but your own self-doubt."

"You really think so?"

"Yep, my employer was once just like you. Now, he's the smartest person I know, and if it wasn't for him," she points to the airship sitting in the courtyard. "Things like that wouldn't exist. He believed in himself and leads the Third House in Rose Harbor, making him extremely powerful. Your future is in your hands. You just need to clear the doubt from your mind."

He looks down at her, holding his hands. *I'm enjoying this too much and he noticed!* She lets go suddenly. "You have some work to do, and I need to get the countess's dinner going. She's going to want it soon." Turning to Tia, she hands her the map. "Could you take this to Crystal up in the sanctuary? She might be interested in it."

"I'll take it and Chuck to William. I think Crystal is busy up there and he would more likely to know what to do with this."

CHAPTER 19

(Unfinished Business)

Crystal and Zarra are still repeating the simple kata Master Monzulo had taught them. Both are breathing hard and sweating. The rays of the sun coming through the window casts long shadows and tell them of the many hours that have passed.

Crystal huffs as they both throw kicks. "So, getting over your evil inclinations was a product of your upbringing?"

"Partially. It's a large part of it. The urge to do wrong is always there, and I did a lot of wrong. I stole things just to steal them. I was verbally and physically abusive." Zarra and Crystal are almost completely in sync as they talk.

"What changed you?"

"I don't think it was any one thing, honestly." They go through the motions. "I wasn't punished any more or less harshly, nor treated any differently than the other children. Even though I was the daughter of their sworn enemy, they treated me better than my biological parents." Zarra breathes in and exhales, feeling her heart beating. "But I was so angry about everything and one day my adopted mother asked me *why*?"

Zarra stops her exercises, getting Crystal to halt, too. She turns to the Dark Elf, sweat rolling off her brow and down her smooth cheeks. *Her skin looks so soft...Wait, where did that come from*? She mentally shakes it off. "So, what then?"

"I couldn't come up with a suitable answer." She glances at Crystal, just as sweaty as she was with her braids having come undone and matted from the activities. "All I knew was that I was angry all the time, but even I didn't ask myself that question. Was it from being a minority in a city of Tree Elves? Was it because I needed to lash out at what I thought was a bad lot in life?" She shakes her head. "I was treated good; even though I was different. Was given every opportunity, despite who my real parents were."

"What happened next?" Crystal hands her a small towel and wipes off her own head.

"She sat down, and wrapped her arm around me, giving me a hug, like she did every day. But that time, I didn't resent it. It felt right for the first time in the eighty years that I was there. I asked her if I could do something with my life. Be someone besides a pretty princess hiding away in a tower." Zarra dabs away the sweat on the back of her neck. "And she smiled at me and told me to follow my heart. That's all they ever asked of me." She sits down on the floor and Crystal takes her place next to her, two halves of a monochrome coin.

"That's when you started training to be a knight?"

"Yep. I could take out my aggressive actions creatively, and then, an Elven paladin took me under his wing as his squire for fifty years. Teaching me about chivalry, and knighthood, and the good word of Johnathan. My whole life changed at that point. If I could do this, then anyone could. I didn't have to be like my people. I could be whatever I wanted." She turns to Crystal. "Why are you wanting to know how I got over my dark past?"

Crystal casts her eyes to the ground. "I used to be the good one. The one who loved life, who wanted to do *good*, but I was naïve. I felt the draw of my evil side for the first time in Mossy Fields. The Black Rose attacked us, poisoned and tried to kidnap me. They tore my dress, leaving me exposed." She looks at Zarra. "I felt hate, genuine hate, for the first time then. I was ready to kill, but William stopped me."

"He's a good man. You're very lucky to have him at your side. I can only hope to find half the man William is to marry me."

Crystal smiles and nods. "The second time I felt the pull was in Black Rock, when I witnessed..." She stops and tears fill her eyes. "I witnessed William die, saving me, so I could escape."

"I remember you mentioned that back on the ship, but didn't want to press the issue."

Crystal nods. "I went berserk. The rage inside me was all I knew. I was watching my body do things, but I wasn't in control." She looks at Zarra. "I even breathed ice at my enemies as if I were an actual Dragon. Tyra and Tom pulled me and Williams's body out of the fighting. For the next day, I was in such grief that all I could think about was hurting those who took him away from me."

"That's when you and Olovira planned his resurrection?"

Crystal turns her still tear-filled eyes to her and nods. "I committed an act that, by all rights, should have ended in my execution. The lady who did this to me." She motions to her horns. "Knew a ritual to bring him back to life, but to perform it, but needed a willing soul to take his place in the afterlife. I was so grief struck and felt so horrible for putting William in the situation that got him killed, I offered myself."

Zarra reaches out and takes Crystal's hands, faces her. "That sounds like the noblest of causes. To give yourself for another is never wrong, especially for one you love."

Crystal nods, feeling Zarra's callused hands in hers. *They kind of feel like William's but smaller.* She swallows, giving her a moment to find her words. "Olovira gave her soul to bring back William's. I didn't know she was going to, and I was ready to die for him. Which was silly being I barely knew him for two weeks, but I could feel he was special."

198

Zarra wipes away a tear and just nods her head. "Sounds like you made it out of your dark place."

Crystal shakes her head. "No. It's always there, at the edge of my mind. I was able to suppress it with jubilation and dating, and the promotion." Her tone gets dark. "But it sank its teeth into my soul in Portstown, and it hasn't let go since.."

Zarra still holds Crystal's hands in her own, comforting her. "I heard some of what happened from reports that came in. I'm sorry you went through that." She gently squeezes. "I can't fault you on your feelings. I don't think anyone could have gone through that without their soul going a little dark."

"You don't understand." Crystal lets her feelings go. "There is more to the story than I spoke of on the ship. I had Tom bring back a book, a book that was evil. It was so bad that Tia couldn't go near it. A book of Necromancy." Crystal's eyes blur with her tears as she bears it all out. "I animated the dead, learned spells I wasn't ready for. I feel like I let some monster take over, all for the power to destroy those who had hurt and disfigured me."

Zarra let her hands go and wraps them around Crystal, giving her an embrace hug as she weeps. "But you didn't. You fought it off."

Crystal embraces Zarra in return. *She's so nice and caring, like William. I feel better with her around.* Both feel a connection with the other as they share their feelings. "That's why I asked how you got over yours. I'm still hurting people and I scare myself because that part of me enjoys it. Tia's been helping and now Master Monzulo's guidance has been helping."

They break their embrace. "And you can add me to those who want to help you."

"I shouldn't need help. I was meant to be strong enough on my own."

"You should always let those who love you help you, even when it's not required. They wouldn't be offering if they didn't desire your presence." Crystal and Zarra both turn and see that Master Monzulo had returned.

They both stand up and bow respectfully, muscles aching from the strenuous exercise. "Master," they say in unison.

"I think we can call it a day. You both have made much progress." He holds up a finger, walking around them. "And tomorrow we will start on a new exercise that will build on what you already have learned."

"Master, I will be leaving in the morning. Tomorrow is my birthday and in a short few days, my wedding. So, I can't stay. I really want to, as your teachings are helping me, but I'm afraid my other life calls me."

"That is the way of things. Practice what I taught you and remember that with focus, you can overcome anything. Now you go and have a wonderful birthday." He smiles happily and motions to the exit.

Zarra pulls at her robe. "Where do you want these wushus at, Master?"

"They are yours. Keep them so you can practice. Don't wash the belt, but the wushu you should. The more you train, the dirtier the belt gets, showing how practiced you are. Think of it as a way of keeping track of your physical progress."

"Thank you, Master." The two say in unison again, getting them both to giggle as if so strange they are in time like that.

"I will see you before you depart and thank you for all the help."

They get changed and take their wushu's back to the ship with them. They see Penelope holding Chuck's hands in the cafeteria and Crystal just shakes her head.

Zarra notices the subtle movement. "What's the matter?"

"Chuck has Shadow wondering what she really wants in life for the first time in years. They might not be an item, but she's feeling the pull of wanting to settle down herself."

"Is that so bad? Everyone deserves happiness."

"Yeah, they do, even you."

"What do you mean?"

"Earlier, you said you could only hope to marry a man as good as William, but you shouldn't hope. There is someone out there for you. Maybe you've met them already, or have yet to, maybe not even born yet as long lived as you are."

"You don't understand, Crystal. I'm a princess and don't get to marry for love. I marry for political maneuvering." They walk through the ship to their quarters. "I was telling William the same thing. My fate is to be shackled to some man or woman for political gain of the Silvian Empire, not for my own happiness."

"You can't get shackled if you don't go home." Crystal turns and puts her hands together, then points. "You can come with me to New Haven and help me take down the Black Rose. By then, we can figure out how to help you best."

"I would love to come along. I've been craving to use my skills instead of hiding at home. Fighting that owlbear was thrilling."

Crystal tilts her head. "But it almost killed you."

"True, but I was defending the defenseless, helping those in need. It's my calling." The two of them make it to Crystal's door. "Would you like to join me for a bath? You're covered in sweat, just like me, and I can feel the water calling me."

"Sure, sounds like fun. Let me grab my bathing suit and soaps."

They get their things together and head down to the bathhouse. They walk inside and there is no one present. "Perfect." Crystal removes her clothing.

Zarra looks at the ivory beauty and her hourglass shape. *William is one lucky man. I bet he can wrap his hands around her waist and get his fingers to touch.* Crystal drops into the water, letting out a moan of pleasure as it covers her body. "So, why do you prefer to bathe nude, even with others around you?" Zarra slips out of her clothes, leaving just her emerald-green suit on, and steps down.

Crystal runs her eyes over her new friend. *She looks great. Why aren't guys throwing themselves at her?* Crystal tells her tale as she did the others and finishes it with how liberating and good it feels, and how she refuses to be ashamed of her body.

Zarra nods along, feeling the warmth of the water on her skin. She lifts a hand out of the water and lets it flop over at the wrist. "I can see that when you're alone, but this is public. Aren't you self-conscious of others looking at you?"

Crystal undoes her braids, pulling the gold ribbons from her hair and tossing them to the deck. "I used to be, but the only people who will see me in here are other girls." She shimmies, letting herself sink up to her chin. "And I hope they've seen themselves naked and wouldn't be too upset over me." She turns to her obsidian counterpart. "Aren't you in the least bit curious about how the water feels without being covered up?"

"It's not proper."

Crystal's right hand comes out of the water and waves the answer away like shooing a fly. "I got that argument from William too, and Tia, and Shadow."

"And you got them all to go bathing without a bathing suit?"

"Yep, Tia and Shadow in this very pool."

"No way." Zarra's head tilts in thought, then points down in the pool. "Tia, the shy priestess, took her clothes off and got into this pool?"

"She didn't exactly take them off on her own. I used my spell to remove them, giving her little option but to jump into the water. I feel a little bad about it, but it got Shadow to follow on her own." Crystal looks back up, letting the water flow around her head. "I didn't ask them to after that. It's not for everyone, I get that. I'm just funny that way."

"Everyone has their quirks." Zarra reaches up and undoes her own braids, pulling the jeweled clasps off and letting her hair cascade down her back as if it was freshly spun copper wire. She sits upright and turns her back to Crystal. "I'll meet you halfway and only take my top off. You have me curious enough and I don't think I'll get into too much trouble with my god for being a little spontaneous." Crystal grins, hearing some excitement in the Dark Elf's tone. "I haven't done anything like this, so I'm half thrilled, half afraid."

Crystal carefully reaches out with a clawed tip hand and undoes the string holding Zarra's top on. She carefully removes it, tossing it to the deck behind her. *The water does feel different to with it off and can see why Crystal enjoys it.*

They talk for hours, going from subject to subject, laughing, crying, trading stories of their childhoods until Penelope walks in after it's dark. The sarcasm was so thick in her tone, it could stop a train. "I'm glad you two told us you were down here and saved me a trip up the mountain to find you."

They exchange glances and both say 'sorry', getting them to giggle more. Crystal flippantly waves the accusation away. "You know me, Shadow, should have checked here first."

Penelope grabs the bridge of her nose and sighs. "Yeah, you're right. Dinner is ready, countess."

Crystal sits up. "Guess the fun is over." She shrugs. "We will be up there in a few minutes. I was just enjoying a nice hot soak after all the training. My muscles hurt, but I will wash up real fast and be up there, ok?" Penelope nods and departs. Crystal partially gets up out of the water and turns to grab the soap and hands Zarra some. They get to cleaning up, get dressed and head to dinner. They are all together in the mess hall and Crystal turns to Tia, speaking between her bites. "I need your help with something. You too, Zarra."

Tia looks up. "Help with what?"

"I need you two help to find some books about this thing Emperor Marcus mentioned and this torch thing you said you saw twice now. I'm wondering how old Olovira really was and if she had any materials on the gods." She stops, pointing her fork at Tia. "When I was in there, nothing grabbed my attention." She waves it at her and Zarra. "But you two being religious, maybe you will feel something call out to you."

"That makes sense." Zarra swallows and picks up her napkin. "Maybe that artifact of yours from Daniel might point the way?"

Tia nods. "Can't hurt."

Crystal laughs, dropping her fork on her plate. "I forgot she even had that."

William scans the table, going to each of them but stopping at Crystal. "Need any other help, or just them?"

Crystal smiles and leans into him. "Offering to carry my schoolbooks again?"

"That, and I haven't seen you all day. I've missed you."

"I missed you too. If you want to come along, I'd love to have you. You can reach things I can't."

Zarra puts on a fake smile. *I yearn for what they have, but I know once I get back, I'll be forced to get back on my ship and go home to be pranced around like some prize pony. But what if I never made it home?* They finish up their meal and head to Olovira's old house. Crystal walks in and turns on the magical lamps, and has them follow her to the library.

Zarra keeps her hands close to her side. "This place is much bigger inside than out. She had some real power to make an extra-dimensional space inside a building like this."

"And she gave it to me. Not sure why, but she told me to use it wisely. So that's why you're here." Crystal points them in different directions. They walk about the room. "We are looking for books on the God's war, or information on the gods. Anything that could lead them to figure out why Daniel is trying to change his church, pass on this so-called *torch of love*, and why there are so many gods missing."

Tia holds her artifact up as she walks and feels it tug to the right and up. "I've got something." William gets to her first, and she points to a book she can't reach. William brings it down and hands it to her. "This thing is drawn to it, and it's giving off positive energy, but I can't read it."

Crystal takes the book and opens it, gazing at its pages. After a few moments, William snaps his fingers, and she shakes her head. "It's Draconic."

"What does it say?"

"The cover says 'Shards of Divinity'." She flips through the pages. "Whatever that means. Good job Tia."

They go back to their search, and after several hours, Zarra reports she's found something as well. She pulls the tome off the shelf and it hits the floor as its weight is more than its size it portrays. She reaches down and hefts it. *Is the cover made of lead or something?*

Crystal and William come rushing over and she looks at the cover. "It says the war between the heavens. We are onto something."

"It's heavier than it looks."

"Probably has hidden pages, then. Means it has secrets, and that means there is a password or an item that unlocks those pages. I got my work cut out for me." She looks at them. "It's really late, and this should keep me busy for a few months." She takes the book from Zarra and turns to Tia. "I will get to the bottom of your problem. I promise."

CHAPTER 20

(Royal pains)

The next morning, Crystal awakens with William cradling her from behind. His massive arms almost completely encase her and she's never felt so safe. She lays there looking out the window at the snow-covered mountains. *In a few days, we will be married at last.* She turns her head slightly and is careful not to stick him with her horns. Even though she's been living with them for almost nine months now, and with him for the last few in her bed, there are still accidents.

He awakens with a smile on his face and kisses her neck, sending goosebumps down her body. "Good morning, birthday girl." She slides her smoothly scaled leg along his, nudging him to roll over onto his back.

She twists and climbs on top of him, letting her hair hang down past his face on either side, leans down and kisses him passionately. "It's about to be." Running her hand along his hairy chest. She leans back, sitting upright, when there is a knock. Her face contorts to a scowl as she casts an icy gaze towards the door. "So, I get to kill someone within sixty seconds of waking. New record." She slides off the bed and picks up her nightgown. William puts his pants on as Crystal's taloned feet clack hard along the metal floor.

She opens the door. "This better be damn important!" She pauses and sighs.

Tia is standing there, her hands drawn up defensively. "Countess, it's seven a.m. We need to depart soon if we are to make it home and get ready for the party tonight."

Crystal shakes her head and looks at the floor. "You couldn't have waited to like eight to come to my door?"

Tia puts her hands down. "Eight? Why eight?"

Crystal sighs and shuts the door on Tia. "She needs to get laid or something. I swear." William stands looking for his shirt, and she digs through her closet trying to find something to wear. She holds up a red dress with gold embroidery and some inset gems. "What do you think of this one, darling?"

William freezes. His eyes dart about. *Why does she keep asking me? Think of something...* He holds a hand out to his side in a half shrug. "Honey, you're so beautiful. Everything looks wonderful on you."

She smiles and looks over her shoulder. "As true as that is, I'm trying to get your opinion."

He puts a red shirt on. "You know, I don't know anything about clothing. You look great all the time. Besides, I know you. You're not wearing that to the party tonight, anyway."

She drops it to the floor and digs again. "True enough, but you're going to have to start taking an interest in what I'm wearing."

He walks up to her and wraps his arms around her from behind. "I'm more interested in what you're not wearing." He leans over her, giving her a kiss on her forehead. "Just pick something so we can get going."

She frowns. "Maybe I should ask Zarra. I know she has good taste in clothing."

He rubs his nose on hers. "Not a bad idea, actually. You're both royalty and women."

Crystal counters jokingly. "Maybe I'll marry her instead."

He kisses her again and steps away. "It will look good on you."

She nods and takes her gown off and slips on a black and gold dress. "Button me up?" He's reaches over her front and takes the two strands of cloth that form a thin V from her beltline to her neck. Wrapping it around the back of her neck and closes the button, it's the only cloth covering her back to her waist. He smacks her on the rump, getting her to smile. "You know how to make a girl feel wanted."

They get breakfast and everyone is wearing their traditional outfits, but Zarra is in some commoner's clothes. "Are you needing a dress, Zarra?"

Zarra looks askance at her. "What for? We are just having breakfast."

William lets out a short laugh. "Guess she's not giving you advice on fashion sense, either."

Zarra sits upright and frowns. "What's that supposed to mean?" Tia and Penelope perk up, wondering why Zarra sounds like Crystal.

"I didn't know what to wear today and Will wasn't being very helpful. So I mockingly threatened to ask you, being you're a princess, and should have good taste in clothing."

William cuts in. "And you show up in commoner's clothes, something she would rather go naked than wear."

"It's not that I don't have good taste, but I'm trying to avoid people knowing who I am. Wearing a fancy dress will let them know who it is they are looking at."

Finishing breakfast, the work crew starts the day. William informs them they will send the ship back, so they won't be left in the cold, but the countess needs to return to Rose Harbor. They understand and should have the foundations for at least one barrack built and at least a dozen cabins repaired by it's return. A Female gnome in a black wushu grabs Crystal's attention.

"Countess, Master Monzulo wants to have a word with you before you leave."

"Thank you." She looks at everyone else. "I'll be right back."

Crystal exits the vessel, spotting Master Monzulo standing there with a long box covered in a golden silk cloth. She bows to the Grand Master. "We are about to leave, Master, but for you, I will delay my departure."

"I won't keep you long, Crystal. I wanted to give you something for your birthday." He holds it up to her. She smiles and bows again and reaches for the cloth, but he stops her. "That is part of the gift. It is fragile, so be careful with it. I hope it helps you on your journey."

She reaches out and takes the box, cloth and all. "Thank you again, Master. I will be back to get more lessons. I promise you."

He turns and Tom, who is now wearing a black wushu, followed closely by Tyra, is on their way over with their things. "Actually, Tom will take over your training. He might be a little different, but he is one of my best students." Tom gets up to Master Monzulo and bows. "And he's ready to be called a master himself. I have nothing left to teach him after all these years. But he can teach you, in his own quirky way."

"So you're just Master Tom?"

"No, my title is Master Ryuu."

"Tom Ryuu, is your name?" Crystal smiles at him, holding back her laugh. "How did you get a first name of Tom?"

Tom sighs. "My full name is Ryuu Tomio, or translated to Treasured Dragon, but to keep it simple for visitors who speak common, I go by Tom."

Crystal gets curious. "What does your name mean, Master Monzulo?"

"It means whatever you want it to. Just like others who are here, I value my privacy."

Crystal's face is covered in confusion. "I don't understand."

"When I first came here seventy years ago, I was a fugitive. I made up a name and stayed here among the monks. Originally figured I would just hide here a little while, but their ways grew on me. I learned and, in time, realized it was a better life than the one I fled from. So, I never uttered my old name again. The man I was all those years ago is not the man you see today, and now, they are my family." He motions to encompass Tom, Tyra, and to the monastery. "These are my brother's sisters, daughters, sons, and grandchildren to me now. I'm living proof of what you seek is possible."

She nods her head and Tom points to the cloth. "You need help with that?"

"I got it. Thank you for the offer, Master Ryuu." She smirks and heads back up the ramp. The crew finishes unloading for the day and Crystal takes the box to her cabin. William looks at it. "What is that?"

"I don't know, to be honest. It's a gift from The Grand Master." She places it on the table and removes the gold silken cloth. Under it, there is a long cherry wood box that's three feet long, only about a foot deep and wide. Laying the cloth on the bed, she undoes the brass latch opening it. Inside is a tea making set that looks a lot like the one she used yesterday. This brings a smile to her face as also in the box is a supply of tea and a note of instructions.

She explains it to William, and he smiles. "So, you're making tea for us?"

"Tonight." She reaches up and pats him on the cheek. "Right now, we have several hours before we get home, and I want to get your armor fixed." She takes the wands of repair from a drawer. For several hours, she works over his armor and burns through one wand, spending all its magic, leaving it a fancy electrum stick. She examines her work, and all the damage is gone. "Good as new." She tosses the used wand into a box.

William smiles and looks it over. "Yeah, it is. You're an amazing woman." He turns to her and runs his hands along her shoulders. "Is there anything you can't do?"

"Well, besides trying to get over my anger issues?" She picks up the book Tia found. "I've got some reading to do."

"What does this religious stuff have to do with the Black Rose?"

"Nothing. This isn't about the Black Rose. This is about Tia."

"I'm not following."

"Tia has had two visions now, mentioning Daniel and some *torch of love.*"

He sighs. "And you've been obsessed with it." William sits down next to her. "Why?"

"Because Tia, and everyone else, deserve to be in love. She has feelings for my brother, and I know he has them for her." She opens the cover. "But from the vision descriptions, it sounds like they aren't supposed to be celibate, but somehow, that's how they interpret it."

"So, you're going to take on the Black Rose and the church of Daniel?"

"The Church isn't fighting me. They are going through their teachings to see if there was a screwup. Tia still has her powers, even though she's going against her vow. This tells me we are on the right track." She looks down at the book. "And I have time to figure this torch thing out. I'm wondering if the gods aren't too dissimilar from us."

William throws his hands up. "That's nuts. They control everything."

"I'm not doubting that." She flips to the next page. "But maybe they aren't perfect. If they were, why was there a war between them? Perfect people don't go to war."

William sits there and nods. "I'm not going to even pretend to understand the gods."

"Maybe that's the point. They are powerful, no doubt, but what if they aren't as perfect as they claim to be, and just hide behind the mystery?"

William looks out the window and can see the city is close, the midday sun's rays reflecting off the silver and gold spires. "And we are home. Put that down and look at it later. It's time to have a wonderful birthday."

They land on the field and disembark but one of Marcus's retainers is waiting on them. A short white ageing man in his fifties wearing a nice suit approaches Crystal. "Countess." She greets him. "Emperor Marcus requests your presence."

"Right now?"

"Yes countess. As soon as he spotted your ship coming in, he had me waiting for you."

"Then let's not keep him." She takes William's arm and tugs him along.

They walk into the palace following the old man and they don't head towards the throne room. This puts William and Crystal on edge, and they exchange glances. They've been around each other so much that they can tell the other has the same question. They follow along till they reach a large room with Marcus sitting inside with some other people they don't know. A mahogany table sits at its center with the flag of the Rose Empire carved into it's surface. It's lined with gold and adamantium, making the whole design pop out with the natural colors.

Marcus stands up, and waves them over. "Countess, Captain, glad you made it home. Can't wait to hear how the monks are doing." His smile fades. "But first I have some news you're not going to like." He motions to some chairs and they sit down. "That Black Rose woman has been talking to us since your intimidation stunt, that lead to find others that were planted in the city."

A Dwarf with a general insignia gives Crystal a tablet with some papers attached and she looks them over. William is looking over her shoulder. "Are they serious?"

The Dwarf nods. "As far as we can tell, yes."

Crystal flips through pages. "What's the plan, then?"

"You take the *Bastion* and a load of troops to Portstown and inform them of what's going on. If this timetable is right, you'll barely beat them there. This gives you a week to get there, deploy the defense forces and then you take the ship the long way around." The Dwarven general rolls out a map on the table. "We have some details of the area. What we are going to do is have the *Bastion* land at the base of the mountain here." He points just north of the small mountain separating New Haven from the rest of the continent. "And you will travel there. Get in touch with the New Haven government and see where they stand. March under a banner of truce. If they have nothing to do with the Black Rose, you are authorized to start treaty negotiations for at least keeping each other at peace. If you think you can do more, you can try, but let's start simple."

"And if they aren't so friendly, I won't be tortured again. I'll die first." William puts his arm around her, calming her down.

214

"If you don't report to the *Bastion* within two weeks, the captain will deploy a rescue attempt. Since we are the only ones with flying warships, New Haven won't have a way to defend. They take out some key buildings, demand your release, then leave. Then we will be at war."

She looks at William and back at Marcus. "I'm not going to put on a brave face and not say I'm not scared." She puts her hand on her chest. "But why me?"

Marcus interrupts, his voice dominating the area. "You've had amazing success with Portstown, and the Black Rose knows you're here. If you stay here, they will keep coming, but if you can turn New Haven against them, then maybe the Black Rose will be cut off." Marcus leans forward on his elbows. "Being you've been fighting them for a year now, you know more about them than anyone. If you and your people pull this off, you will be heroes."

Crystal slumps. "I don't care about being a hero. I just want the people to be happy and safe."

"And that's why you're perfect for this. You love your people, and they know it." Marcus stands up and crosses over to her. "And you will have the gratitude of an empire behind you. If you can secure more than a peace agreement, it will mean that we will need a central power structure for the Bacarian continent."

"What do you mean?"

"You heard of Mithport, right?"

"Yea, they are the empire's largest importer of mithril, onyx, and some rare crops."

"That is correct." He leans down, putting his face close to hers. "It's on Titania, and the duke there was once like you. Someone I took an interest in and he did some good work for me." His tone gets softer. "And since he discovered those treasures there, he now runs multiple towns for me." He sits on the table in front of Crystal. "You don't have to do all this at once. Getting a peace treaty is good enough, and I want you to pick a place on Bacarian to start up your own town."

Crystal just stares forward, feeling her heart race. "Anywhere I want?"

"Yes, anywhere you want." He places a hand on her shoulder, getting her slowly to look up at him. "But the closer to being centralized it is, the better off it will be. As a wedding gift and as a thank you from a grateful Emperor, I will build you a house for you and your husband. Anything you want, just give it some thought."

Crystal gives him an impish grin. "Even a palace like yours?"

"I don't know if the empire has the budget for that, but you can meet with my city planner, and I'm sure you can come up with something reasonable." Marcus stands up and motions for them to stand. "But no matter what, your safety comes first. Don't take chances over a fancy house. You have a long time to get this done, but the Black Rose must be stopped now."

"When do we leave?"

Marcus looks back at his generals and back at Crystal. His face can't hide the regret. "Tomorrow. Any later and you will be too close to the Black Rose army when they arrive. And since we know they have spies, we must give them as little warning as possible."

She slumps back down in the chair, casting her eyes to the table. "But... my wedding."

"I know, I know. I hate doing this to you and William." He sighs heavily. "I feel awful this is happening to you and I wanted you to have a wonderful birthday, so instead of leaving now, you leave in the morning." She looks up at the Emperor and he can see her trying her best to seize up her tears. "Crystal, we've been through a lot together and I think of you as one of my own."

He kneels next to her, and this gets gasps from others in the room. He gently places a hand on her arm. "I know how much this has to hurt." She faces him and he takes her into his arms, embracing her as he would his own child. "When you get back home, you will have a wedding worthy if a returning countess. That is my decree." He breaks his embrace and can see her crying, knowing he broke her heart. "Life has hard choices, and sometimes destiny is out of your control." He looks down into her icy blue Dragon eyes. His voice is somber. "I know this more than anyone."

She tries hiding her sadness with sarcasm. "My birthday is getting off to a great start."

"I think it will brighten up once you get home."

He stands about to turn away when she interrupts, leaping to her feet. "The workers at the Monastery, they don't have a place to stay with the cold weather. I promised them I would send the ship back since I wasn't planning on coming back." She widens her arms out at her sides. "They are going to need that ship back."

Marcus smiles down at her. "You're a true leader, Crystal. You look out for your people even when faced with your own crisis. The new airship, Opal Star, is ready to fly and has been doing test flights since you left." He sits back in his chair. "I had it loaded with more supplies to send north. General Hardforge here will take over the Monastery operations and make sure things stay on track."

"Thank you, Your Highness. That makes me feel better."

"Now go enjoy your party. I have other matters to tend to." Crystal and William file out of the room, escorted by the aging man. They get out front and the Hellstromm's car is waiting there.

William leans down and speaks into her ear. "Looks like the Emperor wasn't the only one watching for your return."

She smiles. "Glad to be home."

Marcus dismisses everyone from his presence and watches Crystal from the window. Skylar appears once again as if cued. "She didn't take the news too well. Maybe you are pushing her too hard?"

He shakes his head. "There is a new piece on the board, and I'm going to use it to ensure things go as planned."

"And how are you going to do that, my love?"

He grins, kissing her tenderly. "With a simple message to the right person." He observes Crystal and William getting into the steam car. "And positioning this new piece exactly where it needs to be."

CHAPTER 21

(All Good Things)

The evening sun touches the ocean, casting its fiery rays across the sky. The rainbow shimmer of the dome is all too familiar, but being so long away from home, so alien too. She looks out the window, not talking. William knows she's usually chatty and her silence is chilling to him. "Penny for your thoughts?"

She turns back to him. "I'm just upset that our marriage in on hold. What we are about to do is very dangerous, and if something happens this time, I want to at least be married first." She swipes a tear away.

He leans over and kisses her, holding her face to his with his large, comforting hands. "Then let's make sure nothing happens this time."

"I'll hold you to that." They ride in the car for several minutes and can see the Hellstromm manor coming up. "I wish I had a chance to invite Zarra. After spending all that time around her, I like her." She sighs. "But she's probably back on her ship and about to leave port."

"Yeah, I'll miss her too. Didn't know her long, but she was fun to have around." They pull into the manor and Cline is waiting for them. Crystal gives him a hug, something that completely catches him off guard.

She lets go and looks up at him. "I missed you."

"Who are you?"

William explains as she takes his arm. "It's her. She's been doing some things with the Grand Master, Tia and Zarra." Cline has a quizzical look on his face and shakes it off.

Tia watches as Crystal and William are taken away by an older man inside the palace. "Wonder what that is about?"

Penelope stands next to her watching as well. "Must be important if the Emperor had someone waiting for them."

They continue to unload their things and four silver knights wearing full armor and helms, bearing the Crest of the Silvian Empire, arrive. They stand there as Zarra comes down wearing her emerald and silver armor, the gash marks still present. One of them points to it and starts speaking Elven. Tia and Penelope exchange glances, both understanding what they are saying.

"She was attacked. I knew this was a bad idea to let her leave alone."

The second knight nods in agreement. "She's in charge. What choice did we have? Maybe now she will come home."

She marches up and tosses her bag to one of them. She replies in common. "I had fun. These people are worthy and I'm sticking around."

This first knight replies, still speaking Elven. "Princess, you were attacked, and your armor is damaged. Return home…" An armored backhand crosses his visor, shutting him up.

Zarra points a finger at his face. "You will speak common in their presence. Speaking in anything else looks like you're trying to hide something, and it besmirches my honor." She pokes him in the chest plate. "And furthermore," she points to herself. "Last I checked, I outrank you. I'm the Princess," then points to him, "you're the knight. If I don't ask you for a suggestion, don't give me one, understood?" The four of them straighten up.

Tia and Penelope turn away with looks of surprise on their own faces that Zarra can be as ruthless as Crystal. Penelope whispers to Tia. "Don't get on her bad side."

Chuck comes down the ramp and stops next to Penelope. "What would you like for me to do?"

She looks up at him. "Have you decided what you where you want to go?"

"Yeah, I want to go home, but I want to help you find the Black Rose first. Being I've been there; I should be a big use for you."

"That you will. I'll get you a nice hotel room for the night. I'm not sure what the plan is for the next few days, probably end back up at the Monastery helping with relief." She goes back to checking the supplies coming off. "Be ready when someone comes for you, ok?"

"Ok, Penelope. What should I do for now?".

"Help unload. Be useful."

Several minutes go by and Zarra and her escort is visited by a dignitary of Emperor Marcus and they leave for the inside too. Penelope tugs on Tia's robe. "It's Crystal's birthday. You should go get Andrew from the Church and meet us back at the manor."

Tia nods. "Not a bad idea." She looks to the palace. "How long do I have to get back?"

Penelope looks distant. "I have to make the cake, and there is dinner as well. Two hours till it starts." She holds a hand out, shrugging with one shoulder. "Plus, we have to make up for Providers' Day and start figuring out a wedding cake." She looks up at the Half-Elf and lets out a deep sigh. "I've got my work cut out for me this week."

"Yeah, you do, and you're right. I should get going. I'll be back with Andrew as soon as possible." Tia and Penelope hug and Tia walks off as she always has. Tom and Tyra are helping with the ship and gather their horses. Grabbing their things, the four mount up with the horses availed them. Along the way, they get Chuck a room and pay for a few days. Leaving him there, they go onward to the Hellstromm manor and start setting up for Crystal's party.

Tia strolls along the streets, staying in well-lit areas, still wearing the chain mail under her robes. She arrives at the church to see that services are wrapping up. Sitting quietly in the back, not wanting to cause a disturbance, and can see Andrew at the front with Lyndis, leading the prayers. Twenty minutes pass by and the Church bell strikes, signaling its six p.m. and services are over. The sun has completely set and the only light in the church is the candles. The flames flicker, and as the common people walk past, their shadows dance in the candlelight. Lyndis, Andrew, and the other clergy now perform individual prayers and small talk with those still hanging around.

Andrew notices Tia sitting in the back and whispers to Lyndis. She looks and Tia raises her hand shoulder high and waves back. Andrew pats his hand on Lyndis' shoulder, signaling his departure, and walks quickly towards Tia. As he closes in, Tia stands, and they embrace. *I want to kiss him so badly, but I know it would cause a stir. Now I know how Crystal felt around William this whole time.* They hang onto each other for several passing moments and they break apart. "I missed you."

"I missed you too." He grins at her. "How was your trip to the monastery?"

"Eventful. Me and Crystal learned how to 'breathe' and make tea. Penelope made a new friend." She looks into his eyes. "And we found some books that might help our cause."

Lyndis walks up, overhearing the last part. "Some books you say? About?"

"You remember the Emperor mentioned a war between the gods? Crystal, Zarra, William and I found some texts about it. At least we think we did. She's going to be looking them over and see what happened in the past. Maybe it will explain my visions and why Daniel is allowing us to break our vows."

"I have news on that front, too." Lyndis sits in the pew and motions for them to do so as well. "I've been going through our church history and our older scrolls." She sighs. "And you might be onto something. The vow of celibacy didn't become a thing till about two hundred years ago. The texts from that period didn't mention a change, but how the clergy interpreted did."

"Weren't old enough to know the church from before those times."

"No, actually. I was only one hundred and seven when this supposed event happened. It wasn't till after that, I came to Rose harbor at one ninety and joined. By then, the new way was the only way with everything else forgotten."

"So. what does this mean?"

"It means that even though the texts haven't changed since the church's birth, the way they were interpreted has." She looks at them. "I'm at a loss. If I get in front of everyone and say their vows were for nothing, they will look at me like I'm a heretic." She shakes her head. "I'm looking for suggestions."

"We can start off subtly. Any new initiates coming in won't take the vow of chastity, since that's not what Daniel wanted." Tia locks eyes with Lyndis. "You have the texts, right? Call a meeting and we can show what we found and how we could have been mistaken. Get their opinions and let's figure something out."

Lyndis looks at Tia. "You've changed since you left us all those months ago. You're more confident than before, more sure of yourself. What happened to the shy girl who wouldn't challenge anything?"

Tia looks down and pulls at her robes. "I think all of us have changed. Some for the better, others for the worse. The Emperor has us out there representing the empire and working for him. This shown me how much larger the world is." She looks away from Lyndis "It's a big place, and I'm glad I'm getting to spread the word of Daniel to other places."

Andrew interrupts. "I hate to break this up, but it's getting late, and my sister is waiting for us. We should go."

Lyndis waves them off. "You two have fun. I have much to think about." They nod and head to the manor.

The young couple enter the manor to find their friends and family waiting. Crystal smiles and runs to her father, giving him a tight hug, then moves to her mom. William's smile matches hers, as his own parents are there as well, along with Tia, Tom, and Tyra. One of Penelope's line cooks enters and informs the group that dinner will be ready soon, and Ms. Hellstromm's cake should finish by the end of the meal. Crystal and William sit on the love seat, with him wrapping his arm around her. They talk for some time about the monastery and Tom's promotion to master.

"We also found some tomes about the gods I'll be adding to my study list."

"Oh, speaking of, I went through those books a little and found some interesting spells." Jasmine leans closer to her daughter. "And none of them were trapped, but nevertheless, be careful with them."

Crystal holds up a finger and puts her glass down. Pulling the rod from her handbag, she gives it to her mom. "Shadow found this in the camp of the Black Rose."

Jasmine's eyes widen as she looks it over intently. "Haven't seen one of these in a while. A Rod of Mass Teleport is hard to produce." She casts her gaze at her daughter. "This could be cursed. I'm glad you brought it to me first." Crystal looks away and down, and Jasmine's eyebrows furrow. "Tell me you didn't use this already."

Crystal doesn't make eye contact, and grips at her dress. "I had to, to save William, Tyra and Zarra." She takes a deep breath, then looks up at her mom. "We were attacked by an owlbear."

"Why didn't you just blast the thing with your magic?"

Crystal looks back at the floor. "Because I couldn't."

"That doesn't make sense. Why couldn't…oh, well, never mind." The room gets quiet and Crystal turns pink and looks away.

Jack quickly jumps in to deflect the conversation. "Why would they leave an owlbear by the monastery?"

William answers, keeping things going. "Because they knew if their attack failed here, we would learn of the attack on the monastery and come running."

Gerald places a hand on his chin and looks thoughtful. "Makes sense. Booby trap the area around the camp so if you lose, your enemies don't get the spoils."

"And I fell for it. I sent Shadow there and when she didn't come back, I went after her. I shouldn't have done that."

"Don't beat yourself up. You had to do an investigation to see where the enemy came from. It's common sense to see how your enemy works." Gerald looks at his son, making a circling gesture with his hand. "William, she was right, wasn't she?"

William nods and squeezes her a little, trying to comfort her, running his hand along her arm and shoulder. "It was. You care about those around you."

"Cheer up, sweetheart." Jasmine hands the rod back. "It's your birthday and in a few days, you're going to be married. So be happy."

Crystal and William exchange glances, and Crystal buries her face in his chest and cries. Confusion is on every face in the room. Tia looks at William. "What's wrong?"

William strokes Crystal's hair as she continues to cry. Looking down at Crystal's head, he musters the words to speak. "The wedding is postponed for now. This thing with the Black Rose and New Haven is getting big." Her tears soak through his shirt. "We have to leave tomorrow. There is an army making its way to Portstown. As per the treaty, we must send reinforcements. The Emperor thinks with the Black Rose fighting in Portstown, it would give us time to talk to the leader of New Haven."

"That's rough. It really is." Jack sighs heavily. "But that's the nature of politics." Jack puts his arm around Jasmine. "But the payoff is usually worth it. You're a countess and have some real pull in the empire. More than me, and that's saying something."

Crystal turns her face out of Williams's chest, and her makeup is running. "I'm sorry, this is supposed to be a happy day, and the reason for it is also ruining it."

"Then let's make it a happy day then, and when you get back home, you will get a wedding that the whole town will talk about for years." Jack leans forward and pats her on the leg. "The Emperor himself promised you, right?"

"And he said he would help me with designing my home, and if I got New Haven to sign a peace treaty, I could pick any place on the Bacarian continent and start up my own town." Crystal wipes away her tears with a tissue.

Jack, Jasmine and the rest exchange looks. "You know what that means?" Crystal shakes her head. "Getting to establish your own town means he is seeing a lot of potential in you. If you pull this off, you might get control of that continent on his behalf."

She brightens up. "You really think so?" She dabs around her eyes. "That would be outstanding, but why would he do that?"

A feminine voice speaks from the doorway. "Because you remind him of himself back then." They all swivel at the new voice and an emerald knight is standing in the doorway, holding a small box with a ribbon wrapped around it. Cline stands behind her with a smile. "May I present, Princess Zarra Silvian."

Crystal runs up to Zarra gives her a huge hug. "I thought you went home." Crystal breaks the embrace and stands back. Zarra reaches up and lifts her helmet off, letting her red copper hair flow down her back and exposing her obsidian black face and ruby red eyes for all to see.

"Nope, I escaped once again, and I'm joining you on your trip to New Haven. By the time they know I'm gone, they will be a full day out of port." She shrugs. "Besides, the Emperor said that since I'm not a citizen of his, he can't sanction me going along." She holds a finger up. "But as a princess and member of the royal House, he doesn't have the authority under the treaty to stop me, either. So, if you will have me, I'm willing to come along."

Crystal's smile grows. "I would love to have you along! Wouldn't be right for me to force Tia to practice martial arts and be forced to drink awful tea on the road alone."

"Thanks for looking out for me." Tia quips sarcastically. "Taking the *misery loves company* thing a bit too literally?"

Crystal steps back and almost returns to her seat, when Zarra interrupts again, stepping to the center of the room. "I have something here for you, from the Emperor. It's his gift for you for your birthday. He wanted me to give it to you. Guess he had a feeling I was going to sneak off my ship before it left port."

Zarra presents the box and Crystal just stands there, stunned. She scans the room, and Jack motions to open it. Crystal's hands shake as she pulls the ribbon, undoing the bow on top. Zarra waits as Crystal slowly opens it, not knowing what to expect. Inside are two sheets of paper, one much larger than the other, but the smaller one is on top. She takes it out and reads it.

I know how much you enjoyed her, so as a token of appreciation for everything you've done for me and on behalf of the empire, she's yours, so take good care of her. I have several others, so enjoy.

Emperor Marcus Rose

She reaches in and takes out the second paper and unrolls it, then covers her mouth. William is the first to ask. "What?"

She looks at William. "The Emperor is giving us the *Bastion*."

"Us?" He gets up, and she meets him halfway, showing him the document. "This says the owners are William and Crystal Hellstromm." He grins and hugs her. "Guess we need to get back and get married, so I get my half."

She laughs a little and leans up and gives him a kiss. Jack interrupts. "You know, I didn't kiss my wife till we were married."

Jasmine looks down at him and gives him a gentle shove. "That's not true."

He gives her a goofy smile. "Yeah, it is. You weren't my wife till after we got married."

Jasmine's mouth opens as if to respond, and Gerald laughs. "That's a good one, Jack."

"You did not just tell a dad joke at my twentieth birthday party." Taking the box from Zarra, Crystal directs William back to the loveseat. Cline brings Zarra a chair to sit in, so she can remove her armor.

Jack puts his arm around Jasmine. "Got you to smile, didn't it?"

Gerald holds up a hand. "I've got a few."

William buries his face in his hands. "Oh god dad, not you too."

"You know another name for love birds?"

William and Crystal exchange glances and Gerald finishes. "Tweet-hearts." This gets a small laugh from them. "That's a good one, dad. I'll have to remember that one."

Gerald smiles. "Once you two have a few kids, me and Jack will have a lot more to tell you to them." William nods and looks down at his bride to be. "Hopefully we will get started on that sooner than later."

Penelope walks in and announces dinner is ready. Zarra had finished getting her armor off, wearing plain white linen under it all. Crystal looks her over with a look of disdain. "You need a dress for tonight, Zarra?"

"I snuck out with nothing, but it shouldn't be a big deal." Zarra waves the thought away. Everyone files into the dining room, but Crystal holds Zarra back. "Daddy, I'm taking her to my house and getting her a proper dress to wear. We will be back in a moment, ok?"

Jack nods to Crystal. "Don't be too long, or it will get cold, monster."

Crystal takes Zarra's hand and pulls her along out back to the guest house where she had moved all her stuff. Zarra looks down at them, holding hands. *It's so unusual that another person could be this good, but turn bad under extreme stress.*

Crystal breaks her from her introspection. "The stars are beautiful, aren't they?"

Zarra looks up, following the other woman's gaze, and never really thought about it. *My people are from underground. They never really appreciated the sky much. In two hundred and seven years, I never really bothered to look up, uninterested until now. Funny how something so simple of an observation is so easily missed. She really fills me with wonderment.*

They walk into the home, and Crystal speaks the command word that lights the magical lanterns. Taking her back to her bedroom, Crystal lets her hand go finally and opens the large closet. She rifles through dresses quickly, trying to find something that would look good on Zarra's obsidian colored skin. "We are about the same size, but you're, well, you're…" Crystal struggles to be tactful, but Zarra doesn't know where she's going with her words.

"I'm what?"

Crystal motions to her top. "You're larger than me."

"But you said we were the same size, how am I larger…" she cuts off as she finally gets it. "I have a larger bust than you."

Crystal nods. "Which limits what I have because my dresses are made for my extra petite frame." She goes through her closet. "But I'll start digging here and you can get undressed so you can change."

"Just right here?"

"I've seen you topless just yesterday in the pool, so what's the big deal now? Besides, it's not like I'm going to throw you on the bed or anything. We have a party to get to." She pulls out a dress, shakes her head, and puts it back. "And when we get to Portstown, we will find you some new clothes." Crystal voice is full of, pulling an ocean blue evening dress out. She turns around and Zarra is standing there in her underwear. Crystal's heart skips. *She's very attractive… Wait, why are these thoughts back?* She mentally shakes off the thought. Crystal

230

holds it up to her. "I think this will work since the cloth for the top is adjustable with a string in the back."

"It's a lovely color."

Crystal walks around her. "Now this part there crosses the front and ties behind your head, but to make this right, you're going to have to lose the brazier. If you don't want to, I can see if I have a full cover dress, but those are usually not very flexible in the front."

"Actually, I like this dress. It flows well." She turns her head to look at Crystal, putting their faces close, and she smiles. "You have good taste." Zarra thumbs over her shoulder. "Unhook me, so I can get it off."

Crystal disconnects the brazier and Zarra tosses it to the floor. "That feels so much better. It's hard to breathe in that thing." The two of them finish up and Crystal walks her in front of the mirror. The bright ocean blue dress contrasts with her obsidian skin and ruby red eyes. It crisscrosses in front of her, covering her bosom but leaving her navel and shoulders showing. Crystal finds her some silver and diamond earrings to go with it, and helps her with her makeup, using some sky-blue shading around her eyes. Crystal hands her some sky-blue lipstick. "Isn't this a bit much for the party?"

"Yes, it is."

"So, why are we doing it?"

"Because it's fun." She points to the mirror. "Besides, look how beautiful you are." Zarra looks, seeing herself with Crystal holding onto her shoulders with her stark white hands. "You're irresistible, and if we went out somewhere together, William would be fighting the guys off with a club." She laughs and grabs the matching shoes. "Here are the shoes that go with that dress. I hope they aren't too uncomfortable."

Zarra slips them on and looks at Crystal. "Apparently my feet are larger than yours too, but I should be fine. I'll tough it out for the night."

Crystal smiles and fixes her own makeup after all the crying she had done. Then, on impulse, changes into a sleeveless strawberry red dress that hangs to her ankles. She slips on a gold necklace and earrings with rubies to finish the ensemble.

Zarra is amazed. *She changes clothes so fast and looks perfect. She's stunning in her own right. How does William keep his hands off of her?* She grins. *That's right, he doesn't.*

Crystal breaks her from her introspection. "Shall we get to my party?"

Zarra smiles. "It's been a long time since I wore a dress. Thank you for helping me with it."

"No problem. It was fun." They make their way to the dining room.

Everyone is talking and laughing as the two of them come in. The conversations die as all eyes are upon them. "So that's what took so long." Jack puts his fork down with a grin. "I see my daughter found a friend who has a similar taste in clothing as her."

Zarra bows her head. "Thank you, sir."

"No need for that bowing stuff. I might be the head of the Third House, but I work for a living." Jack points to the empty places near William with an open hand. "Let's eat and get to know each other."

Zarra and Crystal take their places on either side of William, and take from the food already placed on the table. Tia and Andrew lead a prayer to Daniel and then they all start eating. Zarra gets more than her fair share of questions, but she gets to ask many in return. She smiles, and laughs, something back in her home, she hardly ever did. *Ditching my escort and staying here with them was the right choice. I feel so much more welcome here than I ever did in the Silvian Empire.*

The night goes on and the cake is brought out by Cline. Tom laughs. "Hey, they made a cake almost as big as you, Tyra." Tyra snorts and lashes out to punch him, but he catches her fist before it lands. "Not at the table. There is a time and place for everything." His tone is more serious than anyone has heard him be.

Cline lights the candles as Crystal glances at Tom. "Taking your promotion more professionally?"

"I didn't want your beautiful cake ruined." Tom gazes at the three-tier white and icy blue cake. "Almost don't want to eat it."

Penelope sounds proud. "It's Dwarven chocolate, with icing brought in from the Silvian Empire, and some walnuts grown in Dorbin. I went all out on this."

CHAPTER 22

(It's my party)

They laugh, and drink, exchange stories into the night. They exchange small gifts for Provider's Day that they missed and Jasmine hands Crystal a long, thin box. "What's this?"

"Something I've been working on for months." Jasmine sounds excited. "Open it."

Crystal removes the thin and colorful paper and opens the wooden box. Inside is a two foot long, snow white platinum rod. At the far end of the rod is an eight-pointed sapphire about two inches in diameter, suspended in the middle of a crescent moon. Diamonds cut to look like icicles decorate it along it's sides. She holds the thing up and looks at it as if it was a scepter. "It's beautiful, mom."

"It's a rod of temperature control." Jasmin sounds somber. "When you had trouble back in Portstown with the heat, I decided to build that for you." She looks at her daughter and Crystal is overcome with emotions.

She reaches out and hugs her mom. "How does it work?" Crystal looks at the inscription.

She points to the first of three gem icicles near the base is a blue diamond. "This one lowers the temperature within a half mile area by twenty degrees for eight hours. You can use this twice per day before it must recharge, or tap it twice to double the effect once." She points to a canary yellow diamond icicle.

"This one does the opposite and raises it by twenty or forty if tapped twice." She takes Crystal's hand and covers the buttons. "Be warned. Forty degree's doesn't sound like much, but at negative forty or plus one thirty, people can die within minutes. Even you're White Dragon heritage can't stand negative forty for long." She composes herself and removes her hand. "It should help you conserve your magic for other things besides enduring the environment and will help everyone around you."

Crystal looks at the wonderful object. "It looks like a scepter to me, mom."

Jasmine grins. "You are a countess now, so why not have something to symbolize it?" She points to a red diamond icicle. "This one casts 'bolt of ice'. It can only fire twice per day, but it's faster and stealthier than casting the spell itself." She laughs. "Just make sure of what you're pointing at is the target. Once it leaves your scepter, it's not anyone's friend anymore." She sounds very serious.

"Thank you, mom, it's wonderful." Crystal gives her another big hug. They play games and drink well into the night. The clock chimes, letting them know it's eleven in the evening and time to get some rest.

Tom pipes up, grabbing everyone's attention. "Where are we all staying?" He motions to himself and Tyra. "Are we going back to Mr. Blakely's manor or just sleeping here somewhere?"

"That's a good question." Gerald addresses Tia and Andrew. "And with what's been happening, it's not safe for you two to walk home either."

"Andrew can sleep in his old room for the night. Tia can have my old room, and we have two spare bedrooms here, so Tom and Tyra have a spot each." Crystal mentions these things casually. "And our house out back has two spare rooms, so Zarra can sleep out there. I'll grab her some of my clothes so she can have something to sleep in and change into in the morning before we take off."

Gerald looks around, then shrugs. "Good of plan as any."

Penelope speaks up. "What about Chuck?"

Crystal addresses her. "We are leaving at eight a.m. Someone needs to grab him at six if he's really going home with us, if that's what he was really wanting."

"It is." Penelope steps to the exit and looks back. "I'll grab him in the morning then and get him to your ship."

"Sounds good." Crystal looks around the room and claps her hands together. "Hate to say this, but we have to end the party." She stands up and William follows. "We need our rest if we are going back out to conquer the rest of the continent."

William offers his arm, and she takes it. "She's right, as usual." The young couple takes their leave as everyone gets up and starts filing to where they need to go. Andrew takes Tia's hands and heads upstairs to show her to her room. Cline escorts Tom and Tyra to their respective rooms.

Jack looks at Zarra just standing there looking at Crystal and William walking away. He walks up to her and startles her when he speaks. "Everything alright?"

She takes a deep breath and letting out, looking down at the floor. "They are so happy."

"Yes, they are." Jack looks at their backs as they go. "And I've been around long enough to know when something is bothering someone." He turns his head back to her. "You didn't ditch your ship because you wanted to vacation with my daughter." This gets her to face him. "And I believe that you're a paladin of Johnathan. So, lying isn't in your nature. My question is, why are you being so sneaky?"

She casts her eyes downward. "It's rather personal to me." Her tone tells Jack that there is much deeper than that. "If I go back, the life I wanted will be over."

Jack reaches out and places his right hand on her left shoulder. This gets her to look up at him once again. "I understand that all too well." His words comfort her. "I won't bother asking for the details, but once your people find out

236

you're missing, they will come looking for you." He lets her go. "And the Silvian Empire has been our allies for a long time. I wouldn't like the idea of a war."

"I left a note with my personal insignia explaining my actions. That I wanted my freedom and that my life was my own and not to blame anyone else for it." She looks up with her ruby red eyes, "There won't be a war, but I won't guarantee that I won't be hunted and dragged home." She looks at the couple walking into their home in the backyard and Crystal turns and waves her on. "Crystal and William and the rest are doing some real good in this world, and I want to be part of it." She turns back to Jack. "Thank you for your hospitality and kind words, Mr. Hellstromm."

"Any time, and I'll have Cline store your armor till morning." He motions her on and she walks across the courtyard finding Crystal waiting in the doorway. William had gone on ahead to bed.

"Everything alright?"

"Yeah, just tired. So where am I sleeping, and what in?" Crystal walks her through the home, showing her the kitchen and the other rooms along the way. They come to a room and Crystal shows her in. A light blue nightgown lies on the bed. "You look good in blue, so I kept with the theme."

Zarra grins and gives Crystal a big hug. "Thank you for your kindness."

Crystal blushes. "It's alright. Us princess needs to stick together. You have a good night." Crystal takes her leave back to her bedroom, turning off the lights. The natural moonlight is bright enough for her Dragon eyes, enabling her to get around. Entering the bedroom, she closes the door behind her and places her new scepter on the nightstand.

Hours go by and William is sound asleep, but Crystal lays there, her head on William's chest, too anxious to rest. Thoughts of the day's prior, and the fact her wedding was postponed, the mission, and many other things run through her mind. She's exhausted and usually falls sleep listing to his heartbeat, but tonight, it's not working. *Maybe what I need is something to drink, walk around a bit and clear my head.*

She slides quietly out of bed and heads to the kitchen, not bothering to cover up. William doesn't wake as she leaves. *Good, he needs his rest. I can always sleep once we are airborne.* She sneaks out the door and walks down the hall quietly. Making her way into the kitchen, she turns the corner and barely quashes a yelp of surprise. Zarra is sitting at the table in the dark drinking some juice and gets a small fright of her own.

Zarra places a hand over her heart and takes a deep breath. "Don't sneak up on me like that" She looks up and notices Crystal isn't wearing anything. Flipping her hand out, she points to Crystal. "Why are you walking around like that?"

Crystal puts her hands on her hips and takes an indignant tone. "It's my house. I should be allowed to roam it however I please, shouldn't I? At least I'm wearing underwear."

Zarra laughs lightly, shaking her head. "I guess so." She takes a drink. Crystal walks over to the other cabinet and grabs a glass, then sits down opposite Zarra at the table. "You can't sleep either?"

"No, too anxious." Crystal sighs, pouring herself some juice. "I have so much running through my head since I got back." She sips her cup and continues. "What's keeping you awake tonight?"

Zarra glances at her half-naked counterpart. "I'm wondering if I did the right thing. I feel I did, but part of me feels guilty about sneaking away from my people."

"You want to talk about it?" Crystal reaches across and takes Zarra's hand. "As Master Monzulo says, sometimes to solve your own problems, you should help others, or something to that effect."

Zarra gives a halfhearted shrug. "I have personal reasons for running away."

"You can tell me." Crystal squeezes her hands gently. "We haven't known each other but a few days, but you can talk to me."

"I know you mean well, and I just want to be a use to someone. It's why I trained most of my life, yearning to be part of something larger than myself."

Crystal pats her hand. *There is more to it than that, but she's not being completely forthcoming. But I'm not going to push the issue. I need her to open up to me.*

"As a paladin, I feel more at home helping the people over being a princess. It's what *I* want to do."

Crystal laughs lightheartedly. "The grand Master wasn't wrong about us."

Zarra tilts her head and glances at Crystal. "How so?"

"You're a princess trying to be a regular citizen, and I'm a regular citizen, albeit a rich one, trying to be a princess. You've defeated your darker nature and became good, and I was good, and now tainted by the evil in my heart." Crystal pulls her hand back and takes a drink, then chuckles. "Yin and yang. We are just circling each other."

"Maybe that will mean we will be best friends someday."

"I think we already are." Crystal lifts her glass. "To new friends."

Zarra clinks her glass against Crystal's "To new friends." They talk about different things, from fashion, to guys, to the mission ahead. Zarra is looking at Crystal when she notices movement outside the window. She whispers to Crystal and points. "There is someone outside." Crystal turns her head, locating the intruder right away.

Her face scrunches and a sinister tone escapes. "How the hell did he get past our security?"

"I need to grab my sword." Zarra motions to Crystal's bedroom. "Think you can get to William?"

Crystal nods her head. "I'll make sure he grabs some pants before his sword, since you're awake."

"Thanks, I guess?"

Crystal makes her way back to her room and wakes William. "What's wrong, honey?"

"Someone is outside. Put some pants on and arm yourself."

"How do you know this?"

She keeps her voice low, watching out the window. "I haven't been asleep. Been up most of the night talking to Zarra. We were having some girl time." He looks at her quizzically as she grabs his shirt and slips it on, draping down past her knees. "Look, some things I can't talk to you about and it's nice having a real woman to talk to. Tia is too shy and sheltered, and Shadow is just not interested." She looks over at him. "And I sure won't talk to my mom about this stuff."

William silences her by placing a finger on her lips, keeping his tone hushed. "I get it, but right now, you said we have an intruder. Let's deal with that first." He stands up and puts on his pants and pulls his sword.

"Careful. Zarra is around here too, so be careful. Don't need any friendly accidents." Crystal holds her scepter like a club. He nods in acknowledgment. *I really wish I would have taken up those shooting practices, but nooo, I have to rely on my magic that I don't have for another few days.* They walk quietly out of the bedroom and, as they get to the living room, and she points to the figures outside.

"Are they your personal guards for the manor, maybe?"

240

"They wear armor. You would hear them walking."

He nods again, making sure she didn't have anyone like this working for her. Zarra walks around the corner, wearing her nightgown and holding her sword. William can't see her in the dark, but he can see the sword and the light blue nightgown floating. This gives him a slight start. "If I didn't know any better, I would have screamed 'ghost' and ran."

"What's the plan, darling?"

"Hard to say." He looks back at Crystal. "I know you're tired. Think you can whip up some invisibility for us and we can get the drop on our party crashers?"

Crystal shakes her head. "Not for another three days or so, I can't."

"Oh, I forgot. Sorry. We can distract them and you can go for help."

"I'm not leaving your side. What if you get hurt?"

Zarra holds up her sword. "I'll have his back. You go and we will hold them till you return with help. Until we get an idea about numbers, attacking without knowing would just get us all killed. At least this way we can get an idea of who they are and know we have backup on its way."

Crystal agrees with them. "Just don't get hurt. Just because we have two clerics in the manor doesn't mean you can get yourselves killed." Crystal makes her way, staying down finding a place she can exit unseen. William makes his way to the window and looks out. Zarra navigates to the back door and holds there.

She opens a window with a small squeak of the hinges, then runs across the grass between her home to the main building. With the full moon, she can almost see as if it was full light and gets a look at the people around the building. She walks quickly and spots one guard face down in the bushes by the back wall.

Shadow personally made sure that entering the main house would trip it and no one can bypass it. All I have to do is open the door without my key and the whole place knows. She reaches down and picks up a rock and is about to smash the lock when a large hand grabs her arm. She goes to scream but finds her voice is silenced by a hand she cannot see. *William?* She wonders. *Can't be. He's back at the house.* Her heart pounds in her chest.

"Shhh." She faintly hears her father's voice and the weight of the hand leave her mouth.

She whispers back. "Daddy?"

"Yeah, I haven't been to bed either. Ever since that attack a few days ago, I've been on edge too. Time to show these people who they are messing with. Stay here, and out of trouble."

"Daddy, be careful. William and Zarra are out there, too."

"I know; I can see them just fine, along with the other intruders. I'm going to give them a demonstration on why you don't mess with the Hellstromm's." She can't hear or see him, but the deep impressions in the grass are the only sign of him give him ambling across the lawn in his power armor.

He's distracted with the intruders. Good. He won't forgive for what I'm about to do. She takes this time to sneak into her father's workshop.

William gets a count from what he can see. He whispers to Zarra. "I've got five here that I can see."

"I count three. If it's a squad of ten, it means two aren't accounted for."

"Something isn't right." The alarm in his voice perks Zarra's ears up. "She should have raised the alarm by now." He hefts his sword, getting ready to make his move as two of the intruders walk up to his front door. One knees down and pulls out some pock picks. *Looks like they want to keep this quiet. Too bad I'm going to make it loud for them.*

The front door opens and William raises his sword, ready to get the first strike. The sound of metal piercing flesh is barely audible, then the second intruder makes a gurgling noise. Blood erupts from his chest, covering everything in the area. He gasps and steps back, watching blood drip from twin translucent blades. The first man turns around and horror crosses his face as the second invader is lifted and tossed aside. Blood drains off the ghastly silhouette of something truly enormous.

Zarra watches out her window as a two-man team comes to the back door and picks the lock. She feels completely exposed, wearing nothing but a nightgown. She readies her own weapon as they open the door and enter slowly. *I don't like sneak attacks, but I'm outnumbered and out armored. I'm sure Johnathan will understand.* The two-man team quietly pull short swords, leaving their revolvers holstered. *Not a bad idea given the tight quarters in here, but they are there for one reason: to kill us.*

She follows them, and they walk into the living room and stop. They exchange looks and Zarra can see their faces twist in fear, as if death itself was walking on their graves. She edges around and spots another intruder outside the front door being held at least two feet off the ground. Blood drips from a pair of spectral blades protruding from a man's chest. She steps back, dread filling her soul, as the man's body is cast aside, splattering blood onto something that she couldn't see till that moment. The other man standing in the doorway pulls his gun, but then his arm is raised into the air along with him and he screams. The terror in his voice shakes everyone to their core and draws attention from the other intruders. Gun shots ring out over and over as he continues to scream.

Guards scramble from the noise, and the man continues to scream. The gun clicks as all six rounds have been fired. Zarra and William hear bones snap as the man's arm twists and bends unnaturally. The two men in front of her turn around, but she doesn't give them the chance to flee. She strikes, opening one's chest, and with punches the second, sending him over the couch. William takes the opening to dash across the room as the man on the floor stands and tackles him back down.

The man in the doorway continues to scream an anguish but the tone changes from that of pain to that absolute dread and William and Zarra turn and see why. Power armor painted with the Third House's colors appears to them all, the invisibility finally breaking. Copper fittings and rubber hoses run from the pneumatic cylinders in the arms and legs and its helm is the true visage of horror. The eye slits glow red and gems on the side of it glow a hue of colors, but the visage is unnatural looking, as if born from the abyss itself. With the invisibility gone, the noise it makes returns as well. The hissing and clanking noise sounds haunting as valves dispel super-heated steam.

William swallows hard. "What in Mechas' name is that?" Gunfire erupts and bullets bounce with sparks off the gigantic machine. The strange helm turns in the direction the shots came from and raises his left arm. A loud bang and a puff of steam erupts from under the hand. The intruder's chest explodes from the impact of the large caliber cannon round. Jack turns back to William and Zarra. "You two, stay in cover." He turns, carrying away a still screaming man by his broken arm. "This is my house. I'm the one they need to deal with." The heavy clanking of the metal feet echoes across the courtyard, punctuated by rifle and pistol fire.

William grabs Zarra. "Now I know where Crystal gets this from."

"Gets what?"

He takes her into another part of the house that's easier to defend. "The need to instill as much terror into her enemies as possible to break them. Her father is operating the exact same way." He turns to Zarra. "I'm glad he's on our side because, if not, I think I would have loaded my pants and died of fright."

244

"I think it's those blades protruding from his arm that are the real threat."

They are interrupted by Jack's booming voice, magically enhanced to be heard clearly. "This is my House. Come out and surrender, and you will be arrested and taken to jail. If you fight." He holds the other man a full four feet off the ground by his broken bleeding arm, screaming. "This is what's in store for you." He drops the man to the lawn and places a heavy metal boot on the man's back. Zarra and William shutter hearing the bones snap under Jack's weight.

Zarra and William exchange glances. "Stay here." He runs over and grabs the guy lying on the floor. "Look, I don't fully grasp why you and your people are here, but I know you heard things that aren't true. I don't want to hurt you, but someone convinced you to attack me and my friends and family."

"It's because you're evil. That out there is the *very* epitome of evil."

"That epitome of evil out there is protecting his home, just as you would if someone attacked yours. He builds farm equipment, transportation vehicles, and other life-changing items to make everything better."

"He also makes weapons of war."

"So do tens of thousands of other people in this world. At least he uses his intellect to help the common man more than hurt them." William drags him to his feet. "But this can't be because he designed a few suits of armor and a few weapon designs." William hauls him off his feet. "I know you heard things. I've talked to others with the Black Rose. The best way to get someone attacked is to make them sound like it's a good idea to attack them."

Zarra walks up and pulls William's arm down to put the man back on his feet. "My people used the same tactic thousands of years ago to demonize the Tree Elves." Zarra sighs. "We were told by our government that they were evil, when in fact, it turned out it was us. We just didn't see it."

"What does that have to do with me?" They look out and see the other members of his team surrender, throwing down their weapons.

"Because when you spend your whole life being told lies about the enemy, it's hard to see the truth. It took a wise man to show us, the Dark Elves and the Tree Elves, that we were both wrong. That just because we are different doesn't also mean we aren't the same. We both had the same goals, the same wants and needs, the same drive, but our ways of doing them were different."

She looks at the man with her ruby red eyes. "We almost destroyed ourselves because of a difference of ideas instead of compromising and accepting them." She steps back. "We were lied to about them and they were lied too about us. Instead of sitting down like civilized people, we just accepted it and let it fuel a war that should have never been."

"How do we know what you say is true?"

"You can't." William lets him go and steps away. "But at some point, the fighting must stop."

"It will stop when you're dead and the Demon Emperor is overthrown." He pulls a dagger and launches himself at William, but Zarra is faster, striking him down before he makes it two steps.

She sighs, letting her weapon drop to her side. "People can't be saved when they refuse to open their minds to other possibilities."

William places a hand on Zarra's shoulder, and she feels the warm comfort of the large man. "You stay hidden. I'll go talk to dad."

"But I can help…"

He silences her with a shake of his head and points to her nightgown. "Not looking like that." He looks outside and watches the guards taking the men into custody, and Crystal glides across the yard and stands next to the metal behemoth. William walks up moments later. "How did you know?"

"I worry about the people in this manor and had a special alarm set. If a guard doesn't pass certain points on his patrol at certain times, the alarm goes off. As soon as one wasn't reset, I knew immediately that something was wrong." He turns to them and waves them off. "You two go back to bed. I'll double the guard and have these people taken to the station for questioning."

"Thanks Daddy." Crystal takes William's arm and walks back into their home.

CHAPTER 23

(In the air again)

Early morning comes and Penelope gets out of bed. *Going to be a different morning. For once, I'm not cooking breakfast.* She walks to her dresser and pulls out her clothes and tosses them on the bed. She changes from her nightgown and hides her weapons up sleeves and in unusual places, including one in her hair as an ornament. Exiting the manor, she gets on her riding dog, and takes to the streets.

She rides through town, and it's mostly quiet. The sun hasn't crested the mountains, and the stars are still out, but the smell of many different breakfasts is in the air. She arrives at the hotel and walks past the security unnoticed. Climbing three flights of stairs, she knocks on his door and waits. *Why isn't he answering?* She knocks again and when he fails a second time; she sighs. *He's probably asleep.*

She pulls out her lock picks and starts on the door. It doesn't take long when the lock gives and she can enter. She closes the door behind her and finds him snoring away. *I better make sure there isn't something bad waiting for me. Better look around first.* She checks under the bed and in the closet, and less obvious places and breathes some relief. *All clear. Good.* She calls up to him, trying to be loud enough to be heard, but not disturb others in other rooms, but he doesn't wake. *This guy can sleep through a stampede.* Using the blanket as a handhold, she pulls herself up onto the bed.

She looks down at him as he lays there asleep in his shorts. *He's cute, too bad he's Human. I might have let myself get attached to him.*

She reaches down and grabs his shoulder and shakes it, causing him to react. He opens his eyes and sees her standing there over him and fear rips through his body, jerking him awake, flinching to the head of the bed. He gasps a few times and looks and can see it's Penelope. "You just about gave me a heart attack."

"I need you up. We are leaving early for Portstown and then onward to New Haven. So, if you want to get home, you need to get dressed."

"How long do I have?"

"We must be at the palace by eight. If you're going to get breakfast, you need to make it fast.".

He gives her a childish grin and her heart jumps a little upon seeing it. "We could have breakfast here before we leave. Just us and we can talk before we go."

What was that? Is he asking me on a breakfast date? She smiles back at him. "I guess so. Let's head down and get something, then."

"Or we could order something and have it brought up here?"

Her heart skips again. "I don't think that's a good idea." She's turns to jump down, but he reaches out and takes her arm. She spins in reaction to his touch, and he pulls her down with little effort. Their lips connect and her first reaction isn't anger. *His lips are so soft, and his stubble feels weird on my face.* Her heart pounds. *Why aren't I breaking away? Why did I let him pull me down so easily? I'm a trained assassin. I can easily get away.* She presses harder against him as her body overrides her mind. *He's Human. I've tried this before and it didn't work out.* They both inhale hard. *But it's been so long since a man shown interest in me. What if this is genuine?* His hands encircle her face, brushing along her long ears causes her to feel something she hadn't in a long time. She wraps her hands around his neck and face. *No, this is wrong. It's not possible.* She pushes him back as far as her tiny arms can and breathes heavily. "I…I can't do this."

"Why?"

"I told you why." She looks away, unable to look him in the eyes. "Even if I had feelings for you, which I don't, we are incompatible and you're twice my size. I came here to get you ready to go home, not to fraternize." She continues to breathe hard, trying to get composed.

He sighs disappointedly. "You can't blame me for trying."

She hopes down, her heart still beating in her long ears. "Get dressed, and let's go have breakfast before you miss your ride home."

"You're cute when your ears turn pink." She stops but a moment and then continues out the door.

Tia wakes up in Crystal's soft bed. She stretches and sits up, letting her long blond hair flow down her sides. *This is the most comfortable place I've ever slept. I really don't want to get up, but the day calls to me.* She stands up and walks to Crystal's old bureau and looks at herself in the mirror. The white nightgown Crystal bought her is sheer, and she turns pink from the image greeting her back. *This thing leaves little to the imagination, but it's for sleeping comfort, I suppose.* She sets up her altar and prays. Not long after, a knock at the door startles her. She opens the door and her heart flutters. "Andrew? I… I was doing my morning prayers. Would you like to join me?" He looks her over, causing her to swallow. *Oh Daniel, I'm exposed like this.*

He smiles. "Yeah, I would." He leans in and gives her a kiss. Her mind races and pulls him in, and he closes the door with his foot. An hour later, Crystal walks up to Andrew's room and knocks on the door.

After several minutes, she gets a scowl on her face. *It's not like him to sleep late like this.* She knocks again and doesn't get an answer. *Hope he's ok. After last night, I need to be sure.* She cracks the door and does a quick look, noting he's not inside. *You sly dog.* Her impish grin appears as she shuts the door. *And you're supposed to be the good one?* She stifles a laugh and walks over to her old room and places her ear against the door. *Sounds like they are talking. I better knock.* She raps on the door and the voices stop. She can hear them scrambling inside that causes her to giggle. Tia answers the door in her traditional robes, but her face is flushed. *I know that look. What was happening in here?*

"Crystal!" She pulls on her robe and looks around frantically. "Is dinner ready?"

Crystal smiles so big her fangs show, and Tia's face reddens more. "You mean breakfast?"

Tia laughs nervously, trying to smile. "Yeah, I mean breakfast. You're right."

"You ok? You seem a bit..." The grin grows. "Nervous? Can I come in? It is my room, after all."

"Yes, of course." Tia steps out of the way. She looks over the room and observes Andrew kneeling on the floor and putting up an altar.

"Good morning, sis." He stands. "You sleep well? You look tired." He walks over and gives her a hug.

She looks up at him with a sly smile, seeing his dark tan skin redder than it should be. "Doing some... praying?"

He glances at Tia and back down at his sister. "Yep. Figured I could spend some quality time with my girl and do our morning prayers at the same time. I have too, since I don't get as much quality time with her as you do with William."

Crystal tilts her head and looks up at him slyly. "We can fix that."

"How?" Tia and Andrew say in unison, then she blushes even more so.

"Come with us on the *Bastion*. We are going to be eight days in route, and you can check up on the church in Portstown. Should be there for about a week before we leave for New Haven. That will give you two full weeks of being in Tia's presence." She casts her gaze at Tia. "And then he can take you on a proper date."

"What would dad think?"

"He trusts you more than he does me." Crystal smiles at Tia with a partial shrug. "But we all have our faults."

"What do you mean?" She turns and looks back at him and gives him a look that she knows more than him.

She fixes his collar. "Let's get you packed up, Andrew. I'll make sure you get a room with Tom and have Tyra moved in with Tia with Shadow. Zarra is using William's old room." She walks to the door and places a hand on the doorjamb, turning her head to look at them askance. "Unless you want to be placed in the same room together?"

Tia and Andrew exchange glances and Andrew sighs. "No, sharing a room with Tom is fine. I highly doubt I could keep myself honest if we shared a room."

She lets her hand drop and looks away. "I'll make the arrangements. Let's get some food."

They get breakfast and pack the car. Crystal grabs all of her tomes, including the two god books to take with her. They say their goodbye's and they head to the Palace. The sun's rays filter through the dome, casting a prismatic rainbow effect on the city below. Sounds of horses and steam vehicles putting around fill the air along with the smells of thousands of different dishes being prepared.

They arrive at the Palace and unload with the help of the ground crew. Penelope arrives on her riding dog with Chuck walking beside her. "I see the new couple finally made it."

Chuck looks down at Penelope. "See, she's see's it."

Penelope glowers. "No, she's teasing me because it gets a rise out of me and she thinks it's funny."

"Are you sure?"

"I'm sure." She dismounts, and an attendant takes the dog to the stables.

Walking out back, she hands her stuff off to the ground crew, then gets the captain's attention. "I have to go inside for a moment and speak to the Emperor, but be ready for lift off when I come out."

She enters the palace, looking as regal as possible with a royal purple dress with matching make up. Her scepter in her hands and extra jewelry to pull it off makes her look as if she was a member of the royal family. She enters the throne room and Marcus is standing in there with two of his wives and some others that look like officials. Crystal notes one is Skylar, and the other is an Oriental woman from Shesoa she's unfamiliar with.

Marcus waves her over. "Ah, countess, enter, please. You look stunning today. What's the occasion?"

"We are preparing to depart, but I was hoping to have a word with you in private about a few things real fast, if that would be alright?"

"Of course." He looks at his wives. "Excuse us, my beauties, we will be in my office."

She walks in with him, and he closes the door. He motions for her to sit and takes his place behind his desk. "What's on your mind?"

"A few things I need to ask you, but none of them are mission critical. I don't know if you will even bother answering."

"I'm glad you've gotten this comfortable around me. It's been so long since anyone has treated me as a friend and been so casual." He leans forward on his elbows, clasping his hands together. "What's on your mind?"

She returns his smile. "What's the deal with Zarra? She arrived at my home with that deed to the ship, and thank you for that. I love it." She looks down. "But why is she skipping out on her people? Is she in trouble?"

"Yes, and no. I'm not completely sure, but I think she's afraid of something back in her kingdom. She wouldn't tell me, but she wasn't lying when she wanted to be part of something bigger and wanted to help." He reaches over and pulls her chin up to look at him, and their eyes meet. "But only *she* knows why she's running."

Crystal swallows, and her hands tense. "Are we going to get in trouble harboring her here or, by extension, am I going to get into trouble taking her with me? I don't want to jeopardize the Empire for a runaway princess."

"No, we aren't, and no, you won't. As far as the treaty goes with them, she has the full reign of our empire and can do as she pleases if she follows the law. She's not running from us and has broken no laws. She can do as she pleases."

Crystal lets out a long breath. Marcus suspects she was holding onto for some time, and her shoulders slump a little. "Last thing before I go. A few days ago, while I was here with Tia, you mentioned a war between the gods, and the surviving gods had to pick up the slack for those who were lost."

He does his best to suppress a grin, but she notices a slight crack. "Yes, what about it?"

"I was doing some looking and found some tomes that mentioned the war in the heavens that have some secret pages and a book that mentions shards of divinity. Do you know anything about them?" The neutrality of his face caves and the grin forms. *I knew there was more to this, and he has the answers.*

He leans back, looks away for a fraction of a second and back. Waging one finger at her, he gets into it. "All I can tell you about that you're delving into something that few know about, and even fewer can comprehend." He leans down, and he gets quieter so only she can hear. "I know you and Tia are solving a mystery about Daniel, but you've stumbled into something larger than yourselves. Take care with what you find." He stands up and motions for her to do so. His tone changes from secretive to mirthful in an instant. "Now you need to get your ship. I'll give your father the specs to build your own landing site at your manor, so when you return, you can land there instead of here. No need to have you tracing steps through my palace every time you want to joy ride."

She turns to leave; him following her out. "About that. Am I going to need to replace the crew since they are your soldiers?"

"For now, no, but I will contact your father to have some of his people trained to replace them, but for official ops, my military will run the ship."

"Thank you, Your Highness. You might want to increase your own security as well. Last night, we were attacked again by the Black Rose, and if they are getting past our security, it won't be long before they figure yours out, too. We can't lose you."

He nods. "I saw the report as it came in this morning, and it is disturbing. My security is way beyond anyone else, so I'm very safe." He walks her out past his wives and onto the airfield. She steps onto the ramp and turns around as to speak, but he beats her to it. "When you get back, we will talk more. Bring peace to the empire and make new friends." She waves and walks up the ramp as the mooring lines are tossed aside as the door closes.

Marcus returns to the throne room, and Skylar stands there alone. He grins at her. "She's picking it up fast."

Skylar wraps her arms around the large man. "How soon do you think till she joins the family?"

"Hard to say. Her power grows by the day and with it seeping outwards more and more, soon she will have to realize it herself, or there will be a need for intervention."

She walks up to her room and along the way, and finds William and Zarra talking in the hallway. William takes her into his arms. "What kept you?"

Crystal glances at Zarra. "I had to be sure that our special guest was clear to go with us." She gazes back into William's eyes. "I just wanted to be sure that we weren't going to be chased by her people, our people, and dealing with the Black Rose."

Zarra wipes her hands on her pants. "And what did you find out?"

Crystal shifts to look at her. "The Emperor told me that as far as he's concerned by the treaty, you can do what you want and he's not actively keeping track of you. No one knows you left with us except a few ground crew. You're free."

Zarra smiles and reaches out and gives Crystal a big hug. Crystal wraps her arms around her as well. "Thank you."

She notices William grinning and they break their embrace. Crystal holds her at arm's length, looking over her busted armor. "Bring your armor by and I can fix that. Can't have you in damaged armor trying to protect me, can we?"

Zarra looks down and pales a little. "I'll bring it over right away." She walks into her room and Crystal looks at William once they have privacy.

"What's with that goofy smirk you had?"

"You seem to have this attraction to huggers."

She can't hide her own smile. "Some are better than others, I suppose." She pats him on the side. "Let's get settled in so I can do some heavy reading."

A few days past, Crystal, Tia, Zarra and Tyra, with Tom's help, practice some martial arts. They tried to get Penelope and William in on it, but they showed no actual interest. Crystal catches Penelope hanging around Chuck more often, teaching him some things he can use once they get to New Haven. When she's not doing that, William is giving him some basics in combat. With all the troops on board and extra combat suits for the coming conflict, everyone needs to be ready.

Tia, Zarra, and Crystal are all sweating heavily and breathing hard, performing their moves in their wushu's. Tom had the foresight to grab a few extras before they left the Monastery so Tia could have one. "I've been looking through those books you two found and I think I'm making some headway." Crystal breathes heavily, going through the motions.

"Really?" Tia wheezes, trying to keep up. "What have you found out so far?"

"The war in the heavens left several gods dead, as Marcus told us. That's why there are so few churches these days. In the end, the god of destruction was killed, but not long after, a new god took his place called Xavral the destroyer. God of destruction, torment, and death. The old god that held those powers seamed to of vanished. Even his name was lost to his old followers."

"That is interesting, but what does that have to do with me, Andrew, and Daniel?"

They continue to go through their motions, with Tom correcting their movements, but not butting in on their conversation. "As it happens, gods have their own divine tools they use to enhance their powers. The old god of Destruction used a sword, with a black flame, and turned everything to ash that he touched with it. This Xavral has the very same sword. It's

257

reasonable to believe if a god was using a tool designed for a different god's power, it could be misused."

Zarra picks up where the thoughts are going. "What you're saying is that Daniel's message is to fix the problem with his church; there has to be a new god of love before he can pass this torch thing?".

Crystal huffs. "Basically, he's not supposed to be the god of Love, but is doing his best to fill in till a new one arises. This might be what's wrong with the world. According to the book, the gods of Love, Evil, Magic, Destruction, Gnomes, Travel, Nature and War were killed in the exchange." She breathes deeply, to formulate her words. "It's wrote that Morgana, the goddess of assassins and manipulation, helped Provider put things back together. With her help, he maneuvered those who could be worthy to prove themselves." They turn together and she continues. "And roughly seventy years ago, a new god, the God of War and technology Mechas, came into being along with a New Goddess of Nature and Agriculture, Vetrix. This is also when Xavral appeared."

Tia and Zarra nod, following along, but Tia presses more questions. "What you're saying is to get to be with Andrew; I need to figure out how to create a new god of Love?" She inhales deeply, letting it out slowly. "Why didn't you say so? Should be easy." She doesn't even try to hide the sarcasm in her tone, getting a quick chuckle from Zarra.

Crystal continues unabated. "In the second book, it talks about these shards of divinity. They are created when a god dies. The power in their body turns into a shard of divine power and falls to Delveon, waiting for someone worthy to come along and take up the mantle."

"It can't be that easy." Tia tells her. "Just pick it up and you have their power?"

Crystal shakes her head. "That didn't make sense to me either, so there is context missing, or the information I need is in the hidden passages I can't unlock. Until I gain access to those

258

hidden passages, our search for a new god of Love is going to be difficult. Olovira didn't tell me, nor leave any clues on the password to gain that information, so it might be impossible."

Zarra sweeps her arm down to the floor and up again. "Does your book tell you where these shards are?"

"Not really, but if the shard drops where they died, when it's just gathering information on where a god had supposedly died. Also, there must be other ways to create shards, because where did they come from before the gods?" She shakes her head. "Thinking like that can give someone a migraine."

"The chicken or the egg paradox." Tom holds his hand up. "Let's take a break for tea. I believe it's Zarra's turn today to make it for you three." The three of them collapse to the ground.

Tia lies on her back, chest heaving. "Why do you never have tea with us, Master Ryuu?"

"Because the tea set Master Monzulo gave Crystal only contains three cups, and I'm not a big tea drinker." They exchange glances. "The tea is to see how your training is coming along." He points to them. "And you three are the best to judge where your peers stand. If their balance isn't right, you can tell in the flavor."

CHAPTER 24

(No Town like Portstown)

Eight days have passed since they left Rose Harbor, and Portstown can be seen on the horizon. The captain announces they will land soon. Crystal reflects on the days past, staring out her window. *William and Zarra love to spar. Watching them move is like watching a lethal dance. She can bend and flex in ways I didn't think were possible, and William's overwhelming size gives him reach. Something she isn't used to. Those two are quite the armored pair.* She glances at the tea set, her thumb bouncing on her tome. *And Tom has been keeping us all busy, not to mention Tia and Andrew have never been happier.* She watches the white buildings of Portstown get closer. *Just wonder what's going on with Shadow and Chuck. For her to keep denying she's interested, she finds excuses to train him in something. I think I need to investigate her for once.* She stands, closing her book, and tossing it to the bed. *Time to get dressed for my appearance.*

She walks down the boarding ramp, William hanging on her arm, looking regal in the royal purple dress she wore a week earlier at the Palace. The morning dawn casts long shadows, and the air is cool, but not freezing. *It feels odd wearing the same thing twice, but I rather like this dress.*

Baron Tenishar glides to the landing site at the embassy, followed by Captain Motsana and his guards. He bears his fangs and extends a hand. "Countess, welcome back. I hope you had a pleasant trip."

"I did, Baron Tenishar. As soon as we heard about the Black Rose making a second attempt, we brought troops, weapons, and supplies as per the treaty. We make good on our promises."

He points to her scepter. "I see you have a new accessory."

"Yes, my mother made it for me for my birthday last week. She thinks being a countess means I should have something regal looking that could double as a weapon if I get into trouble again."

William bows. "I'm going to see to getting the troops and supplies to the Baron's fortress so they can prepare. Plus, I'm going to have security around here increased for our own benefit."

She waves her hand dismissively, trying to keep things formal. "Thank you, Captain." She takes her place next to the Baron as they walk away from the ship towards the embassy's door.

The rest of Crystal's companions disembark and the Baron points to the emerald knight. "You have another body guard?" He leans down. "Can't take too many precautions in these uncertain times, I suppose."

"Yeah, she's something like that." Crystal walks in step with him. *I wish I could brag that a princess is with me, but she's been very adamant about being unknown, and I can't say I blame her. I like her too much to expose her like that.* Crystal gives a subtle nod. "She's been training with William and she's already great with a sword. She's amazing, talented, and honorable." Crystal can't hide her smile thinking about it.

"You can never have too many good people around you." He motions back to the ship. "What have you brought for us?"

"In a day or so, another ship will arrive with more troops, as this isn't a cargo vessel, but a frigate. We brought two hundred troops and another ten power suits. They will be assembled today, even if it takes all night." She looks up at the Baron. "The real question is, do the Black Rose know about these steam powered armors? If so, they might just try to cut you off from your fields." She gives him a quizzical look. "Are there any reports of New Haven navy ships headed this way? Would be evidence if they are working together."

"None of our vessels reported any New Haven ships in our waters, but that doesn't mean they aren't preparing to attack. The ground assault might pull personnel away from the coast, giving them a numerical advantage to send in ships. As a precaution, I'm keeping scouts posted out there as early warning signals."

"That's a great idea. I take it this isn't the first time something like this has happened?"

He shakes his head. "And won't be the last. It's a 'wait and see' kind of game." He looks down at her. "And our scouts in the field report that the Black Rose army isn't too far off. They are pulling multiple cannons with them, so they should be here in a few days instead of weeks. I'm afraid you're going to have to leave tomorrow to get ahead of them instead."

She sighs, accepting the new information. "Why would they assemble an army to assault your town? I get it, they have the numbers, but why Portstown?"

"We did snub them, take your offer, and joined their perceived enemy." He lets off a deep laugh.

She holds her hand out and makes a crushing motion. "Guess so, and we will show them why you don't mess with Rose Harbor and its allies." They stop and look at the work that's being done. Zarra and William are pointing at paperwork and start assigning troops to wagons. Penelope brings Chuck down the ramp and says something to him, keeping his attention on her, and Tia and Andrew exit next and she points things out to him. Tia looks excited and takes Andrew's hand and leads him to the stables to pick out a horse.

Baron sounds confused. "I see your Priestess, has a boyfriend. Is that allowed in their faith?"

"I think so. According to the texts, there might have been a misinterpretation of how they are to conduct themselves, so the church is letting them date. If Daniel gets angry, he will strip them of their divine powers. If not, then they will start a happy life together while still worshiping him."

"Dangerous gamble when facing blasphemy."

"Could be. At worse they get kicked from the church and they will start their own family and still be happy, I think." She tilts her head, looking at the large Catfolk. "What wouldn't you do for the one you love?"

He stands there watching the troops get into formation and seeing William pat Zarra on the back as they move out. "Almost nothing. I would face down an army if I had to." He places a large paw on her shoulder. "I'll let you get back to your duties, countess. I will take my leave. Glad to have you here."

He takes a dozen steps, and she calls out to him. "Baron?".

He faces her. "Yes, countess?"

"Does your library have a significant history section?"

"I suppose so. Why?"

"I want to learn about your people's history while I have a chance."

"I'll have directions drawn up." He points at her before resuming. "As long as you make it to dinner tonight in you and your friends' honor."

"Wouldn't miss it for anything."

Penelope gets Chuck from his room that he's been sharing with the other soldiers. He looks happy but distant. "Everything alright?"

"Yeah, just glad to be so close to home. Once you guys drop me off, I won't ever see you again, will I?"

"Don't say that. Who knows what the future has in store for us? Me and William have taught you a few things that will help you and who knows, maybe you will be a big name someday. I'll be able to look back and say, 'that guy had a crush on me when he was just a kid'."

"You keep calling me kid. How old are you?"

"You know it's not proper to ask a woman her age, right?"

"Yeah, but I'm not proper, am I?"

"Twenty-nine."

"You look no older than twenty."

"Thanks." She blushes and can't hide it. Even her ears turn pink. "Let's get you a room inside the embassy and out of the way. I'm sure the Baron will want to have Crystal and the rest of as guests for dinner, but I'll have something prepped for you before we go." He gathers his few things and follows her out.

"Thank you for what you've done for me. I feel real dumb believing the Black Rose that you are all evil." He follows her down the ramp. They can see Crystal talking to the Baron and they head towards the embassy doors.

"Misinformation is one of the best weapons anyone can use. Getting people to believe what you want instead of the truth is how many conflicts start." She looks up at the young man. "You aren't the only one fooled by it, and you won't be the last. Even the wisest of people can be led to believe something false, if it's put together well. All we can do is to be open to new ideas that could dispel the lie and expose the truth."

"Sounds like you've had a lot of experience in that field."

"I was a thief, remember? I lied to survive and got good at it. I'm just glad I got a second chance in life to correct my mistakes. You have a chance at a good life before you made life ending mistakes you will regret later." Crossing the courtyard, they make their way inside and up some stairs, and she reaches a room and opens it for him.

He walks in and she stands at the entrance. He places his stuff down and turns to her. "You can come in, if you want."

She shakes her head. "I have other duties to perform." *I've gotten so good at lying I can almost convince myself they are the truth. He's a good man and I know if I walk in there, I might just make a decision I'll regret.* She points down the hallway. "There is a bathhouse downstairs, and a recreational area. You can ask any of the service maids here for directions."

William and Zarra are fully armored and look as professional as possible. They go over the manifest, making sure everything that went on is coming off. Zarra is careful not to reveal who she is in such a foreign land. *I've never seen people like this and don't know how they will react to my presence. In fact, I don't know how to react to them.*

She surveys the area slowly to not bring attention to herself. *They are a people of carnivores with razor-sharp claws. Why they need weapons on top of them is beyond me, but Crystal walks among them as if she belongs, and they treat her with reverence.* She looks upon Crystal and her beauty, showing a grace that she's worthy of the royal treatment she gets. *Why can't I find someone like her or William instead of being on the run from my empire?* She shakes her head, clearing her mind. *If I stay away, I can't be used as a political tool. I refuse to accept that as my fate.*

William interrupts her train of thought. "You ok?"

"Sorry what?" She glances up at him.

"I asked you if you are going to be joining us for a banquet tonight. I'm sure either Crystal or Baron Tenishar is going to throw one before we take off for mountains near New Haven."

"Yeah, I'll have to do some dress shopping. I don't want to keep wearing Crystal's clothes."

He puts his hand down on the paperwork. "How about you and Crystal go with Tia and Andrew out on the town, do some shopping and a little site seeing and be back here at sundown for dinner?"

"You're not coming along to protect her?"

His chuckle echoes from within his helm. "I trust you with her life. I know we've only known each other a few weeks, but you've proven to be as capable a fighter as myself."

He places his large hand on her shoulder. *I'm so glad he can't see me blushing.*

"And I respect Johnathan for his choice in paladins. With you here, I can perform my other duties and not worry about her. She's safe in your hands."

"Thank you, William. It means a lot coming from you."

"Be on your way. Although you might want to change into something less formal if you're going to be trying on dresses. Putting that armor on, taking it off repeatedly will become tiresome."

She drops her tone to barely a whisper. "What about me being a Dark Elf? How will they react?"

"If you're in Crystal's presence as one of hers, these people will treat you very well. They think of her as their own family, and us by extension." Zarra nods and heads back into the ship.

266

Crystal casually strolls over to behind William with the baron gone. She reaches up and covers his eyes, giving him a start. He looks down and sees her ivory white arms contrasting lightly against the red of his armor and smiles. "What can I help you with, honey?"

"Where did Zarra run off to? You two looked pretty friendly there for a moment and she fled."

"She went to get changed. Figured you two would like to do some dress shopping real fast before whatever dinner is planned tonight."

"You know me so well." She spins him around and removes his helm, seeing his sweaty face. Then holds it with one hand and pulls him down with the other, kissing him passionately for all to see. He wraps his massive arms around her and he slowly dances with her with music only they can hear. She then informs him of the change in plans, with the Black Rose army being closer than expected.

Tom and Tyra descend the ramp. Tom smiles at Crystal and William dancing. "She's getting closer to finding herself again."

"Do you think it's from the training you've been having them do?" Tyra casually carries their stuff across the courtyard.

"It's helping. Master Monzulo was onto something, having them practice our ways a bit. She needed to take her mind off the pain and fear that they put her through. By having her meditate and focus on something else, her soul is recovering."

Tyra watches as Zarra goes by and waits till she's out of earshot. "What do you think of Zarra?"

"I think the training is helping her, too. I felt a lot of inner turmoil fading. Zarra and Crystal make a hell of a pair, if you ask me. She's as passionate and determined as Crystal, but she applies it differently. She's in good company with us." They walk up the stairs and spots Penelope leaving in a hurry down the

267

other steps. "Now her, she's got some internal issues she's working through."

"How so Master Ryuu?"

"She's trained to be a living weapon but is noticing she still has feelings and doesn't know what to do with them." They walk into their old room and toss their stuff down with a plop.

"Think we could help her?"

He shakes his head negatively. "No, she's on her own on this one. I think even asking her if she wanted help would bring a confrontation. It's best to let her figure out her path before offering guidance."

Tyra places a hand on Tom's head and gets serious. "Since you've been granted the rank of master, you've changed. You seem more responsible."

He tugs at his new black wushu. "That's because of the circumstance of me being granted that status. I don't feel I deserve it, but now that it's been thrust upon me, I must fill those shoes." He looks up at Tyra with a boyish grin. "But don't think I'm still not my quirky self. I just understand the burden I was given, doesn't mean I'm going to keep comments to myself."

"How do you think your makeshift Dojo is doing? It's been almost three weeks. Do you think they are still training or descended into chaos?"

Tom lets out a long sigh, letting his lips flap. "Guess the only way is to go and find out."

The two monks descend the stairs, the sounds of Tyra's hooves echoes along the walls letting everyone know they are coming and clear the way. "You sound like you're expecting the worse, Master Ryuu."

"Can you just call me Tom? We've been friends too long to be this formal."

268

"Oh, how the tables have turned." She claps him on the outer shoulder. "You, who've bucked authority, are now the authority, and don't want to be reminded of it."

"The irony isn't lost on me." As they get back to the courtyard, Tia is descending with Andrew, her in a new green dress, and him in a proper suit. "Looks like those two are finally getting to go on their date."

Tyra sounds more somber. "Think you will ever find someone, or will you end up like Master Monzulo?"

"That's the strange thing about destiny. You don't know where it's going to take you. Just enjoy the ride while getting there."

"Spoken like the man himself."

Tom hangs his head. "Only gone a week and I'm already sounding like him?"

This gets Tyra to laugh and is interrupted by Tom's stomach. "Dojo or food first?"

He smiles. "Can't train on an empty stomach, can we?" He watches Andrew and Tia move along. "But let's avoid going where Tia and Andrew are going, but not too far. We can be their secret bodyguards."

Tia and Andrew get into a small carriage provided by the Portstown officials. Tom and Tyra follow behind on foot at a distance, keeping watch.

CHAPTER 25

(Life Changing)

Crystal watches as Tia descends in her beautiful new green dress, with Andrew on her arm. The late morning sun striking it, making her look radiant as a newborn star. Somehow, she can feel Tia's and Andrews's connection as they smile at each other. William breaks into her thoughts. "They look really happy."

"More than you know. I don't think either thought they would find the other. To find someone who completes you is a rare event these days." She turns and looks at William. "I'm glad the Emperor stuck us together. I might have bounced from loser boyfriend to loser boyfriend. Even though the first few days I think I hated you." She's still swaying her hips, standing on his boots as they dance with no music.

He nods in agreement, looking deep into her eyes. "At first, you drove me nuts. I'll admit that much. You still do at times." Her jaw coming unhinged gets him to laugh. "But you grew on me. I can't imagine a life better than what we have now." William looks thoughtful. "It's like the Emperor knew we needed each other."

"How would the emperor know we needed each other? That's silly."

William tilts his head and gives a half shrug. Motion caught in the corner of both their eye's gets them both to spot

Zarra descending the ramp in royal blue commoner's shirt and pants. Her sword hanging at her side and a silver holy symbol hanging from her neck. "Looks like you and Zarra have some shopping to do. I need to get back to getting these war machines operational. Your father has a way of making war a scary thing. Glad he's on our side."

Crystal grins. "Mom doesn't like his war inventions. That's why he's put so much effort recent into agriculture and common goods." She steps off his feet. "Daddy thinks if war was so scary and brutal, that it would end. No one would want to go to war out of fear."

William laments. "Seeing him defend his home, it worked. They surrendered over facing the horror he was wearing."

She gazes at Zarra. Her obsidian black skin and red copper hair contrasts with the pristine white buildings around her, making her so beautiful to look at. *She's so innocent looking, but the blade at her side tells just how dangerous she really is.* She turns back to William and gives him a kiss goodbye. "I'll see you tonight for dinner. I'll get something we match in. Been wanting to change my looks a little."

"You're perfect the way you are."

"Is that before or after my transformation?"

"Uh both?"

"How do you mean, both?" She puts a hand on her hip and continues to interrogate putting him on the spot. "Either I was perfect before, or I was perfect after." She blinks at him.

He holds his hands up when Zarra walks up. "What are we doing today?"

"Oh, hey Zarra. All set to go shopping with Crystal?"

"Yep, I'm excited. Been a long time since I had done anything like this, and I'm glad I get to go with someone who's open about their opinion, and not just telling me what I want to hear."

Crystal smiles at Zarra, then shoots William a look that tells him he's off the hook for now. "Let's get going. It's almost lunchtime and I'm hungry." She turns to William. "You sure you don't want to come to lunch with two beautiful girls? Maybe get other guys *jealous*?" William blushes a little, but Crystal catches Zarra blushing, too. Her skin lightening up around her face gives it away. *That's interesting. Why would she be blushing over that comment? I need to examine this more too. So much to do while I'm here.*

"I have a lot of work to do, so you two have fun. Just stay out of trouble."

Crystal blows him a quick kiss, but looks at Zarra askance as she turns away, paling a bit more. *Am I missing something?* She grins and hooks Zarra's arm like she would his. "See you later, you hunk of a man you!" She turns to Zarra. "Let's get going on our date, shall we?"

The two of them walk in sync from weeks of training together, following each other's movements. With the light, sparing under Tom's tutelage, is taking their training farther than Master Monzulo had. She holds her left hand out in a slow waving motion. "I know this wonderful sea food place near here. They have so many ways to serve sea bass that you will swear you died and went to the Provider's Table." Zarra glances back at William as he bends and flexes, picking up large pieces of machine and carting it away.

Tia and Andrew ride in their carriage till they get to a restaurant she was telling Andrew about. He gets out first, then offers his hand to her, helping her down. She blushes heavily, having never been treated like this before. *I feel so exposed in this dress, but I want to make him happy.* He smiles at her and takes her arm, escorting her into the establishment. A light melody can be heard in the background, played by a band of bards as people eat for lunch. They get a seat near a window and a Male Sand Elf brings them a menu. "What would like to drink, ma'am?"

"I'll take some hot green tea, please."

He turns to Andrew. "And you, sir?"

"Tea sounds good, actually."

The Sand Elf bows. "I'll give you two a moment and will return shortly."

Andrew looks across the table at Tia, looking so seductively in her dress. He can't keep his eyes off of her as she reads the menu. He's always admired her from an arm's length, but now, he has a chance to get close to her. "So, you know this place. What's good?"

"Just about everything, so order what you would like. I'm going with the Murgh Makhani. They have a breading they use that's just to die for." He nods and looks over the menu.

The waiter returns with two cups of hot green tea and sets them down. Pulling out a small parchment, he addresses her first again. "Have you figured out what you wanted?"

"I want the Murgh Makhani, with a salad, and some calamari."

He turns to Andrew. "I'll have the Rogan Josh, with the salad and small Malai Kofta. I hope I'm pronouncing that right. Thanks."

They hand over the menus and the waiter bows. "Excellent choices."

She smiles as he reaches across the table and takes her hand. "I won't lie. Part of me is scared that Daniel will disapprove." He looks deep into her green eyes. "But I wouldn't trade you for the world."

She turns a light pink. "I love you and Daniel. I really hope I'm right too. It's because of him I met you." She leans

273

forward. "Am I wrong for already picturing our lives together forever?"

"I don't think so. I've caught myself thinking about it too." She stands up and leans over the table, prompting him to follow suit and they kiss.

Tom and Tyra set up at a smaller dinner and watch the new love birds from afar. He orders some pan-seared salmon with some white sauce and Tyra goes for the salmon and honey pecan sauce. Biting into his, he moans with pleasure as the flavors saturate his taste buds "This place will never get old with me" He leans back, patting his belly. "If I don't watch myself, my sea of chi will become an ocean."

Tyra nods, monitoring Tia and Andrew. "Do you think Crystal was out of line challenging their church like that just to get those two hooked up?"

Tom shrugs, taking another bite. "Nothing changes if you don't challenge the status quo." He swallows and grabs his glass of water. "She's really gung-ho when it comes to the matter of the heart. It's like she enjoys being a matchmaker."

"Any idea why she went from raising the dead to mending the heart? I would think that's a major swing."

"If you recall, Master Monzulo told her and William to pursue happiness and love long before then. After his resurrection, she was all loving on him. She didn't go dark till she was almost tortured to death." Tom looks at Tyra. "She's just taking her natural want to love to the next step and wants others to love too. She's healing, and she wants the world to heal with her."

Tyra nods. "I don't know. It seems overzealous." Tyra points a fork at Tom. "Think she will ever get rid of her emotional scars?" She takes another bite. "I see it in her eyes from time to time, the anger, the hate, the rage caged inside looking for a way to escape."

274

Tom thinks about between bites. "That's why she must do this training. Tia and Zarra are having huge effects of keeping that cage locked." He put his fork down and clasps his hands. "But I noticed Zarra has her evil caged very well, but it was on the edge of getting loose till Crystal came into her life. It's like they need each other to shore up the other's defenses."

Tyra looks up and can see Crystal and Zarra walking in and to their table. "Hey, you two having lunch too?"

Tom motions to the chairs. "Yes. Are you wanting to join us or looking to eat together alone?"

Crystal steals a breadstick. "We were going to eat on our own and talk about girl stuff. We can join you if you don't mind, however."

I think she wasn't expecting to see us here. How interesting. He shakes his head slightly. "No, you go ahead. Me and Tyra were talking about other things and need to get to the Dojo, just to see if it's still there."

Crystal continues to smile. "Ok Tom. You two enjoy yourselves." She takes a bite of the breadstick, spins, and finds another table. Tom looks to Zarra and can see she's happy just letting Crystal be the center of attention. *Everyone is staring at Crystal. I know she's something of a celebrity, but this is almost creepy. At least she's happier than she has been in a long time.*

"Tom!"

"Huh?"

"I was talking to you, but you're staring at them like everyone else. What's wrong?"

"I was just thinking about how happy she is. The day she tried to kill herself was a low point just ten months ago, and now she's laughing and smiling like it didn't happen." He looks at Tyra. "As far as everyone else, I don't have a clue. Maybe because they look like monochrome opposites and the most unique and beautiful women in the city?"

Tyra looks at him. "And I'm not unique and beautiful?"

"All things are." He then stuffs more food into his mouth. Tyra raises an eyebrow.

Crystal sits opposite Zarra as a female Catfolk waitress walks up with some water, then her eyes widen in surprise. She speaks in felinese. "The Sky Lady?!" Crystal looks to her and then to Zarra, who shrugs, not knowing what is going on.

Crystal responds in felinese, cutting Zarra out of the conversation. "I'm sorry? What did you call me?"

"I'm sorry." She fumbles with the menus. "It's just an honor to have you eating here with us, Sky Lady. What can I get for you?"

"I would like to know why you're addressing me as 'Sky Lady'?"

"Sorry, I mean no disrespect. What would you like to order?"

"Strawberry juice to drink." She holds up the menu. "And I want the Portstown Shrimp Skillet, and a side of fried calamari." She hands the menu to the Catfolk.

She turns to Zarra. "And you, ma'am?" Crystal translates for Zarra and the waitress.

"Strawberry juice sounds good. I'll have the Ginger Halibut with the Brussel sprouts and some calamari myself."

"Right away." She nervously and quickly walks away.

Zarra cocks her head and overhand points to the retreating Catfolk. "What was that about?"

Crystal slowly shakes her head and eyes go wide. "She called me 'Sky Lady' for some reason and acted as if I was important." She locks eyes with Zarra's. "Well, I am important, but she acted like I was royalty or something, not just a countess."

"What's the phrase for 'Sky Lady' in their native tongue?" Zarra looks around, seeing Catfolk, Sand Elf, and others looking at them.

Crystal keeps her tone low. "Gagana Mahilā."

Zarra looks back at Crystal. "My hearing is great, and that's been uttered more than a few times around here." She leans in, speaking low. "Are you famous around here or something?".

"Well maybe. I spent eight months here, bringing Portstown into the empire, and helped defeat an army that tried to wreck the town. I preached that love, understanding, and unity would keep us strong." Crystal places her hand on her chest. "I had a huge ceremony and everything at the signing." Catfolk lady brings their drinks and sets them down nervously. "I can see why people would know me."

Tom also watches the gathering shift and hears the murmurs from where he's at. Tyra glances at him. "I know what you're thinking, but I smell no hostility from them" She scans the crowd. "More like, jubilation?"

"But why?"

Tyra shakes her head. "That's a mystery."

Crystal and Zarra talk a bit about recent events as their food arrives. She stabs a tentacle and points it at Zarra threateningly. "I want to truth about why you ran away from your home. I want to help you, but I can't if you don't tell me."

Zarra nods, taking a bite of her food. "I will. Just not here." She leans in close to keep her voice low. "It's personal and don't want it to be public knowledge. I was going to tell you when we were alone again sometime."

Penelope goes to her room and closes the door behind her. She takes her canary yellow dress out and hangs it up to be ready for tonight. She looks at it. *I wish I had more opportunities to dress up and look nice.* She looks away from it. *That's not my lot in life.* She mopes about her room. *It's boring not having anything to do. Guess I could go get Chuck. He would love to go out.* She shakes the idea from her head. *No, he will think it's a date and he will try to kiss me again.* She flops down on her bed. *How did I get here? The first guy to show an interest in me in nine years and he's the wrong size.* She closes her eyes hard. *I need to get my mind off him. I need to go do something.*

She gets up, checks her weapons, and leaves, walking out to the embassy. She notices that the only one still around is William and the ship crew. *Where did everyone go? Have I been lost in my own mind that everyone took off and I didn't even notice?* She huffs, her mind drifting back to him again. *Wish I would have never rescued him.* She walks to the ship. *No, that's wrong. It was the right thing to do, but sleeping next to him in that hole and then letting him kiss me in that hotel room has had me distracted for almost two weeks now. I'm going to get killed by not paying attention.*

She's so lost in introspection that William almost steps on her, stirring his ire. "HEY!" He looks down and his face softens. "Sorry Penelope."

"Sorry Captain." He can't help but sense the depression in her tone. "Is there anything I can do to help?" She looks up at him. "I need something to do; since I'm not the one cooking tonight, I'm just bored."

He smiles. "I know that feeling. That's why I'm working on these things rather than going with Crystal and Zarra dress shopping."

278

"I understand. I only had to go with her once dress shopping and I'll admit it was fun. Do you know what shop they went to?"

"Sorry, I don't." He hefts another large piece of machinery and walks down the ramp. "Find Tyra. She can find her anywhere on this planet."

"Yeah, that's true." Penelope smiles. "Any idea where she is?"

William puts the part down in the courtyard and brushes his hands off and looks around. "She's…" He scans the area. "Not around here. I thought for sure she was going to help me unload."

"So neither of us has a clue where the others are." It's a statement more than a question and he picks up on it.

"Looks that way." He walks back up the ramp, lifting what looks like a large mechanoid leg. "I thought you could track? Why not just run her down? She's probably eating somewhere since it's lunchtime." He places it with the other parts in the dirt.

"It's a start. Beats standing around here all day." She goes to leave and hears Chuck calling her from a distance. *Is he stalking me now?*

"Penelope!" He runs up to her and William. "Anything I can do to help you two?"

She goes to respond, but William beats her to it. "Yeah, she's looking for Crystal. Maybe you can help her, since you're taller and can look over the crowds."

Chuck agrees. "I can do that. It's not like she can hide. She's quite unique."

"And she has Zarra with her, so there is no way you can miss those two." William waves them on. "You two have fun, me the Dwarves and Gnomes here have our work cut out for us."

Chuck looks down at Penelope and holds out his hand as if she's supposed to take it. *I want to take it, but I just can't. I need to drive him off somehow.* She fakes a look of disgust. "uch." She walks past him. "Let's go find our wayward countess and princess."

He puts his hand back and follows along. William grins. *Crystal is right. It is fun to tease sometimes. I just hope she doesn't kill him.*

CHAPTER 26

(Divine Confusion)

Tia and Andrew finish their meal and decide to take a mid-day walk. They dismiss the carriage back to the embassy and head to the church instead. Along the way, they hold hands, laugh and are amazed at street performers. "This place is absolutely amazing. I can see why sis likes it here so much."

Tia grins, taking in the cool sea air. "I'm glad we got them as part of the Empire. I love it here too."

"Are you wanting to move here after all the conflict is over?"

"I don't know. I think Crystal will need me for some time. She's became a good friend and even got us together; I would hate to leave her behind."

"Guess we will have to see where Daniel leads us." They arrive at the Church of Daniel and can see a few new people.

They are greeted by a light tan skinned Female Sand Elf and bows her head. "Welcome to the Church of Daniel. How can I assist you?"

Tia smiles, remembering this convert. "I'm Tia, recognize me?"

The priestess looks her over and gasps. "Yes, I remember you." Her ears twitch and tilts her head. "Where are your robes?"

"It's hard to explain, but I'm on a date." She motions to Andrew.

"But your vow? I thought that meant you can't have relationships."

She presses her hands together. "Yea, we thought that too, but we spent some time going over the scrolls after I had a vision from Daniel that told us otherwise. Somewhere over the last few centuries, our teachings were misinterpreted." She motions for the convert to walk with them to the head priest. "In order to keep from tearing the church apart, we are running an experiment. If Daniel really wanted us to take that vow, then he would strip our powers away. If not, then we are on the right track for redemption."

They get to the back and walk into the head priest's chamber. The old graying Human looks up from his desk and recognizes Tia and Andrew immediately. "Welcome back to Portstown." He stands and notices that neither are dressed properly. "Did you leave the church?"

"No, Yaris." Andrew sits down and explains the whole experiment to him and Tia presents the artifact proving their claim to of been in contact with Daniel.

He ponders a moment. "I get that. I think it's blasphemy, but I can't fault you for your reasoning. So have either of you lost your gifts?"

"Not yet. Been almost two weeks since we started. I've had other visions since then telling me I'm on the right path, so I hope I fulfill my task and we can all be happier."

Yaris nods and sits back down. "A bit late for me, but I have no regrets. How long are you going to run this experiment before Lyndis lets everyone know the vows don't have to be honored?"

Tia and Andrew trade glances. "We don't know. She hasn't told us. Just that we are ok to date and be a couple. If Daniel is still happy with us after a few months, maybe?"

"Don't forget about us. We need to keep informed." They get up to leave, but he stops them with another question. "Have you heard of this new religion that's taking off around here?"

Tia and Andrew exchange confused glances and turn back to him. "No. What religion?"

Yaris shrugs. "It's not big, maybe a hundred people now, but they worship someone they call 'Sky Lady'. She's supposed to be a love deity. None of their 'clergy' have any divine magic yet, so I don't know what's perpetuating its expansion." He leans forward on his elbows and clasps his hands. "And now you come here and talk about Daniel passing this 'Torch of Love' off to someone soon. It can't be a coincidence."

Tia has a look of concern on her face as the term. "Sky Lady sounds familiar, but can't place it. What can you tell me of this 'Sky Lady'?"

"For a religion, it's not well organized. It's more of a superstition than anything else at this point. No holy writings, no holy symbol, no divine powers. All they seem to agree on is she's from the sky, and promotes love, unity, peace, and fertility." He rolls his hand over a few times. "You get the idea."

"Is there a description of what this *Sky Lady* is supposed to look like? Like we know, Daniel is a middle-aged tanned man with black hair and brown robes. Or Johnathan, a large knight wearing white and red armor wielding a glowing sword of Justice?"

The female Sand Elf speaks up. "The only physical description I heard of her is she's a pure white woman with blue eyes, black hair and embodies the very epitome of beauty."

Tia and Andrew's eyes both widen in shock and they realize they know someone who matches that description. They look at each other and speak at the same time. "Crystal?!"

Crystal and Zarra finish their meal and go to pay, but the Catfolk lady is refusing to take her money. "I'm not a freeloader.

Please take the money." Crystal shakes her head and looks at Zarra. "I can't believe I have to force someone to take money. What is going on?"

"That's ok." The girls hear a deep male voice from behind them. "It's on the house for such honored guests." Zarra looks up and Crystal turns and can see a large tiger-like Catfolk standing there.

"But I don't want to use my position to take advantage. You have overhead and servers to pay. I don't want the special treatment, please."

He smiles and accepts finally. "You're truly a wonderful person. Everything I've heard about you is most definitely true. Thank you for visiting my establishment. But I can't in good conscious, take your money." Crystal and Zarra get up and walk out, thanking him for his hospitality.

After they get outside and into the street, they make their way to a nice dress shop Crystal had visited before. Crystal tilts her head at Zarra. "Was that as strange for you as it was for me?"

"No, I think it was way stranger. They barely noticed me, and being that's what I've been wanting my whole life, it felt odd when it actually happened." Zarra relaxes, letting her shoulders slump a little. "What's this Sky Lady they kept calling you?"

"I've only been called that once before here, ten or so months ago. When we first landed, I was escorted through the town by a retainer and a Catfolk kitten girl steps out in front of me and handed me a white Lilly." Crystal recalls as they walk into the dress shop. "I asked her if that was for me, and the little kitten girl told me yes, 'a white flower for the lady of the sky'."

Zarra nods to herself, looking around and takes notice of other people inside also dress shopping. As she scans the area, others are taking fleeting glances in their direction, like at the eatery. "You think that's why they call you Sky lady?" She admires a colorful green outfit with a sheer orange cloth and holds it to her obsidian skin. "What do you think of this?"

284

Crystal glides over, and a look of approval crosses her face. "Ooooh, that looks good with your skin tone. The orange compliments your hair and the green just jumps out. Wonder if it will fit you as is?" Zarra shrugs, holding it to her body, but Crystal takes it from her with a huge grin. "Let's go ask." They take the outfit to a desk where a Catfolk female is standing.

"Can I help you?"

"Do you have a place where she can try this on? We aren't sure if this will fit, but it looks close."

"I could take her measurements real quick and compare them, or I can alter something to fit."

Crystal turns to Zarra. "If you want, I can hold on to your sword while she does that. Shouldn't take too long." Zarra nods and removes her weapon and hands it to Crystal. The Catfolk lady walks Zarra to a more private area and takes out her measuring tape.

"Arm twenty-five, neck nine, shoulder thirteen and a half, chest thirty-two D, inseam twenty-three, waist twenty-eight, hip thirty, and height sixty." She holds the dress up with a smile. "One moment and I'll get the measurements off of this and see how close they are." Zarra dresses and steps back out. Her eyes widen watching Crystal being approached from behind by an older looking Catfolk woman, along with her daughter. Zarra reaches Crystal about the same time as the elderly woman.

The elderly lady speaks in felinese. "Excuse me."

Crystal spins and response in kind. "Yes?"

"I couldn't help but overhear that you're the Sky Lady." She holds a hand up and weakly points. "Are you really her?"

Crystal glances back at Zarra, letting her eyes go wide and her eyebrows rising. Turning to face the elderly woman again, she keeps her tone soft. "I've been called that. Why?"

Zarra, not understanding anything these two are saying, interrupts. "What's going on?"

The Catfolk lady looks to her and back to Crystal, but Crystal translates. "She's wondering if I'm the Sky Lady, so I told her I've been called that a few times now." She looks down and remembers Zarra's sword. "Oh, and you can have this back."

Zarra takes it and the Catfolk lady speaks up again. "Could you please do something for me?"

Crystal shrugs, and Zarra sighs from being left out of the conversation. "I suppose so. Why?"

The elder woman pulls her granddaughter up by the hand to stand next to them. "Ask her."

Crystal and Zarra exchange glances, but before either could say anything, the young girl speaks, looking down at her belly. "Could you bless my unborn litter to be healthy?"

Crystal's eyes widen, not understanding what it is she's being asked for. The shock of the question gets her to speak in common instead of felinese. "Could I, what?"

Zarra picks up on this. "Don't leave me in the dark here."

Crystal looks at Zarra, and can't hide the confusion and uncertainty in her words. "She asked me to bless her unborn litter."

The young Catfolk girl pleads, reaching out and taking Crystal's hand. "Please, I just want them to be healthy and happy. That's all."

Crystal and Zarra exchange glances, both confused, but Crystal wants to avoid a scene with a crying girl. She smiles, giving in. "Of course. You just caught be off guard, I'm sorry." Crystal slowly places her hand on the young girl's belly and can feel the babies inside moving and kicking. *It's amazing, really. I hope this will be me soon.* She makes up a prayer on the spot, after seeing Tia do it dozens of times. "May your children be healthy and strong. I bless thee." Then she removes her hand slowly, keeping up her smile. The two Catfolk women smile and thank her, bowing their heads and walking away. Crystal turns to Zarra. "That was way more awkward than I cared for."
286

The seamstress walks over and holds up the outfit. "It's a little big for you, but it should give you a good idea of how you would look. Wouldn't take long for me to alter it if you like it. My dressing room is over here." She waves Zarra to follow.

Crystal stands outside the small room but notices she's getting more stares. *What is going on around here? I'm wondering if I shouldn't go back to my ship and wait this out.*

Penelope and Chuck walk the streets and she occasionally climbs a pole and looks out over the throng of people, getting a chuckle from the young man. "You know, you could just ride my shoulders and be above it all as we walk."

She looks down at him. "We will file that under plan N." She tries to sound uninterested. *He's right, but if I take him up on his offer, he will rub my legs as we walk. If he started touching me like that, I might like it too much.* She looks down at him and he just smiles up at her. *My god he has such a cute smile, and his lips are really soft...* She shakes her head and looks over the crowd again. "I think I see Tyra. She's about six blocks away."

Hopping down, Chuck catches her before she hits the ground. She looks up at him and he smiles, setting her down. "Didn't want you to get hurt."

She beams up at him. "Thanks. That was sweet of you." She turns away and starts walking. *I can't believe I said that. There was no way would have gotten hurt from such a short distance. I leaped from roofs higher than that.* They cut through the city's marketplace, but it's so crowded that it takes much longer than it should, but reaches the place where she saw Tyra. They both look around and don't see the giant, hairy woman. "She couldn't of went far."

She walks up to a Catfolk waitress and gets her attention. "Oh, I'm sorry, I didn't see you there. I'll get you a table."

"I don't need a table. Just need to know if you saw a large Minotaur here with a Human monk?"

"Yes, I remember them. They talked to the Sky Lady a few moments who came her with the Black Elf before departing."

"Did this Black Elf have red copper hair?"

She nods her head in affirmative. "Yes, she did. They also left not but a few minutes ago, right after the monk and the Minotaur did, but they left in different directions."

Penelope turns to Chuck. "She was just here."

"Tyra?"

"Crystal."

"I thought we were looking for Tyra?"

"To find Crystal. She's supposed to be out dress shopping and I wanted to join them."

He grins at her, looking her over. "You don't look like the dress wearing type."

"I was bored with nothing to do. Look around. Do you see Zarra or Crystal?"

He turns about, scanning the area, but shakes his head. "As short as those two are, they wouldn't be visible in a crowd like this." He looks down at her. "Sorry."

She sighs then goes back to bugging the Catfolk lady. "Which way did the Sky Lady and her Black Elf friend go, and are there any clothing stores in that direction?"

"There are a few." She holds a finger up. "Give me a moment to take care of my patrons, and I'll draw you a map."

"Great."

"Why don't we get lunch while we are here? Food smells good here and dinner is still pretty far away."

His suggestion sets off a growl from her stomach. He smiles right afterwards, letting her know he heard that. "Fine, if she's shopping, she will be there for some time." They find a table nearby and get seated. The waiter, a light tan and white furred male, comes and sets some water down, and brings her a special chair just for their Halfling customers. He smiles. "And what can I get the happy young couple today? May I suggest stuffed salmon fillets? They are stuffed with bits of crab, some cream cheese with a nice side salad with a choice of dressings."

Penelope holds up a finger. "We aren't a couple, just friends." Chuck's smile fades a bit, being reminded that every advance he makes is being deflected. "But that does sound good, actually."

"And what to drink with your meal, miss?"

"Orange juice."

The waiter nods and looks at Chuck. "And for you, sir?"

"I'll take the same. Haven't tried it before, so why not?" He holds up the glass of water. "And I'm fine with water to drink."

He writes it all down and walks away. Penelope picks up her own glass. "I take it I'm paying the check?"

"No, I'll cover it."

This gets her to raise an eyebrow. "How exactly? You don't have any money."

"Actually, I do." He pulls some cash from his pocket. "William and Crystal gave me some money while I did odd jobs around the ship while we were in transit." He looks down at her. "She said I would need it just in case something came up." He picks up his water and takes a drink. "Guess she was right." He looks at her, and catches her hiding a smile.

CHAPTER 27

(Mistaken Identity)

"Crystal?" Yaris stands and sounds doubtful. "Crystal Hellstromm, the countess? What does she have to do with this?"

Andrew holds his arms out and lets them flop down. "She fits that description perfectly."

"You know how many people fit the description of gods? Middle-aged tan skin man describes you Andrew, if you were another fifteen years older."

"But you must understand how unique Crystal is. I've only seen two people who I know match that description: Crystal and my mother." He leans down and puts his hands on his desk. "I know she isn't this goddess lady. But if she's being mistaken for being the Sky Lady as some kind of avatar, then she could be in danger, or worse." Andrew looks at Tia. "She could perpetuate that she is this person trying to gain favor somehow. I think she's above that now, but still."

"Yeah, she would *never* do that." Tia stands up straight. "We better find these people and straighten them out. At least point out that Crystal isn't their goddess before things get worse."

Andrew continues her point. "Do they have a church or someplace where they worship?"

"Not exactly. There is a building they sometimes meet at, but no set schedule. I can give you the address and you can go talk to them."

"Not a bad idea."

Yaris grabs some parchment and a quill when Tia stops him. Her heart is racing as if in fear. "We shouldn't do this."

"Why not?" Yaris continues to write. "If it's a false religion, we should put a stop to it."

Tia shakes her head. "I don't understand it, but right when you suggested us going there, I got a bad feeling that it's the wrong course. Something I feel deep inside scares me at the thought." The artifact sitting on the desk glows white for a moment, as if punctuating her words.

"So, Ms. Moonglow. What do you suggest we do about this new religion, then?"

"Nothing. Let it play out." She stares off into nothing. She blinks and looks at him. "We could be witnessing what Daniel has been telling me all along."

"But you think the new Love goddess is the countess?" He makes it sound insane.

"No, I think she's supposed to perpetuate it with her self-centeredness. Spread the word inadvertently until the actual god or goddess appears to the followers."

Andrew wags a finger. "When I was studying to be a priest of Daniel, that's how he started, too. In the early beginnings of our religion, we didn't have a symbol either, no powers, but a single man spread the word. Now we are all connected to our god, spreading the word as he did."

"You're more informed than I am, so I'll sit on my hands and watch this play out." Yaris hands them the parchment. "But you should at least talk to her, let he know what could be happening."

Tia shakes her head. "We shouldn't mention anything, but finding her is a good idea. If anything, just to keep her safe. Last thing we need is some fanatic thinking their goddess is bound to the mortal plane and thinks they need to 'free her'."

"What a colossal pain in the ass this is!" Andrew looks over the paper. "Crystal, you should have stayed home. So where do we begin?"

"We must find her. Let's head back to the embassy and try to keep her there?"

"Fine, let's get going. That's going to be a long walk." Andrew takes her hand. She picks up her artifact, and they bid the Priest goodbye.

Tom and Tyra watch Andrew and Tia exit from across the street on the way to the dojo that's just a few blocks away. They are practically running as they negotiate the street. "That's interesting. They look like they are trying to run from something."

Tyra grumbles. "Should we run them down and find out if they are, ok?"

"Not a bad idea. The dojo can wait and I'd rather find out it's nothing, then leave it and find out they are in danger." He looks at her. "Let's go."

They have no trouble catching up to the couple after they haven't made it but a block. Tom grabs Tia from behind, laying a hand on her shoulder. She lets out a yelp of surprise and spins in place, and Andrew draws his hand back, ready to defend her. "TOM!"

He grins. "Who did you expect?"

"We have to get back to the embassy and make sure Crystal doesn't leave."

Tom and Tyra exchange glances. "Well, two questions. Why is it important she stay at the embassy, and what if she already left?"

They give Tom and Tyra the rundown on the new religion, and their concern is that Crystal might be mistaken for this deity. "I think we overheard something about this. We were at the seafood shop across the way from where you two ate when Crystal and Zarra showed up for some lunch date thing." He shifts and glances at each of them. "And several of the people there started acting strangely." He casually throws a hand outwards with a slight shake of his head. "But we didn't feel they were in danger, more like they were fascinated and thrilled they were there."

Andrew grabs Tom's shoulders. "Do you know where they were going after there?"

Tom and Tyra both shake their heads negatively. "Neither one mentioned anything to us. I just figured she was there for lunch with Zarra."

Tia steps forward nervously. "But no William?"

"No. William is military; he's making sure those new machines are operational. Besides, it looked like they really wanted a girl's day."

"And they didn't take Ms. Penelope?"

"She was with Chuck last we seen. She was leaving his room as we were coming in."

"This is a big city to find those two in." She turns to Tyra and takes her hand. "Are you up to it, Tyra?"

Tyra pulls her hand away and scowls. "I'm going to buy you people a dog, just so you will stop using me to track with." She scoffs. "But yea, I can find them."

Zarra steps out of the dressing room looking a bit embarrassed, but Crystal whistles in appreciation, and bites her bottom lip. The green top covers her from the shoulders to just below the breasts, leaving her muscular stomach exposed to the waistline and her arms open. The bottom starts at the waistline, dropping to the floor. Sheer orange cloth covers her from the shoulder to the floor. Decretive white flower patterns adorn the dress along the belt line and along the frills at the bottom. Orange cloth crisscrosses from the waist to the mid-thy on both sides, accenting her legs. Crystal can't hide her anticipation. "Turn all the way around. Let me see how you look." Zarra does a slow spin, her muscles flexing under the tight cloth and along her mid rift. "You look amazing." As her back comes into view, Crystal can see it is completely open except for where it attaches at the top and halfway points, held on by a cloth string. "How does it feel?"

"Breezy in the back, but comfortable. Being this is a warm climate town, I can see why it would be fashionable. It breathes well."

"And that forest green goes very well with your skin and with that copper hair of yours. You're going to make people drool."

"You think so?" Zarra looks around herself.

"If I was your boyfriend, I would carry a large stick to keep the losers away." She giggles. "You want it? We can have the seamstress make the minor alterations, so it fits at its best." Zarra smiles happily and nods in agreement.

The seamstress takes payment and makes after a short time finishes the work. Zarra puts it back on, making sure everything looks right. "It's wonderful." Zarra admits. "Guess I should change back and I can wear it tonight."

Crystal walks up to her, taking a hold of Zarra's hips and turning her about getting a closer look. "Or you can wear it out. See how many heads unscrew trying to look at us as we walk through town?" She hands Zarra her sword.

"Sure, I like that idea." She puts on her sword belt. The two of them exit into the mid-day sun and the breeze causes goosebumps to appear all over Zarra's skin. "Bit chillier in this dress."

"You need me to protect you from the cold?"

"If you wouldn't mind." Crystal smiles and does her incantation and motions with her hands for the environmental spell. She touches Zarra on the back, feeling the goosebumps go away. Zarra looks relieved. The two were about to leave when a dark-skinned Human female approaches them.

She bows her head, then looks at Crystal. "It is true. You're the Sky Lady."

Crystal glowers, and her annoyance is reflected in her tone. "Why does everyone keep calling me that?"

She bows her head in reverence. "Because, goddess, you haven't told us your real name yet. So that's all we can go by."

Crystal shakes her head. "I'm not a goddess. I'm a countess." She looks at Zarra, but she just shrugs.

"It's ok, goddess. I'm a faithful follower. You don't have to use that cover around me, but if you're unsure, you can follow me back to our humble church and meet others who seek your guidance."

Crystal groans. *Why me?* She casts her eyes at Zarra. "Shall we figure out this whole thing?"

"As long as we can figure it out fast. We have a banquet tonight and I need a bath."

Crystal assumes an air of authority, tilting her head up. "Take us to my church, then."

The dark-skinned lady looks up and smiles. "Right away goddess, would you like to try some of our perfume we've made in your honor?"

"Sure, but it better be good or I won't be happy."

She sprays a little in the air for them and Zarra grins taking in the scent. "That smells like fresh lily. It's very good."

Crystal agrees with a nod. "I concur. Wonderfully made."

"Thank you, goddess. It contains a mild aphrodisiac for attracting a mate, or keeping your current one interested."

"That's a good idea. Sure, I'll wear some, anything, to drive William wilder."

The young woman sprays a little on Crystal and Zarra and the two of them smile in appreciation. "This will work on either sex, actually."

"Really?" They exchange glances and follow her for several blocks into a busier part of town. Zarra taps the woman on the shoulder. "You make that yourself?"

"No, one of our members has an apothecary. He heard your message like we all did and made several perfumes to help generate some money for our budding church." She sounds proud of their members. "He's also a florist, so he makes arrangements for marriages and parties. He's a big supporter."

Crystal nor Zarra detect any hint of deception from the young lady. "What's your name?"

"Dahlia." They don't travel far and arrive at a medium-sized building that looks like it used to be a store. Large front windows face the street and no markings on it, just a sign that says 'Church of Love' on the front. They can see several people inside with makeshift pews set up and a lectern being used as a podium. They walk inside and Dahlia announces she has found the Sky Lady for all to hear. The people inside turn and look upon Crystal and Zarra.

Zarra swallows, taking the scene in, but Crystal walks forward, holding her arms out. "How is everyone!"

Andrew, Tia, and Tom follow Tyra back to the place where they ate lunch. They run into Penelope and Chuck, who are having lunch together. Tia approaches them. "Aww, you're so cute together."

This makes Penelope turn bright red and Chuck lets out a short laugh. "Why does everyone keep saying that? He's not my type." She slams her fork on the table in anger.

Tom leans down, whispering in her elongated pink ear. "I don't buy this display for a second."

Her head spins and gives him a dirty look, then addresses the others. "What do you want?"

Andrew speaks up first. "Have you seen Crystal? She was here earlier, maybe an hour."

"No, someone told me she was going to a dress shop that way." She points up the street. "But Chuck here got hungry and wanted to eat before we went and found her. Guess he's not too keen on dress shopping with a woman."

"Actually, I would love to see you in a dress and help you pick one out. I heard your stomach rumble and figured I would be nice and treat you."

Andrew steps over and pats her on the back. "It's about time you found a good man who will treat you good."

Penelope lets a squeaky growl escape. "I'm never going to get to live this down, am I?"

"I'll stop." Tia pulls Andrew back. "But you seem so lonely. I thought I was helping. Sorry."

"So why is everyone looking for her again? Was she kidnapped? If so, where's the pile of bodies those two left in their wake?"

They all sit down and explain what's been happening with the goddess thing and how it might connect with Tia's visions. Chuck is in a state of disbelief. "She went from countess to goddess?"

"She's not a goddess!" Tia waves to the public, who turned at her outburst, and lowers her voice. "But these people think she is. To keep her from harm, we need to get her home. All it takes is for one weirdo to think the reason they don't have any divine gifts is because she hasn't shed her mortal coil, and then send her on her way."

Chuck's eyes widen in realization. "Oh, that's bad."

Tom slaps Tyra's back. "Well, with this information and Tyra's legendary tracking, we should find her soon enough." They all set off and leave, tracking Crystal and Zarra to the dress shop they were in.

Penelope and Andrew go inside while Tyra paces, trying to pick up the scent again. She grumbles. "I lost it!"

Tom walks over to her and grabs her arm. "Lost what?"

"Her and Zarra's scents." She holds her head. "All I smell are flowers all over this place. It's giving me a headache."

Tia examines Tyra's nose. "You don't have any idea where she went?"

"Not with Tyra's nose not working. Maybe Penelope can find clues. From what I've seen of her, she can find anything."

Penelope interviews people inside, looking for Crystal and Zarra. The dress shop owner has a wide smile. "Yes, the Sky Lady was very nice, as was her friend. They bought a beautiful forest green dress that looked wonderful on the Black Elf. The Sky Lady sure knows how to make someone irresistible."

Penelope sounds annoyed. "Besides the dress, anything else you can tell me? I believe the Sky Lady could be in danger if I don't find her."

She places a finger on her chin and looks up. "I remember her blessing a young girl to have a healthy litter while she was waiting. She is truly wonderful."

"So where did she and the Dark Elf go?"

"After they left here, they were stopped by a dark-skinned lady outside for a few minutes and then left with her." She holds her hands apart. "But I don't know where to."

Andrew walks around while Penelope does her thing. He doesn't get much better answers than her, though. "Great. We need to do a citywide search for her."

"We will find her, Andrew. I could find her In Rose Harbor when she wondered off, remember? I can do that here, too."

She steps outside with him and Tom shakes his head before she can even ask the question. "Why not just visit the church? If they are so into her, maybe we can get some answers from them?"

Penelope looks at all of them. "It's common sense to head there first."

Andrew's eyes widen and pulls the paper from his pocket. "Yaris, did give me the address.."

Penelope takes it and scolds him. "You had this, this whole time, and didn't tell me?" He gives her a nervous laugh and shrugs helplessly. "Someone should get William before we proceed. We don't know what we are getting into."

The worshippers stand up and murmurs to each other and slowly approach. "Is it really you?"

Another man bows his head. "She looks just like the description."

Zarra leans in close and whispers. "What are you doing?"

Crystal whispers from the side of her mouth. "I'm getting answers, and according to Shadow, it's easier to get answers if they trust you."

Dahlia smiles. "We are your people. We are ready to spread your word. Tell us what we need to know." She bows her head again and waves to the lectern with her arms.

Zarra follows Crystal to the makeshift podium altar thing as she stands behind it. Zarra keeps her tone low. "I hope you know what you're doing."

Crystal puts on her best smile, exposing her fangs, but talks with her lips closed at Zarra. "You and me both." Crystal looks over the congregation. *Is this what Tia and Andrew deal with every day? This is intimidating. I rather face down the Black Rose over this.* The people inside all sit and give her their undivided attention. "I have a few questions, and I know you have questions for me. Let's share, shall we?" She places her scepter and handbag down, leaving her hands free.

She gets a series of nods and everyone is smiling, hanging on her every word, waiting for her to speak. *This is eerie and fascinating all at the same time. I want to puke, but I love the fact they hang onto my every word.* She clears her throat, giving her time to formulate her words. "Love, the reason for everyone to exist, the reason for being, and is the strongest force of all." He holds up a hand with a single finger raised, pointing to the sky. "Love can conquer countries. Love can conquer hate and overcome differences." Crystal holds her arms out and forward as if inviting a hug. "So, I ask you, why do *you* gather here?"

There is a moment of silence and Crystal looks out over them and someone finally answers a young Catfolk male. "Because we seek *love* for ourselves." He scans around him as others are focused on him now. "To show that war and conflict isn't the correct way to go."

After he finishes, another speaks up, a female Sand Elf. "I'm looking for a man or woman to share my heart with. I'm lonely, but find contentment here."

Others share their feelings, but Crystal is getting an understanding of why they are here. "I know you have questions. What do you want to know about me?"

A female Human speaks up. "Are you really the Sky Lady?"

"I'm not sure what you mean by 'Sky Lady.' I don't live in the sky, if that's what you are asking."

Another speaks up. "Are you the goddess we have been seeking is what she means."

"Me, personally?" Crystal contemplates. *I don't know how to answer that. If I tell them the truth with a no, then they could get angry and turn on me. If I tell them yes, then they will stalk me and it's a bad idea to impersonate a god. Guess I'll improvise with a bit of both.* She places her hands on the lectern. "That is not a simple answer. I speak for her, but I am not the goddess herself. Like a prophet, I suppose."

"So that's why you appear as you do?"

"I was born this way, and can't change how I look if that's what you're asking."

Dahlia speaks up from next to her. "What's the goddess's name, and what does her holy symbol look like? When will she grant us the ability to spread the power of Love with her teachings?"

"When she is ready, she will reveal all to you. For now, she must obtain the Torch of Love first to solidify her power." Crystal looks at them as they murmur to each other. *I'm not exactly lying. From what I know, this could be true.* She continues, silencing them. "But I can help ease some of that now. I would love nothing more than to speak with you all now." She speaks from her own heart, hoping that others will understand what she means.

Crystal takes a deep breath, trying to get her heart to calm down. Her nerves are on edge. "Love is the most powerful of emotions. Love is neither good nor evil. For love," she raises her right and points to the sky with a finger once again. "Can lead to both joy and jealousy." She brings her arms in a self-hug. "Love can bring nations together." She makes a tearing motion as she separates them. "Or tear them asunder." Her heart jumps, spotting her friends walk in the door. They all make eye contact and see Crystal at the lectern, Zarra standing behind her and to the right, a half-dressed bodyguard.

She continues as if nothing happened. "But most often, love is the joining of hearts, of family, friends, and more." The congregation turns and looks at the newcomers but says nothing. Dahlia waves them over with a smile and points for them to sit and listen. The group exchange glances and all came to the same conclusion. That not a single one of them has any idea on what is actually happening here. With a simple exchange of glances, they all just sit down and wait. William sits up front and Crystal looks to Zarra, tilting her head, signaling her to take her place down there with the others.

Zarra sits and leans into William and he whispers. "Sit-rep?"

She shakes her head and whispers back. "Way too much to explain, but she's not in any danger." She tilts her chin up at Crystal. "I think she's enjoying this, or actually is believing she is who they say she is. Hard to tell."

An Elven man speaks up. "Sky Lady!" He holds his hand up, making it easy for her to zero in on him. "In my culture, for many millennia, it's believed that you can love more than one partner. I've often heard from my Dwarven and Human counterparts that to take more than one, you're dividing your love. Doing so lessens the love for all involved. Is this true? Should it be avoided?"

Crystal smiles, glancing at William and Zarra sitting next to each other and her fear leaves her heart. "You ask one of the hardest questions for anyone, and to be fair, there is no correct answer." She leans forward on the lectern, placing her hands on either side. "Love is multiplied by each person you feel love for." She takes in confused glances and looks. *Guess I need an example to make them understand.* She holds her hand out, pointing to the older man. "Do you have more than one child?" He nods. "Is your love divided between them, or do you love them equally?"

He nods his head. "Of course I love them all equally."

"That same principle can apply to partners, but it is trickier." She blinks and leans back. "That's the simple answer. You love them all the same amount, no matter if you have one or ten. Love doesn't have a finite amount." She looks at them all. "You love your friends, don't you? You love your parents, your siblings, your children, your pets." She lets go of the podium and holds her arms to the side, open but not down. "The genuine issue of loving more than one partner at a time is 'does that hurt them or someone else? If they feel they should be your only partner, then your love for them should respect that. For if you're taking another partner and don't respect the feelings of your first, then you never loved them." She places her hands down. "And cheating on them hurts them deeply, defies their trust."

He follows up. "So, all relationships should be between two people?"

"Again, not a straightforward answer." She glances at William and Zarra. "If you find yourself falling for another, confess to your first partner. Remain honest with them about your feelings, but take their words to heart. If they think they too can love this other person, then you all should have that conversation. Make sure everyone involved understands and agrees." She takes in a deep breath to compose herself and turns back to him. "But it's important to discuss it with your partner first. If they want just you in their life, it should be respected. Breaking the bond of love with someone will almost certainly lead to hate and resentment."

She grips the lectern again. "Love is a complex emotion. Just be careful not to mistake lust for love. They are very similar and can be mistaken in the heat of a moment. A mistake that can have deadly consequences. Don't take such things lightly." She smiles. "But true love will always honor what your partner wants. Once you've committed to a person, that commitment should be cherished, not used for selfish means."

Someone in the back calls out. "Can you love someone who hates you?"

"Absolutely." She speaks without hesitation. "In fact, love is the only cure for hate. For without love, hate will lead only to one outcome, complete destruction. There are many ways to hate." Crystal grips the podium again and looks down for a moment, feeling it in her own heart. "Hate consumes the soul, drives you to do things you will regret." She looks down at her hands, remembering them blood soaked. She fights back tears, thinking of the terrible things she has done because of hate. Looking up, she does her best to keep the tears at bay. "Hating things is easier than loving them. Hate is used to persecute someone for their race, their class, their origins, even the ideas they hold, and is a way to control others."

Tom nods at her as she looks at him. *She's finding her inner peace at last.*

"But love!" Her voice rises, and she holds up a hand. "Love is harder to do. To love someone who is physically different; to love them despite what they can do for you; to love them even when their ideas, beliefs, or politics make no sense to you is how you get unity. Humans, Elves, Dwarves, Halflings, and the dozens of other races have proved for centuries now that love can overcome those differences." She gazes out over the congregation, noticing more have come in from the streets. "Just because everyone has different ideas on how to solve a problem doesn't mean everyone else is wrong. It's just a perspective that should be respected, not to give hate a reason to destroy." She steps away, looking tired. "I wish I could speak more, but I must be on my way. Love each other, and if someone hates you, love them back. The best way to stop hate is to stop giving hate a reason to exist."

She steps away and down, walking up to William, who stands. He holds her chin up and they smile at each other. "I'm glad I got to see your first sermon."

She pulls him down by his cuirass, bringing his face to hers and kissing him passionately. "I meant every word." She glances at Zarra and at him again. "But I need a bath and to get ready for dinner tonight." She takes his right arm and Zarra falls in opposite her on William's left. Andrew looks at Tia. "Are we sure these people aren't right about her being the goddess of love? If I wasn't completely sure, having grown up with her, I wouldn't have any doubts."

Tia shakes her head. "I don't know myself. I've only heard passion like that from Lyndis." She takes his hand and pulls him close. "Maybe she will be a clergy of this new god and was it trying out?"

Chuck speaks up. "I think she did great. Goddess or not, I liked it. Maybe if we got the Black Rose to listen to her, they would just dissolve."

Penelope chips in. "The big problem with the Black Rose is they hate others based on ideas and false information. Crystal is right, we should be supportive of others' ideas, for even when we don't like them, or even bad. Showing love and compassion to turn those bad ideas away is more constructive than just to hate out of spite."

Andrew gets up, holding his hand out for Tia to take, lifting her from her seat. They take each other's arms and follow Crystal out. Chuck stands up and offers his hand to Penelope. She looks at it, then at him. She sighs. *If I act like an ass now, it will ruin the atmosphere. Besides, he's been really good.* She takes his hand, and he pulls her to her feet. *Am I wrong? Am I just cutting myself off for no reason?*

They exit together, and he looks down at her. "Would you like to ride on my shoulders on the way home so you won't have to walk?"

Tom and Tyra walk around them as Penelope looks up at the young man, having stopped him. "Only if you answer one simple question."

"Shoot."

305

"I've rejected you repeatedly. We are physically different, not to mention the age difference, and even if by some miracle I fell in love with you, we couldn't produce any children. Why do you continue to pursue me?"

"Because you should never give up on a good thing, no matter how difficult it is."

Damn, that's an excellent answer. She looks down a moment, hiding her smirk. "Ok."

"Just ok?"

She holds her arms up. "Just put me on your shoulders already." She points a finger at him. "But you don't get to smile about it." Once she's on his shoulders, he smiles anyway because he knows she can't see him.

CHAPTER 28

(Truth shall set you free)

Tom and Tyra head off to the Dojo that they started several months ago. The midafternoon sun starting its trek to the west. Walking among the new students, Tom watches them practicing their skills and giving corrections where needed. He gives a nod of approval to Lyssa Smythe. A tall, fair skinned woman with long brown hair and eyes, athletic build, and eagerness to excel. She was the best choice to leave in charge for the short time he was gone, having absorbed Tom's teachings quickly. When the cultural exchanges were suggested six months ago, she arrived in Portstown where she and Tom met. Unbeknownst to Tom, she is the oldest daughter of the Fifth House and was looking to start her own life.

He glances at her askance, making sure that others don't see. *I remember when I ran into her. Her beauty stunned me, and the fact that her shirt looked too small for her wasn't lost on me, either. She was eager to sign up for my marital arts school.* He continues his rounds. *Back then I would have tried to court her, but now, I'm a master and she is my student. I need to be above such worldly things.*

He watches her, judging how far she has come in such a short time. *She is ready for more. She's a quick learner and a natural at this.* At his direction, Tyra shows the students new throws and Tom takes Lyssa to another room, presenting her with some new teachings from Master Monzulo. He puts his hand over the cover of a book. "In this book, are more advance techniques, kata's and even weapon forms."

He hands it over to her, and she looks through the pages and illustrations. "These *are* advanced." She glances up at him. "I don't know how I'm going to pull these off."

"I'm going to be here for several hours and I'm going to teach them to you, so you can teach the others." He takes the book and puts it down, then moves her to the center of the room. "Let us get started."

He shows her the moves, repeating the motions as she follows along, trying to mimic them. They go through them; him correcting her stances, moving her arms, twisting her to show what muscles to use. Her long brown hair, bound up in a ponytail, flows behind her as she spins and throws out kicks and punches. He goes through the motions with her repeatedly, and as she picks up the technique, he starts on another, spending thirty to forty minutes per new move. "Master Ryuu, why can't you stay and teach us these things?" She breathes hard, going through the motions with him.

"Because my primary mission with the countess isn't over. Once the Black Rose has been dealt with, I will be here with my students."

"But Master."

His sigh cuts her off. "I know, but some things are more important than our personal lives. I wasn't planning on even starting this dojo." He stops, causing her to stop as well. Sweat from the training running down her cheek and breathing hard, but she looks at peace. "You're a natural at this and already picking up on these techniques, but you still have years to go."

She bows her head. "How many books did you bring for me to study? I'm eager to learn and pass it on."

"A few. Master Monzulo had several of our texts copied just for me. It's as if he knew I was going to branch off one day and need them."

"He sounds very wise." She keeps her tone low. "Maybe one day I will get to meet him" She takes her stance and starts doing the motions again. "But I'm happy with the Master I have right here." He takes his place at her side, staying in sync as they maneuver. They work for hours till they are both tired and take a break.

They go out and see Tyra tossing students around the room like they are nothing, but they have broken off into pairs, practicing what she has been showing them. Lyssa leans into him. "She's going to be a wonderful master someday."

"Oh, I agree. She still needs to work on that control, though. I'm just glad I had the walls extra padded just because of her." His comments are proven as she tosses a male Sand Elf into one. He turns to her. "I want to teach you to make tea. I'm not a huge fan of it, but it's a great way to learn to control your chi. It will help you go much farther and would benefit you greatly."

She grins. "Where do we begin?"

"Before I left, I had a tea set made by a local glassblower, but hadn't used it." He pulls out a long thin box and opens it, pulling out the contents that look similar to Crystal's, but in jade green. He sets it up and boils the water. "I'm going to show you step by step, and if you have questions, please ask." He turns and kneels on the floor with the hot kettle placed next to him. He goes through, explaining each step and their function, going slowly. At the end, he pours them both a cup of hot green tea.

She smiles as he hands her a cup. *I love how he gives me personal hands-on training, showing his confidence in my abilities. I will study and train hard, showing his trust in me isn't misplaced.*

The girls decide to go back to dress shopping for a little while, and William and Andrew return to the embassy. By nightfall, they are all wearing all new colorful outfits and carrying bags filled with more. They go their different ways once they walk back into the embassy. Penelope is happy in her new outfit, especially with all the places she can hide her weapons and tools. *The seamstress looked a little disturbed, as I had her adding all kinds of hidden pockets, loops, and other attachments.* She enters her room and tosses the other clothes Crystal had bought her on the bed. She turns to the full-length mirror and runs her hands along her flanks. *This black and blue dress really shows off my figure.*

Her mind flashes to Chuck and how, despite it all, stayed with them even though he must have been bored out of his mind. *Chuck really is doing his best, but it wouldn't fit for us. Besides, once he gets home, I won't see him again. If he stayed, it would interfere with my duties if I became attached.* She flops down on the bed. *Why do I have to keep justifying myself like this? Should just give in?* She sits up. *No, I need something to get my mind away from that handsome man. I need to get back in the kitchen and focus on something else.*

She changes into her chef's clothing and heads down to the kitchen. She exits and spots Crystal and Zarra walking and laughing, speaking of the stuff only women of the ruling Houses would be bothered with. Zarra's obsidian skin is mostly exposed, wrapped in a towel, and both are carrying bath supplies. Penelope waves at them. "Where are you two off to?"

"We are going to the bathhouse to clean up. Unlike you, we don't have a man who will carry us everywhere we go, so we are getting cleaned up." Penelope blushes, remembering her trip back to the dress shop, holding her legs as they walked and then putting her down.

"It wasn't my idea. He wanted to, and you have any idea how hard it is to keep up with you with these tiny legs? I wasn't going to pass up an opportunity to be carried and not having to run." She crosses her arms. "I told you, we aren't together."

Crystal bends down, putting herself level with Penelope. "You don't have to convince me; you have to convince yourself." Penelope looks at Zarra. She shrugs, that suggests that she's not buying it either. "You could come down to the bathhouse with us. I plan on kicking everyone else out when we get there."

"That's ok, I wanted to help with dinner. Thanks for the offer, though. Is William going to be joining you two?"

"No, he has his hands full with my father's war machines. As a captain and ranking member of the Royal Guard, he has his responsibilities to handle the military affairs while stationed here." She turns to Zarra and stands up. "Let's go beautiful. The water is calling me and I don't know what I'm getting another chance to relax."

Penelope watches Zarra lighten a bit. *She just loves to tease everyone around her, getting a rise out of it.* The two travel down the hallway and around the corner and Penelope follows behind, being it's the same way to get to the kitchens. Crystal and Zarra stop at Tia's room and knock, but get no answer. Crystal giggles and walks next door to Andrews's room. When she knocks there, Tia answers. Crystal also asks if they would like to join them in the bathhouse, but they decline.

"We have to catch up on our prayers and I want to meditate a bit. Andrew wants to try it with me and see if he could benefit from some of this monk stuff. I'm going to try to teach him what the grand master taught us."

"If you change your mind, we will have the place all to ourselves. Feel free to come down anytime."

Tia looks at Andrew. "Yea, we will be down in about thirty minutes. Let us complete our prayers first 'Sky Lady'." Penelope and Zarra are surprised that, for the first time, Crystal's flushed pink.

"Don't you start that, too."

The trio walks downstairs, and Penelope breaks off, heading in her own direction. Crystal and Zarra take the second flight down. She continues across the courtyard, walks past the guards unnoticed, and into the cooking area. Tracking down their head chief, a large lion-like Catfolk named Cornelius, and gets his attention. The large Catfolk turns, reaches down and picks her up with a large fang filled smile. "Penelope, I thought I smelled your presence." He hugs her. "How have you been, my tiny friend?" He places her back on the ground.

"Busier than a beaver in a petrified forest." He lets out a deep belly laugh. "I came down to see if you could use help for the feast tonight."

"Even if I didn't, you're more than welcome in my kitchen. I'll have some stools brought in so you can reach everything and provide you with a dinner menu." He barks some orders at his staff, and they react just like they would in her own kitchen back home. "Your recipes have been a big hit at my personal establishment. If you ever decide to stop working for the Hellstromm's."

She holds up a hand, stopping him. "Thank you, Cornelius, but they are my family. I appreciate the offer and it honors me deeply for you thinking of me. Now, point me in the direction I can do the most good here."

Crystal and Zarra walk into the bathhouse and set their things down, spotting four other ladies in there. Crystal snaps her fingers, getting their attention, then motions out the door. Without hesitation, they gather their stuff and leave. Crystal closes the doors behind them, then walks to the pool edge. Zarra drops her towel, leaving just her emerald-green bathing suit and Crystal does her magical disrobe thing, and just jumps in. Zarra slides into the water next to Crystal. Crystal undoes the braids wrapped around her horns and lets it all out, flowing around her in the water. Zarra removes her own hair ornaments and can feel the freedom it brings, just letting it hang naturally.

They both visibly relax and Zarra turns her head to Crystal. "Could you?"

Crystal smiles, not opening her eyes. "Both, or just the top? Are you finally letting yourself go?"

Zarra hesitates a moment. "I'll try it this one time since there is no one else here. I want to be as comfortable in my own skin as you appear to be." Crystal nods and utters her spell a second time, and Zarra tossed the suit onto the wooden floor behind them. The water feels different when she's completely bare. "I don't know how to describe this feeling. Liberating maybe?" Crystal just gives a subtle nod and smiles. She looks around the pool and notices part of the wooden floor by the edge looks pealed up and busted. "What happened over there?"

Crystal cracks open her eyes and leans forward, following Zarra's finger. Her whole body turns a light pink, and she lays back again. Her tone is playful and can't hide the smile forming. "I have no idea."

I don't believe that for a second.

A few moments go by as they both relax and talk about the day's events. "So, we are alone, and you promised to tell me why you're on the run from your own people. Did you commit some high crime?"

Zarra lays her head back on the wood floor, looking up at the decorations on the ceiling. "You could say that. I tried to talk to William a little about this some time ago, but thought better of it. I figured I should take this personal problem alone."

"Master Monzulo says to help yourself, you help others, and you've helped me come a long way, and I want to help you. No one as beautiful as you should have 'worry wrinkles' at a young age."

Zarra sighs. "I don't know if anyone can help, to be honest."

"Try me. If I can't help, I have connections that could." Crystal places her head on the wood, arching her back.

Zarra can't help but smile. "Ok, well here it goes, but don't way I didn't warn you." Just blurts it out. "I ran away because I'm supposed to get married."

This brings Crystal's eyes to open and rotates her head at the copper haired woman. "I take it that means you didn't want to?"

"I don't want to get married unless *I* love the person I'm marrying." Zarra points to her chest. "I hate being a princess." She turns and looks at Crystal. "I know hate is bad, but hear me out." Crystal turns and places her arm on the wooden floor and supports her head, listening intently as Zarra lets it all out finally. The frustration, the pain, the indignity of her position. "I wanted to explore the world, like what you and William are doing, to be the paladin I was destined to be." Her voice sinks. "The day I left was the day they informed me that my life didn't matter. What I wanted out of life didn't matter. I was a princess and my duty was to their empire." She speaks with passion and anger, her hands in motion, displaying those feelings for Crystal to see. "My 'Father'," she says with air quotes. "Decided that I would be useful as a tribute to some prince I've never met for some lame trade agreement with the Sullivan Empire in southern Druso Escaria." She drops her hands in the water, frustrated, the ripples cascading across the pool.

"And you took your family's war vessel, with the crew not knowing why you were leaving, just made something up and took off for Rose Harbor?"

"Yeah, it's way faster being the only steam-powered ship we have. It would take weeks longer for one of our older ships to catch up." She turns and looks at Crystal. "I heard about you and William, and Tia, and how you and your friends are making tremendous changes, not bound by the politics of being royalty. That's something I wanted over some loveless marriage to a guy I never met."

"I never understood arranged marriages myself. I figured they would be unhealthy, but look at Emperor Marcus. He has four wives from arranged marriages and he loves them all and they love each other."

"I should go back and accept my fate?"

Crystal reaches under the water and takes Zarra's hand in her own. "No, follow your heart. What does it say?"

Zarra turns her head slowly, and Crystal can see the tears welling up. "I want to have what you and William have. What Tia and Andrew have. I want someone to love me unconditionally." She wipes away a tear that was about to fall. "I felt awful about for some thoughts I had." She admits depressively. "And hearing your sermon makes me wonder if those thoughts aren't so wrong now."

Crystal squeezes her hand a little tighter, showing she supports her. "What thoughts?"

Zarra looks away. "I'm afraid to say because I don't know how you will react, and I value you as a friend. I don't want to lose you and your council."

Crystal speaks softly to the confused woman, gently squeezing her hand. As she looks into Zarra's ruby eye's it dawns on her what is happening. "You have thoughts of me, or William, don't you?"

Zarra nods, looking down. "Being around you both, watching how you two interact, how you can display your affections and don't give a damn what anyone thinks. I want that too. Thought of you and me and William and myself." She gives off a pitiful laugh. "Sometimes even the three of us." She turns to Crystal. "I'll understand if you want me to leave. I shouldn't be lusting after your man, or you, for that matter. Maybe I should return to my empire and just face my fate head on."

She goes to stand, but Crystal doesn't let go of her hand, pulling her gently back down. "I don't want you to leave." Crystal speaks softly. "Every girl I know lusts after William." Zarra settles back down. "That's why I don't get mad about it. I don't think you're feeling lust. If it was, you wouldn't be about to break down and cry." She gazes into Zarra's eyes, feeling the connection between them. "And I have something to confess myself." Crystal moves so they are sitting shoulder to shoulder, resting against each other.

"The day I met you, and you removed your helm, you about floored me with your beauty." Crystal's heart feels as if a weight is being lifted. "I never met someone like you before. You were unique like me."

"You never met a Dark Elf before?"

"I have with mixed interactions. Some good, some bad." She casts her eyes down and looks back forward. "But you, the copper hair, the obsidian color, the regal stance, and wearing heavy armor, while being a paladin of Johnathan, you're something special." Crystal turns to the princess. "When you asked to come along, I was overjoyed. Finally, someone who was like me, unique, beautiful, and from royalty. Someone I could talk to, interact with, have an actual girlfriend who I could talk about guys with and go dress shopping without having to hold a wand to."

"I'm happy about that, too. Getting to train with you, and be around you, be part of your everyday life, and help with your recovery."

Crystal nods in agreement. "I started having feelings for you, too. I didn't realize the extent of them till the day you put my dress on for dinner and helping you with your makeup. You were just radiant. I never thought of a woman as a potential partner before, so I buried those feelings." She shrugs. "I'm with William and just as I said earlier, if I love him, then I shouldn't act on my other feelings. And I love him more than life itself. I know how I would feel if the rolls we're reversed."

Zarra nods. "So, you can't love me." She sounds defeated. "I understand."

Crystal pulls her chin up, getting her to lock eyes again. "I didn't say that. Love isn't something that can be divided. I said that too, but I'm not a hypocrite, nor am I going to commit blasphemy in my own church." Zarra snorts a laugh, and Crystal wipes away a tear from Zarra's eyes with her other hand. "I won't cheat on William, but if he also has feelings for you, then maybe we can work something out." Crystal lets go. "And you already confessed you had liked him. So two of the three things to make this work are in place."

"So how do we get him to love me, too?" She pauses. "And why does that sound unethical?"

Crystal smiles, and this gets Zarra to smile too. "He's a man of honor. I've seen him doing his best to avoid looking at you when you're working and showing off your body. He's interested, but like me, he could be doing his best not to be seem tempted. It's how he was raised. It took me months to get him to come to bed with me the first time, and I had to corner him in his room and then drag him back to mine."

Zarra has a good heartfelt laugh. "You dragged him to your bed to get him to break his code of chivalry?"

Crystal shrugs, feeling Zarra's taking her hand. "Sometimes you must take the chance. If he would have rebuffed me at that point, I might have given up. I loved him so much that I didn't care about protocols and being proper anymore. That was the day we got married, and we both know it. The ceremony we had planned is a formality."

"So, what's your plan to find out? It's not like he's going to just admit it. He might reject this just to keep you from getting hurt again."

"I'll dance with him tonight, and you wear that new red dress that shows off your figure. Be alluring and see how many heads you can turn. Then, after we dance, I'll ask him to take your hand and dance with you." She rubs the top of Zarra's hand. "And you're right, he will resist at first, but I'll let him know how much I love the idea of you dancing with him. If he understands the message I'm sending him, he will dance with you, signaling to you and me he's on board."

"What if he dances with me anyway, just to be nice and didn't catch your innuendo?"

"Can always ask him bluntly?" She lets go of Zarra's hands and throws her arm around Zarra's back. Zarra relaxes as they sit in the water together. "Look at the bright side. Even if William decides this isn't something he wants to do, we will still be the best of friends." Crystal's impish grin returns as she tilts her head to look at Zarra. "As the Goddess of Love, I'll be actively looking for someone for you to knock boots with." Crystal just blurts this out, getting Zarra to laugh hard.

"You're not the Goddess of Love, but if you sure know how to make people believe it."

"Are you sure I'm not? Maybe I'm fantastic at hiding it and finally decided to come out." She glances askance at her Dark Elven companion with a smirk. They both laugh and splash at each other and having fun.

"We need to get cleaned up if we are going to get to dinner. Wash my back for me?" Crystal gets up and bends over to grab the soaps and wash clothes. Zarra looks at the ivory woman's perfect body and suppress' her thoughts. She turns so Crystal can get started.

Zarra thumbs at the spot again on the floor. "So, what *really* happened to that wooden floor over there?"

"I happened."

She sounds confused, but loving the feeling of Crystal running her hands over her back and shoulders. "What do you mean?"

"As in me and William alone in the pool late at night with no one around."

It takes a moment, but it finally hits her. "How did you do that?"

"I'll show you." Crystal gets Zarra to turn around. She stands up and bends over, reaches out, and stabs her claws into the wood where the damage is.

"I don't under…Oh, OH." Zarra looks at how Crystal is standing to do that. Then her whole body lightens a bit as it dawns on her.

Crystal laughs and sits back down. "Don't tell anyone. They might get mad that I ruined the floor."

"What are we going to do about me being married off to prince wrong?"

"That's a good one. I guess I'll hide you in a tower somewhere." They both laugh. "But in all seriousness, maybe the Emperor can help. I'll beg, cry, plead, or whatever I must, to get you out of it, but I don't know what we can do. I don't know marriage law for the Silvian Empire like he does." She takes Zarra's hands. "I promise you will not be in a loveless marriage. You deserve so much more than that." They pack up their things and get dressed. "In fact, I'm going to get the ball rolling by writing a letter to the Emperor explaining the situation and give him a head start before we return. Maybe he has a legal scholar I can pay that can figure this all out."

Zarra's voice fills with hope. "What about in the meantime?"

"Let's see if William has it in him to love us both at the same time." Crystal takes Zarra's hand and walks back to their respective rooms.

CHAPTER 29

(The Future Beckons)

Penelope finishes helping Cornelius and takes her leave. "I have to get changed for dinner." She pulls on her now filthy rose jacket. "Can't wear this or I will be mistaken as a member of staff."

Cornelius smiles, reaches down and picks her up. She would normally be upset, but has known this Catfolk and it's his peculiar quirk. He gives her a hug. "Don't be a stranger. Next time you're in town, I must show you my new establishment." He puts her down knowing she doesn't like it, so he keeps it brief, and continues. "I had an offer to open a restaurant in a hotel, but I can't run so many places at once. I told Xander about you and let him sample some of your recipes, and he loved them."

"I wish I had time to meet him, but I would just tell him as I told you, I'm loyal to the Hellstromm's. I'll be happy to sell him my recipes for his own chef to mimic, however."

"He will be disappointed, but that's life, right? You Halflings are always about business. Enjoy your night." Cornelius smiles, bearing his fangs. She tries her best to mimic the gesture, but has no fangs of her own. She makes her way back to the embassy, happy to of made a difference in dinner service and for clearing her mind of the day's events.

Crystal and William emerge from their chamber looking like the royalty they claim to be. She's in a crimson red dress, a long V cut from shoulders to beltline, revealing the center of her torso and midriff. It shimmers and sparkles as she walks, with the sides of the dress cut to allow her to walk freely and show off her legs. Two braids wrapped around her horns, hang down with gold rings woven into the ends. Several other braids hang from her head to the small of her back, also braided around themselves, making one long strand. Her makeup matches her dress with a light brushing of blush and red eyeshadow, making her eyes that much more appealing.

William is wearing a black jacket and pants, with a crimson red undershirt and black tie. The sleeves end with cufflinks of gold, with onyx gems topping them. His hair is styled, parting along the right side and trimmed up back to being short and military like. He even trimmed up his beard, so it wasn't as scruffy looking. Penelope has to do a double take on how regal they look, but is taken aback as they stop and knock on Zarra's door. She steps into the hallway and she presents herself like the princess she is.

Zarra wears a ruby red dress that matches her eyes. It crosses her chest and is held in place by small strings with the back completely open to the beltline. Her arms and upper body are open with a decorative pattern of semi-precious stones decorating the top, accenting her natural curves. Her entire torso is open except for a small bit of cloth attached just above the bellybutton and leading down into the dress itself, covering her legs. It too has semi-precious stones along the belt that shine when the firelight hits them, dancing on their own. Her copper red hair is braided in three parts, two hanging from the front with silver rings and the third larger one hanging down between her shoulder blades. Silver ornamentations pin the style together, adding an accent to it all. *Even color coordinated, they stand out.*

"What do you think William, isn't she beautiful?"

Penelope shakes her head. *Of course she is. He better bring his sword to keep the other guys away from them both.* She heads inside before they notice her. She removes her own clothing and freshens up a bit and puts on some lily scented perfume Crystal had given her. *It smells amazing. How does Crystal find this stuff?* She gets dressed, getting her new canary yellow dress on with the long open sleeves and V cut showing off her own body. She instinctively hides a few blades on her person. *You can never tell when you might have to use them.* She does her makeup and is a bit out of practice. She hasn't needed to use such beauty enhancements, but knows it's expected of her for tonight.

She exits and can see Tia in a new dark blue dress and Andrew wearing a black and dark blue suit escorting her. *They look very different from usual, but well-coordinated and uncomfortable.*

Penelope falls in step behind them, and they descend the steps to the bottom floor. Just before she takes her first step, she hears someone behind her. "Penelope!"

She turns and Chuck is standing there in a black suit and white undershirt. *He looks formal, but given he didn't have a lot of money, this must have cost him what he had left.* His hair is cut and looks proper and he even got a shave. *He cleans up well. Very handsome.*

"I wasn't invited to this dinner of yours, but I got dressed anyway. Can I at least escort you over?"

She smiles, and doesn't understand why. Something about this makes her happy. "Sure." He glides up to her and offers his arm. *Why did I say that?* She takes it the best she can. *Because even for a Human, he's cute and shows interest in you.* They start walking and Chuck continues. "Why don't I join you as your date? Everyone else has one, and I don't want you to look out of place."

"Zarra doesn't have a date."

"That's true, I guess."

322

"Walk up to her and ask her to take your hand. I need some entertainment tonight."

He shakes his head. "She's too fancy for my tastes, and well out of my budget." He laughs. "But you're perfect as you are."

He smiles at her and she can feel her face getting a little warm. *Oh, Provider, no, I'm blushing at his comment, aren't I? Are my ears turning red, giving me away?* She glances away. "Thank you, Chuck." They get outside and she can see Crystal and Zarra bracketing William as they talk and laugh, both hanging off one of his arms. Then Crystal turns back and makes eye contact with Penelope and the smile on her face widens like a hungry cat. *I might as well accept my fate at this point. She's got me.* She resigns to herself. "Chuck?"

"Yeah?"

"Who gave you that suit?"

"William did. He was told to get me something nice for tonight in case I got invited in." Crystal turns back laughing, having seen the look on Penelope's face as she now knows she was set up.

They enter the Baron's fortress and are guided to the dining hall as honored guests. A band plays, and a long rectangular wooden table covered in all kinds of food sits to one side, allowing an area for dancing. Crystal and her friends, along with Baron Tenishar and his dignitaries, sit, feast and talk. The night goes on, and Crystal and William slow dance together, alongside Tia with Andrew and, surprisingly, Penelope and Chuck.

William grins and gazes into Crystal's blue Dragon eyes. "I'm shocked that Penelope is dancing with Chuck." He holds Crystal close with one hand behind the small of her back and the other at the center of her shoulders.

Her arms are wrapped around his neck as she looks up at him. "I wouldn't be much of a Goddess of Love if I couldn't get something as obvious as those two together." She gives him her impish grin.

He raises an eyebrow in puzzlement. "Still on that kick, I see."

"Girl has to have goals, doesn't she?" Moments pass and they continue to talk. "Since I have your undivided attention, I have a very serious question to ask you." She turns her voice down and explains the situation to her betrothed.

"Wait? You love me and her?"

"Yes, I have strong feelings for her." She pushes herself closer to him. "But I will not pursue it unless you love her, too. I've told everyone I will die for you and I meant that. If you would rather us stay just us, then I'll accept that and help her find another." She cranes her neck back, looking up at him. "But before you decide, dance with her as you would dance with me."

"But why a dance?"

"I've seen how you look at her, or should say, 'don't'." She grins. "You get embarrassed when she's close by and puts herself in compromising positions. Just like you did before we got together. That's how I knew you liked what you saw." She swings her hips in time with the music.

"I didn't fall in love with you because of your beauty." He does his best to keep his voice down, but sounds flustered. "It was the fact you were willing to sacrifice yourself for me. That showed me how much you actually cared. After that, I knew you were the one for me."

"And Zarra has given up her entire life to be here with us in the pursuit of love." She places her face against his chest. "And she unexpectedly fell for both of us." She gazes back up at him with her icy blue eyes. "And I started feeling it while we were training together, and you can't say she's not honorable."

He nods. "I just don't know." He glances in Zarra's direction. She looks at the dancers and looks lonely and depressed, but strikingly beautiful. "I do find her attractive." His

324

admitting brings a smile to her face. "And she is a very wonderful person, but still, I don't know. Elves might do multi-partner relationships, but it's rare in Humans, almost like it's taboo."

"Tell you what, darling. You dance with her like you would with me, and don't hold back and give it a serious try." She glances at Zarra for a moment and then up at him. "And after you finish your dance with her and you can honestly say you have no feelings for her, I'll drop the matter entirely." She smiles at him. "We will stay mutually exclusive to one another forever."

William smirks. "And what if I do?"

"You're a man. Do something a man would do when he has a beautiful woman in his hands." She giggles as he runs his hands along her back. "At least talk to her as you two dance and see how you both feel about the matter."

"And how would this work, exactly? We are supposed to get married. As far as I know, once we are married, neither of us could marry her. She's royalty."

"We are definitely getting married, even if I have to drag you to that altar." She leans into him and pulls him down. Her face is just inches from his. "Love finds a way, darling. It did for us."

"Then the next dance is hers." He grins and looks at the obsidian beauty. "How would this work?"

"It would work just like regular couples, I suppose. Just the bed will have to be bigger?" She shrugs. "Emperor Marcus would know; he has five wives."

William holds back a laugh. "Yeah, I guess if he can handle five at once, I could with two." He kisses her on the nose. "Trade out with her and we will talk, see where we sit with this situation, but I make no promises. Love and lust are two different things. We must be sure about this."

"Using my own words against me? You learn fast, darling." The song finishes moments later, and Crystal motions for Zarra to come over to them. A smile appears on her face as she crosses the dance floor.

Tia and Andrew hold each other close, watching the other dancers and how lovely of a party it is. "Tonight is our last night together." Tia sounds depressed. "Tomorrow we leave for New Haven and hope to put a finish to this whole tragedy."

"I want to come along." Andrew holds her tighter. "I worry about you."

She smiles, gazing at him with her green eyes. "I worry about you, too, but you have duties here preparing for the assault. They are going to need experienced healers for the wounded that will come in." She pats him on the chest. "And while you're here, you can figure out more about this Sky Lady Love Goddess person." She shakes her head in disbelief. "I knew Crystal was full of herself, but even I didn't think she would try to impersonate a goddess for a kick. She's going to interfere with this new religion, and it might have unforeseen consequences."

"I didn't think she was capable either, but after hearing her speak so passionately about love, you could almost believe she was the prophet." He chuckles. "Maybe she will become a priestess and do both arcane and divine spell casting."

Tia bursts out a laugh and covers her mouth to stop it. "I can see that now her screaming some evocation, then pray for healing, healing, then throw out a bunch of ice projectiles, and putting up a protection ward. She wouldn't know what to do with herself." They both get a good laugh, thinking of Crystal mixing her up her spells and prayers.

Andrew looks at Penelope and Chuck and how odd they look together. *She's only waist high to him and they are doing their best to look normal.* "You think those two are an item, or is she still humoring him?"

326

"It's too hard to tell." Tia examines the couple. "Sometimes I think she's going to kill him. Other times, I think she's waiting for him to kiss her. They are an enigma."

"I think it's cute. They are very different, but even with her reservations, she's giving it an honest try," Andrew observes. "For as long as I can remember being around her, I've never seen her date. I had my questions if she was more deeply religious than us."

Tia smiles and nods, placing her head against his chest and he holds her close, dancing slowly with the music. "Let's not worry about them. Just hold me close while we still have a chance." She notices that Crystal and William had stopped dancing and Crystal walks away from him, signaling to Zarra to stand up. The two of them meet halfway and talk a few moments, and Zarra has an enormous smile on her face. Crystal takes a spot next to the Baron as Zarra walks up to William.

"That's nice of William to dance with her, being she came here alone." Andrew looks down at Tia. "He's a good friend to her, and Crystal looks to be supportive of it."

Tia looks closer at how William is holding Zarra and shakes her head. "Friends don't hold each other like that." She flicks a finger as if to point and Andrew turns to look again. William places his arms around her back and shoulders, and she rests her hands on his chest and hip.

Andrew sighs. "This 'Love Goddess' thing has gotten into her head. If we aren't careful, she's going to believe she truly is, and it might get bad. I knew she was self-centered, but after all she's been through, this can't be good."

"I'll have a few weeks with her when we are headed to New Haven. Maybe I can intervene and try to convince Zarra and William to help me."

Chuck and Penelope hold hands since it would look awkward with him placing his hand on the back of her head.

They dance to the music the best they can. "I told you we would look silly."

"I know, but I would rather look silly with you, then be with anyone else."

She shakes her head. "You know, it's that kind of talk that makes it harder for me to keep you at a distance." She glances around at the other dancers. "But it doesn't change my mind about us."

He smiles down at her. "I won't stop trying, however."

"I wish you would. I feel bad being here with you because it's like I'm leading you on." she looks up at him. "Don't get me wrong. If I were Human, or you were a Halfling like me, I could see it working. But look at how different we are." She motions to herself and then to him a few times. "Crystal and William have a size difference, but it's still close, at least. They can kiss each other and wrap their arms around each other." She looks back down. "This is why we are incompatible. Even if I let go of all my reservations and had the same enthusiasm as you for this, our difference in size is our limitations."

Chuck asks slyly. "So, you're saying because you can't kiss me easily, we can't be together?"

"Among other things, but yes. Look at us dancing. I can't wrap my arms around you because I'll be hugging your belt. Don't tell me that wouldn't look disturbing."

"I understand, but as your friend says, love is powerful."

"You just don't understand."

"I do. You're concerned over something as insubstantial as a height difference." He smiles, trying to put her at ease. "And I'm willing to overlook such things." His eyes widen realizing what he had just said.

She gives him a disapproving look, making him sweat, but can't hold it and laughs. "I'm going to confess something, and you will keep it to yourself, got it?"

Chuck's heart leaps. "Sure, I promise."

"A long time ago, when I first arrived at Rose Harbor, I did date a Human. He was sweet, intelligent, and a great lover." She dips her head. "But when I needed him most, at my deepest failing, he wasn't at my side. He left me to flail on my own." She holds back her tears. "After that, I didn't date a Human again. With no other Halflings that I liked in Rose Harbor, I just buried myself in my work, and being the best cook in the city makes me feel wonderful."

Chuck finishes, running his hand in her hair. "And I come along and awaken those feelings again." He nods. "I'll leave you alone then."

He moves to pull away, but she holds onto him. "No, no." They look at each other. "I enjoyed our kiss back at the hotel, and the way you're always trying to be there for me." She does her best to gather her thoughts. "This is not a confession of love. I just think our worlds are too different." She looks towards Crystal and watches as she walks away from William and motions to Zarra to stand. They meet halfway and exchange words. *Whatever Crystal told her must have been good for Zarra now has an enormous smile on her face.* Crystal then sits down next to the Baron and strikes up a conversation with him and Zarra makes her way to William, but looks nervous about it. He wraps his arms around her, like he did with Crystal, and she reaches up and rests her arms on his chest and hip. "There is something you don't see every day."

"What?" Chuck follows where she's looking to. "How lucky can one guy get?"

Penelope scowls at him. "Don't get any ideas."

Chuck looks back down and continues to smile. "You're all I need." She can feel her face getting warm.

Zarra walks up to William and she can feel fear in the pit of her stomach. *What am I doing? Elves in multi-person relationships are commonplace, but Humans are much more reserved. What will others think of this display? Maybe I shouldn't be doing this, no matter how much I want to be with them. What will their parents think?* He smiles at her and she smiles in return nervously, as he wraps his arms around her. She feels little jolts of pleasure as his hands touch the small of her bare back and shoulders, embracing her. She reaches up and places her arms on his chest and hip. *I've wanted this moment for so long, but I want to be respectful of their personal lives. I'm glad we had a heart-to-heart talk, but even my courage has its limits.*

William holds Zarra as the same as Crystal, just as he promised. Her obsidian skin is silky smooth, but she lacks the scales he's used to along Crystal's spine. She smells of lily and it pleases him with her being so close. "Crystal told me of why you're on the run and what you're looking for."

"My 'father' informed me he was negotiating with the Sullivan Empire about a peace treaty, and that I should be looking to being part of that treaty." He feels her hands twitch, and she looks away for a moment. "I know exactly what that means." She looks up at him, searching his brown eyes for understanding. "When I confessed to Crystal how I felt, I expected her to get angry."

"But she didn't, and I can tell you're surprised to be in my arms right now expecting me to of been angry for being forced into this?"

She nods, confirming his assessment. "Humans aren't like Elves. My people don't look at relationships the same way. Coupling with more than one person isn't unusual there." She turns with William as the song continues. "But hearing Crystal talk about it at the makeshift church made me wonder if Humans could actually accept it." She places her forehead against his massive chest. "I don't mean to burden you with such things."

"You're not burdening me." He just holds her, moving in time with the music. "I pictured me and Crystal growing old together, having kids, and taking over her father's business ventures." He rubs his hand along her spine, comforting her. "But me and Crystal are in control of our own destiny, free to make those kinds of life decisions. It must be truly horrible to be told you have to marry someone that you don't even know."

She can feel him holding her tighter, feeling his kindness as he tries to understand. "That's why I fled. I stole the only steam ship in our navy under false pretenses, then ditched them to be here. I'm running, like a coward." She pulls back to look up at him again. "But after being around you two, seeing how you two can argue and tease, and laugh, and support each other, I wanted that too. Could I be happy like that?" She takes a deep breath, trying to calm her beating heart.

Tears well up, but she holds them in check. He finishes her thought. "And being around us for days on end, laughing, joking, training, and confiding in you, you felt more for us because in your society, it would be acceptable."

Her smile, having faded away, returns. "I don't mean to put you in a difficult position. To be honest, unless I stay on the run, hidden, I'll be dragged back to my empire, either forced to marry that clown, or have my title stripped from me and placed in prison." She sounds as if accepting her fate. "Not exactly an 'honorable' thing to do. If Johnathan takes my powers for being a coward and not facing up to my duties…" She trails off.

"I think it's braver, being here locked in my arms, confessing your feelings, not knowing how I will react. It's not cowardice to retreat from horrific circumstance." He places his hand on the back of her head, cradling it. She smiles, looking up at him. "And there is nothing dishonorable about retreating from a position that's indefensible."

She lets out a brief chuckle. "Spoken like a true military commander. Guess I could look at it like that."

"You know I can only marry Crystal. Even if we were to get together and get this to work between the three of us, I don't believe there is any legal avenue for us. By law, I can marry more than one partner. They put this in because of the Elves in Rose Harbor believe as you do, so that's not the problem. I just don't know of any non-Elves to have used this law to do so."

"Then what's the problem if you can take more partners?"

"You're a princess from another empire. If somehow we had a good relationship, and it got to where marriage is something all three of us wanted, there is no way your father would sign off on it."

She nods, and her smile fades. "Crystal said something about writing a letter to the Emperor about getting legal help along those lines, I think." She pauses as a new song starts up and he moves his hands to her exposed love handles and they continue their dance. "But if it's going to be too difficult, then I guess we can finish our dance and I'll be on my way."

"I didn't say that." Speaking with an upbeat tone. "I'm willing to see where this goes. The prospect of having the two most beautiful women the world has ever known, being at my sides fills me with happiness."

Her spirits lift. "What are you saying?"

"I'm saying if it wouldn't cause a huge scene. I would kiss you right now to show you I cared, but not everyone will understand, and I would rather let Crystal fill them in before causing a possible diplomatic incident in front of the Baron." She grins, but he continues. "I'm not saying that I love you, but I care deeply about you and you have my trust. It's just too early to tell if it's love or not."

She couldn't be happier. "I understand, and I'm glad we've made this step together." They finish their dance and walk over to Crystal, Zarra still holding William's hand. Crystal looks to Zarra. "So, is it our turn?"

"Our/Your turn?" Zarra and William ask at the same time.

"To dance. I should get to dance with my girlfriend, too." William raises an eyebrow as she drags Zarra back onto the dance floor. *We are getting a lot of looks, but that is to be expected with me.* They get out there and Crystal and Zarra both look confused when trying to figure out what they should do. "So who leads?"

Zarra shrugs. "In my culture, the older woman does in the relationship, but you would be considered the first in the relationship, so it's up to you?"

Crystal nods and places her hands on Zarra's hips, and Zarra places hers on Crystal's shoulders as a new song from the band ques up. "Well then, I'll lead this time. You can have next." They laugh and talk, circling each other.

Baron Tenishar leans over to William. "Something I should know?"

William shakes his head. "I'm not sure if I could explain it, but they look like they are having fun."

CHAPTER 30

(Prepare)

The party ends and they all head back to the embassy, giving farewells to their Catfolk hosts. Getting back to their room, William informs Crystal and Zarra he must change and do his rounds, leaving the two girls alone in the room. Crystal grabs a pen and parchment and pens her letter to the Emperor explaining their situation and their current plan for handling the Black Rose. She finishes and seals it, ready for the captain of the *Opal Star*. "I'm thirsty. I'm going to grab some strawberry juice. Do you want anything?"

Zarra sits down at the table. "Yeah, I'll take some."

Crystal reaches up, stretching to grab a few cups, and Zarra can finally look and appreciate Crystal's beauty without being embarrassed. Crystal gets the juice from the cooler and pours them both a drink. "I had fun dancing tonight. We were the center of attention." They reach out and hold each other hands across the table.

Zarra finishes her drink and looks into Crystal's eyes. *She said to take a chance and see what happens.* She leans forward, still holding Crystal's hand, and pulls her closer. *I can't believe what I'm about to do.*

Zarra lets go and cups Crystal's face and draws her in. Their lips make contact. Crystal slowly closes her eyes, drinking in the moment. *Her lips are so soft compared to Williams. This is intriguing. I never knew it could be like this.* After a long moment, they gaze into each other eyes as they separate. "That was amazing, but we should get to bed soon if we are going to get up to leave tomorrow."

"Did I do something wrong?"

Crystal tries to compose herself. "Not at all." Her smiles grows wider. "I could do that all night, but we really have an important mission and we need our sleep."

"Then I better get back to my chamber then." They kiss goodnight, and Zarra heads to her chambers.

The next morning, they prepare to leave and the *Opal Star* lands in the courtyard of the Baron's fortress. It is much larger than *Bastion* and drops its loading ramps. Hundreds of Rose Harbor troops disembark along with weapons and supplies. William escorts Crystal to the ship where her dark green skinned, Half-Orc captain is seeing to the unloading. Spotting the countess and her escort, he closes the gap to greet them.

She introduces herself first. "I'm Countess Crystal Hellstromm." Then waves her hand to the massive man at her side. "And this is Captain Blakely."

"Captain Throrg Zedan." He takes their hands, shaking them.

"Pleasure to meet you, Captain." She pulls a sealed letter from her handbag. "This needs to get to the Emperor as soon as you're done here. So put it in your safe and don't forget about it."

He takes it and laughs. "I have something from the Emperor to give you to you as well." He hands over a small sealed box to Crystal.

"Thank you, Captain. I'll let you get back to work. Thank you for your service to the Empire." They walk back and Penelope runs into them, limping.

William points to her leg. "You alright Ms. Penelope?"

"I'll be fine, just a little sore. Been running all over, getting ready to leave, and might have pulled something."

William nods. "Have Tia or Zarra look at it and get some healing."

"I'll be ok. Too much to get done the next few hours before takeoff." Crystal bends down, looking her over. Penelope is about to say something when Crystal stands up with a grin and puts her arm back in Williams. "What?"

"Nothing." She turns to William. "Let us be going, darling."

They leave Penelope there and Crystal spots Tom and Tyra walking into the embassy gates. "Wonder where those two were all night."

"The dojo most likely, training their students while they had a chance." He looks down to at her. "Speaking of, don't you, Zarra, and Tia have some training to do this morning?"

"We are going to do that on the ship after we take off." She looks up at him, eyes wide. "Is my Vardo loaded and the transport wagons?"

"Did that last night. That's why I was gone."

"What would I do without you?"

"Tease someone till you start a war." She shoots a glare at him and changes a few shades of pink out of anger and embarrassment.

Captain Motsana and two squads of Portstown's guard arrive, handing William a document. "Reporting as ordered, Captain." He stands rigidly. William looks it over and Baron Tenishar assigned two squads as promised.

"Welcome aboard, Captain Motsana." He takes Motsana's hand. "You ever been to New Haven?"

"No. Never had a reason to go till now. Going to be a learning experience." He waves back towards the fort. "We have two wagons of supplies and heavy winter gear. It's going to be cold that far north this time of year."

Crystal perks up. "How cold?"

"Zero, maybe a little above."

William glances down at Crystal. "Better make sure we are prepared, then."

"My scepter can help a little, but we need to figure something out." She turns him towards her. "I'll take Zarra and Tia and see if we can find some wands, or some other magic items that can help with the weather."

William stops her from leaving. "We need to get going. If we take off too late, that incoming army will see us and know we have brought reinforcements."

"And if I don't, people *will* freeze to death. I won't be long. It's not like I'm going dress shopping."

"They are soldiers. They know the risk. Besides, we have winter gear for them."

"At zero, that's not enough, and I'm not letting them die walking in the snow. Give me one hour to find something that helps."

They stare each other down for a moment and his shoulders slump. "Fine, one hour." He bends down and hugs her. "Your heart is in the right place. I admire that about you. Just don't get stuck preaching to your 'followers'."

"I make no promises about that." She taps his armor with the long, thin box. "One hour. If I'm not back, send Tyra to kidnap me." She looks down and realizes she still has the box in her hand. "Oh, let's see what this is first." She opens it and inside is a note and some insignias.

Countess, I forgot to do this while you were here, so it falls on you as my proxy to fulfill some duties. Inside are some rank insignias and you must present the commissions on behalf of the Empire. The list is attached to who gets what. Enjoy your flight to New Haven and come back to me in one piece this time.

Emperor Marcus Rose

She pulls the list from the box and reads over them and smiles. William peeks around the note. "What is it, honey?"

She looks at him. "Emperor Marcus has some orders for me, and for me to issue them to you.

"Oh really? What orders?"

"ATTENTION!" William and Motsana and all troops in the area snap upright, and bring all the crew members in the area to a halt as well. Zarra, Tia, and Andrew all turn to see what the commotion is about. She steps in front of William and pulls an insignia out of the box. She speaks loudly and with all the authority she can muster. "I, Countess Hellstromm, on behalf of the Rose Empire hereby bestow you the rank of major and grant you all rights and privileges of the rank thereof." She removes his captain's insignia and replaces it with the insignia of major.

She then steps in front of Motsana. "Captain Motsana." She bears her fangs. "On behalf of His Majesty, Emperor Marcus Rose, I hereby grant you the honorary rank of Captain in the Emperor's Royal Guard, with all rights and privileges of the rank thereof. Furthermore, I place you in command of Rose Harbor forces here in Portstown. Congratulations." She pins Williams's old insignia to his uniform.

Captain Motsana looks confused. "I was already a captain."

Crystal nods. "But of the Portstown guard. Now you're one of the Royal Guard. Gives you permanent command of the garrison here." She smiles at William. "I hope I did that right. It was my first time. At ease."

"You did fine." William runs this thumb over his new insignia. "So I'm a Major now." They turn towards the ship.

"Major pain in the ass." She slaps his butt. "Guess the Emperor likes how you took down the Black Rose at that fortress and saved my life. Showing good tactical strategy and ambushing the Black Rose here at Portstown made you look good, too. Get this ship ready to leave, Major." She hands him the box and her voice drops to a seductive growl. "I'll be back with what we need." She turns and shouts for Zarra and Tia, "C'mon ladies, we have to gather some supplies that aren't standard issue."

They make their way through the streets, quickly gathering extra winter gear. They find a place that sells magical wears and enters. Crystal goes through and starts picking things out. She holds up some wands. "Wands of Fireball? Nice."

"What do you need that for?" Tia examines a bandolier loaded with healing vials. "This would be much handier."

"Grab that too, then. As much trouble that finds us, we going to need that."

"This could be useful." Zarra holds up a gem of life sensing. "Be nice to see ambushes before they happen."

Crystal smiles. "My father has one of those gems built into his helm. Next time we are home, I can have him build you a similar setup into yours."

"Think he will? I don't want to impose."

"If I ask him, he will. Especially since it will be for one of my bodyguards." They continue to look around and she finally breaks down and asks the shop keep if he has a staff of temperature control.

"No, such things aren't in demand." He leans on the counter. "What are you needing to accomplish?"

"I'm trying to protect my troops from the harsh weather up north. I don't want them to freeze in the subzero temps."

He nods, then points a finger at her. "I got something you might use, but it's expensive." He walks over to the wand section and pulls a wand of environmental protection. "Holds fifty charges. I have several of them."

She interrupts him. "I would need a hundred of them for my troopers."

"Allow me to finish countess." This brings her ire. "If you combine that with this," he holds up a rod of mass range. "You slot the wand in here." He demonstrates how it functions by placing the rod over the tip of the wand. "And then instead of it being a targeted effect, it's a blanket effect. Rod holds two charges, so that will give you about eight hours straight protection for just two wand charges a day."

She takes it from him, looking it over. "How many of these rods do you have?"

"Just the one, I'm afraid."

"Is there a way I can force the rod to recharge somehow? Like manually?"

"Sure, you need a sorceress, but it can be forced."

"I'm a sorceress. How do I get it to work?"

"Just hold it in your hand and you can pour your magical energy into it and recharge it, but if you're not very strong or experienced, it could put quite the drain on you. So be careful."

"I'll take it, the wands of fireball, this life gem and the bandolier." She looks at Zarra and Tia. "Anything else we need? William is expecting us back so we can lift off."

"This magical aid kit. I want that." Tia hefts a heavy bag up onto the counter. "I don't ask for much, but this contains some things that could get us out of a lot of situations."

"Oh, that reminds me." She turns to the shop keep. "Wands of repair. How many you have?"

"I have four, I believe."

"Sold, tally this up and send the bill to Baron Tenishar with the note of empire expenses." She bags the stuff.

"You can't just walk out of here without paying. I'm not 'sending a bill'. I want the money now."

She turns to him and Zarra and Tia can see her getting redder, then the white returns. "For the love of your countrymen, I need these supplies. I'll tack on an extra ten percent as compensation for your inconveniences if you could find it in your heart to help your countess."

He looks at all three women and sighs. "Fine, for the love of the country, I'll do it." He writes up the receipt and hands it to her, "But I want your seal here so the Baron knows I'm not making it up." She smiles and agrees, stamping her signet on the ink pad and then to the paper.

Penelope makes her rounds, sweeping for dangers and checking crates for unauthorized alterations. She doesn't have too long and is crawling around the supply carts when she hears Chuck enter the cargo hold.

"Penelope?" He tries to whisper, but way too loud to be called one.

He knows I'm trying to work here. She sighs and crawls out from under a cart. He's walking around looking lost. She climbs silently around the crates and finally gets up next to him. "I'm working here." This gives him a start, having not heard or seen her coming.

"Sorry babe, just figured I would offer my help. I want to be useful to you." He holds his arms out. "I don't exactly have a job around here like everyone else."

"I have to be sure in here that everything is checked by me personally." She leans closer and whispers to him. "So, I can't exactly get help. Why not ask Captain Blakely? See if he needs anything."

"It's major now, or at least that's what I heard as I came in here. The countess promoted him."

Penelope speculates out loud. "Order for that came from the Emperor. She doesn't carry rank insignias with her."

He shrugs. "So, I should go help Major Blakely?"

She nods, but before he can turn away, she grabs his shirt and pulls him in close to her face. "Morgana, help me if Crystal finds out about us, because you're calling me a lover's name in public. If she finds out because you can't keep this to yourself, I'll never speak to you again."

"I don't understand, I thought, because we…" She presses her lips against his, silencing him for the moment and he wraps his hands around her body.

A few moments pass, and she breaks away. "If *she* finds out what we did, I will NEVER hear the end of it, and my life will be a living hell. So as far as anyone is concerned, we are not a thing." She lets go of him and hops down. "I have work to do, and so do you. Get to it." He smiles and walks away with a whistle. "And don't whistle. You might as well be advertising our arrangement."

He exits the cargo hold, climbing the stairs and walks along the hallways, not really paying attention to where he's going, and runs into William. "Hey, watch where you're going!" William turns and sees it's Chuck.

Chuck sounds a little down. "Sorry Major, I wasn't paying attention. I'm preoccupied. Won't happen again."

"What's wrong Chuck?"

"I can't say. I made a promise."

That sound suspicious. William looks down at the smaller man. "Made a promise to who?"

Chuck looks thoughtful a moment and goes to speak, mouth opening but closing again as he thinks better of it. "I don't think I can say that either, to be honest." He looks up at the Major and can see he's not amused. "I'm sorry sir, I gave my word and I don't want to look untrustworthy if I break it."

William looms over the kid, placing a hand on his chest to prevent him from retreating. "You're not making it sound any less suspicious when you're trying to hide something from me."

"I know." Chuck looks back down at the deck plating. "If the countess wanted you to keep something to yourself, would you tell anyone or just accept any heat tossed your way?"

"The countess is having you keep something from me?"

"No, no, sir." Chuck chuckles nervously, looks away and places a hand behind his head. "I don't know what to say. It's just an example."

"It's Penelope, isn't it?" Chuck's eyes widen and his head swivels around. William smiles. "That's a yes. She break your heart again?"

"Not exactly, sir."

It's William's turn to be shocked. "You and her?" His eyes widen in disbelief. "Really? But she had all these reasons that actually made sense."

Chuck holds his hands out, and fear pours from his lips. "You can't say anything to the countess. Forget you even ran into me." He's in a full-blown panic. "If it gets back to her and Penelope gets teased, I think she would kill me."

"Who, Penelope or Crystal?"

"My luck, it would be a race between them. Penelope for letting the secret out or the countess for taking advantage of her friend."

William raises an eyebrow. "Taking advantage? This sounds interesting." He stands there stoically.

"I really should be going." Chuck tries to leave, but William's massive hand stops his movement again.

"How did you take advantage, exactly?"

"She was lonely, I didn't know. I was just persistent trying to get her to like me, and last night, I woke up with her in my bed, ok?" He keeps it at a whisper. "I didn't force her there and to be honest, I thought she was there to murder me, so my heart about came out of my chest when she woke me up." Chuck looks up at him. "But she spun a sad story of being lonely and how I've been such a good guy..."

"And she doesn't want Crystal to know because she's been teasing her for weeks now about you two and it's coming to be." Chuck nods and William pats him on the shoulder. "Ok, I'll keep it to myself. I know what Crystal is like when someone gives her something to annoy them with." He lets Chuck go and goes to check on Penelope. He climbs down the stairs into the cargo hold and looks over things. His armor echoes off the walls, letting Penelope know he's there.

She comes out of hiding. "Hey *Major*. Congrats on the promotion." She walks up to him, still limping a little.

"You sure you don't want that looked at? Looks like you could have *pulled* or *stretched* something."

I don't like the look of that smile or his tone. Something is up. She smiles back. "I'll be fine soon. I just overdid it with my morning stretches before starting breakfast."

William walks the cargo hold, and she does her best to follow along. "Does everything check out? We ready to go, or should I have Chuck come down here and help you? There is a lot to do here with you injured."

I think he knows, but how? She keeps up her smile. "I'm almost done. He doesn't need to be down here. Should be finished in the next half an hour."

344

"Sounds good. The girls will hopefully be back soon, and we can take off. Then you and Chuck can go back to *faking* not being in a relationship." He looks at the shock and embarrassment on her face.

"How?"

"How do I know? Who doesn't? You two danced last night, held hands, you invited him along to be your date. It's obvious you have feelings for him even when you try too rational them away."

She shakes her head. "No, if everyone knew, Crystal would be on me like a dog with a new chew toy." Her brows furl and points up at him with a finger. "So don't pull that cop crap with me to get a confession. How do *you* know?"

William can see the anger is real. "Chuck." Before she comes unhinged, he holds up a hand. "He was acting suspicious and I more or less intimidated it out of him."

"And I sent him straight to you." She shakes her head, realizing she gave herself up like that. "I should have told him to stay in his room."

"I won't tell her, but if she catches wind that he's hiding something, she won't be as gentle getting it out of him as I was. If you want your secret to stay that way, better get him to keep off her radar."

CHAPTER 31

(Cold White North)

The girls return with their supplies and are greeted by Captain Motsana. "Countess, everything is ready to go, and the troops are loaded." He falls in step with her as they board the ship. "Major Blakely is on the bridge awaiting you, and I had our town's history brought to your quarters. Baron Tenishar mentioned you were interested in it, so he had it all pulled from the library."

"Very good Captain." She speaks with an air of authority. "Join your men. We will lift off as soon as I reach the bridge." She dismisses him with a wave of her hand. He bows and walks away. They make their way to the bridge door and Crystal stops. "Tia, could you see to Shadow? She was walking with a limp and could use your help. I need everyone top notch from here on out."

"Sure thing, countess" She makes her exit, leaving Crystal alone with Zarra.

"Any orders for me?"

Crystal looks around and finds they are alone, then reaches out and cups her face, drawing her in and giving her a passionate kiss. "Take this stuff to my quarters. After that, we will figure something out. I'll probably be outside on the deck watching the ground go by." Zarra nods, takes the items, and walks away. Crystal watches her intently as her hips sway, then turns about and enters the bridge.

William smiles. "Buy me anything?"

"We got all kinds of goodies. I believe we are set to take on anything." She turns to Captain Zylra. "Let's go Captain." She holds her hand out and makes a fist. "I have an empire to build and a cult to crush."

They loft into the air and once underway, Crystal walks out onto the deck but, William leaves the bridge and heads back to his cabin. He enters and can hear Zarra in the other room. He knocks on the joining door and she opens it. Grinning, she places a hand on his chest. "What brings you here?"

"Crystal is out on the deck, so I came here to check on you. Having second thoughts?"

Zarra smiles and pulls him down so her lips can meet his. They wrap their arms around each other. *I'm so glad I went on this trip. I found what I was looking for.* They separate and smile at each other. "How's that for an answer?"

His grin doesn't fade. "That was an excellent answer." He stands up. "Wish I could stay, but I have duties to perform."

She nods. "Guess I'll join Crystal on the deck."

He caresses her cheek, then exits their room. *I can't help but wonder if we are doing the right thing or not. If it wasn't for the uncertainty of our futures, I could see this being a wonderful thing. I hope this isn't all in vain.* He takes some steps down towards the armory. *But I care about them both. No mistaking that feeling.*

They have several days traveling over the sea, taking the long way to New Haven, staying just within view of the shore, navigating around. They avoid any New Haven ships at sea or being spotted from the shore. Tia, Zarra, and Crystal continue to do their training, with Tom finding their balance and getting over their inner turmoil. Zarra and William learn more about each other as they train and Captain Motsana also spars with the troops to help strengthen their bond together.

The mountains cutting New Haven peninsula off from the rest of the continent come into view on the fourth day. They are covered in snow and ice and the air is frigid. Crystal, laying back on a deck chair, enjoys the weather as she continues to read. Using the history books from Portstown, she cross-references from the books about the gods. She's more curious now than ever since her odd experience with the people in Portstown and wondering if there could be a connection.

Night falls and a waning moon getting close to half is coming up. The only other light is coming from her lantern next to her. Zarra walks out on the deck wearing a tight-fitting outfit and caring some strawberry juice. Crystal smiles, knowing she must be freezing in that. "Do you mind, sweetie?"

Crystal chants her incantation for her environmental spell and Zarra bends down, laying her lips on Crystal's, transferring the energy. Zarra stops shivering, and a look of contentment settles over her. "Thanks." She hands Crystal a drink and sits in the chair next to her. She points to the books. "Find anything useful?"

"Took a colossal risk kissing me out here. It might confuse people to see us doing that." Crystal sips her drink.

"I don't see why we should hide it. We love each other. Who cares what the others think?"

"I agree with you. It shouldn't matter." She sets her cup down. "But everyone knows I'm betrothed to William, so they might get confused on why I'm kissing on the Silvian princess. It's more of an 'I don't want to be asked uncomfortable questions' consideration." She shrugs. "But if you don't want to hide it, I'll happily come out."

Zarra shakes her head. "I understand the complications. Will there be a time we won't have to hide it?" She shrugs. "Will and I spar alone down below, but it slowly turns from training to

348

talking and being close to each other. He's truly a one-of-a-kind man."

Crystal reaches over and pats Zarra on the hand. "Yeah, he is, and of course there will be, and it won't be long. If you were a regular woman, we wouldn't have to hide it at all. It's your status as a princess that puts this into the weird category." She turns and looks at the obsidian beauty. "I would love nothing more than to shout to the world how much we all love each other, and damn anyone who is against it." She slides her hand against Zarra's. "But till we solve the royalty problem, it has to be a hush-hush thing."

"I could solve that with a single letter to my 'parents'." She continues seeing Crystal's intrigue peek on her face. "All I would have to do is renounce my status and citizenship to their empire. Then I'll be a nobody and we could date, kiss, and live our lives."

"Let's make that a last resort. If this doesn't work out, you shouldn't be giving up everything over it."

"What do you mean?" Zarra sounds concerned. "Are we having a rough patch already?"

"No, baby. I enjoy every moment together with you. Just life is full of unforeseen circumstances." She turns her full attention to Zarra. "I don't want to imagine a life without you in it, but you shouldn't make any radical changes unless it's a last resort." She sounds very confident. "I'm sure the Emperor can help us." Zarra smiles, her white teeth so prominent in the dark. Crystal changes the subject and casts her gaze upwards. "Let's just enjoy each other's presence and the view of the sky from here. Have you ever just looked up and gazed at it all? Wondered how many stars there are, and why there is a thick band of them so bright and long in the middle?"

Zarra stops looking at Crystal and lays back and looks up at the sky, taking it all in. *I remember back at her home of looking up then. She has an eye for this. The beauty, the purity of it.* The bright band of stars stretching from horizon to horizon with a few wisps of clouds. "As a Dark Elf, I never really appreciated the sky." Her tone is filled with melancholy. "Where I was born, there is no sky. Just the stone walls of the caves and tunnels."

"And when you were adopted by the Silvian's, you didn't look up in wonder this whole time?"

Zarra shakes her head. "I did, but I didn't have any real wonderment about it till you. To me, they were just stars. Lights in the sky. Didn't matter." She waves her hand above her, indicating to the blinking lights above her. She lets out a small chuckle and turns to look at Crystal. "But now I'm seeing things from other views, and I'm glad you have this kind of wonderment to point out to me."

Crystal looks at the lantern and turns it off and then tugs on Zarra's hand. Zarra stands up and, seeing the smile on Crystal's face intensify. She continues to pull until Zarra is kneeling on the deck chair over Crystal. "What happened to not letting people find out?"

"You think they can see you in the dark at that distance?"

"The Dwarves might." She gasps as Crystal wraps her arms around her, pulling her down. Zarra whispers a short incantation of her own and a magical darkness envelops them. "Now they can't."

William, Chuck, Penelope, and Motsana sit at a table in the conference room going over Chuck's map he drew and comparing it to maps the captain brought. They speak for hours, getting as many details out of Chuck as they can, as he points out on the map all the places he remembers.

"They must be here in the ruins of Old Haven." William points on the map. "You said it was a swampy area, so it's the only place that would make sense."

The captain nods his head in agreement. "I concur with that assessment. It would make sense to hide in the ruins, being no one would dare go there after its fall."

"What happened there? Why is it abandoned?"

Chuck answers. "The sea level rose about two hundred years ago or so. It swallowed the town, killing thousands. According to myth and legend, three beings of incredible power clashed there in a bid for ultimate dominance. The power they exerted was so great it caused the sea to rise and created the mountains that cut the peninsula off from the rest of Bacarian."

"And that's why it's off limits. The people of New Haven say it's cursed and don't speak of it." The Captain finishes.

William nods, but it's Penelope that speaks up. "Did anything like that happen in Portstown?"

"No, we weren't devastated like that, but we noted the new mountain range in our history books and Delveon itself shook as if it was being ripped apart. We chalked it up to normal seismic activity." Captain Motsana leans over. "So, when we heard about what happened to Old Haven, we thought an earthquake destroyed it, and they was spinning us a story about these beings to drum up sympathy."

William taps the map. "But now we know about the war between the gods happening in that time period and could lend credence to their story."

"I think that's a fairy tale, too." The captain straightens up. "But that's a personal opinion."

"Very well could be. I won't fault you for that. Just exploring all probabilities." William stands up. "Penelope, Chuck, when we get to just outside of the town of New Haven, you two are going to infiltrate. Get a hotel room there for a day or so, check things out. Find out who's in charge and get us an idea if they are hostile to Rose Harbor and/or Portstown. If the Black Rose has taken over there, we won't be able to go in and any chance of a peaceful resolution will be pointless."

"If they are hostile, then what?"

"We must call in the *Opal Star*. She might be a freighter, but she has sixty cannons. Between her and the *Bastion*, we can mount an attack from the air and devastate the city's defenses. Sink what we can in her ports and run. This will give us an advantage when we bring in more troops to take over, destroying the Black Rose for good."

"I don't think they will be hostile. I live just outside of town on a farm, but it's far from where we are going in at." He blows out some air. "But they look at Rose Harbor as indifferent because of the distance." Chuck sounds hopeful. "You should be able to work with them and might get lucky and they might hate the Black Rose as much as you do. They have been trying to start a war that New Haven has no interest in, could have made them bitter."

"I hope you're right, but that's our primary goal is figuring out New Haven's disposition to us. If they will hear us out, we can work with them. If not," he shrugs. "Plan B, for *Bastion*." He points at Penelope and Chuck. "It's all on you two. Gather what you can, just don't spend all day in the hotel room." Penelope doesn't look amused.

Captain Motsana addresses them as well. "We should land in the morning sometime, dress warm, temps are going to be bad out there."

William waves to the door. "If that's all, then dismissed. Grab some food while you can."

Everyone leaves the room, except William. He continues to look over maps and reports, looking for anything he could have missed. Focused on his work, he didn't see Zarra walk in. He bolts upright when she speaks, her voice sounding concerned. "Crystal sent me to find you. It's almost ten p.m. We were going to have dinner together, but you didn't show."

He leans back in his chair, pinching the bridge of his nose and closing his eyes. "Sorry, hun, this mission has me worried. I want to minimize risks and make sure we are prepared. Don't want anyone to die without a good reason."

She walks over to him and sits in his lap. "You're a great man and an excellent commander." She wraps her arm around him and leans in, giving him a passionate kiss. "But you need to eat. Let's go, and we can all talk about it over dinner."

He smiles at her. "You're right. I'm lucky to have you two in my life." He motions with his arm, palm open, for her to lead the way. She stands up and they walk together to their chamber. "So where is Crystal? Usually, she's the one coming and dragging me away."

"She's cross-referencing some information she found in Portstown history with those books about the gods and their war. We were on the deck when she made a discovery and had to run back to your quarters and check something else."

He nods. "I think I know something of New Haven's history that Chuck told me that could help as well."

They arrive, and dinner is waiting for them. Crystal partially started and looks guilty, having snuck in a few bites before their arrival. She smiles at them as they take their seats and the three of them talk about their discoveries. After hearing the news about New Haven, Crystal puts a few more pieces together. William unfolds his napkin. "Zarra said you made a discovery?"

Crystal bounces in excitement. "Yes. In the war of the god's tome I have, it talks of a shard forming when a god dies, right?" They nod. "Well then, there should be a shard there. If the events of two hundred years ago, lines up with the stories in this tome, then a divinity shard could be there."

William holds up a hand. "But we need to deal with New Haven."

Crystal sounds aggressive. "Maybe we shouldn't bother with New Haven at all. What we want is in the ruins of the old city. We should just fly in there, bombard the place, and go in and kill them, then take the shard."

Zarra counters. "But you don't even know if this shard thing is there."

Crystal shakes her head. "I'm almost certain of it. All the events fit. It should be there."

William counters with his own reasoning. "But it could be gone. Someone could have taken it and left by now."

She nods in agreement. "But they are worshiping the new dark god Xavral from that location. Which tells me it's still there." She looks across the table at him. "And if it is, I'm taking it for myself."

William and Zarra exchange glances and he can't hide the worry in his voice. "To what end, honey?"

"It's a source of divine power. If I could figure out how to use it, I could use it to make changes, real tangible changes."

"I don't know about that." Zarra sounds concerned. "If anyone can just pick one of these things up and become a god, that would cause a lot of problems."

"It doesn't work that way, at least not from what I read. With the pages that are sealed away, I can't find the information I need. It could take me years, or I might never figure it out. It might all be a dream and I'm grasping at nothing."

William pokes at his plate. "Let's finish and get to bed. Tomorrow is going to be a long day. We have time to talk about your ambitions later, honey."

The next morning, Crystal and William are awoken by a call from Captain Zylra. They get dressed and head to the bridge where she's waiting for them. "Countess, Major, we're here." She points to the ground where the road going to New Haven is below them. A blanket of snow covers the area for as far as they can see.

William swallows. "What's the current temperature outside, Captain?"

She looks up at him and can tell by the look on her face he's not going to like the answer. "Negative five, sir."

Crystal comments out loud. "Thank the Provider I'm Half-White Dragon."

"That's not helping." William turns to the captain. "If we are where we planned to land, then it's a three-day trip by horse and wagon to the City of New Haven."

"I feel sorry for those people who were fooled by the Black Rose to walk in this. If they didn't take the same precautions, I did for our troops…"

William nods. "I'm glad you did. I just hope you bought enough to keep us alive long enough to complete the mission."

She mutters, looking at the thermometer. "Me and you both."

The loading ramp is lowered, and the cold air hits them like a hammer. Even with the environmental protection spells making it easier on them, the biting cold is still harsh. Everyone is bundled up but Crystal. Troopers hitch up horses and make ready, coving them with blankets. The sky is overcast, saving them from the blindness that accompanies the snow when the sun is out, but fear it could mean more snow coming in. The Vardo is placed at the center of the convoy, giving it the most protection.

As they are about to depart, Captain Zylra hands Crystal an odd-looking object. It's a small electrum box with a curved cone on the end, about an inch long and half an inch in diameter. "What is this?"

"That is the latest in magical communication. The captain of the *Opal Star* handed these to me." She points at the box going over it. "You hit this gem here in the middle and it will connect with a paired gem here on the ship. Then all you do is talk into it and it will send your message to us. So if you need help, or just want to see how my day is going, you can just call."

Crystal looks down at the small device. Her excitement is evident. "That's amazing. Getting to talk to someone who isn't there? Who made this?"

"A gnome in the Forth House. He was trying to build something else, apparently, and this was a happy accident. He was going to toss it out when one of his staff said it could be useful. They brought it to the Emperor, and it was handed it to me for this reason."

She looks at the tiny box. "This could revolutionize the world. That gnome is a genius. This is way better than a telegraph." She climbs up into her Vardo still intrigued by the portable speaking device, and William closes the door. Tia is inside and Zarra is riding with Penelope, acting as Crystal's personal guards. Tom and Tyra walk with the troops. With it now empty, it lifts off and heads into the mountains to hide. The only clue is the impressions of the landing gear in the snow.

They follow the road as best they can. Carts get stuck in the deep snow, and it doesn't help that the road wasn't well maintained. The hidden dangers under the snow make it so much worse on them. Crystal curses as her things are tossed about and complains about delays as cartwheels break and must be repaired. The daylight dwindles, causing the temperatures to fall. Crystal uses her scepter to bring the temp up forty degrees' expelling its magic for the day, giving her a break from having to recharge the rod. Evidence of the Black Rose having been here is morbidly apparent with how many frozen corpses they find along the way.

With the delays and the temps falling, William orders the convoy to break for camp and get fires started. "Ice has built up on all the wagons and needs to be removed. We keep this up and things will break down faster."

Zarra calls down to William. "You need help with camp?"

"Any help is appreciated, so do what you can. I'm going to talk to Captain Motsana, see where we are at. I don't think we made it that far."

Crystal lays in her bed exhausted with Tia tending to her. "You're really overdoing it with this." Tia informs her. "You keep this up and you might start having health issues."

"These men are depending on me to keep them alive." She turns her head to face Tia. "It's an odd feeling; having others depend on me." She looks at her clawed hands, having removed her bracelets to channel more. "I feel more important now than ever, but it's such hard work." She swallows and winces from it. Her body taxed from all the magical power she had to funnel into the device that empowers the wands that keep them alive.

"Then you need sleep and rest. You keep this up, you won't make the trip to New Haven." Tia wipes Crystal's forehead. "Now get some rest." Crystal nods and closes her eyes, trying to get some sleep. Penelope enters and Tia holds a finger to her lips, getting her to nod and slip silently into her own bed.

Tia exits holding her new staff for balance in the snow. She walks into the camp and finds William, Zarra, Tom, Tyra and the Captain, along with several troopers by the fire eating rations and whatever they can cook. She sits down next to Zarra, but William speaks up first. "How is she?"

"Exhausted, hurting, but has high spirits. She's happy to be helping. I'm wondering if there isn't something else wrong with her. She's usually more self-centered, so this is an odd change for her." Tia holds her hands out to keep warm.

"Maybe this is a good thing." William pops a smoldering piece of ration in his mouth. "She's been through a lot and with the teaching of Master Monzulo and Master Ryuu, she's growing up more."

Tom nods in agreement. "And tea is getting a lot better for all three of you." He looks at Tia and Zarra. "I'm proud of you girls for working so hard."

Zarra bows her head to him, then turns to William. "I'll take night watch along with Dwarves on that shift. With my ability to see in pitch darkens, it would be best to put that gift to good use."

William nods. "Thanks for volunteering." He turns to the others. "We are going to head off early, get some rest, and keep the fires burning hot."

CHAPTER 32

(Perils of the Wilds)

Crystal wakes up, feeling the stove heating the Vardo with Penelope passed out in her own bed. She feels much better but is still weak. Peering out the window, she can see fires with troops huddled close to them and wonders if her scepter's power has worn off yet. *Guess I need to cast the environment spell again for the troops.* She opens the drawer, but the environment wand and rod attachment are missing. *The other wands are still here. Tia must be doing the work right now to let me rest.*

She goes back to her bed and picks up the book about the gods and closes it and puts it aside. *I've been on this god kick thing for too long and been silly.* She glances back at it. *But I have to know how to help Tia.* She breaks back into her book.

The door opens and Tia steps in, shaking off the snow and seeing Crystal is up and reading the tome. Tia sounds angry. "I told you to rest."

"I am resting." She holds the book up. "Just some light reading while I lay here."

"I know you better than that. There is nothing light about you and studying. You need to let your body rest, or it will break down on you. I've seen you when you think you're worthless." Tia hangs her head. "I don't want to see that happen to you again."

"And I don't want to go back there again." Crystal puts the book back down and lays back. "I just feel like I should be doing more. You and William, and Tom all work so hard and I'm just being carried along."

"But you've always been carried along. Why does it bother you now?"

She shrugs and giggles. "Been through a lot over the last year. Can't be a leader and a goddess if no one looks up at me."

Tia shoots her a look. "You keep that up and you're going to develop another complex."

Crystal laughs weakly, looking up at the ceiling. "Just trying to stay positive. People have died because of me, a war is brewing because of me, and my wedding got canceled because of the things I did. I've got a lot of problems. Why can't one of them be a net positive for me?"

"You've done a lot of good, too." Tia sits on the bed next to her. "And this war that's 'brewing' started before the Emperor even selected you to go on this trip. Stop blaming you're self for that. If it wasn't you, it would have been someone else." She grabs the bowl of water and rag. "And the fact you're spreading the word of love and understanding is a good thing. You could have easily destroyed that church, but you didn't. You embraced what they were and made it part of you."

Crystal turns her eyes askance to look at her as Tia dabs her forehead. "Thank you for being there for me. For helping William pull me from the brink of doing something I would have regretted."

"Then take my advice now and go back to sleep. Doctors' orders." Tia stands and covers her up. Tia leaves the Vardo, but Crystal just lays there and stares at the ceiling for long hours, wondering what the future may hold.

The smell of cooking eggs awakens Crystal from her bed. Rolling over, she can see Tia asleep, slumped over in a chair next to her. *Poor thing. She must have sat there making sure I was alright as I slept.* She looks out the window to see the overcast sky. *This is my kind of weather, but not for those under my command.* Fires still burn, keeping the troops and horses warm, but they are already setting things up to get back into motion.

Penelope sets a plate down at the table, bringing Crystal's head around. "Breakfast is ready, countess."

Crystal stands, awakening Tia as she tries to get around her. "Thanks Shadow." Penelope puts down two more plates and sits herself, and Tia joins them. "How far do you think we have to go?"

Penelope shakes her head. "We didn't get far yesterday. This weather is brutal up here."

Tia swallows some bacon. "Why would anyone want to live up here?" She glances at Crystal. "I mean normal people. You would love it here, I'm sure."

Crystal smiles. "That I would." They eat in silence till she lets out a sigh and puts her fork down.

Penelope perks up. "Everything alright?"

"No." She stands. "I have work to do. Breakfast was wonderful, but I'll finish it when I get back inside." She reaches into the drawer, pulling out the wands and rod. She steps out and walks up to William and Zarra.

William turns and sees her coming with the wand in her hand. He turns and whistles, getting everyone's attention and making a circling motion above his head to get the troops to gather. "That time again?"

She nods her head. "Yeah. Are we ready to depart?"

William looks around. "Should be road ready in thirty minutes." The troops gather and she does her thing, forcing the rod to go beyond its limits, pulling from her own magical reservoir to keep it going. She breathes heavily after finishing and William escorts her back to the Vardo. "Can Tia help you with that so you're not pushing yourself so hard?"

Crystal shakes her head. "Can't take the chance if we get into battle, or an accident." She pats him on the chest plate. "I'll be fine Will." She gazes up at him. "In fact, I'm going to ride on top of my Vardo again. This way, I can keep an eye on everything."

He places his hands on her shoulders. "That's probably not a great idea. What if the enemy spots you up there and decides to shoot first?"

She waves her hand at the snow and freezing troops. "You think someone is going to be waiting for us in the freezing snow, hoping to get a shot at me? I've seen the frozen corpses along the road. There is no way someone is out here waiting."

"All the same, I rather not risk it." He looks her in the eyes. "I… I don't want to take that chance. If I lost you again…"

She reaches up, cupping his face and pulling him down. "You won't lose me again. I'll wear something in white, so I blend in, ok?"

William scowls. "I'm not going to win this with common sense, am I?" She stares up at him. "Fine." He exhales and she can tell he's not happy. "I'll send scouts out to make sure of things." She smiles, but he raises a finger to her. "But if I get so much of an inkling, you're in danger…"

"I'll go back into my house. I promise."

Afternoon comes and Crystal rides atop her Vardo, enjoying the weather. As she's preparing to reuse the wands, the scout that was left behind rides up in a full gallop and pulls alongside William. He gets a look of concern on his face, and he moves to Captain Motsana and speaks to him. Penelope trades glances with Zarra and Crystal. "Wonder what is going on?"

Zarra shakes her head, watching William and Motsana move to others in the group relaying orders. "Can't be good, whatever it is. A commander rarely discusses things with subordinates over nothing." She casts her gaze up at Crystal. "Be careful up there."

362

Tyra speaks up, overhearing from below. "She's never careful, but she's getting better about it."

Crystal sits up and looks down. "What's that supposed to mean?"

William finishes his rounds and rides alongside the Vardo. "Penelope, I'm going to have you give your seat to another trooper. Then you three, please get into the Vardo and keep the door and windows shut for your protection."

"What is going on, major?" Zarra points to herself. "And why am I being caged up when I am more capable than most of the soldiers here?"

He glances back over his shoulder, then up at her. "Our scout spotted a few dire wolves, and they have been following us a while now." He holds his arm up, bringing the convoy to a halt. "But if there are a few, it means there has to be a larger pack following them."

"That's not a reason to keep me out of the fight!" She stands. "Is it because I'm…"

Crystal places a hand on her shoulder, stopping her rant. "If I was to guess, it is to protect me. If the pack is too large, he's leaving you to protect me and get us home."

He dismounts and waves a trooper over. "She's right. We can't afford to lose her, and I don't want to lose anyone here, but I'm prepared to give my life. You three and Tia have to survive to get home."

Zarra climbs down and continues her protest. "I'm prepared too."

"And I expect nothing less with Crystal, if I fall."

Crystal's eyes well up. "Don't you dare die on me again! I can't lose you a second time." Penelope and Crystal climb down and William escorts them to the back. Crystal casts her protection spells on him, making his already formidable armor magically enhanced. "When do you think they will attack?"

"Hard to say. Could be minutes, could be a day. They will stalk us till they see an opening and then we will be in the thick of it. Just stay in there and don't be foolish. I can't focus on instructing the troops if you're in danger." He places his forehead to hers and whispers. "You two take care of each other. If I know you two are safe, I can command with a logical mind without fear." He gives her a kiss and helps her into the back.

The darkness arrives, but Crystal is deep in her books. Tia sitting by her side listening to her mutter. "I think this shard thing might have something to do with your predicament."

Tia looks at the book but can't make heads or tails from the Draconic. "I thought it was just a source of divine power. Whoever holds it becomes a god."

Crystal flips the page. "Not exactly." She taps a passage. "The shard only reacts to someone who is worthy of its power. So, it will not grant just anyone its gifts."

Tia looks down at the book. "How do you know if you're worthy?"

"That's just it. I think it's part of the sealed pages I can't get into. I'm going to have to take this home and with mom's help, maybe we can crack the enchantment sealing the important stuff away." She flips through the pages, muttering to herself.

Penelope speaks over her shoulder but doesn't take her eyes off the woods outside. "How long has it been since the rear scout reported in?"

Zarra stands up, grabbing onto what she can to keep from falling over and gazes out a window herself. "Too long." She glances back. "And we should stop for the night soon."

"Maybe then I can get better studying done. All this bouncing around really makes it difficult."

Tia glances at the other's, then back at Crystal. "I'm sensing more than just frustration over your studies. What's really wrong?"

"Nothing!" Crystal snaps, slamming the book shut. "I just need to do my research." She pushes her hair back behind her ears. "And it's hard to do when I'm cramped up in here and everyone is distracting me."

Zarra sits down next to Crystal on the bed opposite Tia. "We all love you, Crystal, and we know you love us in return. We've all been through a lot, and you've been through more with them than me." She sighs and places her hand on Crystal's back, rubbing her scaled spine. "But even I can see something is really bothering you, and it helps to talk about it."

Crystal looks down at the floor and feels the other woman's soft hands. "I didn't like it when William talked about sacrificing himself again. It brings back so many painful memories." She looks down at the floor to hide the tears welling up again. "But he's doing his duty, and that's why I fell for him in the first place." She looks at Zarra, staring into her ruby red eyes. "I don't want to lose those I love."

Crystal turns to Tia. "And I don't want those I love, not getting to experience what wonders of love I have. That's why this is so important to me. I don't do this for myself but for you and Andrew. I feel you're meant to be together, and if Daniel helps me, I can free him of that torch and bring you two together finally."

Penelope goes to scold her for thinking like a god again when shouts outside erupt. All four look out and see the troops bringing the wagons around like a fortification. Tyra walks up to the window and opens it, sticking her face in. Snow is present on her fur. "Someone spotted a gray figure in the area, thinking it could be one of the dire wolves, and signaled the alarm. William is stopping here for the night and ordered the start of campfires, thinking it will deter the beasts."

Crystal stands. "Does he need any help?"

"He wants you to stay in here knowing you and Zarra will both want to charge out and do whatever you can, despite the danger. He sent me here to remind you to stay put." She turns as the chopping of wood.

Crystal goes from sad to angry at being treated like a child. "Remind the Major that I'm the countess, and I will do as I please."

"He said you would say that and told me to remind you that Emperor Marcus put him in charge of military actions, and you were to adhere to them, or something to that effect." The sounds of a tree falling gets her attention. "I'm needed elsewhere. Stay here, please." She turns and walks away.

Crystal puts down the book about the gods and picks up her book on Cyromancy and flips through the pages, searching for something. Tia looks over her shoulder looking at the pictures of snow and ice inscribed with the writings. "What's that?"

"If I'm going to be stuck in here, I might as well do some pleasure reading." Crystal leans back, diving hard into the book's contents.

Tia exchanges glances with Zarra, who is still sitting there and shrugs. They watch out the windows and the snow is falling hard. Crystal shows no interest, burying herself in the book's mysteries.

Fires burn all around and the darkens is only held back by the light they cast. Penelope opens the pantry. "Guess I'll start on dinner. Need something to cut the boredom."

Penelope is setting the table when the first signs of trouble hit. Screams of alarm and gunfire from outside get everyone to look out the windows and what they see is terrifying. Wolves, as large as horses, leap into the light, teeth stained pink from troops that have died or have been wounded in the initial attack.

William pulls his teal-colored sword and grips his shield. He opens his mouth to issue orders, but a large beast leaps at him, taking him off his horse. It violently shakes his arm, pulling it from the socket and forcing him to drop his shield. He stabs with this sword, going deep into the beast's side repeatedly, trying to get released. An Elven soldier empties his pistol into it, then charges in, shoving a spear deep into its flank and pushing it off his fallen commander. "Thanks." The Elf offers his hand and as William reaches for it, another wolf jumps him, ripping his head from his shoulders, showering William in blood. Captain Motsana and his troops rally, using their Patas to keep the wolves at bay. Shouting his own orders, he points to him getting Tom and Tyra's attention. They turn to see three more moving in on the Major's position.

Tyra launches herself, slicing with her Katana, taking the beast's head clean off. Blood freezes as it hits the ground, and the large body falls over. Tom lances out with Sia rapidly stabbing, puncturing as much as he can to slow another. The beast turns biting his leg and bringing him to the ground. Tyra hears the snapping of bone as Tom lets out a yelp of pain and he's violently flung about. William gets to his feet and picks up his sword, his left arm hanging to his side, limp. His armor wasn't designed to stop from being pulled apart like that. The wolf lets go of Tom's leg as William slams into it. The giant wolf bounds to its feet and bares its teeth. Tyra braces against his back with Tom on the ground, unable to stand from the broken leg, preparing for the circling wolves to make their move. He readies himself as the wolf in front of him lunges at him and is struck by a beam of yellow and blue, freezing it solid and shattering as it hits the ground.

Crystal puts her book down and stands up, startling everyone else in the Vardo. "Are you really content with sitting here and watching them get slaughtered out there?"

Zarra stands, holding her hand out. "I'm under orders to keep you safe."

"And you're not part of the Rose Harbor military. You don't have to follow those orders." Crystal turns and looks at all of them. "I'm going to help them."

They stay silent, and she turns to the door. Zarra steps in front of her and places a hand on Crystal's chest. "Please, don't go out there. I don't want to see you get hurt."

Crystal looks down at Zarra's hand and back up again, then points past her. "I'm going out there to save my man and troops."

"I'm supposed to keep you and the others here safe. I gave my word." Crystal reaches down, takes Zarra's hand, and pulls it away despite how hard she tries to keep it there. *What is this? She just moved my arm like I wasn't trying. How strong is she?*

Crystal then nudges Zarra aside and steps past, grabbing the door. "Come with me and keep me safe, then." She turns to Tia. "And we have wounded. Don't tell me you're going to sit here and let people die."

Tia shakes her head. "That's not fair. You know I wouldn't do that."

"Then grab your staff and the med kit we on a rescue mission."

Penelope holds her arms out wide, helpless. "What about me?"

"I don't know how deep that snow is getting. You might be stuck in here. I'll find Chuck and maybe he can come get you?" Penelope does her best to hide her feelings on that matter.

Captain Motsana swings his Moplah, slicing deep into a wolf as it lunges. Not being able to stop it, the beast bites a woman's leg clean off. She screams and blood stains the snow red and drops her weapon and latches onto what's left behind. He steps over the Catfolk female as their medic starts triage and trying to stop the blood flow. "We are all going to die." She cries, her tears freezing to her fur covered face.

"We've been in worse situations. Stay brave!" The captain stands over her, deflecting another attack. *But at the moment, I can't really think of one.* He does a fast count and there are still nine of these things that he can see, with four dead, but their own wounded and dead count are mounting. His head swings around, hearing the Vardo door open, and Crystal descends the steps, followed by Tia and Zarra. "Chuck!" He spins to the captain's voice. "Protect the countess!"

Chuck nods and runs to the Vardo, firing off shots as he goes. Crystal holds up her hand. "Get Shadow first. I'm off to help William.

He turns and calls into the Vardo. "Penelope?"

"I'm here." She steps out, pulling her revolver. "I'm going to regret asking, but can you give me a ride? The snow is getting too deep for me to walk in."

He smiles. "Sure thing, babe." He picks her up and places her on his shoulders.

She hands him down some ammo. "I'll shoot, you reload." She pulls his head back. "And no funny business in front of the countess."

Crystal holds her scepter up and points it at a wolf. "Mom said this thing could fire some ice rays, lets see what it's got." She depresses the red diamond icicle and the blue gem at the end glows purple, then at the tip of the scepter a yellow beam lances out and slams into the flank of a wagon missing. She frowns. "I really need to learn to aim."

Zarra shrugs. "You need more practice with it, that's for sure." She points towards William, Tom, and Tyra. "Think you can hit that one?"

Crystal can see the wolves circling and shakes her head. "Not with this, but I know what I can use." She speaks an incantation, scooping up a handful of the snow, adding it to the magic she pulls from her blood and her hands glow yellow. She points and a beam of solid yellow and ice blue swirls from her fingertip, tracking its way to the dire wolf in front of William as it leaps, changing it to a statue of solid ice. Falling to the ground, it shatters as if made of glass. He looks towards the direction of the beam's origin to see Crystal standing there, finger still outstretched. She smiles at him, then her eyes roll back and she collapses.

Zarra turns and drops to the ground, grabbing her. "TIA!" Tia spins to see Crystal is on the ground.

She races over. "I told her she had to recover." Tia kneels in the snow and Crystal lays there semi-unconscious.

"I'll be fine in a moment; I think I overdid it a little. Save them. Zarra can protect me while I recharge."

Tia opens her magical healing kit. "I have to save you."

Crystal grabs her and drags Tia down. "Save the wounded, but patch up William first so he can fight. Don't make me say it again."

Her orders chill Tia to her core. "Yes… countess." She stands and makes her way to William.

Zarra stands and pulls her sword as one wolf breaks away from the group and comes at them. "I'll die protecting you." Her sword glows red as she prays. "Holy Johnathan, guide my blade and grant me favor to defending the ones I love."

Penelope looks over the battle. "We need to find the Alpha. Once it goes down, the pack will break off. Might buy us a few days if not drive them off completely." She points her pistol and fires. The bullet strikes one wolf, blood spraying into the air. "Get us closer to the captain so we can help them. They don't have the fire support William and the Rose Harbor troops have."

They close in, Penelope handing her revolver off to Chuck and he hands her up his and reloads. "Are you sure we can fight these things with small arms?"

She aims, firing several rounds into the head and a wolf, dropping it, and looks down. "Depends on where you aim."

They trade guns again. "And how do you know about driving these things off?"

They get to Captain Motsana and his troops still firing away. "And old story my grandparents told me. They were always talking about how their grandparents had to deal with giant wolves and snow beasts." She takes aim, blasting another wolf in the side. "But we don't get much snow in Woverly. Too far south." A wolf lunges at them and Chuck ducks back, causing them to tumble. A large blade swings out of the darkness, hitting the beast in the face. Blood explodes over Chuck's face.

"Thank you two for the help." They look and Captain Motsana is standing over them and the wolf growls back. The wolf flinches back as he swings again, and it takes advantage, biting down on the captain's extended arm and pulls him off his feet. It drags him backwards and starts its death shake, ripping his arm completely off. Another trooper reacts, driving her spear into its flank, causing it to drop the severed limb and retreat. Penelope and Chuck get to their feet and rush over to the captain. He looks at the bloody stump in shock. He looks at them. "I've been disarmed." His eyes roll back and collapses to the ground.

"MEDIC!" Tia's head swivels around and looks at the Catfolk trooper waving his arms.

She's using her staff to heal William's arm. William flexes and can lift his shield again. "Better." He glances at Tyra. "Tyra, escort Tia to Captain Motsana now! I got this from here." Tyra nods and scoops her up and carrying Tia faster than she could run. Zarra holds off two of the enormous beasts as Crystal lies on the ground. "Tom, you wouldn't know some secret monk technique to fix that in a hurry, would you?"

"No, but Tia left her medical bag laying here. William, kick it to me and I'll see what I can do on my own." William slides the bag to Tom, and he reaches in, looking through it. "This looks promising." Looking over a glowing yellow concoction. He pulls the stopper out and takes a whiff. His face scrunches up and he holds the bottle back. "Why does the best healing have to smell horrific?" He downs the drink and makes a disgusted noise, then jumps up. "Stuff works fast."

William moves, trying to keep his two in front of him. "We should move towards Crystal, combine our strengths." William looks in Crystal's direction, taking his eyes off the wolves, and they lunge forward. William turns and gets his shield up just in time for its massive jaws to latch onto the hardwood. It yanks hard, dragging William off his feet. Tom reacts, jumping to William's aid and stabbing the wolf in its muzzle. It yelps, letting go and retreating a few steps.

Crystal stands up and wobbles, regaining her balance. A wolf leaps and in a panic, Crystal shoves her scepter forward, setting off the second ice ray. The yellow beam lances through the wolf and, in an instance, is encased in solid ice.

Zarra glances back at her, not letting the other two wolves find an opening. "You ok baby?"

"Yeah, cover me while I prepare something new." Zarra watches the two wolves circle, and one lunges in for her. Zarra places her red glowing blade in its path, cutting deep into it. The second rushes in at Crystal with Zarra occupied. Crystal speaks an incantation and bolts of pure ice flashes from her fingers. Large shards of ice pepper it's face causing it to fall immediately to the ground. Large, bloodstained icicles jut out in all directions from its skull. Crystal falls to the ground but remains conscious. She grabs her head, and her breath is labored from the exertion.

Zarra hits the wolf as it bites into her left shoulder, puncturing the armor and digging deep into her flesh. *This is how it ends? As dog food defending a woman who knew she needed to stay in the carriage.* A large shadowy figured that looks like an Ogre comes out of the darkness. It raises its weapon, and Zarra can feel the evil exuding. *Ogre's too? Where did the Ogre come from?* She closes her eyes, waiting for the fatal blow. *Johnathan, accept my soul and the souls of my comrades.* She feels the wolf's bite release and no strike. Opening one eye and the shadow-like Ogre is wrestling the wolf, striking it with its sword.

Turning, she looks at Crystal holding her hand out, wreathed in black energy. "We need to get to William and that medical bag before you bleed out."

Zarra takes it and stands up. "What's going on with that Ogre?"

Crystal stays quiet as they amble to Williams's side. He watches the shadowy Ogre stabbing the wolf, killing it. Crystal's hands become darker, and she weaves them around. A shadow like figure of the wolf emerges from its corpse. William turns and gives her a dirty look, and she shrugs and points her hand at the other wolves in the area. They hear the report of Penelope's revolver going off again and can see in the firelight; the wolves are retreating.

Tia gets carried to the captain, and the blood is pouring from his wound. "Where is his arm? Someone grab it and bring it here." Tyra hefts her Katana and Penelope fires, catching one of the colossal beasts in the leg. The Catfolk female brings it over and Tia reattaches it at the shoulder. "I hope this works." Praying, her hands glow blue as she holds the severed limb to his body, enveloping him. She pulls a potion from the bandolier and hands it to the Catfolk, and she pours it on the wound. Tia continues to pray as the limb reattaches itself to his body and he lets out an agonizing scream and his bones and ligament fuses back together. The glow stops and she topples over, breathing hard from the experience.

Penelope points her revolver. "Chuck, I see the alpha, the gray and white one there. Get me into the air!"

Chuck grabs her and hoists her back onto his shoulders. "Now what?"

"You spot a rifle lying around?"

He glances around and sees one laying in the snow. He kicks it up and hands it to her. "Now what?"

She looks down at him. "Hold it for me so I can aim. It's too heavy for me like this." He holds the front of the gun as she looks down the site. The alpha circles, and she follows, taking aim at its head. It arches its back, and she fires before it can leap. The rifle kicks, throwing her to the ground, but the shot embeds itself into the alpha's head, dropping it where it stands. The other wolves back off, no longer hearing the calls of their leader and retreat into the forest.

Crystal looks around at the wolves retreating and dismisses the shadow Ogre and wolf. She holds Zarra as she collapses to the ground from the blood loss. William grabs the medical bag and Crystal lays Zarra's head in her lap, stroking her blood-soaked copper hair. "Stay with us. William is here with the medical bag. You're going to be ok."

"It's so cold."

Crystal nods. "It's from the blood loss."

Zarra shakes her head. "No, it's negative ten and my environmental spell wore off some time ago." She laughs and winces. "Could you please?"

Crystal laughs too and starts her incantation and her hands glow white, enveloping Zarra's body. She smiles and reaches up, touching Crystal's face, spearing blood on her cheek. Her eyes close as William applies the medicine. Crystal cries and looks at him. "She's going to make it. She's still breathing. He takes her shoulder pauldron off and gains access to the wound directly, placing a healing salve on it, and Crystal continues to stroke her hair.

"I'm sorry, William." Crystal looks down at Zarra. "I should have stayed in the Vardo, but I was worried about you." Tears freeze to her face. They take stock and Tia pulls the life gem from her robes and starts searching for survivors.

CHAPTER 33

(New Haven Woes)

The next morning, Zarra wakes up in Crystal's bed next to her. She looks down and notices Crystal's arm draped across her. Looking around the room, she gathers what information she can. Penelope sleeps in the overhead mother's attic as usual and Tia is asleep on the divan. Her left shoulder is still hurting, but the wounds have all been closed. She smiles and moves to get more comfortable, waking Crystal. She whispers to Crystal as she opens her eyes. "Sorry, I didn't mean to wake you." She beams. "Guess this means our secret is out?"

Crystal smiles and shakes her head. "You were wounded, couldn't let you sleep on the dirty floor, and I'm a countess, I'm not sleeping on the dirty floor. As small as we both are, we could reasonably fit in this tiny bed." She takes her tone down to a whisper. "That's how I reasoned away their suspicions." Crystal leans in and giving her a quick smooch.

Zarra lays her head on Crystal's chest and looks out the window at the troops packing gear and burying the dead. "How bad was it last night?"

Crystal sighs. "Tia was able to find a few that survived, but were horribly maimed. She stayed up all night with the medics patching who they could together, but we lost a grand total of twelve. Captain Motsana's sword arm is going to need a lot more treatments to be useful again. Even though Tia reattached it, it's not working as it should. She spent most of the night dealing with wounded."

Zarra looks up and sees the blood stain still on her cheek from last night and then notices her clothes are stained, too. "It must have been bad. So now what?"

Crystal strokes her copper hair, still matted with dried blood from last night. "We press on. Complete the mission." She looks down. "Then I get my own town, my own castle, and get married to William, and hopefully an answer on how to include you in our lives if you choose to stay with us."

Zarra nuzzles Crystal's chest, feeling her through the fabric and hearing her heart beat. "I would like that."

They cuddle in the bed, stealing these moments together till they feel Penelope rousing in her overhead bunk. Zarra sits up and Crystal lies on her side, hand propping up her head. The curtain separating Penelope from them opens, and she looks out and sees Zarra and Crystal are up. "How are you doing this morning, Zarra?"

"Sore, wondering why I woke up here." She holds her shoulder. "But glad to still be alive."

"I'll get breakfast started then." She stretches, then hops down, gathering stuff for it. "What would you like for breakfast, countess?" Crystal casts her gaze at Zarra for a moment, then back to Penelope. She picks up on this subtle gesture. *What was that look about?*

"I would like an omelet if you wouldn't mind, and some milk. Going to need the energy today."

Penelope turns to Zarra. "And you?"

"I'll take one as well." She turns to Crystal. "So, what are you planning on reading today?"

"Not a lot. Today is repair armor day. Me and Tia are going to be burning through these wands of repair getting you, William and everyone else, back up to full fighting strength."

The sun comes out for the first time in two days and the whiteness of the snow is blinding. They wrap scarves around their heads to limit the light coming in and Zarra is blind to such intensity. She opts to stay inside the Vardo with Crystal and Tia repairing armor. The three of them talk about the contents of the god books, and how she thinks she's getting closer. Crystal asks Tia and Zarra about religion, needing their knowledge to help understand what it is she's reading.

The next two days are uneventful, with the wolves not returning. They arrive an hour outside the walls of New Haven, and pull way off the main trail and set camp in the woods. William pulls a horse around and has Chuck and Penelope brought around. "Alright, you two. You know what you're supposed to do?"

Penelope nods. "Get in and find out their stance on Rose Harbor."

"And get an idea of standing army size and capability. If they are in league with the Black Rose, any intel on what they are capable of is helpful."

Penelope nods again. "Anything else?"

William crouches down and hands her some gold coins. "Hopefully they haven't converted to gold back notes like we have and these still have use. Get a hotel for the night and bribe anyone you think might have information." He shrugs. "You're supposed to be visitors, so act like tourists." A grin appears on his face. "Just don't act like honeymooners."

She snatches the coin purse from his hand and gives him an angry look. "That's uncalled for."

Chuck mounts the horse. "Don't worry, sir. I live in a village not too far from here. I know who to look for. Probably helps that I know the local language here too."

William hands Penelope up and places her on the back. "That will be helpful."

Chuck turns and looks at her and winks. They ride off, Penelope clinging to Chuck. Crystal walks up and stands next to William, watching them go. "For someone who swears they are incompatible, she looks thrilled to be hanging onto him."

This gets a laugh from William. "Let's hope they get the information we need so we know how to proceed. If they are hostile to us, we could all end up dead or prisoners." He turns and they walk back to the Vardo. "Let's be ready to run if it comes to that."

Chuck and Penelope approach the gates and are halted by the guards. They wear standard steel gray heavy armor with a purple and white cloak covering them with the city's standard on it.

He steps up next to them and speaks in Poshlovish. "Names?"

Chuck smiles and answers. "Chuck Petrovich, from Bortsova."

"Bortsova? That's half a day's travel from here. What brings you to New Haven?"

Chuck thumbs at Penelope. "She wondered into our village and almost frozen to death. Said she was part of some pilgrimage and, from what I can tell, is the only survivor. My family and I nursed her back to health, and we figured she would do better here than in our little town."

The guard nods and looks at the Halfling. "And your name, Ms.?"

Penelope is stunned. *They are speaking my native language. But why? How? What is going on here?*

He coughs. "Are you going to answer me?"

She fakes a smile and responds shyly and responds in Poshlovish, but with her unique dialect. "Sorry. Still recovering from my ordeal."

"That's all fine, but I need your name."

"Olivia Goodbody."

He puts the parchment down. "Are you wanted for something?"

Penelope can't hide the shock. "No, why?"

"Because that's not a Halfling sir name. So why are you dodging the question?"

Wait, how does he know that? She looks down. "Sorry. Just I've been through a lot and don't feel comfortable."

"It will be alright. You're safe here." He smiles at her and speaks softly. "But I still need your real name." He steps back and waves them down. "If you two could dismount and follow me inside where it's warmer, we can ask a few more questions and figure out where you should go.

This means they could have a Zone of Truth put down. I've beaten those before with the training I was given. They dismount and follow the soldier inside, and it is warmer. She looks around and studies the small office. Nothing out of the ordinary and no glow that a zone normally puts out. *I don't see anything to show it's here, but it could be hidden by other means. Just need to remember my training.*

Henry's words echo in her mind, flooding back as she finds a chair. *"The trick to beating a zone is to structure the lie in a way it's still truthful, but meaningless. Don't forget that you aren't compelled to speak, so you can omit what you don't want them to know."*

The guard takes his seat and picks up his pen and looks at Chuck. "You're from Bortsova?"

"That's correct, sir."

The guard writes the information down. "How long have you lived there?"

"My whole life. I was born there, my father retired from the guard here, actually. Kabinov Petrovich. Have you heard of him?"

"Yes, I knew him. He was a good man." He leans forward on his elbows and stares at Chuck. "But I don't remember him talking about a boy named Chuck."

"My full name is Chavrik Petrovich, but Chuck is easier on people to remember."

He nods and starts writing. "I remember him talking about you, Chavrik. Thanks for clarifying."

He turns to Penelope. "And you are?" She's about to answer when he continues. "And be truthful. You're in no danger here unless you're a known criminal."

Penelope smiles. "Penelope Grzeskowiak." She holds her smile. *Yep, zone of truth in place. I'm going to need to be creative.*

The guard smiles and writes it down and then puts his hands down on the desk. "See, you're not in trouble. That's not a name that's on my wanted list." He picks his pen back up. "And how old are you, Ms. Grzeskowiak?"

She glances at Chuck and sighs. "Thirty-five." Chuck's eyes widen a little and glances at her.

He writes that down too. "And where are you from?"

"Black Rock." She keeps her smile. *Which technically I am, I came from there, to Rose Harbor, to Portstown, to here.*

"And what brings you to New Haven? I know it's not a pilgrimage, so I'm guessing refugee?"

She nods her head. "A group of friends of mine were in a battle that took over Black Rock, where these people called the Black Rose started attacking everyone." She hangs her head, looking at the floor. "In the aftermath, me and my friends left and come to New Haven."

He writes it all down. "Black Rock is Rose Harbor territory. Why did you and your friends move so far away from here? Don't get me wrong, we have no love of the Black Rose here either. Just home sick?"

"Guess you can say I was wondering about the place. I haven't really been in the city proper itself ever in my life and looking to find out more."

"And how did you and Chavrik here meet?"

"He found me in the snow, slowly freezing to death, going through the remains of a knocked down tent. I was looking for supplies and valuables. I was all alone at that point." She looks back up and to Chuck. "Glad he found me."

He looks at Chuck. "You found her digging through a tent?"

Chuck nods. "Yeah, I held her at gunpoint point till she convinced me she was harmless and that we should work together. I felt bad for her and wanted to help." He turns to her, then back at the guard. "And that lead us too here."

He nods and focuses back on Penelope. "What happened to your friends?"

"I got separated from them. The snow is deep and I'm short." She slumps in her chair, thinking of ways to beat the spell. "But all they did was tease me, so I'm glad I'm not around them now."

He nods and continues to take notes, then looks down at her. "What do you hope to find here in New Haven, Ms. Grzeskowiak?"

"Answers, I guess. I've spent a long time getting here and I'm hoping to find out if it was all worth it in the end." She looks at the guard. "I'm self-sufficient and I have skills." She places her hands on his desk, leaning forward, almost pleading. "I'm a decent cook, and sure, I can find employment here if I look hard enough."

"You sound like you've been through hell. Why not go home to Chernyvask on the coast south of here?" She tilts her head. "Well, unless you don't want to go home. We do have Halflings that live in town."

"There is nothing there for me. That's why I'm here. I worked with other races before and very adaptable."

"Very good." He stamps some paperwork and hands it to her and Chuck. "These are your papers. It's your ID, place of origin and general description. These are used to get yourselves established and entry into the city if you leave." He looks at Chuck. "I'm surprised you didn't already have some."

"I do. I just forgot them till we were just outside the city and was too late to turn back."

"Well, enjoy your stay." He stands up and grabs some parchments. "Here are some hotels in the area that are cheap that rent rooms by up to a month for those immigrating here." He looks at them both. "Unless you're doing more than just looking for a job?"

Penelope perks up. "What do you mean?"

He hands the papers to them. "You're not the first couple to pass through my post. The whole forbidden love thing. You're safe here. Welcome to New Haven."

They walk out and Chuck mounts up, then leans down and picks up Penelope, placing her behind him. *Wonder if this is what Crystal felt when she was always on the horse with William?*

They get a few blocks, and Chuck speaks up. "Thirty-five, huh?"

Penelope shrugs. "Told you not to ask a lady her age, but with that spell up, I couldn't exactly fudge that." She grips him a little harder. "Don't tell me after all this, my age is a problem."

"No, I still think you look no more than twenty."

She's glad he can't see the smile on her face. *Can't believe I'm old enough I could be his mom, and he still wants to be with me. Guess he's the real deal.* They ride into the streets and the roads are mostly clear of snow. Small piles are here and there and horse-drawn wagons are everywhere. Houses made of thick dirt and wood are most prevalent on the outside, but as they get further into town, they are replaced with nicer looking homes made of a high-quality wood and better architecture. They get to a hotel that looks decent enough but not overtly fancy and hitch their horse. They walk inside and approach the counter.

The nice fair skinned blond woman smiles and her blue eyes meet Chuck's and she speaks in Poshlovish like everyone else. "Hello sir, you need a room?"

"Yes, for me and my friend here." He indicates to Penelope.

She bends forward and looks over the counter. "I'm sorry, I didn't see you there, miss." She sounds genially apologetic and smiles. "Single bed I take it?"

Penelope turns to Chuck, and she smiles. "Yes."

"Sign here and have her sign below that. You two will be in room four." She points to her left. "How many days will you two be here?"

Chuck signs the book. "Let's go day by day. It depends on how fast we can find a job. You know how it is." He hands it down to Penelope, and she signs it.

She grins, taking the registry from Penelope. "That I do."

Are we that obvious? Why hasn't Crystal teased me about it yet? They take their key, and Penelope notes there is only one, and head to the room. They open the door and it's musty, and they check it out, but it's clean.

"So now what?"

384

She jumps up on the bed so she's closer to his height and pulls his face down, bringing his lips into contact with hers. They kiss long and passionately till she finally breaks away from him. "Now we have to figure out who we need to talk to about the status between Rose Harbor and New Haven." She runs her hands over his chest. "That guard didn't sound happy about the Black Rose, so maybe that's a good thing and we can use that. So first we need to know who's in charge around here."

"I can answer that. His name is Rogozin Lavrenenti Vladimirovich. He's a Wood Elf who took one of our names to fit in. He's the Lord of the land. When Old Haven was destroyed, the people had to move. He was gracious enough to let them rebuild on his land if we paid a tax to him. The town has its own mayor and such, but he's the one who pulls all the strings."

Penelope takes her coat off, tossing it to the floor. "What can you tell me of him?"

"He's a gracious Lord. Been around forever. He lives in a castle at the edge of town, but it's not very big."

"Is it possible to get an audience with this Lord Vlad?"

Chuck shrugs, letting his own coat fall to the floor. "Not that I know of, but that doesn't mean it can't be done."

"For now, we need to find out the political situation first before we jump that far ahead." She smiles at him. "But if I know people like that, they don't come out till it's closer to dark." She raps her fingers on Chuck's chest. "So, we have time to kill." She pulls him close again. *I'm breaking orders, but I don't really care.*

Hours go by, and Penelope watches the sun go down from the window. She turns, looking back at Chuck, his arm laid over her. "Time to work. Let's get some food at some low-class establishment and see if I can find the underworld here." They get dressed and head out. It doesn't take her long to find the underbelly of the city, finding an establishment that looks run down, but still open. Entering, they find a table and she looks around, finding a rotund blond woman wearing a blue corset that makes her large breasts look even larger by pushing them up. She's flanked by several well-dressed people and watching everything. After half an hour, Penelope noticed several people visiting her and then leaving again. She looks over her glass at Chuck. "That large blond lady knows things. Everyone is going to her, so she's in charge around here." She takes a sip of the cheap mead.

Chuck leans in, keeping quiet. "Wouldn't it just be easier to talk to the officials? Just walk into a government building and ask?"

"It would. Because if they don't like Rose Harbor, they would just arrest us on the spot." She looks at the mead in disgust. "We would find out real fast."

"So, what's the plan? We are just going to ask her what's going on around here?"

"Sort of. Chances are she doesn't know directly, but knows someone high up that would. She's going to want something in exchange to arrange such a meeting in secret." She looks at Chuck. "This means anything from bribery to having to murder someone. So if you want out, now is the time to speak up."

He shakes his head. "I'm with you to the end." Penelope looks down. Chuck reaches out and takes her hands. "What's the matter, baby?"

"I don't know. It seems silly after thinking about it."

"What does?"

She looks up at him. "Us. I dreamt one day I would have a restaurant of my own, kids, and things going for me."

"But being we are incompatible; we can never have kids."

She nods, looking down. She grips his hands. "I'm not having regrets." She smiles up at him. "You're considerate, willing to adapt like me, reliable." She looks around and seeing other couples that are mismatched like them. "Guess if others can find happiness in the oddest of places, why can't I?"

Chuck smiles, and leans in, giving her a quick kiss. "I only want you to be happy and fulfill all your dreams."

She grins and looks over at the woman, seeing she has no clients now. "We need to make our move, since we have an opening."

They approach the woman and one of her larger guards gets between them, placing a hand on his chest. "Hold it right there. What do you two want with Katja?"

Chuck looks down and up again, holding his hands out. "Just seeking some information about the state of affairs. We aren't looking for money or items."

The large blond man smiles "Everything has a cost." He turns to Katja, and she nods, waving them on, but he doesn't take his hand off. His tone drips with menace. "Try anything, so much as twitch in a way I don't like, and you're both dead."

They get to the table and Penelope stands on a chair so she can be seen. Katja lights up a smoke and locks her blue eyes on Penelope. "What is it that I can do for ya two? I can tell you're not from around here."

Penelope raises an eyebrow. "How do you know that?"

"I have my ways. The clothing you're wearing isn't from 'round here. I would guess Rose Harbor, or somewhere in them parts." She picks up a pastry and takes a bite. "What business do ya 'ave here in New Haven?"

"I'm just needing to know if New Haven is itching for a fight with Rose Harbor. Maybe someone who is sympathetic or at least neutral to Rose Harbor, willing to talk to us?" She reaches for the pouch, but the guard's movement tells her that's a bad idea. "I have gold and am willing to pay for the information."

"Isn't she cute?" Katja puts on an ironic smile. "I don't know 'bout the politics, but I know someone who *is* sympathetic to Rose Harbor." She takes another bite and savers the sweet taste. "I could possibly... hook you up with an audience with 'im, but I need something of equal value, don't ya think?"

"Like what exactly?"

"In the dock, there is a ship, the *Rosina*. On this ship is a very special item I've been trying to get my hands on for some time, but it's in the captain's quarters." She finishes her pastry and smacks her fingers, then casts her gaze back to the two of them. She leans forward, steepling her fingers. "It's a locket. Gold, with a sapphire embedded in it with a gold chain. Bring it to me, and I'll make sure ya can see the man you're needing, but ya only have till morning to get it. The *Rosina* leaves port in then and heads to New Bufort, and won't be back for two weeks. So how badly do ya need this audience?"

Penelope nods, understanding. "I'll have it for you first thing in the morning." She looks up at Chuck. "Let's go." They get outside and Chuck looks down at her, but she answers him before he can ask. "We need to locate this ship, get the layout and get a guard count, look for possible ways in and out."

"So, how are we going to pull this off?" Chuck shrugs as they walk. "That's a large ship for us to check."

She looks at him. "We aren't. I am. No offence, love, but you're about as silent as a stampeding bull."

"What will I be doing while you're taking the risk?"

"If things go bad, I'll need a distraction to get out. That's where you come in. If the guards are alerted, I'll need you to make them go the wrong way."

His voice rises. "How do I do that?"

"You're smart. You will figure something out." They cross the small city and come to the docks. She looks at the ships and none flies the New Haven flag, but those of nations she's unfamiliar with. "Which one is it?"

They walk along the docks, the freezing cold biting them to the bone. He reads the names till he finds a large plum purple and white freighter with the name *Rosina* on the side. He nods at it. "That one"

"That's huge. I've got my work cut out for me."

"Just be glad it's a galleon class sailing ship. The captain's quarters are always on the top deck below the wheelhouse. It's just getting there."

"We have time to plan that part out. Let's get some hot beverages and find a spot we can watch from. Get an idea of the guard's rotations."

CHAPTER 34

(Darkness)

Zarra and Tia sit in the Vardo talking and repairing. William, Tom, Tyra, and Captain Motsana take stock and keep the troops in line. They can't light fires this close to the city without being discovered. Crystal is exhausted, keeping that magic rod charged so they can keep everyone alive. She rests in bed with Tia doing her best to keep her comfortable. Zarra puts down another piece and tosses the spent electrum stick to the side. "Crystal?" She casts her gaze in Crystal's direction. "I was wondering about something."

Crystal tries to prop herself up, but Tia pushes her back down. "Sure, Zarra. What's on your mind?"

"I've been quiet, wrestling with this internally for a few days and I have to know."

"About?"

"The night the wolves attacked, an Ogre, made of shadows and dripping with evil, came out of the darkness and saved our lives, killed a wolf, and then vanished."

"Guess you need to know more about me." She looks up at the ceiling. "I summoned the shadow to protect you. I couldn't risk casting a spell that could have killed you and it."

Tia takes her hand away from her head and steps back as dread fills her soul. "You're summoning shadows?" Zarra's eyes widen in surprise.

"You remember that book you destroyed?"

Tia nods. "Yeah, it was evil. I'm glad you let me."

Crystal turns her head to Zarra. "Zarra, I hit a low spot in my life. Tried to kill myself. William, Tia and Shadow kept me from hurting myself. Then I used Tom to bring me a book of necromancy. Figured if I couldn't get them to kill me, I would do it myself through magic." She lays there as the feelings flood back into her mind. "As I studied the book, looking for anything, I found many dark passages of powerful magic. Reanimation, resurrection, and other things. The Black Rose tortured me for days and has been tormenting me and my friends for months. All I wanted to do was hurt them back. I hate them with every fiber of my being and didn't care what I had to do."

Zarra looks at Tia and back to Crystal, covering her mouth. "I remember report about you almost dying, but I didn't know it was this bad."

Crystal lets it out, tears coming to her face. "They broke me while I hung there helpless. Burning me, cutting me, ripping my scales off, and more. I wasn't going to give them anything, but inside, the only desire I had was to kill them all in ways that would be the thing of nightmares for generations to come." She flexes her clawed hands, shredding the bed sheets. "I learned the dark secrets of that book. *All* of it. It's locked inside my mind now forever, held in the very magic that flows in my veins."

The tears stop and her eyes turn hard. "I thought I could resist using such power." She turns and looks back at the ceiling. "But I used it to rip the soul out of an Ogre that was about to kill William. I couldn't lose him again. Then I reflexively summoned him as a shadow when we were attacked in Rose Harbor." She turns back to Zarra. "And then again to save you, but this time, I took the wolf as a shadow, too. Something about one of my creations killing another grants me the ability to steal their spirit to use it to my own ends."

Crystal cries again. "I understand if you two want to leave. I'm not a good person. As much as I try, that part of me will always be there." She covers her face with her clawed hands. "I've tried so hard to bury it, to be loving and kind, but I still call on that power."

Tia takes Crystal's hands and pulls them, getting them to lock eyes. "You call on it to save loved ones. To use evil in a good way isn't something to be ashamed of. Only if you use it to for power and gain." Zarra nods in agreement. "Just as you said, love can be both good and bad, and your love caused you to use an evil thing for good reason. Let your love for others guide you is what you said, wasn't it?" Crystal nods. "And that's what you've done. We aren't going anywhere." She leans down and gives her a hug.

Zarra looks at Tia. "Could you take the Captain, his armor? I'm finished with it. I'll watch over Crystal while you're gone."

"Sure." Tia gathers up the newly repaired pieces and steps out.

Zarra sits on the bed next to Crystal, stroking her face, wiping away the tears. "I'm not going anywhere. I'm with you and William till the end, I promise. Thanks for telling me about what happened, and I'll be here to help you along."

Crystal reaches up and takes her hand that's holding her face. "I don't deserve you, or William, but I'm glad you're in my life." She struggles, trying to sit up.

"You're going to hurt yourself; you need to stay down." Zarra presses her hand against Crystal's chest, forcing her back down.

"I need to finish a project I've been working on."

Zarra tilts her head. "What project?"

Crystal points at a small white leather bag. "It's in my handbag. It's a small box."

Zarra looks around and finds the two feet by six-inch by two-inch box and looks at it. It has dials and gems, springs and several hinges for different compartments. "What is it?"

"It's a magical device I've been working on slowly over the month or so. It's almost done."

"What's it supposed to do?"

Zarra hands it to her and Crystal opens it. "It's a peace keeping device. If it works like I believe it will, it will make peace between us and the Black Rose by making them see the light of their errors."

Zarra smiles and leans over when the door to the Vardo opens, getting her to prop herself up and look normal. "Well, peace is good."

Tia steps up and sees Crystal working on her trinket some more. "Working on your fancy timekeeper thing again?" Tia sits down at the table. "You need your rest. Work on that later

"I'll be fine. It's almost done, anyway."

"What's that for, anyway? You never told me."

Zarra paraphrases Crystal's words. "It's a device to get people to see the light of peace."

"I can't get the Black Rose to see reason without some help, but with this, they should be convinced the Emperor isn't the demon they should fear."

Night hits its peak, and Penelope is dressed in all black, making her the shadow of her namesake. She looks over the dock, with just a handful of guards in their predictable patrol pattern. She looks to Chuck, who is kneeling looks at the docks with her. The moon has just risen, having waned past its halfway point. The only light is a handful of stars peeking through wispy clouds above them. She whispers to check. "I'm going to get going." She looks over at him. "Don't do anything unless they look to be alerted to my presence. Then you do the distraction and get away. I'll meet you back at the room where we can celebrate our victory." She leans over and kisses him. "A kiss for luck." Turning, she stands and makes her way down to the docks.

She darts from crate to crate, peeking out just long enough to see where the patrols are to duck between them. The shadows are her friend as her small size already makes her hard to see, but in the dark, she's all but invisible. She steps out and walks behind a guard slowly, then ducks into a stack of barrels as he turns to go back over to where he was just at. He steps past, not noticing her, and she peeks out again, looking for the next spot. She makes her way to the gangplank and crosses it quickly, hoping no one had seen her.

She peeks back over the side, and no one was alerted to her presence. *So far, so good, halfway there.* She walks the deck, dodging a sailor by hiding between the cannon and the brass monkey loaded with cannonballs. The boat rocks in the water, throwing her stance off and making it harder to stay silent and sure-footed. She slides a bit, knocking over some stuff and getting the attention of one patrol. She darts and hides behind a gantry holding some small barrels of what she thinks is gunpowder for the cannons. The sailor shows up and looks at the mess and curses.

He sighs. "Whoever secured this last did a piss-poor job of it." Takes him a good thirty minutes to clean it up, and she just sits there in the dark, waiting for him to leave. He walks around the area then leaves finally, giving Penelope a chance to take a real breath. Looking across the deck, she counts the steps to the door. Making her way over, she peeks through a window.

Taking out her lock picks, she looks around before starting. She picks the lock, feeling the pins click into place and the tension finally releases, spinning the core letting her know she's in. Opening the door just enough to let her inside and then closing it quietly behind her. The cabin is cluttered with a large table, maps, and trinkets everywhere. *It can be anywhere in here. I'm going to be awhile.* She stalks in the dark, lifting things, checking under papers and doing her best. She searches for almost two hours, pausing every time the man so much and breathes differently.

There is a knock at the door, waking the sleeping man, and Penelope reacts instantly, finding a spot and vanishing. The captain gets up, throwing his thick legs over the side of his bed and walks to the door. Throwing it open, he sounds unamused at the disturbance. "What is it?"

"Sir, just reporting that there is some suspicious activity on the dock."

Dammit Chuck. Too early.

"Thanks. Might be one of Katja's people trying to steal my stuff again. Teach them a lesson if you find them." He slams the door in the poor man's face. Reaching under his shirt, he pulls the locket out and Penelope sees it. He smiles at it, makes a kissing face, then places it in a drawer. He flops back into his bed and she waits for the snoring to resume to come out of hiding.

I hope Chuck got away. Going through his desk, she finds it in a false bottom in the drawer he had pulled out. *Tricky, but doesn't fool me.* She takes the locket, and it's just as she described. Peeking out and seeing it's clear, and squeezes out the door. Making her way back to the gangplank, she looks across the dock and can see a fight going on. *What is he doing? He shouldn't be engaging the guards, but fleeing.* The guard punches him with a gauntleted hand and Chuck hits the ground.

She crosses the gangplank, but the commotion has gotten guards to move in that direction and Chuck gets up. *No, stay down. What are you doing? It's better to get arrested over getting killed.* She crosses the dock unseen but is still watching as Chuck reaches for the guard's sword, but another pulls him and strikes Chuck down. His body collapses and lays limp on the ground. Penelope covers her own mouth, stifling the bloodcurdling scream she would have let out. Tears stream down her face and freeze in the cold. Grief takes over and her heart stops. *You idiot, why did you do that?*

She flees, knowing there is nothing she can do, and heads back to their room. Locking the door, she braces it. She finds Chuck's papers and stuffs them in her bag and takes his clothes. *They won't be able to ID him and will probably wait till morning to search hotels and ask questions.* She tries to get a few hours' sleep, but she can't stop crying. She lays there till she can see light coming through the window. Changing into more appropriate clothing, she sneaks out the window, taking his stuff and his ID papers, then tossing them into a dumpster far from the hotel. *They shouldn't find this stuff that fast, if at all. I won't let them know who they killed.*

Katja sits at her table when Penelope walks in and approaches her. "Where is your friend?"

Penelope's voice is hard, full of anger and loss. "Dead. Killed while trying to get this." She tosses the locket on the table.

"I'm sorry for your loss, Hun." She picks it up and examines it. "But ya wanted an audience wit' the man who is sympathetic to Rose Harbor. He is an Elf named Rogozin."

"The Lord of New Haven?"

"The same. We don't see eye to eye on everything, but as long as I give him some extra cash on the side, he overlooks my shenanigans. When would ya like to meet him?"

"As soon as possible. It won't be long till the guard tracks Chuck to the main gate and finds out where we were staying."

A male voice speaking in the same heavily accented common from behind her, rolling his r's as is common with speaking Poshlovish. "How about now?" Penelope turns not hearing the man come up behind her. "I am Lavrenenti Vladimirovich." She spins in place, seeing a tall, fair skinned Elf.

He speaks Poshlovish natively, but only been practicing common for a year or two. He must be doing this to put me at ease. Penelope still has dried tears on her face and speaks her dialect of Poshlovish. "Not sure if I should say it's a pleasure to meet you or not. My friend died so I could get an audience with you on behalf of my Countess Crystal Hellstromm."

He nods. "Life can be unforgiving, but you were willing to do much for my audience. I've lost friends too. Walk with me, tiny one." They go outside and walk to his small castle, talking along the way.

"We are here because the Black Rose operates from this area. At one point, there were shipments going from Black Rock to here unlawfully."

"Yes, it was a dirty deal done with one of the merchants here and the Black Rose. I was fearful it might have started a full-scale war. I'm glad you're here peacefully. The rumors of your flying ship are truly terrifying." He flicks at his fingertips. "It seems the Black Rose was trying to start an intercontinental conflict."

"How do I get the countess to see *you?* The whole point was to see intentions, then if not hostile, gain an audience to see what we could do about the Black Rose."

They get to his gates and stop. "Fine, little one, I will see your countess." He reaches into his cloak and pulls out a signet made of a material she hasn't seen before. "Take this to her and she and her people can cross safely into the city under my protection. As long as none of your people act with any hostility, you will be safe. You will be escorted by an armed guard to my castle ground where you will stay."

Penelope takes the object bearing his crest. "Thank you."

He leans down, putting his face dangerously close to hers. "But know this. If this is an elaborate trick, none of you will leave here alive. I'm taking a risk showing you compassion. Don't make me regret it."

I believe him. Something about him tells me he is serious about this, but I sense no deception in his words, but I won't let

Chuck's sacrifice be in vain. She goes back to the hotel where their horse is and spots the police there. They go to stop her but she holds up the crest, getting them to stop in their place and back up. "I want my horse." They exchange glances as if unsure what to do. "ME HORSE NOW!" The pain and loss in her voice are clear. They look around and she points to a horse standing nearby, then to herself. "I want my horse."

One of them nods and retrieves it. "Where did you get that?"

"Where do you think? Rogozin gave it to me." She walks up to the horse and points. "Now put me on it so I can leave. I have orders from him." The guard picks her up and places her on its back. She nods, tears welling up in her eyes as she rides off.

Penelope makes her way back to the camp, almost freezing to death along the way. She rides in and William, Tom, and Tyra rush over to her. William looks behind her, confused. "Where's Chuck?" Penelope's face contorts and grief hits her again, bursting into tears. Tyra takes her down and holds her. Tia, Zarra, and Crystal hear the commotion and exit the Vardo to see what is happening.

William bows his head, and he walks to Crystal and Zarra as Tia runs by. "Chuck didn't make it." Zarra covers her mouth and Crystal bows her head.

She's going to blame me. Just another body added to the Black Rose's count that I have to make up. Crystal walks up to Tyra, who is still holding Penelope. "I'm sorry."

Penelope looks at her and hands her the crest. She tries to speak through the pain in her chest. "This will let us into the city unrestricted. I tried it. The cops were terrified of me while I held it. We are to meet a man named Vladimirovich. An Elf who owns the land we are standing on."

Crystal holds it and can feel the magical power it holds, calling to her blood. The crest bears a Dragon breathing fire in

398

one panel, and mountain on the other. The pattern is reversed on the bottom. *Maybe they worship Dragons?*

Penelope is set on the ground and she looks up at Crystal. "You can bring him back, right?"

Crystal shakes her head slowly. "I'm sorry Penelope." Penelope's blood runs cold, only hearing Crystal call her by her real name in the worst of situations. "That spell is gone for good. Destroyed when Tia destroyed the book that contained it. Maybe we can find someone here in New Haven that can help you bring him back? Maybe the laws are different here."

Penelope hangs her head, walking away and climbing into the Vardo. She sees the device on the table. *Where have I seen something like that before?* She ignores it and climbs into her hole, closing the curtain.

Crystal nods to William. "I'll ride with you up front. Zarra, stick close to us. Let's move out. Every second we waste is time for the Black Rose to find out we are here." They mount up and take off, not wasting time getting to the city. As they get close, William advances first, waving a white cloth, showing they are not an attacking force. Zarra holds her hand up, stopping everyone, letting William and Crystal proceed. They get to the gate, him still holding the white cloth for truce. The guards walk up to them, hands on the hilts of their weapons, ready for any deceit.

Crystal holds up the crest and speaks loudly and firmly. "Lord Vladimirovich is expecting me and my retinue at his castle. Please escort us to his castle so we may avoid any unforeseen complications."

The guards exchange glances and look's at the wagons behind them. "And you are?"

"Countess Crystal Hellstromm of Rose Harbor on a mission of peace, love and understanding between our peoples."

"Welcome to New Haven countess. Enjoy your stay."

They are escorted to the castle where the Lord is waiting, wearing a deep red and gold outfit, but much lighter than the surrounding people. Some other people stand there looking official and have some rank insignias she's not familiar with. William dismounts and helps Crystal down. Zarra gets down as well, and the other troops keep their weapons stowed as ordered. "Welcome, countess, to my humble home and city. I extend to you full diplomatic rights and courtesies to you and your companions as long as they cause no interruptions from now until you leave." He turns swinging his arm in a sweeping motion as if inviting her to join him at his side. "I believe we have much to discuss."

His common is deeply accented, but I understand him just fine. Kind of interesting how he speaks. She smiles, extending a hand to him. "If any of them screw up, you will have to beat me to them to extract punishment." He extends a hand and takes hers with a smile of his own. "Come with me, countess. Let's talk and I can show you around and speak of some of the history of *our* people."

She looks to William and Zarra and they both know there isn't much they can do at this point. She falls in step with him. He's taller than her, but not as tall or as muscular as William. They talk and he shows her paintings and tapestries and speaks of their history behind them. *I'm actually enjoying his company, but it's almost as if there is something familiar about him. I just can't put my finger on it.* She speaks to him about her mission of love and compassion. How she is trying to bring peace when war seems to be what everyone wants. "Your city is small, but exquisite. The architecture is unique. Would you be interested in a trade agreement, perhaps? I don't know how strong your economy is here, but trade with the Rose Empire could help you significantly."

"And how do you know we need help with our economy?"

"Everyone's economy needs help. The more places you trade with, the better it gets."

"It's true, we don't have a net positive right now. Ever since you and Portstown joined together, they have been trading with you more than us, and that hurts." He guides her down some spiral stairs.

"We didn't intend to hurt your economy when I negotiated for Portstown to join the Rose Empire." She widens her hands in front of her, keeping a genuine smile. "Baron Tenishar didn't mention you had a trade agreement, or I would have made sure it stayed in the agreement to make our talks easier. I know you're interest in obsidian and coal from Black Rock."

He smiles in return. "Some of my people are, and I'm sure if we were buying from you, it would make them happy again." He walks up to an enormous door, way bigger than any Human would ever need.

"I could fly the *Bastion* through these doors. Why would anyone need doors this large?"

"I want to show you something I know *you* of all people would appreciate the most." He pushes open the door a crack and they walk in.

Crystal is absolutely floored by the site. She walks in with him, and they walk up an immense pile of gold coins, gems, art, and more. Magical fire casts sparkles from the piles of gold and gems all around her. It's a massive treasure trove that triggers her Dragon's blood at the massive hoard. She takes it all in as the gold and treasure goes on for thousands, if not more, feet in all directions. "This is beyond words."

His language changes. "So, tell me, countess." His tone shifts from friendly to apprehensive with a tinge of malice. Then turns to face her. "What is your real purpose here?"

She smiles, trying to dispel his fear and distrust. Her language reflexively changes with his. "I'm on a mission of peace and love and want to stop the Black Rose." She looks about the room. *Wait, we are speaking Draconic!* Something inside her clicks as she realizes exactly where she is and why her blood feels so at home here.

Her eyes widen and she fearfully steps back, as the Lord changes shape raw fear grips her as she backpedals more. Her heart lodges itself into her throat, watching him change into his true form and an Old Red Dragon. *He's gigantic!* Fear grips her soul, and she turns to run, but he effortlessly knocks her to the ground, scattering coins and gems in all directions with a massive claw. He flips her over onto her back, then she tries lets out a scream and clinches her eyes shut, but fear has frozen her voice. The sound of shattering stone echoes in her head as his massive claw comes down on her. She opens an eye, realizing she's still alive, but he has pinned her to the floor. The massive claw all around her with two of them on either side of her horned head. Pure horror fills her, making her feel cold on the inside for the first time in her life. *I'm a White Dragon in a Red Dragon's hoard. I'm already dead. My body just hasn't accepted it yet.*

He places his nostril to her face, inhaling; the wind rushing past her face whipping up her hair. His massive Dragon eyes, larger than her body, stare down at her. She can feel the heat from his breath and his claw. *With a single snort, he can erase me from existence. What is he waiting for?*

The deep resonating of his voice echoes off the golden hoard. "Why are you here?!"

She's living through her worse possible nightmare as terror races through every part of her body paralyzing her. *I wouldn't be able to move, even if he wasn't holding me down. I'm doing my best not to lose control of my body completely.* She swallows, trying to find the courage she knows isn't there. "To spread peace and love." Fear oozing from her every pore as she knows her fate already.

Flames burst from his nostrils, missing her face by inches. The heat causes her to sweat even more. "That's not all. Speak the truth and you walk out of here, instead of your friends spreading your ashes over some mountain somewhere." He bares long serrated teeth that are longer than William is tall, shoving them inches from her face.

"My secondary mission is to establish trade relations and possible empire expansion to include New Haven as part of the Rose Empire."

"You're still hiding something."

"I want to destroy the Black Rose by any means necessary."

His nostrils get right next to her face and she closes her eyes, thinking of William and Zarra. "I believe you." She feels the pressure of his enormous claw come off her chest, the stone floor crumbing as it pulls it up around her head. She peeks an eye open again. He steps back, the ground shaking, and making it difficult for her to stand. He lies on top of his gold and looks down at her. The fear she felt vanishes as his voice becomes civil again. "Let's speak of your intentions."

William checks on Penelope and she's still crying from her cubbyhole in the overhang. *I feel so guilty and powerless sending them in there. She's a trained operative, but Chuck had no reason to go.*

He closes the door and Zarra walks up behind him, giving him an armored hug as the armor clangs together. "You must make decisions that can end and save lives every day as a commander. If you hadn't done this, we wouldn't be standing in here right now getting the opportunity we needed."

They get their gear and Captain Motsana informs him that a squad will stay with their gear and rotate out while getting some rest. One official, a short brown hair, tall woman, with blue eyes, wearing the standard steel gray and plum purple and white cloak of the city, walks over and introduces herself, breaking the uncomfortable silence between them. "I'm Sergeant Plaksina Svetlana Konstantinovna" She holds her hand out in friendship to William then Zarra.

Zarra bows her head. *Her common is actually really good with almost no accent. She also stands much taller than me, making me feel really kind of tiny.*

William smiles and takes her hand. "William Blakely. Nice to meet you, Plakan Svet," he stops knowing he's butchering it. "I'm sorry I'm not used to such extravagant and multi-syllable names like this. Your city is new to me along with its culture and I don't want to be insulting."

Zarra takes her turn, shaking the larger woman's hand. "Zarra Silvian."

"You may call me Sveta if that makes it easier on you." She bows her head and smiles. "Most people from outside our borders have a hard time with our names, so I'm not offended." She turns her head to the castle and back to them. "The Lord has offered you full diplomatic courtesies. As far as anyone here is concerned, you and your friends are protected by us. If you're hungry, or tired, we are to assist you in any way we can. All our facilities are at your disposal."

William steps forward and holds up a hand. "Actually, I have a question. Last night one of mine was killed while in here. I'm not sure what he was doing, but his name was Chuck. I would like to retrieve it and return it to his family."

"Of course, sir." She waves them to follow. "If you would follow me, I will take you to our morgue and you can identify him." Her tone is very dignified. "I'm sorry for your loss."

CHAPTER 35

(Win and Loss)

He mounts his horse, and she gets on hers. "Captain, I'll be back in a few. Hold things together here. Make use of their hospitality and get the men fed and rested. We don't know when we will take this fight to the Black Rose." The captain salutes and starts barking orders. Zarra returns to the Vardo to get Tia and Penelope. He rides with her and it's not long till they reach their destination. They walk inside and the personnel let them through unimpeded. He addresses a man in a white outfit. "Have any of these came in recently, like the past day or so?" They exchange glances and Sveta repeats what he says in Poshlovish. One of them nods and takes them to a table and uncovers the body. William looks at it and looks at Sveta. "This isn't him. Is there anyone else?" She turns and repeats his words and they both shake their head and say something back to her.

"They say that we could check the hospital if they were still alive and passed. They have their own body storage there." He nods and waves to her to take him. They make their way to the hospital and check with them. They inform him no one had died, but they had a patient brought in under police custody last night who's being treated. William and Sveta have the man show them where this person is.

The police have two guards posted outside the room as they approach. They place their hands on their swords as they see the incredibly large knight clanking his way down the hallway, huge compared to them. Sveta waves them down and informs them he is a visiting dignitary and wants to see the prisoner. They step out of the large man's way and he nods, entering the room. Chuck lays there, bandages all over him. He looks up at William with his one good eye, the other being swollen shut. He sounds as weak as he looks. "Sir?"

William slowly looks over at him. "It's going to be alright, Chuck. I'll have Tia come by and patch you up."

Chuck shakes his head and his voice cracks. "Please, don't. I'll be fine."

"Why? You must be in a lot of pain. Besides, Penelope will be thrilled you survived. She thought you were killed and hasn't stopped crying in hours."

Chuck closes his eye and lays there. "Its best you all forgot about me. Leave her to believe I'm dead."

William can't believe what he is hearing. "That's nonsense. It's obvious she has feelings for you."

"And I do for her too." Chuck swallows and the pain of such is clear on his face. "But she wasn't wrong about is being incompatible. She dreams of children someday, to teach what she knows to them, own her own business." He looks back to William. "She wants so much from life, and she's not going to get that with me." He closes his eye again. "I love her, and will always have a place for her in my heart, but this is the right thing. She should get to live her dreams."

"Are you sure about this?"

Chuck nods slightly. "I'll just go home after I'm better, but I'll probably be spending time in prison first."

"That won't happen. I'll make sure you're released when you get better." William reaches out and takes Chuck's hand. "For what it's worth, you're a good person. Thank you for your help. Goodbye, my friend."

Lord Vlad rakes up a handful of gems and coins and then motions for Crystal to rest upon it. This gets an odd mix of feelings in her as she sits down and leans back on the wealth. *It's not very comfortable, but the Dragon in my blood sings with all the treasures surrounding me.* She smiles, glancing up at the gigantic Red Dragon. *He could have killed me and not only would no one had ever known, but could even of claimed justification. He's after something that only I can give him.* She does her best to get comfortable, and addressing him with the most respect she can muster. "We could start with a simple non-aggression pact. I know we are so far apart that aggression is virtually impossible, but this will at least show that we as representatives of our peoples aren't wanting to go to war." She crosses her legs and holds her knees, interlacing her fingers. "And that will make it easier later on for us to establish the trade agreement that will benefit both of us."

He snorts and small wisps of flame come from his nostrils. "I agree. A non-aggression pact would be mostly for spectacle, and you're not wrong that it would put people at ease. I won't fault you there." He moves, allowing some gold to cover his body. "But for a trade agreement, I don't see it working. It would take months for wagons to travel all the way from Veldar, and ships would take weeks." He raises his head and yawns, flames trickling from his large open maw. *Let's see if she will divulge the information on their airships to use as a bargaining chip.*

"Not necessarily." Crystal counters, leaning forward and resting her arms on her knees, feeling the gold shift under her. "The Rose Empire has been buildings airships for trading with Portstown. It wouldn't be hard to put more people to work and build a few dedicated to your city."

His lips peals back with a smile, revealing those huge teeth of his. "I've heard rumors of your flying ships. I'm eager to see one myself, for as rumors are just that till they are confirmed." He shifts, raising his head and stretches, cascading the gold around him and partially burying his body and contentment crosses his face.

"I can arrange that. Your courtyard is large enough for my ship, the *Bastion,* to land in. If you were to assure it's safe passage and have your people not shoot at it, I could give you a tour."

This perks him up. "Your ship? It's not a military vessel?"

She places a hand on her chest, and her tone shifts, sounding important. "Yes, I own the *Bastion.* It's my personal yacht."

He raises himself, letting the coins cascade down. "Really?" His teeth grow in an enormous smile. "Well then, I'll make arrangements, but I think our little dance needs to turn a little more informative. I know you're here to extend the olive branch, but I also know there is much more about it than that. The Black Rose is currently entrenched in Old Haven, and they cause me problems here, but not on the scale they have caused you." He shifts his stance to peer at her with those enormous eyes of his and backs into his hoard, causing more of his treasure to cover him. "But you're a White Dragon, and I know you personally wouldn't travel all this way when you could send a fleet of your flying ships and just wipe them out." He points a giant claw at her, coming within inches of her chest. "So why are *you* here, Ms. White Dragon?"

So, pinning me to the floor was just to see how I respond to force. This is the real interrogation. I bet he's been around for thousands of years. My best bet is just to be honest. He can vaporize me if he if I lie to him. She shifts but looks him in the eyes, showing no fear. "Personal vengeance. They almost tortured me to death, killed the love of my life, and threatened my family. There is one other thing that is true." His head tilts and shifting one eye to look at her. "And I'm seeking a special gem, a shard, if you will, that I think is somewhere in Old Haven."

Vlad's head tilts down and gets inches from her body, making her uncomfortable. He motions with his oversized claw that is more of a curiosity than a threat. "Would you happen to have a description of this *shard* that you seek and what it's supposed to be?"

He knows something. Better play along. She looks down a moment and then back up at him and holds her hands out several inches apart. "Let's see, from the descriptions I've read, it's about a foot or so long, thin, about an inch or two in thickness, and has a pearl white color to it with a feint glow."

"And what is it supposed to do?"

"It's written that it was the remains of a god, but the book I have on the subject doesn't tell me what it does." She holds a hand up, staying his next words. "I already know your next question and that answer is I'm trying to help a friend find love. Her church doesn't allow for relationships, and we stumbled on evidence that says otherwise. I'm hoping by finding this shard, I can use it to change the church and let my friend be happy."

He moves back a little. A grin crossing his scaled face. "I'm surprised White Dragon that you care about your friend that much that you're willing to put your life on the line for another's happiness."

"Are you saying I'm lying? I believe everyone should have a chance at love, even you." She leans back on her hands again, looking more relaxed than she feels. "She has done much for me. It wouldn't be right if I didn't try."

He laughs, and it echoes in the large underground cave network. "You impress me." He stands, the coins sliding from his back and onto the ground in a jingle of noise. "But I regret to inform you that there is no shard like that in Old Haven, and hasn't been for some time."

She stands too as the coins shifting had almost knocked her over. "So you've seen it?"

He grins, showing those teeth again. "I have, and I know exactly where to find it."

Che advances, putting her hands out. "Please, tell me where it is so I can obtain it for my friend." Crystal flattens her dress, realizing how desperate she sounded. "I would be personally grateful for the information."

His grin grows. "Personally grateful? Well then, I want your sworn word, as countess and on your Dragon lineage that if I tell you, that you will give me favorable treatment in our trade agreement, and share the airship technology with my people, as part of said agreement."

He's got me over a barrel. I really need that shard and he just played me like an old harp. I should be ashamed at how this turned out. She stands stiffly, looking dignified. "I accept your terms. As a countess and as a Dragon, I will give you favorable treatment." She opens her hands in front of her. "So where is it?"

He smiles, reaching out and taking her miniscule hand in his massive claw. She doesn't dare resist. "Not so fast, Ms. White Dragon." He takes his other claw and reaches out, pricking her hand, drawing blood, then does it to himself, and presses the wounds together. He recites an incantation and their bodies glow for an instant in blue. "The deal is sealed. You can't back out on your word and I will know, no matter where in the world you are." He lets her go. "Don't disappoint me." He then turns and digs through his hoard. Coins, gems, and magical items scatter about, cascading as she is forced to move or be buried in a golden avalanche. He pulls a glowing shard from the pile, like a tiny splinter in his gigantic claw, and hands it to her. "Now I have fulfilled my end of the bargain."

She reaches out to it and feels the divine power radiating from it at such a close range. *It's calling to me, but why?* She's enamored with it as she wraps her bloodstained hands around it, feeling the energy rush through her body. *What is this I'm feeling? It's beyond description.*

Outside, Zarra and Tia perk up and look around, and catch the medics doing the same. Tia looks at Zarra. "Are you feeling what I am?"

Zarra continues to look around, confused. "Yeah, a divine source nearby, but where can it be coming from? It's drowning out the entire area."

The Dwarven medic scratches at his head. "You feel that too? I'm not alone wondering what in Sturm's hammer is going on around here?"

Tom and Tyra look confused. "What is wrong?"

"There is a divine source that just lit up. It feels like it's all around us, but it's unfamiliar." Tia shakes her head, scanning the area. "I don't know how to describe it. It's like a fog or a heavy wet blanket. It's almost oppressive."

William returns an hour later and only a token force of five guards stands outside, guarding the wagons. *Everyone else is inside, I guess.* He checks on Penelope and notices she has gone from the Vardo. *At least she stopped crying. Wonder what is going on around here that the courtyard is wide open?* One of the Lord Vlad's guards greets him and brings him inside where everyone is at but the soldiers. They are being housed in his personal barracks on the premises. Crystal sits next to Zarra on a large couch opposite the Lord, who sits in a fancy chair of his own. Tia and Penelope sit in a large chair, Tia holding the Halfling, comforting her as best she can.

They look up as William walks in and Crystal leaves her seat and meets him halfway. She embraces him in front of everyone. "Glad you made it back. The *Bastion* will land soon."

William holds her out and at arm's length and stares into her eyes. "Why?"

"Lord Vlad and I talked and… made arrangements. He's curious about flying on our ship as part of agreeing to speak with us about future endeavors. If we handle the Black Rose and dig them out of Old Haven for him, he will be more willing to discuss a peace agreement."

"But bringing the *Bastion* here will tip the Black Rose off we are here." William sighs. "That was a huge tactical error on your part. They are going to be waiting for us."

She bows her head, realizing he's right. "I didn't think about that." She looks up at him. "I was trying to get our relations here solidified. I'm sorry, I wasn't thinking."

"It'll be ok. I'll figure something out. I always do." He brings her back in and wraps his arms around her. "I can't fault you for being you." They sit down as the party continues.

The *Bastion* comes in and lands and true to her word, Crystal guides Lord Vlad around the ship, explaining it was a prototype and more advanced ships are already in service. "Captain, take us up so Lord Vlad can see his town from the sky."

They float upwards and he walks out on to the deck looking down at the city. Crystal stepping up next to him. He speaks in Draconic. "I can see why Portstown was so eager to join. This technology is a tactical advantage over land locked armies." He turns to her. "Even a Dragon would be hard pressed to fight against something so advanced." He looks back out over the landscape. "Glad you're bonded by your word." They set back down and he invites them all to dinner where they feast and they get to know some of the higher up officials in his city, including the mayor and council. He gives them quarters for the night so he can continue talking to her and the future of their people.

They plan out the next day. William goes over the accurate maps provided by New Haven officials. "The *Bastion* is going to fly low and land at the edge of the frozen swamp and they will go in and confront the Black Rose once and for all." He points at different places. "We are going to land here at the edge and move in by foot. Once we engage the enemy and get an accurate location of their fortifications, we will call in the *Bastion* to bombard the area."

Crystal speaks to Lord Vlad alone as William conducts his planning. "As a powerful and old Dragon, why don't you just root them out yourself? Should be easy for someone like you."

He nods in agreement. "It would be, yes." He looks down at her. "But if a rumor of an old Red Dragon lives in the area, it would cause panic." He grins. "Since you're here and your goals align with mine, I'll just use you instead." He points to her handbag. "So has that shard helped you yet?"

She nods animatedly. "Once I had it in my position, parts of the book that were sealed away opened to me. I've learned much and that now I must keep some things to myself. The stuff in that book is not for common knowledge."

"Just be sure to keep your word. I would hate to have to take my gift back." He grins. "You must be special. It never spoke to me." She nods, accepting the warning he tells her as a promise.

William comes by and informs Crystal that they are ready to go. She bids farewell to Lord Vlad, and they exit into the courtyard. Crystal looks at her Vardo. "Will, I need to grab something first." She let him go, rushing to the old red and gold wagon.

What is this all about?

She climbs in, picking up the gem inlaid box and places it in her handbag, then grabs the medical kit. She gets back to the ship and hands him the med kit. "Can't leave without that." They board the ship and Crystal goes to her quarters with the object she built in her small handbag. She picks up the book about the war between the gods and the secret pages reveal themselves to her with the shard in her presence. She reads intently, and Zarra comes in with William. Crystal looks up and Zarra points at the book. "What are you reading now?"

"It's about the war in heaven. Better get Tia in here." William leaves, and Zarra looks at Crystal. "I've been having a hard time staying in contact with Johnathan, and Tia has been getting interference trying to get a hold of Daniel. There is some weird divine presence that's interfering with our prayers."

Crystal stops and looks up at her. "How long has that been happening?"

"Since yesterday. It's started off small, but it's steadily getting larger and it feels like it's all around us. Any idea what it could be?" Crystal looks at Zarra and looks back at the door. She turns and reaches into her bag, pulling the shard out for Zarra to see. "Is that?"

Crystal nods. "Lord Vlad gave it to me, and when I held it, I could feel the power radiating in it. After that, this book started revealing everything to me." She puts the shard back. "It's full of information that's going to help me get Tia's situation figured out."

Tia walks in, escorted by William. "You needed to see me, countess?"

She pats the spot next to her. "Have a seat. I found out something you two are going to want to know." She picks the book back up and opens it. "So the gods of War and Death had a disagreement and Death tried to take war's powers, but the God of Love intervened and tried to settle the two down. Death didn't take too kindly to Love's interference and was first to be struck down."

Tia looks over Crystal's shoulder at the book. "So that explains why the torch is in Daniel's hands?"

"Let me continue here." Crystal points to the words and paraphrases. "The goddess of Nature took up for Love and sided with War in keeping their domains separate. Soon almost every god had chosen a side or abstained. Provider, along with the other neutral gods, didn't want any part of it, disappeared till it was over. Ideals were pitted against each other but not in debate, but in bloodshed. The planet itself bearing the scares of their battles. The sea level rose, and the land masses shifted. Mortals

414

perished, but with those gods dead, there was no place to keep their souls."

Zarra covers her mouth. "That's horrific." This gets nods of agreement from William and Tia both.

"There is more." She taps the pages in the book. "In the aftermath, Provider, Daniel, and the others picked up the pieces, knowing those souls had to go somewhere. Each one who was left alive took on extra roles, waiting for the day that new gods would take their place amongst the pantheon and fulfill the calling. The shards left behind by the death of a god aren't enough to grant a person such divine powers, but must be worthy to wield such power.

Tia continues to stare at the book. "What does that even mean?"

Crystal shakes her head and shrugs. "I haven't a clue, to be honest. I have a lot more studying to do, and if we survive assaulting the Black Rose, I'll find the answers." She turns to Tia, patting her on the leg. "But maybe this is why Daniel is appearing to you now. He knows there is a new god of love coming to take their rightful place, and maybe we are supposed to help him get there. Then you can be happy at last."

"We still have to get the shard, though."

"Actually, I've already got it. Lord Vlad gave it to me as part of our negotiations and the deal I made for it. I'll hand it off to Emperor Marcus, and his religious scholars can figure it out. This religion thing makes my head hurt." She shrugs. "I hope he can figure out who is supposed to have it."

Tia glances at it and then at Crystal. "Do you know which shard that is?"

Crystal looks back at the book. "According to this, only Love fell here as the first casualty. The others fell in other places around the world." She hefts the shard. "So this must be the Love shard given no other evidence to tell us otherwise."

William turns to exit. "I need to meet with the captain Motsana and get the lieutenants and sergeants ready for action. We have no idea what we are facing and should be ready for anything." He leaves the three, shutting the door behind him.

Crystal closes the book. "How's Shadow doing?"

Tia sighs and looks down. "She's pretty broken up losing Chuck."

Zarra sits down. "Yeah, she loved him, even though they were different."

Crystal gets up, putting the book on the table. "I'm going to go check on her. You two should get something to eat before the battle starts."

William walks into the planning room, where Tom, Motsana, and the others are waiting. He looks out the window as they pass over the swamp. "The water around the buildings should all be frozen over, so being quiet will not be much of an option."

"We got that handled, Major. We can be your scouts and not leave a trace of even existing."

Tyra closes her arms. "Speak for yourself. You're not the one who weighs eight hundred pounds. Silent? Yes. Trace? There is no hiding where I've been."

"All the same, you will know when we are near someone, and we can silence them." He walks over, looking at the map. "That is what you're going to want us to do, right, Major?"

"Unfortunately yes. If they alert anyone to our presence, we are all dead. Better them than us and they have this coming." William joins them at the map and points. "It looks like there is an underground network of old sewers that they are using, according to these reports. If they sealed up the walls and pumped the water out, it would make a good hiding place because no one would think of looking for them under the swamp. The captured operatives let us know about it. Just be careful of traps. If they have something rigged to flood the tunnels with intruders, we will be in a lot of trouble."

Zarra walks in and William welcomes her to the table. He goes over the plan with her as well and they toss ideas around. Tom looks at William. "We aren't all making it back, are we?"

William shakes his head. "This could be one way for all of us. If anyone wants out, speak up." He turns to Tom, then Tyra, then Zarra and the other soldiers. They all keep quiet. "Dismissed."

Everyone files out, leaving him alone in the room with Zarra. He looks into her eyes. "You and Crystal should stay here and let me handle it."

Zarra shakes her head and reaches up and places her palm on his beard. "We live together or die together. I have your back, and I know Crystal feels the same."

He reaches up and places his hand on hers. "I love you both. I think after this, we should retire and settle down." He leans down and kisses her soft onyx lips.

"I like that idea."

CHAPTER 36

(Light of Peace)

The ship lands a few miles outside of the old city, bordering the frozen swamp. Alone in her quarters, Crystal completes the device, and slides it into her handbag with the other items. She joins them outside as they assemble and use the wands to protect them all from the environment. As they get ready, Crystal hands the rod of mass teleport to Tia and tells her the command word. "If things get bad, use this and think of the ship. It will bring you right back to here along with anyone close by."

"Why are you handing this to me?"

"In case my hands are full, or I'm incapacitated from over casting. There're tons of reasons and you know the condition I'm in. If I'm the only one who can use it and things go wrong, we could all be trapped. At least if the two of us know how to use it, then it's a greater chance most of us could survive."

Tia nods, looking at the small white rod. "You really think it's going to be that bad?"

"To be honest, with Chuck gone, we don't have a clue what we are facing against. We may have to run and bombard this from the sky." She places a hand on her handbag. "But one thing I know is today Zalreria Pyrewind is getting a one-way trip to hell. That I promise."

Penelope pulls herself together after Tom fills her in with what is happening. They head into the frozen swamp, but it's foggy, making it hard to see. Frozen vines hang from the cypress trees, causing a constant obstacle. She stays a quarter of a mile ahead and on the left side of the group, Tom is on the right and Tyra sticks to the middle, letting her nose guide her. They lose each other in the fog often, so they guess where the others are at as they use compasses to keep them moving towards the old ruins.

Tyra struggles with the frozen mud and slush, her weight making her sink. She struggles and uses the vines to keep pulling herself out. *Why did it have to be in a swamp?* She sloshes, trying her best to keep quiet, and mud and snow are building up on her legs. Breathing hard and climbing over a large exposed root, she comes face to face with another person holding a rifle.

He holds readies it and points it at her "Who are you, and what are you doing here?"

She sighs, and like lightning, she takes the rifle from the man with little effort and then lands a punch, knocking him out and to the ground. She snaps the weapon and tosses it into the slush. "Should have stepped back first."

Tom makes his way silently, and after some time, finds some abandoned homes. The mud here isn't as deep as the cobblestone just below him is still decently strong for being around for two hundred years. He moves along the streets, trying to be as quiet as he can. Finding the first sign of any guards, they don't look to be on to high alert. *They seem complacent. Should be easy.* He works around behind them, and before they know what happens, his Sai kills them quietly. *I hate this, but they wouldn't hesitate to kill me or anyone else.* He pulls their bodies into a nearby building, hiding them from other guards. He leaves and nears the old city government building that's being guarded with more Black Rose.

Penelope finally makes it into town and is so light that she walks on top of the ice without breaking through. Silent as the dead, she readies her blades and dashes from alley to alley, dispatching anyone she can find. She comes up on one member of the Black Rose as he turns and she leaps, grabbing his shirt and cutting his throat, riding his corpse back to the ground. Perking up, she can hear the armored troopers coming with William at the head. She continues scouting and taking out who she finds, till she runs into Tyra, who is covered in mud, slush, and blood. "Bring the whole swamp with you?"

"Hilarious." She points to the door of the building she's standing in front of. "This place looks intact, and I smell a lot of unfamiliar scents here."

Tom speaks up from behind them. "Only way in is through the front door?"

Penelope nods. "Guess that's my job." Walking up to the front door and she holds a hand out, stopping them. She looks over the entire area before stepping anywhere near it and lifts a mat with a dagger tip, finding a trigger plate. *Explains the absence of guards here.* Reaching under with a tool, she snips the string, then lifts it. *They sure don't want company.* She checks the door, picking the lock and opening it just a little, seeing another wire attached to it at the top. "Tyra, hold this door, and don't let it move."

Tyra takes the door and Shadow squeezes through the small crack and looks. A spiked contraption is bolted to the ceiling big enough to cover the whole door. "Close it softly." As the door shuts, the tension comes off the mechanism. She grabs a nearby chair and sets it up so she can climb up and reach the release pin, making it safe. She opens the door, letting them in.

Tyra looks up at the spikes. "That would've hurt." Tom nods in agreement. "I hope this whole place isn't like this or it's going to be a nightmare navigating."

420

"I expect nothing less from these people." Penelope looks up and can hear William and the troops fighting it out with a few they missed. Moments later, Willian and Crystal walk in, followed by the others. "What kept you?"

Crystal thumbs back out the door. "Picked off a few stragglers. There isn't much of an army here, so that's a pleasant surprise."

William pushes in, taking the area in. "Doesn't mean they aren't around. Let's stay vigilant and find an entrance inside. According to Chuck, they had it hidden inside an office under a desk. So let's start looking."

"And let's be careful." Penelope moves out into the room. "Just getting through the door were two traps. Do not mess with anything. We don't know what nasty surprises are in here."

They search, and traps get set off, killing a lieutenant and two troopers just from picking up inconspicuous objects. Two of them by contact poison just lifting an object and the third by a mechanical spring-loaded spike coming out of the floor, impaling him. Tia shakes her head, knowing she can't do anything for them as it kills them too fast for her to counter. "What have we gotten into?"

Zarra shakes her head. "I don't know, but what kind of people use things like this?"

Crystal crumbles something in her hand. "Those who don't deserve a trial." One sergeant finds the right desk and moves it, exposing a passage way down. He calls out, letting everyone know and William, Penelope, and Crystal all gaze down the hole.

"I'll go first." Penelope puts a dagger in her mouth, making her words sound funny. "I'm the least likely to set traps off and need to check for them down here." She climbs down. As she gets to the bottom, she looks at her gloves and sees they are wet. She warns them. "More of that contact poison on the ladder, wear gloves or clean the rungs off."

Crystal spouts a quick incantation and the ladder glows yellow and looks new. "There, the poison should have been removed by me using my clean spell." They climb down and see the tunnel branches off in two directions, and it's dark. The walls are damp and the water isn't frozen here, but an ankle deep sludge. Lichens and mosses grow along the walls and the smell is very unpleasant, Tyra feeling the effects worse than anyone.

"I'll take the Portstown guards and head this way." Captain Motsana tells William. "We Catfolk see just fine in the dark and can get the surprise on any enemies."

William nods, and Crystal creates a ball of light with her magic. They pull weapons ready for anything. Penelope navigates ahead, disabling trip wires hidden below the water as they slosh through. She holds her hand up as she comes to a large underground chamber lit with lanterns. William and the rest make their way slowly and whispers. "What is it?" Crystal douses her light not to give them away.

She whispers back. "Looks like some kind of library. The shelves aren't very tall, but there are a lot of books and lanterns. I note five people inside that I can see."

William looks at Tom and Tyra, and they nod and step around quietly. Penelope pulls her daggers and the trio enter, moving silently. Zarra takes a crossbow from a trooper and takes aim, waiting for the moment to strike. Penelope leaps out, planting her daggers deep into the back of a lady, riding her to the ground. The man next to her turns and Zarra takes him out with a crossbow bolt to the neck, dropping him where he stands. The third turns and runs, but Tom beats him to the exit, hitting him hard enough to knock him out cold before he hits the ground. Another lady screams, but is cut short by Tyra, who cuts her down with her Katana. The last remaining Black Rose member throws his hands I the air, surrendering.

Zarra hands the crossbow back to the trooper. "Glad you brought these along. Much quieter than the rifles."

Crystal walks over, clicking her bracelets and letting her claws come out. He holds his hands up, showing he isn't armed. "I surrender."

She stabs him through the chest with her claws and he makes a gurgling noise as blood pours around her wrist. Absolute hate drips from her mouth. "Your people don't take prisoners, but to torture them. Feel grateful I'm not returning the favor." He collapses to the floor. She flicks the blood away and looks around at the disapproving faces of everyone there. "What? We weren't sparing anyone, anyway. They are all guilty of all manner of heinous crimes. We can't exactly give them a trial here."

William takes her hands. "Maybe you should go back to the ship. This is too stressful for you."

"I will see justice done, even if it's by my own hand. I won't let the ones I care for and love be at their mercy."

Tia hugs her from behind. "We love you too. But don't go back down that road again. You don't have to hate, remember?" Crystal nods and waves them on.

Captain Motsana and his people break off, taking a separate way. They move silently through the moss covered and dingy tunnels. The lichens have a slight glow giving them a little light to navigate by and any Black Rose they encounter is taken down silently. They make a few turns and come to a large chamber that's well lit. Captain Motsana looks in and see's many figures inside. He moves back and tells his people they have the element of surprise, and it looks to be a good chunk of their forces. "We have a chance to deal a major blow here to their numbers." They move forward silently. Unlike Willian and the Rose Harbor troops, they don't use bulky and noisy heavy armor, allowing them to keep their stealth. He motions and they move in low, crossing the floor fast.

He raises his Moplah and cuts down the closest enemy, and Talwars and Patas come to bear on the enemy. Cutting them

423

down quietly, but the after that, the surprise is over. The clashing of swords and armor echo in the tunnels along with shouts in various dialects giving orders. He catches another word on his Moplah and harmlessly turns it away, and countering with a swing of his own. The ring of metal on metal come in from all sides as he flashes fangs as blood flies.

The Catfolk are slowly pushed back, and more reinforcements arrive from other tunnels sooner than he thought could be possible, but retreat isn't an option. His troops fight harder, dropping one after another, as limbs, weapons, and bodies hit the ground. More Black Rose fall, but his own troops are falling too. He has several cuts that got past his armor, weakening him as well as he faces overwhelming numbers.

He looks about the area and notices half of his troops are down, but the Black Rose has lost far more. That doesn't stop the fanatics as they keep throwing themselves at the Catfolk, uncaring that they are dying to their blades. *They must be trying to bury us alive with their dead.* More come in armed with nothing more than knives, or unarmed and just picking up any weapon nearby. He slashes with the enormous sword, cutting them down one after another till he is but one of only six remaining Catfolk in the room. The dead litter the floor and they are surrounded back-to-back with each other, but the enemy stops advancing.

He looks around and they part allowing a tall smooth gray skinned woman wearing a black and red cloak and mask. A short necklace with the black flamed sword hangs from her neck. The unholy symbol of Xavral. Her voice is calm, almost arrogant. "You must be Captain Motsana. I've heard so much about you." Her eyes are crimson red like pure blood, and there is nothing gentle behind them.

"And you are?"

She holds her hands up and apart at the shoulders. "Zalreria Pyrewind. Priestess of Death and Destruction, that is Xavral."

424

His tone fills with anger. "You're the one who sent the troops to destroy my people. I'm going to enjoy watching you die."

She smiles, her mouth the only part of her face besides her eyes exposed, and it makes his blood freeze in his veins. She wags her finger. "On the contrary Captain. You're going to watch Crystal Hellstromm die, for you will be the one killing her."

"There is nothing that would make me willing to do that." He raises his sword and a blast of black energy strikes him from her outstretched hand and he collapses to the ground.

"Not alive anyway." She waves flippantly. "Kill them. I'm going to spend a little quality time with my new pet here." The Catfolk fight the last man, taking down way more than they had left, making the Black Rose victory a costly one in the end.

William and the rest hear the noises stop as they come to another chamber. "Either Motsana won, and they are on the move again, or they are all dead, meaning we need to finish up here."

Crystal looks about the room, casting her spell to see magic, and the circle on the floor glows and several instruments around the room does to. "This must be where they sent Chuck and the others to the Monastery. It's as he described, remember?" Crystal continues to look around. "Her lab has to be nearby. We smash that and she's crippled, unable to do anything to us, at least for a while."

Zarra calls out. "Over here, there is an imperfection in the wall."

The Dwarven lieutenant agrees with her. "I see it in the stonework, but how to open it?"

"On the wall, I see a rune that glows with magic next to where you are standing."

Zarra and the Dwarf look but shake their heads. "I don't see it."

Crystal walks over and points at it, but they still don't see it. She goes to place her hand on it and a voice, cold and dripping with contempt, calls from behind them. "I wouldn't touch that, if I were you, countess." They all turn and see Pyrewind. "It would be very hazardous to your health."

Something about the woman's words makes Crystal believe her. She makes no attempt to hide her disdain. "And you are?"

She smiles and even William reflexively steps back. "Zalreria Pyrewind. I believe you've been looking for me."

Zarra grabs Crystal, knowing she would charge in head first to kill this woman. Pain and anger drips from her fangs. "Oh, you have no idea how badly I've been wanting to meet you."

She walks into the light better and Captain Motsana walks in behind her, but he is moving oddly. William can't place it, but the pure evil dripping from the woman tells Zarra and Tia all they need to know. Tia shouts a warning. "That's not Captain Motsana."

The gray lady turns to her. "But of course it is." She pats him on the head like a pet. "He's the person you left to be killed by me. And now, he wants his revenge for letting him die so horribly."

Captain Motsana charges at Crystal, making a noise that isn't natural, but William intervenes, colliding with the reanimated remains of their friend. Zarra gets in front of Crystal, guarding her. Others move, but the gray woman speaks up. "Stop right there, anyone tries stopping them, and you all die." Black Rose troops move in around them, wielding guns, crossbows, and other weapons. "I want to see who wins, so I know who to keep."

William slashes out with his sword, but the Captain catches it with his Moplah. He circles, lashing out much faster than William can counter with the smaller Catfolk having those inhuman reflexes. His armor is more than a match for the Catfolk's sword, doing minor damage. William grabs the Catfolk's arm, pinning it, and brings his sword down, killing him a second time. William lets go and the captain falls. He turns to Zalreria, his own anger tainting his tone. "You'll die for that."

She smiles, raising her hand and starting an incantation and her hand glows black. Crystal knows from the book of necromancy exactly what it is. "STOP!" Zalreria turns to the interruption and holds her spell. Crystal cries, knowing how this must end. "I'll surrender myself if you let them go. I won't resist and give you any information you want willingly." She looks at the Zalreria. "If you let them leave."

She smiles, but sounds unconvinced. "You're really willing to do all that for them?"

"Yes." Tears fill her eyes, knowing what she's about to do.

William raises his voice. "You can't be serious!"

"Quiet Will."

Zarra's mouth gapes. "But countess!"

Crystal steps around Zarra slowly walking towards Pyrerwind "That goes for you too." She looks at them. "I love you all, and I will do anything, make any sacrifice, if it means you live another day."

William walks to her. "Don't do this."

She steps in front of him, putting herself between him and Pyrewind. "I have to Will. I must bring peace and love to our world. It's on me. Promise me you will tell you and Zarra's children about me." She kisses him, then pushes him away forcefully. Spinning to face her with tears in her eyes, she grits her fanged teeth. "Do we have a deal or not, Pyrewind?"

"Why shouldn't I kill them and just take you by force? Would be fun."

"Because you know how powerful of a sorceress I am, and I'm willing to bring this place down on all of us if it means killing you. They are keeping me from destroying everything right now."

She puts her hand down. "You make a fair point. I accept. They are free to leave."

William walks back to Crystal. "Don't do this. There is another way."

She pushes him away again, and he knows she's made up her mind. She looks at Tia. "Remember the ship. Get as far away from here as possible. Warn the Emperor." She turns and walks over to Zalreria.

Zarra drags William away, but he points at Zalreria. "Don't think you've won. I will hunt you down to the end of Delveon." He looks at Crystal, pain welling up in his chest. "I'll come back for you. I promise."

Crystal shakes her head. "Don't." She looks away. "Don't let my sacrifice be in vain. Go back to New Haven and tell Lord Vlad that my word won't die with me."

Tia holds the rod and, with a word, vanishes in a flash of light, taking everyone with her. Zalreria grins, turning to her prisoner, shackling her hands so she can't cast. "Very noble of you." She walks around the short girl, dragging a finger along her shoulder. "I know one of my disciples tortured you for days." She shoves, pushing Crystal to the ground. "But the simple days are over." She reaches down and takes Crystal's handbag, and kicks her over.

"Give that back. I surrendered to you so we could make peace. I was hoping we could talk and come to an understanding."

Zalreria opens the bag as Crystal gets back to her feet. "Oh, what's this? You have some interesting trinkets." She pulls out the glowing shard first. "What does this do?"

"It's my night light. I use it to see in the dark."

Zalreria laughs. "I'm not sure if I should believe you or not." The shard calls to Crystal, wanting her to hold it once again. Zalreria pulls out the copper and steel box covered in gems. She holds it up. "What's this?"

"My magic lock box. Keeps the most important secrets safe."

Zalreria looks down at it. "How do you open it?"

Crystal scoffs and looks away. "Like I would tell you."

Zalreria walks over and shoves it into Crystal's chest, forcing her back. "Open it, or I'll send people to murder your boyfriend and make you watch."

Crystal bows her head. "Fine. I need the shard. It's the key for this." Zalreria looks at her for a long moment. Then hands it to her. Crystal holds the shard and uses it to press a yellow gem on the side of the box. There is an audible click. "There. The first lock is disabled, but you still need the combination."

She reaches up when Zalreria takes it from her. "What is it? And what is in this box that needs this kind of locking mechanism."

"Press the red gem, turn the dial to ten, and then slide the pin back."

"You didn't answer my question." Crystal stays quiet and Zalreria punches her, causing her to cough up blood and collapse to the ground.

Crystal wheezes from the floor. "One of my father's best-kept secrets." She coughs again. "Just please don't open that. You're problem is with me, not with him."

Zalreria follows the instructions, and the box opens, exposing three wands inside banded on both sides by iron. A ticking noise can be heard coming from it. She glowers at Crystal. "What is this?"

Crystal grins, grasping the shard tight. "I didn't lie. It's one of my father's greatest secret." Zalreria looks down at the device and back at Crystal. "See you in hell, bitch." The timer stops, the bands on either end pull down and the wands inside crack.

William and the rest appear several miles away at the ship outside the swamp. He turns to Penelope. "We need to regroup and go after her. We aren't leaving without her."

Penelope nods. "I'll go straight to the captain to get us…" is all she gets out when a flash of bright white energy penetrates the fog. In under a second, the fog is dissipated, and trees are uprooted by the pressure wave of intense heat knocks down everything in it's path. Mud, snow, and trees fly outwards from the epicenter, knocking them all to the ground. Broken and charred trees become lodged in the ship's side, and splinters of wood penetrate personal armor. As fast as it came, it's over, leaving all their ears ringing and feeling as they have been hit by a train. They slowly pick themselves up and look as all the trees, as far as they can see, were flattened to the ground. They look up and see a mushroom shaped cloud rising miles into the sky.

"CRYSTAL!" William screams and charges towards the swamp, but is stopped by Zarra, Tyra, and Tia. "Let me go. I have to help her." His tears flow unchecked.

Penelope shakes her head. "I know what that was."

William looks down at her. "It was that box thing she's been working on, wasn't it? That was the thing her dad told us about."

Penelope slowly nods, watching the mushroom grow into the sky. "I've heard that story a dozen times. Even Cline told me about it when he was running the House, that Jack never lies."

Zarra looks at them. "Fill me in?"

Penelope looks up at her, and her eyes are filled with tears once again. "Tactical magical bomb. Snapping an overloaded wand creates an explosion of energy. Jack figured out how to make it into a weapon that magnified the power into something truly abominable. I never thought it was true, till now."

Zarra leans in. "It's impossible to snap a wand. The magic makes them indestructible."

Penelope shakes her head. "You're seeing proof that Jack can do the impossible. Noone should possess such knowledge."

William fights to get free. "Maybe she's alright, built some kind of safety in it?"

"She's gone, William." Tia can't hold back her tears either. "She sacrificed herself so we may live. To put an end to the Black Rose." Her own tears of grief and anger flow and freeze on her face.

He collapses to the ground. "I could have been the one to set it off, not her." He tosses his sword and shield away, gripping his head. "She didn't have to."

Zarra places a hand on his shoulder, letting her own tears flow with everyone else. "No, it had to be her. The only way to get us out of there was to use herself as bait." Zarra kneels next to him. "She did the bravest and most noble thing anyone could have done, and she did it out of the love for us." She wraps her arms around him, the agony of losing her best friend filling her chest.

They are all mourning at this point, but Penelope brings them to reality. "We need to get the ship repaired and off the ground before we will all freeze to death out here. Without Crystal's environmental magic, we won't last long out here. Plus,

431

we don't know what the aftereffect of that weapon is. Let's not make her sacrifice in vain." She hands William his sword and shield. "We lost too much on this trip. Let's not lose more."

They board the ship, and the damage from the debris isn't too bad. Two dead, seventeen wounded from ruptured steam pipes and broken glass. They cut the pieces of tree that are lodged in the ship's hull and patch it as best they can. They spend several days making repairs while grieving their loss. William, Tia, and Penelope tell stories Crystal about the good and the bad, and how they are going to miss her despite her flaws.

William hasn't slept since her passing, as his bed feels empty without her there snuggling on him. He walks the ship, trying to keep busy and his mind from it, but his bed doesn't feel right anymore. He sleeps in his chair in his office with his head on his desk. On day three, he has a dream, surrounded by a white plane in all directions. He looks around and sees nothing but white in all directions. Then a hand from behind him grabs his shoulder. He turns and sees her. The pain of loss hits him once again. "Crystal?"

"Yes darling, it's me." She kisses him. "I don't have much time. I just wanted to say how much I love you, and to stay strong for Zarra and Tia." She softly strokes his tear covered face. "Tell them that everything will work out in the end."

Grief overwhelms him and tears rain from his eyes. He reaches up and takes her soft hand. "But I can't go on without you."

"I am not gone as long as you keep me here." She places her hand on his heart. "And there is something else you should know." She steps back and pulls a torch from out of thin air. The warmth of Love radiates from it.

"Is that what I think it is?"

"It is. Daniel gave it to me." She pulls him down, kissing him once again. "I'll be waiting for you."

He awakens sobbing again. "What does it all mean?" He sits there and moments later, Zarra walks in, looking flustered and confused, shutting the door behind her locking it.

She can see on his face that she wasn't the only one who experienced the dream. "You saw her too?" She sits down in his lap and throwing her arms around him.

He nods and looks into her eyes. "She told me to be strong for you, and everything will work out."

Tears well up in her eyes. "She spoke similarly to me. Said to embrace you, to be there and hold you when you needed it most." She looks deep into his brown eyes. "I love you." She cups his face pulling herself to his lips.

CHAPTER 37

(Of Love and War)

The last thing Crystal remembers is the bomb detonating and getting to see Zalreria incinerated with her at ground zero. She stands in a plane of white that goes on in all directions endlessly. "So...this is the afterlife?" Her arms flop to her sides. "How dull." She glances in all directions, her voice doesn't echo here. "Guess being bored for all eternity is a suitable punishment for someone who was entertained for her short twenty years."

A male voice speaks from behind her, causing her to spin, her white dress flowing with her. "You aren't being punished." A man made of pure golden light stands before her, white robes and a staff in his hands.

She looks down. "How did I get in a white dress?"

"Here you can look however you want. Your imagination is the only limit."

"Really?" He nods. She thinks a moment and her dress turns red and it shimmers as is made of thousands of stars. Two bands of silken cloth hang straight down from her shoulders, covering her chest. It tucks under her belt where it encloses her lower body and drags the floor. The dress is open from the neck to waist, and is sleeve and backless, allowing her to move unhindered.

"What do you think?"

"It matters not what I think, but what you think your worshipers will like."

434

"Worshippers?"

Another voice joins the conversation. "Yes, Crystal. You have a following." A tan man with blue eyes, brown hair, and brown robes appears before her.

"Daniel?"

"That is correct."

She looks at the golden figure. "Then you must be Provider."

A third voice enters the conversation. "She's two for two." She turns and sees a huge red and black mechanical being. Swords and weapons are attached to him, much like how her father's personal power armor, but more aggressive looking.

"You're the new god of war, Mechas, but I don't know you as well as the others."

The mechanical man looks at the others, and they give him a nod. The armor opens and a short black man with dreadlocks steps out, covered in gears, cogs, and rubber hoses. "That's because I've been purposely hiding it from you your whole life."

"DADDY?" She rushes at him, and throws herself into him, crying.

"Yes monster. It's me." He cries with her, holding her tight. "You did me proud at the end. I had always wondered if I raised you right, and you didn't disappoint. Copying the plans to my bomb was slick. I didn't think you had it in you. I was quite disturbed when I found them out of place, meaning you made your own."

A feminine figure appears in a black cloak with a serrated dagger on her hip, and places a hand on Provider's shoulder. She pulls her hood back. Revealing her Elven features. Provider reaches up and pats her hand. "This is my wife, Morgana, goddess of assassins and manipulation."

She offers her hand. "Welcome to the family. It was fun getting you here."

Crystal looks up, crossing her arms. "What's that supposed to mean?"

The Provider speaks grabbing her attention. "Now we need you to practice honing your new powers. While you were on the material plane, you started showing signs of your divine gift and those around you were being flooded by it. Even before the shard was in your possession, your divinity was shining and effecting those around you unintentionally." He holds a finger up. "Remember Master Monzulo's teachings?"

"Yes."

"It works the same for your divine gift for controlling your chi. If you can't control it, then your worshipers will get mixed messages. It takes years to master, but the one thing you have is time." He rests a golden hand on her shoulder. "You're the new Goddess of Love with domain over love, fertility, creation, and magic. You can take on others, but those will be your primary focuses."

"I have a question, well, tons of questions, actually."

"Sure, we are here to help you as you develop."

"How is my father the God of War and still on the prime material plane?" She then follows before he can answer, looking at her dad. "And how did you become the God of War, father?"

Jack looks at Provider and he motions at him with an open hand. "Well, I didn't die on the prime plane, and I gained my Godhood while still there. Remember when I told that story of the scorpion man city? After that day, it spread that I was the ultimate persona of War, that everywhere where I went, I brought war with me. So they started worshiping me as War himself." He shrugs. "After a time, Provider came along and granted me the powers associated with it by handing me the Shard of War."

Crystal's eyebrows shoot up. "So that's why when the people of Portstown were calling me Sky Lady for spreading love, they thought I was the new Goddess of Love?"

"And then it spread to Rose Harbor through your brother's stories and others coming from there."

Provider picks it up from there. "When you grabbed the shard, all your priests and priestesses could actually cast divine spells for the first time, giving credence to their claims." A grin appears on his face. "And from there, it spread like wildfire. The Goddess of Love was finally real." The Provider looks down at her. "And now, you're here."

She looks around the plain white landscape. "Is my future stuck here in limbo forever with only you to talk to while you get to have fun on the prime plane?"

Daniel holds out a hand, and the Torch of Love appears above it. "This rightfully belongs to you now." She takes it. "If you hold it and think of someone, you can speak to them in their sleep. Try it."

She closes her eyes and thinks of William and sees him moving about the ship. He sits down in his chair and starts doing paperwork and she pushes a little, causing him to fall asleep. She visits him in his dream, and she cries as she communes with him. A few minutes go by and she can feel how hurt he is. She then goes to Zarra, then Tia, and the rest. Visiting each one in their sleep, telling them how proud she is of them. After some time, she comes out of it and looks at Provider. "They are so hurt. I tried to comfort them, but I don't know what to do."

"The best way to get an idea of what's happening in the world is to be there."

She flops back into the chair. "Well, fat chance of that. I died in a tactical magical explosion. My atoms are scattered across Delveon."

The Provider leans in, letting his voice lower and it almost sounds familiar. "I wouldn't be much of a provider if I didn't provide, and I owe you a town to call your own."

Wide eyed, her head slowly turns to face him and finally clicks on why she knows that voice. "Marcus?"

"Guilty."

She looks at Daniel. "And I suppose you have a living Avatar too?" She eyeballs him.

He nods. "We all do."

She points at Morgana. "And you?"

Morgana grins. "Skylar."

She looks at each of them. "Then why don't I?"

Jack laughs, getting her attention. "Because you blew yours up with my bomb. Look at the bright side. The shard didn't infuse till *after* you died, so it didn't drop on the spot, but stayed you're your soul here." She looks at him and scowls. "Hey, it wasn't any easier on me watching you use it. I wanted to stop you, but I knew it was the only way you were going to reach your full potential. Your mother is going to be pissed at me, and I'm going to hear about it for all eternity."

Crystal smiles. "And who is mom the goddess of?"

"Nagging mostly." This gets a laugh from Provider and Daniel. "But she's the Goddess of Nature and Agriculture, Vetrix. That's why I started building tractors all those years ago. She had a hand in it."

"And why isn't she here?"

"Because not all of us can get away. Being a God isn't all fun and games, and immortality isn't what it's cracked up to be. Watching friends grow old and pass on, it's not all great, but with your mother alive and at my side, it's bearable, and now you. There is water Marcus has that can extend the age of others, and I was planning on using it on Andrew and his wife."

438

"His wife?"

Daniel answers her. "Yeah. He loves Tia and you know those two are going to get married. It's fairly obvious. Your mother can't wait for him to propose as William did."

Crystal slumps. "And now Andrew is going to be destroyed when William shows up and tells him I died."

The Provider interrupts. "Unless you didn't *die* in the blast."

Crystal raises an eyebrow. "What do you mean? They would have seen that from Portstown."

"As much as you've done to stop the Black Rose, they aren't done, only set back. Your purpose on Delveon isn't over yet. So, I've decided I'm going to send you back."

"How is that going to work? How do I explain that I died in a fiery blast and I appear in front of them?" Before he can answer, she stands up and anger fills her voice. "And you said that resurrection was an insult to the gods."

Providers shrugs, holding his hands out. "It's wrong to take a soul from a god whom has already arrived. Your soul is that of a god and I can't wrong you by taking you from you."

Crystal holds a finger up and is about to complain, but stops and starts again. "What?"

"If you don't want to live again, I won't force you, but I'm giving you the option to walk among the mortals once again." He points at her chest. "The shard has merged with your soul in that explosion. An event I've only seen a few times where a god was created without a mortal avatar attached to it." He holds a finger up, forestalling her questions. "But if you die on Delveon after I restore it, the shard will separate, and you will become a normal soul. If you're here when your avatar dies, you can never again return to the mortal realm. The shard will be with you for eternity. Even I can't break that rule."

"I want to go back." She looks up at him. "But how do I explain that I'm alive after being atomized?"

"You're the Goddess of Magic, too. You'll figure it out." He grins. "Zarra and Tia are going to go nuts now that you've reached full divinity and can't control it. So you will need to come here and hone your gifts."

"What do you mean, come here?"

Provider holds his hands out and turns. "This is your plane. As with your looks, it will bend to your divine will. When you want to come here, you can will yourself here. The shard transfers with you. On Delveon, you will look to everyone else to be peacefully sleeping."

Morgana interjects. "Or in a coma."

They all laugh, and Crystal looks at her father and the other gods. "Guess I could tell them I had a teleport spell built into the bomb to send me away and it malfunctioned and sent me to a different destination? Kinda like what mom did with daddy."

Provider smiles. "See, give yourself some credit. So where would you like them to find you?"

"Where are they headed now?"

Daniel points to the torch. "Look for yourself, Goddess."

She nods and closes her eyes and concentrates, picturing her ship. She can see it but is too close, so she moves back, and it's disorientating. "How do you gods do this? I'm going to hurl."

Jack chuckles. "Makes me glad we can't do that here. It would be gross to visit and find chunks everywhere."

"That's disgusting, father."

"You brought it up."

She looks at the ship's heading. "They are headed back to New Haven. Probably to explain what happened to me and the remnants of the old town. The expanding glowing ball of fire just a few hundred miles away…"

Jack puts a hand on her shoulder. "You'll get the hang of it, eventually. Only took me seventy years." He ruffles her hair. "Kids didn't make it any faster."

"I guess put me in the room I stayed in there at Lord Vlad's castle." She looks at Marcus. "And thank you for everything."

"Just keep the number of people who know you're a goddess to a minimum. Remember what I said about dying again? Your body might be immortal, but you can still be murdered, or have a nasty accident." He informs her with all seriousness. He places his hands on her shoulders, his tone carrying the seriousness of his warning. "But if you decide to give up immortality, you can come to your realm any time and stay forever. Giving up your body completely and letting it die." He looks around. "And you might want to get to designing that soon. Your followers are going to need a place to spend eternity."

"I have to design their homes too?"

Daniel butts in. "And write a holy text or texts."

Her father chimes in, adding to the pile. "And a holy symbol to give to a prophet."

She looks at Provider, waiting for him to just pile on more. He just shrugs. "No one said being a goddess was easy. Just need to focus and choose a name." He smiles. "You'll learn that later. I'll see you when you get back to Rose Harbor and find a nice place to live while the Black Rose plans their next move."

It dawns on her she can tell him now what she really wants. "I want a castle." She grins. "Made of ice for my dream home, and…"

He cuts her off. "Ok, see ya." He waves his hand, and she's gone in a puff of air.

Jack gets back into his armor. "Think we loaded too much on her at once?"

Provider shakes his head. "She can handle it. You did good at raising her."

Daniel laughs. "She's going to be using that torch as a club, you know that, right?"

Provider laughs, picturing Crystal beating on someone screaming, 'love me,' with that torch. "We got a long way with her, but you were right, Morgana. She was perfect to join the family."

She nods. "Game well played." She glances at Provider. "Who's next?"

Crystal wakes up in a bed and bolts upright looking around. She pats herself down and feels she's alive and whole and in her nightgown. Her heart races, not knowing what just happened. *Was it all a dream? Was it real?* She notices her bracelets are gone, along with her clothes and handbag. Her engagement ring is also missing, and she looks around for it. Peering out the window, the *Bastion* looks like it went through hell as it lands in the courtyard. Grabbing a nightgown from the closet, she rushes down the stairs and along the flagstone floors. *I don't know what's happening, but I must know if Will, Zarra and the others are alright.*

The gang plank lowers and Lord Vlad is standing in the courtyard along with Sveta and a few guards. William descends first, with Zarra next to him. Tia and Penelope come down next, with Tom and Tyra taking up the rear. Lord Vlad looks around, standing on his tiptoes as if it will help him gain a vantage point. "Where is the countess?"

William breaks down crying again, trying to get the words out, when Crystal throws open the main doors and runs down the stairs. Tom shouts from the ship above everyone else. "CRYSTAL?!" William turns at the outburst and follows Tom's

442

pointing to see her running in her nightgown across the courtyard.

William drops his shield on the ground and he and Zarra rush past Lord Vlad, running straight at her. She leaps, and he catches her. They embrace and kiss, all three bursting with tears of joy. William lets her go and Crystal turns to Zarra, cupping her face and kissing her as well in front of everyone, not long caring what they think.

Penelope and Tia run too, but Tom passes them like they aren't moving, propelled by years of endurance training. "But how?" William looks her over. "You died; we saw you die."

Tom can't control his emotions either. "How did you get here? It doesn't make sense."

Tia, Penelope, and Tyra catch up surrounding her and bombarding her with questions. Crystal holds her hands out, making space. "Back up, please. I'm glad you're happy I'm alive, but you're going to suffocate me."

William holds her by the shoulder. "Nevertheless, you made us believe you were dead. I even saw you in my dreams."

Tia raises an eyebrow and looks at William. "You had that dream too?

Zarra nods, adding to the conversation. "I did too, yesterday."

Crystal sounds innocent. "What dream?"

William looks back at her. "That you would always be with me, that you're waiting for me."

"And here I am. Waiting on you."

Zarra butts in. and points down. "But how are you here?" She throws her hands out. "Where are your clothes and jewelry?"

"I had a failsafe in the device installed. A teleport spell. It was meant to take me back to you, but the problem with teleport is you can end up anywhere, remember?" She shrugs innocently.

443

"And I ended up here and it must have failed so badly because it only teleported me, nothing I was wearing. So my handbag, my bracelets, my clothes and the magic knocked me out, so I just woke up this morning. How long was I out?"

Tia tilts her head. "Four days. You should have died of dehydration."

"Guess being in a magical coma has its benefits?" Crystal looks around. "But I'm hungry. Who's up for raiding the kitchen?"

Penelope sounds ecstatic. "I'll make you whatever you want, countess."

Lord Vlad clears his throat, getting everyone's attention. "I see how important I am."

Crystal pushes past everyone and walks up to him. She bows her head. "I'm sorry Lord Vlad. No disrespect. They thought…"

"You had died. Yes, I figured that much out." He openhanded points down at her. "And I understand that aspect. My question is why are you wearing a nightgown out here? That's not really doing much to keep you covered?"

She looks down and in her rush, didn't notice that she might as well be naked for all this night gown was covering. She giggles nervously. "I thought I felt a breeze."

William wraps her in his cloak. "Our apologies Lord Vlad. We are just trying to put the last few days together." William informs him. "None of us knows exactly what's going on. But I can say for certain, your Black Rose problem in Old Haven has been dealt with."

"I want to hear all about it." He walks towards the castle. Crystal and William fall in step with him. "The Black Rose operatives here in New Haven have more or less given up, acting as if they weren't doing what they were doing on their own. It's possible they were entranced or under some powerful spell." He holds a finger up. "We are going to investigate the matter further

444

before pressing charges. It wouldn't be right to jail those who aren't responsible for their actions." They walk inside and he looks at Crystal, William, and the rest. "Get her dressed in something decent for dinner tonight." He gives her a wide smile. "As visually appealing as that is, it's not appropriate for dinner." He chuckles and walks away, leaving them alone in the foyer.

Tom and Tyra stay at the ship with Tia. She uses the left over wands of repair to help the crew fix the battered ship. Penelope walks slowly across the courtyard towards the castle. *I'm glad Crystal is alright, but my heart still hurts over Chuck. I need to get my mind off of him.* Walking in, she smells something in the air that brings a smile to her face. *I did promise her a meal.* She follows her nose and finds the kitchen. Looking around, there are mixes of Humans, Halflings, and Elves working together. A smile creeps across her face. *This is amazing, and there are ingredients I don't recognize.*

A woman passing by stops and addresses her in Poshlovish. "Something I can help you with?"

She shrugs. "I'm a well trained personal cook of the countess. I was wondering if I could help and learn some of your dishes."

She smiles, motioning to the tall sink. "Pull up a chair then and wash your hands. I will teach you some basics while we prepare." Penelope smiles finally back in her element.

"The main course tonight is going to be pierogi."

Penelope tilts her head and looks up at her. "That's a Halfling dish."

She leans down and waves her hand to the other Halflings. "It's a New Haven dish. Halflings have been part of our area for hundreds of years. We share everything."

"I'm wondering if my ancestors are from here. I need to investigate more."

Dinner comes and goes, and everyone sits, laughs and carries on, burying deep the feelings of loss over the last few days. Lord Vlad is eager to start the trade agreement, but Crystal informs her she must return to Rose Harbor and report on her activities and let the Emperor know she is setting up the deal. "It wouldn't be right to leave him hanging with no information." She reaches out and pats him on the leg. "But I promise I will be back to negotiate terms and treaties for as long as it takes." They eat something the locals call Beef Stroganoff and a delectable dish they tell her is Chanakhi. "It's amazing. It reminds me of some of the exotic food Shadow prepares for me from her people." She leans back in her chair. "I must be careful." She pats her belly. "I keep running into so much good food, and my figure is going to be shot." After dinner, they retire to their chambers and Zarra and Crystal sit at a table in her room. William leaves at Crystal's behest to go get her a change of dress for in the morning and any old shoes that fit her clawed toes. She sits opposite Zarra and they talk. "You want some strawberry juice?"

Zarra smiles back. "Sure." Crystal gets up and walks over to the small magical device that keeps their food and drinks fresh and bends over opening it. Zarra watches, and her smile grows. *I can see why William can't keep his hands off her.*

Crystal sets the glasses down and pours the drinks and her icy blue eyes meet with Zarra's ruby red ones. Zarra makes her move and reaches up, taking Crystal's face and bringing it to hers, pressing their lips together, feeling the softness. William returns not long after opening the door and noticing that only one torch lights the room. He closes it behind him and spots movement and hears some giggling. He grins and approaches the bed.

The next morning, Crystal sits in her nightgown at the table, writing up some paperwork for a preliminary guideline for the new treaty. She looks up and William is sound a sleep with

Zarra laying on top of him. She grins. *I don't know what got into us last night, but I won't forget it.* There is a knock at the door she wasn't expecting, and it is enough to arouse William from his slumber.

Crystal walks to the door and asks who it is, and Penelope answers from behind the door with breakfast. Crystal slowly opens the door and allows her to enter. William pulls the sheet up and over Zarra, trying to hide her presence. She comes in and sets down the large tray carrying Crystal's and Williams's food. She glances in his direction and notices the blouse and pants that Zarra was wearing yesterday is laying on the floor. As she takes it in, she also takes note that the sheet doesn't look right and then turns to Crystal. Penelope gives her this look of 'unbelievable' as the sight of the room tells the entire tale of what's happened. "You didn't?" Crystal just shrugs, knowing it's pointless to even try to argue or hide the fact.

As if to punctuate the point, the cover gets tossed off by Zarra, who stretches and sits up, places her arms behind her head and popping a few joints in her spine as she arcs backwards. She comes to rest and sees Penelope standing there wide eyed in disbelief. "Oh, are you here to take breakfast orders?" Zarra rotates, popping her spine as if nothing mattered. "If so, I would love some scrambled eggs and some sausage patties."

Penelope turns back to Crystal and she just smiles. "You heard the princess."

Penelope sounds disturbed. "Scrambled eggs and sausage. What to drink?"

Zarra shrugs. "I'll take a tall glass of coffee. Something tells me I'm going to need the boost for today." She leans over, placing a hand on William's chest.

Penelope sighs and turns to Crystal. "I won't be too long. Try not to get started on anything."

She turns, but Crystal reaches out and grabs her shoulder, turning her back around. "Shadow, keep this to yourself, please.

447

There's more going on here than you realize, and I don't want things to get weird."

Penelope tilts her head and points to the bed. "Don't want things to get weird? Not weirder than a betrothed couple making it with a princess from another empire and acting like its nothing new? That *not* kind of weird?"

Crystal turns to Zarra, who shrugs, and William pulls the sheet over his head. She glances back at Penelope. "Well, you got me there, but it's more complicated than that. I'll tell you more later, ok? Just keep this under your chef hat for now." Crystal has a look of desperation on her face.

Penelope sighs. "Fine, you're all adults, so I really don't care anymore." She points a finger at Crystal. "But if you're not careful, you're going to be pregnant before you're married, and that's not a good thing." Penelope takes her leave, shutting the door behind her.

"Speaking of betrothed." Crystal gazes at William and Zarra and motions to come over. They get some clothing on and join her at the table. "When we get home, we need to plan a proper wedding." She glances at Zarra. "And let's hope the Emperor has good news for any future prospects for us."

CHAPTER 38

(New Tidings)

Crystal and Lord Vlad talk over the day and agree to meet in the late spring when the temps are more favorable for their peace talks and she will stay for as long as it takes to seal a deal between their peoples. He kisses her on the cheeks as a formality as it is traditional in his culture and shakes Williams's hand. They board the *Bastion* that's still battered, but repairs are coming along, and lift into the air. They make a heading straight back to Rose Harbor. Crystal doesn't want to waste time going back to Portstown, but sent word with the *Opal Star* about Captain Motsana, and will visit the Baron later in person to explain everything that happened. From the air they look toward Old Haven that's several miles away, but from here can see much of the geography.

William gasps, and Tia covers her mouth at the devastation. Tom looks at Tyra and shakes his head, knowing what it symbolizes. The trees for miles around the town are all flattened and burned black. A crater half a mile wide and as deep, pockmarks the surface showing that everything in the area was erased from existence from the violent magical release of Jack's weapon. Zarra can't believe what she is seeing. "Your father designed a weapon like this?"

She nods, trying not to sound like bragging. "Actually, father's was many times that. I used normal wands in my construction. He used maximized, extended, and multiple damage overlay's in his. From the stories, the blast zone erased everything within three miles of the detonation and the light from the explosion was like dawn was breaking again over the horizon." Her words contain no inflections, no embellishments. Just a cold fact. "I still wonder where he got the idea for such a device, and why he would unleash it on this world." She shakes her head and looks down at the devastation. "I can't imagine a world if this technology got out and into the wrong hands."

Zarra can feel the icy fear of the realization of what she is looking at. "That's beyond terrifying."

"And that's why my father keeps the plans locked up. If it wasn't for him raising me to understand the mechanics of engineering, I would have never figured out how to build it from them." She looks at the group. "And not to worry, I destroyed my copy of the plans once I finished the device. It won't fall into anyone else's hands. War isn't my business." She closes her eyes, unable to keep looking at what she had done. "It never should have been."

Penelope shakes her head too at what she is looking at. "Too bad the shard was destroyed in the blast." She looks up at Crystal. "How are you going to convince Lyndis to let Tia and Andrew to continue dating?"

Tia smiles and looks down at the Halfling, but Crystal is smiling larger than them both, feeling the shard pulsate in her core, having become one with her soul. She places a hand on Tia's shoulder, but looks at Penelope. "Love will find a way."

Several days pass and they pass by a mountain range close to the center of Bacarian and Crystal gazes off the deck, William, Zarra, and Tia standing with her. She looks down at a large lake that's being fed by a river from the mountains and surrounded by some woods and grasslands. The river continues on and she knows the river leads onward to Black Rock. She speaks aloud, catching everyone off guard. "That's where I want my town."

450

They exchange glances, but Tia asks first. "Your town?"

Crystal nods animatedly. "The Emperor promised to build me my home and if I got New Haven to sign a peace agreement and possibly a trade agreement, he would let me set up a town to be the Capital of the Bacarian continent. I want it there, on the shores of that lake. With the mountains, the woods, the plains, and being close other center, it would be perfect." Without warning, she walks inside to the bridge. Soon the ship is coming back around heading to the spot she was looking at. They land on the snow covered the ground, but no one disembarks. She walks the deck smelling the fresh air, taking in the view of the snowcapped mountains and the sparkling half-frozen lake.

The captain rights down the coordinates in her log for Crystal to present to the Emperor later. They leave and she is already calling it home. "We will put the docks on the lake, and the Castle will be on that hill there, overlooking the lake with the mountains in the background. And I should have the streets radiate outwards from the castle, so all roads will lead there." She's very animated and writes things down and they just let her go.

Two days later, they arrive in Rose Harbor; the dome beckoning them home as the bitter cold outside gives way to the warmth inside. The metal on the ship creaks as the temperature difference causes the metal to expand after being exposed to subzero temps for so long. They circle and can see more airships are being built, with another being finished up. The Seventh Houses color shows they got the contract to build and ship for the empire's expanding air cargo fleet. Crystal pulls on William. "I better marry you quick before your House gets above my own."

They disembark and there is an official from the First House already waiting for them. Crystal and the rest follow the well-dressed man into the throne room, where Marcus is standing there. Next to him is an Elven man dressed in green and silver, standing about five and a half feet tall. Crystal is weary immediately, but Zarra stops in her tracks. Her tone carries both surprise and unbelievable coincidence. "Father?"

Crystal and William also stop and look at the Elf and back at Zarra, both knowing there is a conflict brewing. Crystal looks up at William and she holds her hand up, stopping everyone with an air of 'I'll handle this,' as she walks forward alone.

She gets next to the two taller men and they look down at her. She knows Emperor Marcus has her back, but doesn't know the Elf. Extending a hand, she introduces herself. "I'm Crystal Hellstr…"

The Elven man interrupts rudely. "I know who you are." She retracts her hand, seeing he won't be taking it.

"Your, Highness." Marcus speaks calmly. "That was uncalled for. She is my countess and has earned much respect from me and our people. That was unbecoming."

"I want to know why you took my daughter off on some dangerous mission, knowing it could get her killed." There is no hiding the anger and frustration in his speech.

"I didn't have the authority to tell her no," Crystal counters right back, letting a little anger into her own tone. "And I'm glad she came along. She helped to save lives and was a tremendous asset to my efforts."

He looks at Zarra, who reflexively hides behind William. He takes a deep breath and calms down. "I love my daughter." He takes another deep breath, looking at Zarra. "I want what's best for her and want to keep her safe." He turns back to Crystal. "You have any children, countess?"

"Not yet, but I'm hoping to resolve that soon since now I can finally get married to my love."

His voice softens more. "Once the first one is born, you will understand how I feel." He looks at Zarra. "I know Zarra isn't mine by blood, but all the same, I feel my duty as a father to protect her from the dangers of the world."

452

"I don't have to be a mother to understand that feeling." She waves her hand towards her friends. "I laid my life on the line for them, willing to make the ultimate sacrifice to protect them. I know what it means to love someone beyond yourself." She continues to reflect. "Had you known me a year ago, I would have laughed at this current version of myself as being pathetic. To die for someone who isn't family was an absurd notion to me then." She looks them over. "And I'm sure for some of them they would have felt the same way." She puts her arm down and looks down to gather her thoughts. "They are my family. As much as my own parents and brother." She looks back up to the tall fair skinned Elf. "That includes your daughter, Zarra."

Marcus stands there quietly. Letting the Goddess do her thing. He can feel her divinity is still out of control, but she's harnessing it properly and he smiles. *She might think it was all a dream, and her dreams are just odd moments, but she's handling the duality well.*

The Elven man nods, accepting what she has to say. "Zarra needs to come home and fulfill her duties as a member of the royal House. She is supposed to wed as part of a treaty, and she's been delaying it." He looks at her and holds his hand out. "Come, Zarra, we must go."

Zarra stands there and shakes her head in defiance. "I don't love him. I don't want any part of it."

"You don't have a choice, young lady. It's our way."

She shouts back at him. "Then I don't want to be part of your kingdom anymore. I renounce my position as princess!"

He gets angry and steps forward, but Crystal holds out her hand, placing it on the taller man's chest. William pushes Zarra farther behind him. Crystal holds him there. "Your Highness. Why can't you let your daughter, that you claim to love, find her own love too? You don't need an arranged marriage to enforce a treaty, do you?"

He looks down and see's she's being comforting, but her strength and the claws show she is deadly serious. He looks down at her. "You would start an international incident over her?"

Crystal's eyes harden. "Love is worth fighting for."

The tall Elf looks down at Crystal, and then at Marcus. His face softens and nods. "They still aren't royalty."

Marcus opens his hands slightly. "They will be. Are you satisfied, Sire?"

He nods and lets out a defeated sigh. "For now. Let me know when to make arrangements. I must go tell my wife and let the poor prince down that he's going to have to date the old fashion way." He looks down at Crystal, reaches between her horns and pats her on the head. "Take care of my little girl." He winks, turns, and exits, taking his retinue with him.

What was with that wink? Did I miss something? And did he just pat my head between my horns? The sheer audacity! I'm going to string him up with his shoelaces!

William watches Zarra's father disrespect Crystal with that head pat and can only imagine all the different ways she has just killed him in her mind. He turns and looks at Zarra. "Are you clueless as I am?"

Penelope shakes her head "I think we all are."

Crystal stares at the Elven King till he's out of sight, with questions running through her mind from just about everything. She glances up at Emperor Marcus, confused, and he smiles. "I got your letter." He nods his head for her to follow. "Step into my office, countess. We have much to speak on and I await your report." She nods and finds her way in. "David, take them down to the kitchen and get them something to eat. We might be a while."

He steps in behind Crystal and she is already seated. "I have so many questions."

"I know you do, and I'm going to do my best to answer them. I owe you that much."

454

"I guess my first question is the most important. What's up with the King and Zarra?"

Marcus stops and slowly turns to look at her. "That's your... never mind." He takes his own seat. "I got your letter about Zarra, with you and William thinking of adding her to your family." He leans forward on his elbows. "And yes, it's legal here in Rose Harbor because of the Elves and other long-lived races believe in such things. Zarra is a special case, as you guessed." He spreads his hands. "That's why the King was here. When his ship returned without Zarra, he was furious and he came here immediately. When your letter arrived, I showed it to him to show that things are complicated." He leans back. "I had faith in you to complete your destiny, and I told him you and William were worthy of Zarra's affection. So he stayed till your return."

Crystal thumbs over her shoulder. "All of that was for show out there?"

"Not exactly. He was being serious. If you two really loved her for her, then you wouldn't back down, not even to a King. Had you given her up, you wouldn't have ever been judged worthy in his eyes." He leans back forward and interlaces his fingers. "But he wasn't wrong that you're not royalty. So you could never get married."

She squints slightly and raises a finger. "No, you said 'they will be' at the end. What did you mean?"

He laughs. "You caught that? I thought I said that low enough for you not to hear. It was going to be a surprise for later. It still can be if you're willing to wait."

She tilts her head. *There is more, but he wants to keep it to himself. Might be best if I don't press him on it.* She crosses her legs and leans back. Folding her hands over her knee, she speaks as if it didn't matter. "I'll wait. Knowing that Zarra is free and no longer on the run makes me happy."

"I guess there are only two questions remaining, then?"

"Two?"

"Yes, where do you want to build your home and town, and when and where are you going to wed William?"

She grins, rocking back. "I know where I want to build. I saw it as we passed over on the way here. The captain wrote the coordinates down for me. As far as my home I want…"

He finishes her sentence. "A castle made of ice. Yes, you mentioned that."

She leans forward excitedly in her chair. "So that wasn't a dream? I felt it was real, and I can feel the shard inside me, but I had wondered how much of that was real."

Skylar appears from behind Marcus, but doesn't speak. "It was all real, and once you're done with your honeymoon, your formal training starts. You need to pick a head priest or priestess to give your holy symbol too, and from there, your influence will expand. It's difficult what you've walked into, but when the work is done and things are in motion, there is no greater feeling."

Skylar places her hands on his shoulders and grins. "So that leaves the last question. When and where for your wedding?" Crystal smiles, knowing exactly what she wants to do.

Penelope walks out the front when a messenger runs up behind her. "Ma'am!"

She turns to the short Elven man. "Are you talking to me?"

He holds up a letter. "Are you Penelope Grez-co-wak?"

She sighs. "Grzeskowiak."

He looks down at the letter. "Sure. I'm sorry your name is so hard to pronounce."

She holds her hand out. "Tell me about it." Handing it to her, he stands to the side, and she looks down at it. *This was sent by magical means. Someone spent a lot trying to get a hold of me.* She opens it and her eyes widen as it's written in Poshlovish.

Greetings,

> *My name is Xander Zielinski. A mutual friend of ours names Cornelius had mentioned you to me on my last visit. I missed you when I got back into Portstown. If it wouldn't be too much trouble, I would like to meet with you over a possible business venture. I run several high-end hotels in every major city and looking to expand to Rose Harbor this summer. Cornelius spoke very highly of your cooking skills, and I would like to sample your cuisine to add to one of my hotels. If you are interested, I already paid for a return message to reach me here in Portstown. I look forward to meeting you.*

> *Xander Zielinski*

She puts the paper down. *Going into business is a dream of mine.* Her eyes widen in realization. *Wait, Cornelius mentioned us Halflings are always about business, and this guy writes to me in Poshlovish. Could he be?*

Crystal walks up and peers over her shoulder, but Penelope rips it away before she can read it. "I don't know what you're so jumpy about. I can't read that." Her voice takes on a mocking tone. "Is it a love letter?"

Penelope turns her nose up. "It's a business proposal from Portstown about opening my own restaurant, and I just might."

Crystal leans down and gives Penelope a hug. "Let's talk to father. Maybe he will help with an investment." She keeps her tone low. "But I'm getting my town, so maybe you can build there instead?"

As they walk into the main gate of the Hellstromm estate, they are greeted with warm smiles and tears of happiness, glad they had come back to them once again. Tia and Andrew embrace and kiss passionately. They go inside and Penelope's replacement chef cooks them all dinner. Crystal, William, and Zarra talk animatedly about the wedding and how beautiful it's going to be at the Hellstromm Ice Castle. The five girls stay at the table, excitedly picking out colors and looking at patterns while William, Jack, and Andrew sit in the other room. The girls take hours, but they give it a break and walk in and start taking their places around the room.

Before Tia can sit down, Andrew stands up and meets her halfway and takes her hands. William looks at Jack and sees his smile growing. "Tia Moonglow, the love of my life, the sun in my sky, the reason I exist." He kneels, pulling a ring from under his robes. "Will you be the star that guides me forever?"

Tia bursts into tears of joy and once again Jasmine has to watch another child take the leap. Tia is speechless but nods yes as she extends her hand. Andrew places the ring on her finger and Jasmine, Penelope, and Zarra break down in tears. They leap up and hug Tia, welcoming her to the family and congratulating her on the engagement. Jack hugs his son and informs him of how proud he is.

Crystal turns to William, looking deep into his eyes, seeing him fighting back the tears as well. "To think, soon you're going to have to do that all over again."

He grins, turning back to her. "What makes you think I should be the one this time?"

The next morning, William wakes with both Crystal and Zarra on either side of him. *I'm not sure if I'm the luckiest man alive. Marcus warns that the Black Rose hasn't been defeated.* He runs his hands along both of their backs. He looks askance at a solo burning torch. *I just wonder where Crystal got that thing. It's nice, but do we really need a night light?*

William goes and gets them breakfast and brings it back as they go over some basic ideas for the castle. Crystal pours over the plans with excitement he's never seen before. "Once the permanency magic is in place, nothing short of a wish will be able to bring it down. So I have to be sure of its construction." She turns to William. "And when it's done, we can wed in its courtyard." After breakfast, the three of them head to the palace.

Zarra peers over her shoulder. "You're going all out. Even running electrical lines for those new fancy non magical lights and indoor plumbing."

Crystal nods. "I want my city to be the beacon of innovation, love, and technology. Duke Samuel might think he's good in Mithport, but here, my father and his team can run wild with ideas." She sips at some milk. "And I'll even grant special incentives for inventing things that help improve the nation and city, like extending patents to last twenty years instead of the normal ten."

Zarra's eyebrows shoot up, looking impressed. "Gnomes and Dwarves will be happy about that."

Crystal nods. "I have a lot of ideas I think will make everyone happy." She glances up at the clock. "But we need to get to the palace if we are going to meet the engineers and city planners."

Entering the throne room, Marcus stands with his personal architect, a gnomish male named Izit, and an Elven woman calling herself Lura. "Ah Crystal. Are you all ready to go?"

She bows her head. "Yes, your highness. Izit's plans have been very enlightening, and can't wait to discuss some minor changes."

Marcus beams. "Excellent. Then you best be on your way. A countess should run her city from day one. Off you go."

"Thank you, Your Highness." She bows her head again and they exit the palace, off to the location of her future home.

Tia awakens in her room and sits upright. Getting her robe on, she walks to Andrew's room where he has set up the altar for morning prayers. She grins. "I still can't get over your parents calling me their daughter. I finally feel to be part of something so grand."

He brushes her hair back behind her ear. "Yeah, can't believe you. Crystal and Zarra actually figured out what was going on. You three are a great team."

Tia nods. "I think we need to get our morning prayers done. Daniel is waiting for us."

CHAPTER 39

(EPILOGUE)

A month has passed and Crystal, William, and Zarra watch from the deck of the ship as the castle and the town itself come together. Zarra turns as a Dwarven man pulls on her. "Ma'am, the military academy is ready for your inspection."

"Thank you. I will be there shortly."

He turns to Crystal. "Countess, the castle is ready for your inspection as well. The last few permeant spells are about to be placed and Izit requests you look it over before he finishes."

Crystal's eye light up. "I can't wait."

Zarra pats them on the shoulders. "You two go on ahead. I really want to be sure of this academy, then I'll join you on the inspection."

Crystal and William walk across the courtyard, watching as dozens of people prepare for the wedding in just a few days, when she spots Penelope and Xander speaking with an architect. "Those two been practically inseparable." She leans into William. "I think they might be falling for each other."

He shrugs. "I didn't know she was seeing anyone."

"Apparently he's from New Haven, and is building a hotel here and restaurant with her being his star chef. When he heard of this city being built, she convinced him to build both here and Rose Harbor."

"Interesting. Did she meet him there?"

They enter the castle, following Izit in. "No, some mutual friend set them up." She shrugs. "And I thought I was the goddess of Love."

William glances down. "Not this again." She just giggles.

They walk the corridors as the Architect shows them all the intricacies of the building, including their massive bedroom. Entering, William and Crystal take in the room. Large king and a half canopy bed, several dressers, an armure, and ornate oak table and chairs. The view from the bedroom they can see over the entirety of her capital. "As requested, countess. The bedroom here has a view of the docks on the north side, and on the east, a view of the mountains." Crystal and William walk out onto the balcony and talk in the view. "And your personal bathroom has a private pool with temp control, filled with water from that monastery."

She glows and looks over the room and its furnishings. She looks Izit in his eyes and her tone lowers. "Could you leave us?"

Izit nods. "Yes countess. When should I return?"

She growls at him. "Just wait for me in the throne room." He bows his head and backs out, closing the door behind him.

She turns to William and throws her arms around his neck. "I think what this castle needs is to be broken in." She brings him closer to her face. "Right now."

Four days later, the arrangements for the wedding are finished. Everyone is seated facing the ice castle in the foreground and the snowcapped mountains behind it. The lake is close enough that the sounds of the waves add to the majestic feel of it all. Tia arrives with Andrew along with Jack and Jasmine, amazed at the sight from the sky as the castle comes into view. Once landed, they are greeted by Crystal, William and Zarra on the ground. Tia rushes over and hugs her soon to be sister-in-law. "Don't be squeezing me too much. I haven't been feeling well lately."

Crystal takes Tia for a tour, leaving William to show the military academy to Jack. Zarra takes Andrew and Jasmine to look over their new manor's construction is coming along.

Tia Glances over Crystal as they walk through her throne room. "You're not feeling well?"

"No, I haven't in a few days. I think it's all the excitement of the wedding happening soon. I'm all nerves being worried."

"And Zarra hasn't been able to help as a healer?"

Crystal shakes her head. "Her healing magic is limited."

Tia stops walking and turns to face Crystal. "Would you like me to cure you, or at least figure out what's the cause?"

"I'm resistant to magical healing now, but if you wouldn't mind. Feels like I'm fighting more to keep from being sick than anything else." Tia smiles, placing her hands on Crystal's shoulders. "And I've been eating the weirdest things, like pickles and peanut butter. Maybe it's from the weird foods?"

Tia perks up at this latest news. She starts her prayer and her hands glow purple, enveloping Crystal. She runs her hands down and stops at her torso. "Well, this is interesting."

Crystal throws her hands out, frustrated. "Well, spit it out."

Tia fights a smile, but Crystal isn't convinced. "It appears you have a parasite."

"Why are you smiling? Get it out of me,"

Tia shakes her head and giggles. "I can't. You're going to have to wait for it to come out on its own and you're going to have to give it a name."

Crystal's face shows surprise as her eyes widen and looks down where Tia has her hand. "Are you saying?"

Tia nods, grinning largely as to confirm Crystal's joy. "Congratulations, *mom.*" She leans in and hugs her.

They embrace each other for a long moment, then break apart. Crystal tries composing herself. "Can you tell how long ago this happened?"

"Within the last week, you've been busy with William, haven't you?"

"The only time this week was…" Realization dawns on her. "Was when we were in our new room. I forgot to cast my pregnancy ward." She looks at Tia and points a finger, sounding worried all over again. "We cannot tell anyone till after the wedding. As far as anyone knows, this is going to be a honeymoon baby. The wedding is tomorrow, so it's not like it will make much of a difference."

Tia sighs. "I don't like deception, besides how are you going to explain why you're not drinking wine? You can't have that with the baby now."

Crystal nods. "I'll just say that I don't want to take the chance of ruining my wedding dress. That should be good enough, for it wouldn't be a lie exactly."

"Well, let's finish the tour, *mom.*"

It's a bright and warm day for mid-March. Few clouds in the sky as hundreds of people gather from all over. Baron Tenishar and his wife are there along with dozens of other Catfolk dressed in their best. Lord Vlad, and some of his officials are also there, having started negotiations and wanted to see the new town for himself, along with Master Monzulo, having left the monastery for the first time since he had arrived there in seventy years. The *Bastion*, repainted ice blue, is decorated with large white and blue roses hanging from its sides, with 'Just Married' wrote under them. On either side of the castle, a Rose

464

Harbor air ship fly's flanking with cannons pointed outwards. Royal Guards line the premises both from her own personal guard, wearing the white and blue of her new House and Rose Harbor Royal Guard in red and purple.

A huge arch with white and blue roses brackets the altar, with the band playing nearby, keeping guests entertained till the moment arrives. Penelope and Xander sit in the front row, holding hands. William, wearing a royal suit of blue, with white accents holds arms with Jasmine, wearing a dress of pure white. The Emperor wears a suit of Crimson Red and Royal purple, his crown shines in the sunlight and the holy book of the Provider is in his hands, but also a new Holy Book of Vixana is in front of him on the altar. A small gold box sits just behind him, barely visible.

Tom and Tyra wait with the red carpet rolled up, waiting for them to move it for the precession. Standing nearby is the young Catfolk girl who gave the lily to Crystal the first time in Portstown, whose parents agreed to let her be the flower girl for this very special occasion.

The music shifts, and William knows it's finally happening. The heart in his chest pounding harder now than facing even the deadliest of enemies. Tyra and Tom unroll the ice blue carpet and it ends at the altar and they part separate ways. William walks with Jasmine up the aisle as all eyes are upon them from several cultures and cities from across their land. As the music plays, they reach the altar and Jasmin leaves William standing there and takes her seat in the front row. Tia and Andrew walk arm in arm down the aisle next, her blue dress looking amazing, and Andrew looking uncomfortable in his formal wear the same as Williams. Andrew takes his place next to William and Tia stands in maid of honor's place. Next is Zarra, walking with Gerald. The icy blue dress on her looks absolutely stunning, flowing with each step. Gerald looks happy walking with her. As they get to the end, Zarra takes her place next to Tia, and Gerald hugs his son and moves to stand next to Andrew.

The music changes again, playing the music that they have all been waiting on. Heads turn and the Catfolk girl walks, dropping lily pedals along the way to the altar. Crystal comes into view with her father arm in arm. The short black man looks both happy and sad knowing it was time for him to give his daughter to another, giving the responsibility to protect her to another man. His suit of white, with blue accents, is crisp, his black skin a sharp contrast, bringing it all together.

Crystal is beyond beauty. Her ice blue dress and bouquet of white roses in her hands fit the pattern, drawing all attention to her. Her braids wrap around her horns and hang down, decorated with white and blue roses, and a white veil covers her face. Gold accents the dress and gold rings hold her braids down. The sleeves are open, exposing her ivory white skin, and a train of blue and white flows behind her. *I think my heart is about to leave my chest. I'm excited, frightened, and ill all at the same time. I'm so happy but I want to cry. I can't believe this day is finally happening.*

They arrive at the altar and Jack stands there with Crystal as Marcus's voice booms over the gathering. "Who gives this woman to be married to this man?"

Jack speaking loudly and clearly. "I do, Your Highness."

Crystal steps forward, taking William's hand and Jack takes his place sitting in the front row next to his wife, Penelope, and Xander.

Marcus starts with the traditional 'We are gathered here today' speech. He talks of their journey of love together, leading to this point in their lives. Both the hardships and the joys as his voice heard over all else in the area. He picks up the Holy Book of Vixana and reads from its passages. "Love transcends all, for love is a powerful bond that binds people together in harmony despite their origins, race, or identities. For when you love for another, nothing else in the world matters."

When he finishes, he turns to William and whispers. "Do you have the ring?" William turns and Andrew takes a gold and

466

platinum ring from his pocket, with a large diamond with sapphires on either side, and hands it to him. Marcus nods and proceeds as Crystal presents her hand with William holding the ring in front of it. "Do you, Major William Blakely, son of Gerald and Muriel Blakey of the Seventh House, take Countess Crystal Hellstromm, to be your lawfully wedded wife? To have and to hold from this day forward, for richer or poorer, in sickness and in health, to love and to cherish till death do you part?"

William tries his hardest to hold back the tears of joy he feels. His heart races as he does. "I do." He places the ring on Crystal's left hand.

Marcus turns to Crystal, who turns to Tia and hands her the platinum band and holds it out to William. "Do you, Countess Crystal Hellstromm, Daughter of Jack and Jasmine Hellstromm of the Third House, take Major William Blakely to be your lawfully wedded husband, to love and to hold, for richer or poorer, in sickness and in health, to love and to cherish till death do you part?"

Crystal looks at the man of her life with tears welling up. "I do." She slides the band onto his left hand.

Marcus looks over the gathering. "If anyone here has reason for these two not to be wed, speak now or forever hold your peace!" He looks as if dares anyone to speak up. Turning back to them, he grins. "With the power invested in my by the Provider, and as Emperor of this land, I now pronounce you Man and Wife. You may kiss the bride."

William lifts her veil and leans in, cupping her face and giving her a deep and passionate kiss. She wraps her arms around him and the embrace for long minutes as the people gathers clap in applause. They break apart and turn. Marcus places a hand on each of their shoulders. "I hereby introduce to you for the first time, Mr. and Mrs. Hellstromm."

They go to leave, but Marcus doesn't let go. "Not so fast, you two. I have an announcement before you walk away." His voice still carries over everyone and he waves his hands in a downward motion, silencing everyone. "Countess Crystal Hellstromm. I have something else for you. As a grateful Emperor, I have given much thought to your future in my empire. You, your husband, and your friends have done a great service not only to me, but to the people of this continent you now live on." He turns, picking up the gold box and holding it in front of him. "And as such, my parting gift to the happy couple." He opens it, revealing inside is a tiara made of gold and diamonds. "Crystal Hellstromm, remove your veil and kneel."

"What is all this? I don't understand."

Marcus points to the ground, and she removes her veil kneeling before him. He holds the tiara above her head. "I hereby pronounce you Duchess of these lands, and the all the rights and privileges thereof. You are also hereby part of the royal family and, as such, are now part of my monarchy." He places the tiara on her head. He then steps back and waves his hand over the crowd. "Rise, Duchess Hellstromm, and address your subjects."

Royal family? What? Her mind races as her veil is held in one hand, and her bouquet in the other. She's barely keeping herself together as she stands and bows her head. "Thank you, Emperor."

He smiles and keeps his voice low. "Your work isn't over, but take this respite and be happy." He waves them on.

William and Crystal stroll back down the aisle arm in arm, this being the first steps of their life together. They know the darkness hasn't been beaten, but for now, it's driven back long enough for them to make new plans against it. The cannons of the flanking ships sound off, a salute to the new Duchess and her husband as the sound echoes off the mountains in the distance.

She gets to the end of the runway and turns. "See you all at the reception."

TO BE CONCLUDED…

The world doesn't end here. Check out more of Delveon with Legacy's, Chronicles, and Tales coming soon. Book 3 will be out soon to finish the first series, and the others will follow shortly after.

Made in the USA
Columbia, SC
11 December 2023

27474957R00261